# LATENT
# IMAGE

# ACCOLADES FOR JOSHUA GRAHAM

"...A riveting legal thriller.... breaking new ground with a vengeance... demonically entertaining and surprisingly inspiring."
*—PUBLISHERS WEEKLY*

"... A heart-pounding thriller...This gripping novel has it all: faith, hope, conspiracy, legal thrills, heart-pounding scenes..."
*—The Washington Post*

"...Action, political intrigue and well-rounded characters. Graham has created a novel that thriller fans will devour.
*—CBS News Entertainment*

"A haunting tale"
*—Toledo News Now*

"*Darkroom* is a fascinating, fast-paced, beautifully written story of love and war, murder, terrorism, and a dark conspiracy."
—Douglas Preston, *New York Times* bestselling author

"A great mystery, unearthed secrets, and beguiling adventure. Joshua Graham mines an emotional landscape through an entourage of fascinating characters. Read this one—and take a walk on the perilous side."
—Steve Berry, *New York Times* bestselling author

"....a fantastic read in every definition of that word...blisteringly paced, high-tension suspense, characters you bleed with. I can't wait to read more!"
—James Rollins, New York Times bestselling author

"...Pure genius... the most intriguing book I've read in a long time..."
*—Suspense Magazine*

# LATENT
# IMAGE

REDHAVEN
BOOKS

First Edition

Cover design by Dan Pitts

ISBN 978-0-9844526-6-8

*For Katie, my love, the bride of my youth,*
*the very air I breathe*

# ACKNOWLEDMENTS

THE CONCEPTION OF A NOVEL doesn't typically occur within a vacuum in which the author churns out word after inspired word. That is not to say that I do not depend on my Creator for everything I write (or for that matter, my very breath)—indeed, I do, but much of what I receive comes to me by way of people and relationships.

There are always more involved in the process than a simple page in book can list, so I will beg forgiveness in advance for anyone I have inadvertently neglected to mention.

LATENT IMAGE is another Xandra Carrick novel, the main premise of which was inspired by watching the inaugural parade of the then newly re-elected President Barrack Obama. A proud moment for him and his family for sure, but part of me felt anxious for his security as he walked and waved at the throngs of cheering well-wishers. This led me to research the type of protection POTUS (the President of the United States) would require. Of course, one thing led to another and my mind became so filled with ideas, I had to share them with my beautiful wife Katie.

That is when most of my ideas become realities, when I share them with her brilliant, imaginative mind. Knowing the main characters as well as I, she makes so many great suggestions, I can't keep up! But what a blessed problem to have, no? So, thank you, Katie. I would never have been able to become the writer, or the man I am without you.

I also wish to acknowledge my son and daughter who are now of the age that they contribute thoughts to our brainstorming sessions. You'd be surprised how many of the things they've said that have made their way into this book. I'm sure some of you have already seen a few of these "nuggets."

As for research, I would like to thank Mike C.,"The Chancellor", and Michael Nichols of the USMC for their expertise in military logistical and operational procedures. I'd also like to thank Michael Hiebert, and Allan Leverone, my friends, colleagues and two of the authors whom I respect most. Their help and perspective when I went "manuscript blind" and expertise in Flight Control procedures have been a tremendous help in this book.

A few other names I would like to include are Cindy-Lee Samuel, Scott Beaty, and Scott Lowell.

My personal friends, friends from church and family members are all a great part of supporting me in countless ways. You all know who you are. Thanks for your prayers and interest in my humble efforts.

Finally, I want to thank you, dear reader. You are the reason I spend hours toiling over the keyboard. Without your support, and enthusiasm, there would be no point to my writing.

JoshGraham.net

*Revenge, at first though sweet,*
*Bitter ere long back on itself recoils.*

—JOHN MILTON
*Paradise Lost*

# PROLOGUE

WASHINGTON, DC
January 23
2:28PM EST

IN THE CROSSHAIRS OF THE SNIPER'S SCOPE the target shifted in and out of view. The motorcade drifted down Pennsylvania Avenue, Secret Service agents flanking its side, while Vice President Phillip Marsden and his wife Gwen waved to the cheering crowd on either side of the street behind the cold 16-gauge steel tubing of the barricades.

Neither of them was the target.

The sniper swung his scope back to the west, where the glare of the sun blinded him momentarily. He grunted, blinked and reestablished his view. The cold January wind bit at his bare fingers as he felt the trigger and anticipated the diversionary strike his partner would unleash half a block away.

Tuning out the trumpet strains of marching bands, the steady drum beats, and the crowd's applause, he initiated a silent countdown just as Jennifer Bradley, the nation's newly re-elected president strode past the designated spot.

...four...three...two...one...

# ONE

SHE FOUGHT BACK TEARS as she walked across the asphalt, all the while trying to maintain that dauntless smile which some claimed to have helped her win her the election. Snow and broken ice had been shoveled over to the edges of the street so as to afford a clear path for everyone and everything in the procession—the floats, the Marines, the marching bands.

This would be her second term, having by succession fallen into the Oval Office after President Colson's shocking conviction for the Vietnam War atrocities cover-up conspiracy, and his subsequent suicide. Now, four years later, having been elected the first female president should have made this, her inaugural parade, one of the most triumphal moments of her life.

But behind the winning smile, the appreciative waves, she couldn't fully enjoy it.

*If only Ben were here.*

With her left hand holding onto Mikey's, her eyes met his— deep set and blue like his father's. He gave her a nod and such an austere look she might have found it endearing, had the wound not been so deep and fresh. Ben had told him just two weeks ago, *Keep your head high. You're the man of the house now. I need you to look after Mommy for me.*

She'd dealt with leaders of unstable nations, headed up a war on human trafficking and took down cartels, but none of those enemies of freedom, life, and liberty were so cruel as the one that had taken her husband, Benjamin Bradley. Cancer had no mercy. Nor was it a respecter of men.

"You okay, Mikey?"

"Michael," he growled, and continued to scan the crowd. Though only nine years old, Mikey was taking his father's dying words more seriously than any of the Secret Service agents charged with their protection today.

"Just try to smile for Mommy today, you look so serious."

"I hafta look out for you, okay? Daddy said..." he tried to hold back a sob, bit his lip, then turned away trying to cover the fact that he was crying.

"Oh, sweetie..." Jennifer stopped, knelt down and wiped his tears with a handkerchief. This drew the attention of several onlookers, and one or two of the bodyguards. Maya, Jennifer's staff photographer came around discretely to capture this poignant moment evocative of the little John F. Kennedy Jr. saluting his father's casket during that state funeral procession nearly half a century ago.

"I miss him, Mom."

Without a thought for the millions watching both on the sidewalk, and over television, Jennifer wrapped her arms around her son and held him as he wept. She tried to soothe him with a gentle stroking of his hair.

But a deafening boom shattered the atmosphere, sending her to the ground over her son's body.

# TWO

TERRIFIED SCREAMS PIERCED the cacophony of car alarms, cries of panic and chaos everywhere. Jennifer Bradley's first thought was for Michael, over whom she had thrown herself.

"Stay close to me!" She heard herself say, but her voice sounded like she was underwater, her ears ringing.

A pair of hands suddenly lifted her to her feet. Campbell and Jones, and several other Secret Service agents surrounded them as they rushed her and Mikey to The Beast just a few yards ahead. They pushed through a thick cloud of smoke, but not quickly enough for her to miss the severed limbs and blood strewn across the street.

Acrid smoke.

Choking cries.

Shouts of horror.

A bomb had exploded—from the sound of it, maybe about thirty feet behind them.

As they reached the armored limo, Maya was following, camera in hand. Trying her best to stay out of the way, she yielded to the agents covering Jennifer and Mikey, as the door opened.

Jennifer pushed Mikey in first.

"Madam President, you need to get in," Campbell said.

"Maya!" she called out.

The photographer hesitated, stopped to look around as her camera fell and dangled from her neck. Another agent pushed her forward right up to the door, but she turned around in reaction to something in the distance.

Just then, a whisking sound stopped with a dull thud which Jennifer hadn't so much heard, but felt, as she stumbled backwards into the limo.

Maya's head swung back.

Her back hit the side of the car just as Campbell pushed the President inside, covering the door with his torso.

But from the crimson spray and grey matter that splattered on the window, Jennifer Bradley knew.

It was too late.

Maya had been shot.

She shielded Mikey's eyes.

Campbell leapt inside, slammed the door shut and shouted to the driver. "Go, go, go!"

The limo sped off.

In the front passenger side, Jones droned into his walkie-talkie something about POTUS being secure within The Beast.

*Secure?*

Staring at the streaks of blood sliding across the window, a thousand thoughts raced through her mind—the bomb, the victims, the inevitable national panic...

*Oh God, Maya.*

She would process it all later.

For the moment, only one thing mattered.

Mikey's safety.

# THREE

THREE YEARS EARLIER

En route to FULAD-ZERA HEADQUARTERS
Borderlands of Tariqistan
23:46 GMT

*IT IS A BURNT OFFERING, sacrificed on the altar of justice.* What was one more life in the broad strokes of history? Ishmael Al Shihab himself had also been offered up in the name of the greater good. He understood all too well the nature of such matters.

A chill wind rushed through the open canopy of his jeep and clawed at his face. The sun fled over the bare hills of Tariqistan's borderlands leaving in its wake brush strokes of clouds the color of dried blood. Ahmad, his bodyguard, could have driven slower to mitigate the effect of the dirt road, but Ishmael had ordered him to get them back to the compound as soon as possible—not for an important briefing, not for a demonstration of newly acquired weapons or technology, but for something far more important.

Odin's fourth birthday celebration.

It seemed only yesterday that Aiza was nursing, swaddling,

and parading their son around their luxurious home in Kishwar (compliments of the United States Government), prior to his illustrious career as a clandestine operative for the United States Central Intelligence Agency.

Before long, however, Ishmael's usefulness had been deemed expended, and he'd been unceremoniously cut loose. Since then, amidst shattered hopes and dreams, they lived in exile on the run from the enemies he'd made, while trying to keep a step ahead of the CIA.

*Not for long.*

Ishmael had acquired something that would change the tides. Something that would bring him back into favor with the powers that be, and possibly re-seat him in that place of legitimacy and power that had rightfully been his.

As the bruised sky darkened, the temperature in the barren trail had plummeted. Yet a host of stars looked down from above upon this joyous evening, marked not only by his impending shift in fortune, but by the relief he took in knowing that he would soon secure a bright future for Aiza and Odin.

The jeep went over a large rock and nearly rolled. Ishmael gasped, then gripped the door frame to steady himself. "Careful!"

Ahmad grunted his acknowledgment and drove on.

A minute later, they arrived at the concrete walls of the compound. Outdoor lights after dark were forbidden. The only illumination came from the sallow moon above.

Ishmael activated the walkie-talkie and called up to the guard tower.

*"It is not down on any map; true places never are."*

No one recognized the literary reference in his passphrase, and that was exactly how he wanted it. It was clever, if he did say so himself. Since his Harvard literature classes, Melville had become his favorite writer because of that infamous opening line in *Moby Dick*, spoken by a narrator with whom he coincidentally shared a name. It had struck an instant, resounding chord.

"Welcome back, Ishmael," the hollow voice on the walkie-talkie replied.

Ahmad pulled the jeep forward as the gates yawned open.

Somewhere in the obsidian firmament, a hawk screeched as it glided over the concrete bunkers. Unlike many of his colleagues who might have taken that as a grim prognostication, Ishmael was not the least bit superstitious. No, Ishmael was a man of reason, of science.

Knowledge was power.

And he kept that knowledge in a clenched fist, sharing it only with those from whom he would benefit by doing so. Tonight however, after months of risking everything to go dark, infiltrate *Al Saif*, and gain the trust of Massoud Haashir—the most wanted terrorist leader since Bin Laden, Ishmael would regain what he'd lost by disclosing to his handler what he'd unearthed; Haashir's location.

Haashir was the former dictator of Tariqistan and the head of al *Saif*, the extremist insurgent militia responsible for the ongoing terrorist attacks on the provisional government the United States had helped establish. He also came frightfully close to orchestrating a massive attack on the Superbowl at Cowboys Stadium in Arlington Texas. But with Ishmael's help, the Department of Homeland Security, along with several other agencies thwarted it. Yet another of the myriad classified facts of which the general public to this day had no knowledge.

Most significantly, Ishmael and the local Special Forces operatives he'd trained had ousted and driven Haashir out of Tariqistan just eleven months ago. They had proven instrumental to the CIA throughout the entire operation. Nevertheless, Haashir continued to elude capture.

Until now.

Ishmael's men were holding Haashir captive, and were keeping him in a hidden makeshift holding cell just a mile away. Prepared to set Haashir on the altar of the global "War on Terror," Ishmael took comfort in knowing that now, he would certainly be set in a running for the first presidential election of the country he'd liberated.

Regardless of what the United States thought of him.

He was about to become an international hero.

Ahmad stopped the vehicle about fifty yards from the bunkers. Dim candlelight flickered through the small windows, and the door to his apartment swung open.

"Baba!" Odin shouted with excitement, holding the prized Ironman action figure Ishmael had sent him last week. Aiza quickly hushed him, picked him up, and bounced him gently. Muted moonbeams fell softly over her face, her eyes bright and her smile as pure as her heart. A scarlet silk scarf lifted in the breeze. Powerful as his convictions, his principles, and dreams were, they could not compare to the overwhelming love he felt for his wife and son. No one and nothing brought him as much joy.

Unable to suppress the smile stretching across his face, Ishmael leapt down from the jeep, hid his gift—a shiny new iPad—behind his back, and walked slowly towards them.

"*There's* my little treasure!"

Just then, a whooshing sound flew over them.

Sounded like fireworks.

*Whose idea...?*

Before he could chastise the well-intentioned idiot that had set them off for the celebration, a thunderous explosion knocked Ishmael to the ground. A blast of gravel, choking dust and searing smoke blasted over his face, forcing his eyes shut momentarily.

"Odin!" he tried to shout, but the concussion of the explosion had knocked the wind out of him.

Struggling to sit up, he blinked, rubbed the dirt out of his eyes, blinked again.

All he could see was a bright blaze ahead.

The muffled sounds made his head feel as though it were submerged in a boiling cauldron.

Another explosion rocked the ground, a bit further away.

Ishmael tried to stand, but stumbled back onto his hands and knees. His palms landed on what he realized was the body of Ahmad, eyes and mouth agape in macabre surprise. A long piece of shrapnel had impaled his forehead. Ishmael gasped in pain, willed his legs to stand.

As though inebriated, every step took him in an unexpected direction. Despite the disorientation, the shouting and buzz of the invisible aircraft, he pushed into the flames, the choking black clouds billowing from the place where Aiza and Odin had been.

A blast of heat roared and ripped at his face like the claws of a dragon.

"Odin!" He shouted hoarsely, shielding his face with his arm. Aiza!"

Absolutely nothing remained but smoldering rubble. No one could have survived the blast. He now realized what had attacked them, understood the destructive capabilities of its weapons.

The familiar buzz of an MQ-9 Reaper faded. The unmanned drone had been known as the Predator B-001back when he worked for General Atomics in the States straight out of college.

Against all reason, he hoped to find his wife and son alive. The door frame stood perversely alone among the utter wreckage. But he found nothing save for dust and debris. Not a trace of them.

Except for the charred remains of Odin's Ironman action figure.

And two meters away, under a pile of cinderblock fragments, the end of Aiza's red scarf fluttered in the wind. He called out, stumbled over, and proceeded to uncover her broken body, parts of which lay beside his son's remains in a bloody heap, her arm draped protectively over him.

They were gone.

Tears laced with sand and soot stung Ishmael's eyes. He cried out in anguish, ignoring the shouts of people trying in vain to take cover or flee.

Another pass of that accursed drone, another Hellfire missile attack in the distance. It was going to extinguish every life in the compound.

Despair weakened and held him there waiting for the next

missile to reunite them. He wept and rolled into a fetal position beside his family. Then a bitter laugh escaped him. He himself had been betrayed, thrust upon that altar of 'global security.'

In his final moments, clutching Odin's Ironman toy to his chest, Ishmael clung to the mental image of his wife and son.

The Reaper fired one last missile...

# FOUR

PRESENT DAY
*34 DAYS AFTER ASSASSINATION ATTEMPT ON PRES. BRADLEY*

WASHINGTON TIMES OFFICES
WASHINGTON D.C.
FEBRUARY 26
8:45 AM EST

FREDDY KLEIN HAD NO IDEA why the plain white, padded mailing envelope with nothing but his name scribbled on it had ended up on his desk, or who it was from. After eight years working mundane local interest and fluff pieces, finding something as cryptic as this—with no other identifying markers and no clue as to its contents—was both compelling and nerve-abrading.

He nearly spilled his coffee as he tore the envelope open thinking a bit too late, *Hello, Freddy? Anthrax? Unabomber?*

White power did not spill from the envelope, nor did it immolate in his hands.

Instead, a black SanDisk MicroSD memory card fell into his open palm.

He laughed nervously but kept extremely quiet, not wanting

anyone else to know about this. Was it the latest scandal on The Hill? Compromising hotel videos, photos, audio transcripts?

He inserted the media into the SD card reader slot of his Dell all-in-one desktop, double clicked on the SDXC(E:) icon and opened its only folder.

At the root of the directory sat a lone icon with the filename 0225.mp4—a video file which was only about 400MB in size. The chair nearly rolled out from under him as he stumbled, tossed his donut on the desk, and steadied himself into a seated position.

Heart bouncing like a Rockhopper penguin on a hot tin roof in July, Freddy yanked the white earbuds from his iPhone, plugged them into the computer's audio jack, and launched the video.

The initial image nearly made him choke on the last bite of Krispy Kreme wedged in his mouth. He coughed and sputtered and reached for his coffee as a man wearing a black hood stood before the screen between two others wielding assault weapons, their faces obscured by the shadows.

In a digitally modulated voice, the armed man in the ski mask began to speak in English with a slight accent, a blend of Middle-Eastern and British.

"This message is to the female American president Jennifer Bradley, as well as all United States citizens—especially those who elected her into office. For the past several years, the nation of Tariqistan has suffered the humiliation of foreign interference at the hands of the Bradley administration. You have removed and killed our leader Massoud Haashir, and replaced our entire government and society with the corrupt social, political, and anti-religious ways of your own culture—and most heinous of all, the imposition of a process which permitted the election of Nasra Aamal, a young westernized whore who now fancies herself our country's leader.

"We now demand the complete and unilateral withdrawal of all American and United Nations armed forces, diplomatic, and contractor personnel from Tariqistan, as well as the resignation of Nasra Aamal from office, the release of Abdulla al Shabas, Imam of the Free Tariqistan Movement from prison, and the unconditional transfer of power to him.

"You have seven days to comply or we will commence attacks on America and its interests, the likes of which you have never before witnessed. The withdrawal will take place in stages. Within three days, you will first remove all military presence from the capital city of Kishwar. Failure to do so will result in our first strike. You've seen that even your own President Jennifer Bradley is not immune to hatred and assassination attempts by her own citizens." The camera zoomed in tight on the hooded man's face. "Be assured, Free Tariqistan is committed till death, and is capable of more than you can imagine. Do not test our resolve."

Freddy clicked the pause button and the screen held on the speaker's eyes. Swallowing the lump he thought was a piece of his breakfast, he realized that he'd held his breath for longer than he should. Exhaling, he closed the file, then saved a copy of it on his computer.

The shortness of breath, the clammy palms, and the trembling of his body came not from anxiety, but from the thrill of a truly remarkable story—one which just might launch his career skyward.

But as he picked up the phone to contact George, his editorial director, he hesitated.

*It'll never happen. President Bradley won't agree to any of those demands.*

His throat went dry as images of the September 11th attacks on the Twin Towers and the Pentagon filled his mind.

**INAUGURAL PARADE BOMBING SUSPECT DEAD**
By Daniel Weisman
Washington, DC
February 27, 7:05 AM EDT

(Reuters) Thirty-five days after the Pennsylvania Avenue attack during President Jennifer Bradley's inaugural parade, Kenneth McEntee, suspect in the bombing which injured twenty-nine, and killed five (including the nine year old daughter of a participating member of the USMC Band) was found dead in his room at Mercy Hospital. Cause of death has not yet been determined by the DC Coroner's Office, and local law enforcement officials have declined to issue a statement regarding the possibility of foul play.

With the help of eye-witness and social media tips, Federal Officers had tracked down McEntee at Mordor, a cybercafe in Toswon, MD, to where they proceeded with a warrant for his arrest. Patrons at the cafe state that McEntee drew a gun, but was shot twice before he could fire it. He was critically wounded and rushed to Mercy Hospital in Baltimore.

The bombing suspect had remained in a coma for the past five weeks, though doctors reported his condition as steadily improving. His sudden death has frustrated investigators hoping to get a statement, or any other information pertaining to his alleged involvement in the coordinated strike with former Texas sharpshooter Eric Avery, whose attempted shooting nearly killed President Bradley but instead, struck down the Chief White House Photographer Maya Flores. Avery was shot by the Secret Service Counter Assault Team, and pronounced dead at the scene.

Though Federal and other intelligence agencies do not believe McEntee and Avery were linked to a recently exposed paramilitary militia in North Carolina, they are not ruling out the potential connection of the assassination attempt to the growing unrest in Tariqistan, in light of a video message dated February 26th, which threatened terror strikes against the U.S. and demanded the unilateral withdrawal of all U.S. Military, diplomatic, and contractor personnel in seven days.

The threat is believed to originate from the recently prominent terror organization al Saif, which some believe has taken the mantel of Osama bin Laden and al Qaeda.

As of 9:00AM EDT yesterday, the NTAS (National Terrorism Advisory System) has updated its alert status to Elevated Threat.

# FIVE

*SUBMERGED IN FRIGID WATER, unable to scream or breathe...*

*She struggles but finds herself utterly immobilized. Nothing but bubbles of her last breath float out of her mouth, as cold pond water rushes in.*

*Her lungs beg for air.*

*She fights the urge to inhale.*

It's here.

I'm back.

Again.

*The place where that killer impersonating a Homeland Security agent thrust her under the frigid water of a pond in the woods of Southern California.*

*She struggles to free herself.*

*Beneath the murky depths, flashes of light and air bubbles flicker around her eyes.*

*Fighting to get to her feet, she slips, flails about, hands seeking purchase, yet fails to grasp anything but fists full of water.*

*Above the shimmering surface, his outline stands over her.*

*She reaches up for help.*

*But the hands crushing her throat press even harder.*

*The fingers are thin, frail, and at the same time powerful.*

*Unrelenting.*

*The only sound beyond her muffled scream is the splashing of her limbs as she tries desperately to escape.*

*And to her horror, the sound of her killer's laughter penetrates the water.*

This can't be happening!

*But the maniacal laughter belongs not to the impersonator sent to kill her. No, it's not him at all. It's a woman. Someone familiar. She manages to lift her head closer to the surface but still can't breathe. She sees the face of the person drowning her, though.*

*It's her own.*

*In horror, she tries to cry out, claw at her doppelganger's eyes, kick wildly, but the more she tries, the harder the fingers around her throat squeeze.*

*Fleeting air bubbles rush out of her nose and mouth.*

*The light fades into the gloom of a watery grave.*

*And then...*

> *...just as all of existence vanishes into complete darkness...*

*The grip on her neck is gone.*

*A strong pair of arms lift her out of the water, holding her secure.*

*Xandra blinks repeatedly until the light returns to her eyes.*

*At first, she can only discern the presence of a man.*

*Warmth—from his arms or the sun shining on them, she can't be sure—envelope her with reassurance. She draws a deep breath. Lets it out, just as her vision begins to clear.*

*It must be him, who else could it be?*

*"Kyle?"*

*The image fully resolves.*

*Her horror is perfected.*

*It's not Kyle.*

*The man who has rescued her is the last person she could ever imagine.*

*The last person she would ever wish to see again.*

*Ian Mortimer.*

GEORGETOWN
WASHINGTON, DC
February 28
4:29 AM EST

A COLD FILM OF MOISTURE made the sheets cling to Xandra Carrick's back as she awoke with a gasp, and bolted upright in her bed. Drops of sweat dotted her forehead and ran down her neck. Heart jack-hammering in her chest, she drew desperate breaths, her entire body trembling. This caused the bed to make sounds that might imply to her neighbors in the apartment below that she had a guest.

"Oh my God..."

*A nightmare, just a nightmare.*

But no, it was so much more real. In the past three years, since rescuing Nathan Remington's daughter, she hadn't experienced many visions, and those that might have been, she'd ignored. They had either decreased in frequency, or she'd lost the ability to recognize them. In either case, this dream—or vision, if that's what it had actually been—was unlike any she'd ever experienced before, in or outside of the darkroom.

*But Ian Mortimer?*

A bead of perspiration crept down between her shoulder blades causing her to shiver. Wrapping her robe around her, she got up, went to the thermostat to shut off the air er. Why would anyone run the A/C in February?

To her surprise, the thermostat was actually running the heat- er.

At 76 degrees.

She went to the bathroom, still shaking from within because of him—the image, rather—of Ian Mortimer. For several years, she'd avoided any thought of that murderous creep. Why now?

Running a washcloth under hot water, she regarded her reflection in the mirror. Dark circles ringed her green eyes, belying her thirty years. Well, thirty-one this month, but who was counting? She'd have to commit herself to the tender mercies of Elizabeth Arden for her official orientation at the White House today.

After indulging in a hot, longer than usual shower, Xandra decided that though the sun had not yet graced the skies over the nation's capital, she would get an early start. Once again, sleep had eluded her. Only this time, it came back and struck her a blow before banishing her from the Land of Nod.

Her new appointment as the Chief White House Photographer made her nervous because it was really a cover for her unofficial appointment to work with the Secret Service. That's where the real danger lay, as her predecessor had been shot and killed just a few weeks ago at the Presidential Inaugural Parade.

Ironic that Xandra had been offered this position.

Even more so that she'd accepted it, considering what had happened with the Colson conspiracy. After all this time, she still experienced nightmares of the trauma she'd endured. She was either extraordinarily brave, or extraordinarily foolish.

*Where angels fear to tread.*

While most candidates for the position of White House Chief Photographers would have been thoroughly vetted by the White House staff, it was President Bradley herself who had sent the written request that Xandra accept the dual-role appointment.

It could not, however, have been mere coincidence that having met Wade Masterson of the Secret Service after the rescue of then presidential candidate Nathan Remington's daughter, the invitation from the Oval Office had materialized. Regardless of how it had materialize, this was not an opportunity to take lightly.

Still, the appointment struck Xandra as peculiar, considering that she had been the one who brought about the downfall of President Bradley's former running mate.

One of the conditions Xandra had insisted upon was that she'd receive some of the same training Secret Service agents did at the James J. Rowley training center, months prior to her official start date. After all she'd been through, she vowed never to be defenseless again.

After accepting the appointment, they flew her into Washington to acclimate and begin her "secret agent" training. It felt more like boot camp for Mulan. In the past month, she had not only gotten fairly proficient in firearms, but had improved her overall physical fitness and prowess as well.

It might all come in especially handy one day, in light of the recent terror threats by the FTM (Free Tariqistan Movement).

As the steam in the mirror cleared, she flexed her arms to reveal the firm curvature of her deltoids and triceps, evocative of Sarah Connor's return in the second *Terminator* movie. She blew a lock of dark brown hair out of her eyes, and stuck her tongue out at her reflection.

*Not quite as kickass, but getting there.*

Wrapped in her towel, she glided to the vertical blinds over both windows of her corner apartment and opened them. A magnificent view of the pre-dawn DC skyline and the Potomac greeted her. It had only been a month and a half since she moved here and while it wasn't much compared to her apartment up on Central Park West, there was something thrilling about being here in the nation's capital.

Before the window sat her cello, a functional work of art by the 18th Century Venetian master luthier Domenico Montagnana. It had been given to her as an anonymous gift two years ago, while trying to hide from the media limelight of the Colson conspiracy. Grateful, she decided to get back into practicing and gave private recitals for the friends who insisted she return to her musical roots—a balm in the parched land of sorrow after losing Kyle.

The cello must have cost millions. It was a monster of an ax, but the sound was opulent and easily filled any space within which she played it, with its deep baritone rumble.

On the music stand sat the Barenreiter edition of J.S. Bach's *Six Suites for Unaccompanied Cello.*

Unaccompanied.

Solo.

*Alone.*

Just like she had been since Kyle had been murdered in cold blood. Doctor Woods had told her not to blame herself for his death, encouraged her to move on.

It just wasn't that simple.

The sheet music was opened to the *Sarabande* of the Sixth Suite, which she'd been trying to perfect since her days in Juilliard Precollege. But as this particular work had originally been written for a cello with five, rather than four strings, she afforded herself a bit of latitude, though the handicap was not unique to her but common to mostly all cellists not performing on period instruments.

Dad had once accused her of not following through with her dreams and pursuits, citing the cello as a prime example. But glancing over to the vintage Graflex camera he'd given her, which ultimately unlocked that mysterious door into her clairvoyant abilities, she now realized that following through with her photographic gifts had cost her more than she would have been willing to pay. If she'd known, she might never have gone into photography.

Mom was gone, so was Kyle. And Dad was serving time in federal prison for his involvement—albeit unwilling—with the Colson conspiracy. All that threatened to overshadow the excitement of her new life and appointment with the White House.

Shaking off the heaviness, she took in the view of the lights reflecting across the river.

*I've always been fiercely independent, right? Isn't that what Dad always said? I can do this. I don't need friends or a family to make me whole.*

It wasn't so bad, actually. In the short time since moving in, she'd already found her compulsory haunts: Shogun, a fairly decent sushi restaurant and Honest Abe's Coffee Depot, both conveniently located within walking distance.

Taking a deep breath, she shut the blinds.

A full schedule lay ahead starting with a meeting with Adam Finley, the White House Press Secretary at 6:00 AM leading up to her first in person meeting with President Bradley herself. But it was the meeting with Wade Masterson, now chief of the Presidential Protective Detail that wrenched her innards. His email stated that he wanted to discuss some important matters regarding the non-photography duties of her new position.

Considering the recent terror threats issued against the President, this part of her new position gave her pause. Was she in over her head?

The clock read 5:05 AM.

Her car would be waiting for her in about twenty minutes.

Still drowsy, Xandra yawned and stretched, her arms still sore from max pushups (seventy-five, and not kneeling) in two minutes just yesterday during her PFT.

The images threatened to re-emerge—being strangled by the hands of her spectral double, Ian Mortimer pulling her out of the water. That all too familiar numbing tingle and chill which typically accompanied bouts of clairvoyance coursed through her body and to her extremities.

That sense of vulnerability which came with following through on the promptings of her visions always robbed her breath.

Which is why she had chosen to endure the soreness from strength and endurance training, as well as the scrapes, cuts, and bruises received in physical defense techniques training.

She took a deep breath, then exhaled.

Time to get dressed and ready for the day ahead. And to help with the tension she would enlist the assistance of that substance with which she was now bordering on abuse:  Caffeine.

Fifteen minutes later, coffee in hand, she sat in the back seat of a black sedan provided by the Secret Service and was on her way to the White House.

# SIX

THE WHITE HOUSE (WEST WING)
OFFICE OF THE WHITE HOUSE PRESS SECRETARY
6:15 AM EST

ADAM FINLEY THUMBED AWKWARDLY AT THE KEYS of his Blackberry, while Xandra sat in a chair before the large curved desk which wrapped around him in the corner of his office. Behind him sheer white curtains stretched from way up to the trim just beneath the white crown molding.

The fifteen minutes for which she'd been sitting there had been comprised of a polite handshake, two interruptions from his desk phone, one quick exit and return to and from the restroom, and now a text message from his wife for which he was sorry, but simply had to reply.

Xandra took yet another sip of her coffee and glanced at the grandfather clock by the wall. She made a valiant attempt to stifle the yawn threatening to escape her. For a moment her vision blurred with lingering slumber. When her eyesight returned to normal, Finley was smiling at her, his hands folded over his desk.

"Keeping you up?"

She shook her head and blinked. "Sleep's overrated."

"You're going to have to keep on your toes, Xandra. We're going to be spending a lot of time together. Mind if I address you in the familiar?"

"Mind if I call you Adam?" She smiled.

"I've been called worse." He handed her a folder bloated with documents. "That's a brief overview of your duties and responsibilities, though being the professional you are, I'm sure you'll intuit most of it."

With her left hand, she reached over and took the folder. Due to the sheer magnitude of its weight, it nearly fell out of her hand. "I'll take whatever help I can get, Sir."

"What happened to Adam?"

The half empty coffee cup fell out of her right hand and its lid popped off. As of late, she'd been taking her dark roast black, which did wonders for the effect it made on the carpet, the color of the very cream from which she'd abstained.

She bent down and tried to wipe the spill, but it only spread wider and deeper into the plush pile. She swore quietly.

"You'll want to refrain from that sort of language around the President."

She felt the complexion ebb from her face. "I didn't know she was so straight-laced."

"She's is a stickler about stuff like that. From the halls of the White House to the movies we watch on *Air Force One*—nothing risque like Clinton's staff would watch. She's got a nine-year-old son, you know, and he's often within earshot. Oh, and one more thing: Every picture you release must be approved by me."

As a photojournalist, she never had that kind of restriction imposed upon her objectivity. But like Okamoto, Atkins, and Kennerly, she was no longer working for the media. She was working for the President of the United States.

But censure like this? It was like the Nixon days where his photographer Ollie Atkins was kept on a short leash by then Press Secretary Ronald Ziegler. It would more than cramp her, but this level of access was an honor nevertheless.

"I'll bear it in mind." Xandra abandoned her attempt to clean the spill, and retrieved her cup. "Sorry about the carpet."

He grunted, then lowered his glasses and peered over its rims at all the equipment bags at her feet. From one of them, the Graflex protruded.

"Antique?"

"It belonged to my father."

"Ah yes, the legendary Peter Carrick." His half-open eyes belied his feigned interest. "Must've been tough growing up under his shadow."

"Not particularly."

He nodded to the old camera. "Hope you're not going to carry that around everywhere the President goes."

"I just brought it as decoration for my new office." Which was only partially true. It had been damaged, and restored, but if the opportunity arose, she intended to use it once in a while to create some truly unique shots. Her clairvoyance wasn't limited to the darkroom, and she had no problem taking pictures with the classic large-format camera. Contrary to what she once believed, the camera was not the sole vehicle of her second sight.

"Speaking of your office," he got up, walked out from behind his desk, and regarded her many bags of equipment on the floor. "Let's take you down there right now. Need some help?"

Xandra declined graciously, which she would have done even if she believed his chivalry was genuine. She was only half-Asian, but that embarrassment and inability to accept help had been branded in her personality.

*You've been gone four years, Ma, but your influence lives on,* she thought recalling some of their banter in the years before she passed.

Xandra couldn't decide if she felt more excited about being a member of the staff, or the fact that she was about to go to her own place here in the White House. After all these years wondering what it was like working in one of the world's greatest power centers, she was about to find out.

# SEVEN

LIKE A BEAST OF BURDEN, she lugged everything over her shoulders and followed Finley out the door. As soon as she stepped out of the Press Secretary's office, she scanned the corridor. Against the wall sat a red couch flanked by cherrywood end tables with lamps that cast a warm glow on the quartet of paintings directly above and between them.

Donning the aspect of a weary museum docent, Finley waved straight ahead. "Cabinet Room...some pretty spirited discussions take place there." Then looking down the corridor, he pointed to the door at the end. "And that, Xandra, is the Oval Office. Take it in, I'm sure it's quite an experience for you."

As the caffeine coursed through her bloodstream, the thought of being this close to where so much history had been and would continue to be forged, invigorated her. For a moment, she forgot about the imminent threats to the President, and the concerns about her ability to help the Secret Service. She just stared at everything around her and took her time processing it.

*I'm in the West Wing—I actually work here.*

With a dry tone, Adam Finley said, "Well, it'd be rather awkward if you didn't realize that by now."

"Did I just say that aloud?"

"You're on staff, not a tourist," he said giving her a strange look. Then he shrugged, and motioned for the staircase going down to the ground level. "Plenty of time to explore, don't worry. Trust me, you'll be sick of it soon enough."

Xandra followed, but couldn't help but stop and admire the jumbos, the enlarged photos lining the wall of the staircase, each of them taken by Maya Flores, her predecessor. Here a picture of President Bradley with Benjamin Netanyahu, there a shot of her with various dignitaries which Xandra didn't recognize in that short glance as she descended the stairs. But what struck her was how many of them depicted Jennifer Bradley with her son Michael, many with her recently departed husband Ben. These had never been released to the media, as far as Xandra knew. Though they were all smiling, each photo exuded a somber spirit, like the amber skies of a Pacific sunset in Del Mar, evocative of her and Dad's mourning, when Mom had passed away four years ago. Taking down her pictures had almost seemed disrespectful, so they never did. Not in his house in California, nor in her apartment in New York.

"Among other responsibilities, you'll also be in charge of what goes on these walls from now on," Adam said, stopping and turning back to view the photos as well. He muttered, *"though I'm not sure why they chose someone as inexperienced as you."*

She didn't bother dignifying that with a response. He obviously knew nothing of her involvement with the Secret Service.

"Anyway…" he motioned to the jumbos on the wall. "What goes on these walls is now your responsibility."

"Got it."

"You'll get plenty of input from the President, don't worry."

He continued down the stairs. Arriving at the bottom, he pointed to the door on the left.

"Secret Service."

The door was open.

A tall, black-suited man in his mid-thirties, with dark brown hair stood there with a concrete countenance, and nodded to Finley.

Finley leaned over and whispered to Xandra, "That's Wade Masterson of the President's Protective Detail. You'll be seeing a lot of him."

"Right." Ironic—borderline humorous—that the Press Secretary didn't know that she'd already known Masterson a while now.

Turning to the right, they passed the Homeland Security office and stopped between two doors on either side. To the right, the placard indicated Photo Office, to the left, Photo Closet.

"That's the darkroom you requested. You're really into vintage, aren't you?"

"My father's influence, I suppose."

"Lucky for you, the President likes that sort of thing. You know, classic art, classical music, literature, opera. She's had Itzhak Perlman, Yo-Yo Ma, and a whole bunch of other musicians give recitals here."

Best not to mention that she played the cello, though having been vetted by the Service, they probably already knew.

"Maybe you'll give a concert here too, hmm?" Finley's eyes narrowed, barely veiling his sarcasm.

"I'm hardly qualified."

"She's heard your recordings from Juilliard."

"Oh really?" Xandra felt her annoyance rising. "Public record, or national security?"

"What?"

"I was an accused enemy combatant-slash-domestic terrorist."

Adam squinted at her.

"But you already knew that." Of course he did, but he seemed neither put off, nor impressed. How President Jennifer Bradley managed to play in this sandbox full of boys was a mystery indeed.

Finley gave her a faint smile and pointed straight ahead to a small open area where modest colonial-style furniture lined the neutral colored walls. "That's the lobby," he sighed. "Typically, you'll enter through the West Wing's ground floor foyer, through those double doors."

As he spoke, a slender woman about Xandra's age approached slowly from the lobby. She could have been a runway model. With impractically high heels and equally impractical tight skirt, she strode over, tossed her long golden hair back and regarded Finley.

"Adam."

At the sound of her voice, his half shut eyes opened up. Turning to Xandra, he made the introduction. "Xandra Carrick, this is Erica Gordon. She's one of the staff photographers and will help you get up to speed."

Erica reached out to shake Xandra's hand. "Nice to meet you." But her haughty eyes belied her attempt at sincerity.

"Thanks." Xandra offered hers, only to find Erica's hand exuding all the warmth of a dead fish.

Already moving off to the foyer, Finley waved at someone entering the doors. "Ms. Carrick, you couldn't be in better hands. I'll check with you later."

And with that, he was gone.

Erica's flawless smile, blue eyes, and hair as fair as high noon made Xandra uneasy. Xandra took a deep breath and started for the Photo Office—her office.

Erica went before her, produced a card and placed it before the magnetic reader to unlock the door, which she opened, handed the card to Xandra, and then made an ushering gesture. "Your home away from home."

The lights came on to reveal a blank canvas of a desk on the right of which sat a large monitor and USB docking station, keyboard, and mouse. The chair was an executive black leather type and the walls were strikingly bare. Xandra set her equipment down on the desk and looked around.

"In case you didn't know," Erica said, her voice laced with just a hint of disdain as she stood holding the door open, "this office used to be—"

"A barbershop, I've read about it." Xandra laughed in an attempt to break the ice, uncertain if it had been Erica's intent. Something about the way she carried herself with those long legs, and the way she looked down her nose at her when she spoke, irritated her. Nevertheless, she worked for Xandra, and that was all there was to it.

"You'll want to watch yourself," Erica said.

"Oh?"

"I'm sure you know all about your predecessor, how she died?"

"The reports say they were acting alone," Xandra said, hoping to end the conversation with the most popular opinions of the media.

"And the media's always trustworthy, isn't it?" a stern voice said, announcing his presence at the door.

"Wade." Erica smiled at him and gestured to Xandra. "This is the new Chief Photographer."

"Yes, we've met." Masterson stepped forward, leaned down and extended his hand before Xandra could stand. "Welcome aboard."

She stood and shook it. "Nice to see you."

"As you'll be shadowing the President the majority of the time, I'll be briefing you on SOPs at 10 o'clock in my office."

"Great."

"See you there." He turned around and walked out.

Xandra glanced over to Erica. "A man of few words."

"Disregard his rules, and you'll get an earful." Erica's eyes trailed after him. "Though I think he's kind of cute." She turned back to Xandra and handed her a business card. "Anyway, that's my cell. I'm around if you need anything."

"Right. Well, I do have a few questions about—"

"Gotta go. Text me." She pushed the door open and looked back. "Breakfast photo session with the Vice President."

"I'll catch up with you later."

The pretentious smile which never seemed to leave Erica's face, faded. In a low murmur she said, "Just so you know, *I* was in line for a promotion to Chief before your name came up. And I can do this job better than anyone."

The coldness in her eyes chilled Xandra from within, but she remained impassive. "Glad to hear it."

A second later, the plastic smile returned. "Anyway, don't worry. I'll do everything I can to help. Toodles!"

In the space of a breath, before Xandra's retort, the door shut with a dull thud.

# EIGHT

THE WHITE HOUSE (WEST WING)
SECRET SERVICE OFFICE
9:58 AM EST

SHE WASN'T SURE if she should knock, or wait for the door to open in exactly one minute and fifty-two seconds. Technically, Xandra was early, which might send the wrong message. So she stood there and waited.

At exactly 10:00 AM, Wade Masterson opened the door.

"On the dot." Xandra said with a slight grin.

Masterson motioned for her to enter.

Passing a few partitioned cubicles, they entered his office, a spartan cave, which came as no surprise. He shut the door behind him and invited her to have a seat.

"Coffee?" He pointed to a carafe on his desk.

"I'm good, thanks."

"I don't have a lot of time, so I'll get straight to the point."

"Good." Xandra sat tall.

"After last month's assassination attempt, we've been on heightened alert regarding the President's safety."

"Naturally."

"As you can imagine, there's been a spike in threats against her."

"All credible?"

"We don't have a consensus, but I have to treat them that way. It's our mission not only to shield her from, but to prevent any possibility of threats. Which is why we hired you. In fact, I was the one who made the recommendation for the President to hire you as her chief photographer. When the Press Secretary suggested it was time to hire Maya's replacement, he recommended Erica Gordon, who you just met."

"Oh, yes. Erica." Xandra forced a smile.

"However, I all but insisted she hire you."

She knew that the job would entail more than just her photographic duties but was never told exactly how. So when she'd gotten the email to report here today, she was more than ready to ask. "So what does the Secret Service need with a photographer like me?"

"Long story short—your *specialized* skills."

Her stomach clenched.

He'd hinted at it before, but now it seemed he actually knew.

"Wait," Xandra said, a sudden panic tweaking her nerves, "I thought you've been prepping me to become an agent."

"I believe the term we used was Assistant Operative."

"Isn't that something like a junior agent?"

He shook his head. "Look, whether your skillset is based on an exceptional intuition or psychic phenomena—"

"Just stop right there for a second." Her heart was racing. How did he know this much about her? "I thought my training was for self-defense. What exactly are you talking about?"

"You didn't actually call it clairvoyance in your psych eval, but I had a hunch. We've been paying attention to you ever since the Colson conspiracy broke out."

"I thought you worked for the Secret Service, not the NSA."

"Are you trying to be cute?"

"It's called sarcastic."

"Cute."

Xandra sat up tall. "To what extent did this...paying attention go?"

"I've read all the files and transcripts from the tribunal—the testimonies, statements, psych—"

"That's privileged information. What right do you have?"

"You're going to be working with the President of the United States, whose safety and protection is my sworn duty." His tone was firm but not harsh. "So you can be sure I'm going to vet the hell out of anyone who gets that close."

She glared at him, but internally, she felt as exposed as a newborn's bottom.

"Who else knows about my abilities?"

"Besides me, the President is the only person who even has an inkling." Masterson cocked an eyebrow. "I'm not even sure I believe it myself. Why are you so uptight about it?"

"Oh, I don't know, maybe it's the fact that my visions, clairvoyance, second sight—whatever—have shoved me into Colson's cross-hairs, got a friend killed, put my father in prison? If anyone even suspects that I have this ability I'll be in worse trouble than ever. Best case, I'll be harassed, coerced, or exploited. Worst case...well, that already happened four years ago and I never want to go through that again. Look, even if you *don't* believe it's real, you can't tell anyone else."

"I would never do that. Trust me, I understand your concerns."

"Do you, really?" How could he possibly know the effects of what Ian Mortimer and Richard Colson had done to her, to the people she cared about? It wasn't a one-time trauma from which one recovers over time. The constant apprehension was overwhelming if she thought about it for longer than a few minutes. It stalked her, like a panther in the dead of night, ready to pounce at its first sign of weakness.

Wade looked her straight in the eye. "So, can you give me some kind of sign, a reading or something?"

"Excuse me?"

"You know, tell me something about me, my life, past, present or future?"

Xandra smirked. "It's not something you can just turn on and off like a light switch."

"Yeah, I've heard that before."

"Mister Masterson, you brought this subject up, not me. The burden of proof isn't on me."

Fair enough." He raised a placating hand. "The truth is, I need your help."

"How, exactly?"

"You've got the skills, experience, and international credibility as an investigative photojournalist—great piece on Female Suicide Bombers in Iraq, by the way."

In all her flustered thoughts, it never occurred to her to thank him for the compliment. "And?"

"And, with continued training on the side, you can be inserted into various situations as a political fact-finding photojournalist. Sort of like David Kennerly, President Ford's photographer who went to investigate for him on the deteriorating situation in Vietnam. Knowing your predilection for plunging headfirst into such matters, you'll probably want to be doing that from time to time anyway."

"Perhaps." Clever, appealing to her photojournalistic passion.

"POTUS has already approved this. The Secret Service's focus on protection goes hand in hand with our investigative focus. You can help us look into threats against the President. This is a vital part in the planning and implementation of security designs for national events and—"

"Hold on, just back up a little. You said it was my specialized skillset you were interested in."

"I need your help finding the root of something which could be a much more serious threat than two sexist rednecks with guns and pipe bombs—that was just the tip of the iceberg. We're doing all we can to track the source of the most recent threats, but I don't think it's enough. I want every kind of eye on this, even if it's psychic."

"I'm not a psychic."

Wade sat forward. "Psychic, paranormal, prophetic—I don't care what it's called. You uncovered a decades-old conspiracy perpetrated by Richard Colson. If you can use any of those abilities to help protect the President, then I need you on my team."

"But, what about my photography duties?"

"When you're away, your entire staff—including Erica Gordon and a few other competent photographers will cover for you."

Countless considerations flitted around her mind like bats in an abandoned bell tower. This was quite different from simply being a photographer armed with a weapon and some self-defense training. "So, are we talking about spying on terrorists?"

"Getting a little ahead of ourselves, aren't we?"

"I have a right to know."

"Clandestine work for sure. However, you'll never be assigned anything without my personally ensuring your readiness and safety. I'll make sure to get you training in tradecraft as well as..." he started scrolling through a file on his computer. "I see you've gotten some pretty good scores in your firearms and PFTs."

"I may have."

"Here's the situation. We've just received a new terrorist threat demanding that we pull all our troops out of Tariqistan."

"What are the chances she'll agree to, or negotiate the terms?"

"Tariqistan symbolizes all the success we failed to achieve with post-Saddam Iraq. Never going to happen."

Xandra didn't think so either, but wanted to hear from someone within the inner circle.

"What's unique about this threat is that they've given us seven days to pull out, or they promise a strike against the U.S.—domestic or abroad, they didn't specify."

"So what's the President's response?"

"Of course, she won't dignify such a brazen threat. But Homeland, Langley, the Bureau, and all local law-enforcement agencies are on high alert. Meanwhile, tensions are rising with more saber rattling from insurgent groups in the borderlands of Tariqistan.

President Aamal has reached out for assistance and our President has agreed to fly out there to offer her support."

"Really?" Though incredibly risky—foolish, even—it sounded like something Xandra might do herself, if she were in the President's shoes.

"Both the National Security Advisor and I have recommended strongly against it, but Bradley is adamant. Refuses to turn her back on the very people we fought so hard to liberate. I have a bit of a love-hate relationship with her ideals."

"I can see why," Xandra said. She had a feeling she was about to become inextricably enmeshed in a situation, the scope of which was much greater and more complex than she could imagine. "What do you need me to do?"

"With your abilities, you can help uncover whatever we might not be perceiving. I can't leave a single stone unturned in proactively protecting her, wherever she goes."

This was the first time anyone outside of the very few who knew of her clairvoyance ever spoke with her about it so matter-of-factly. On one hand, it came as a welcome validation, an acceptance of who she was without question. On the other, it was so pragmatic an approach, it left her feeling uneasy. He almost seemed to have more confidence than she did in it.

"Listen, Wade. I don't fully understand my visions or how they work. I can't guarantee anything."

"Understood. But you'll do your best, I'm sure."

"Of course."

"Now, first things..." Masterson sat back in his chair, searched his desk and found something in its drawer. "As you can imagine, being positioned as the President's photographer can be hazardous."

"I don't have to imagine. I saw what happened to Maya Flores."

"Exactly." He slid an SD card across the desk to her. "I've uploaded a few encrypted PDFs on safety protocols for you to study, especially when POTUS travels and you're inside the Bubble."

"The Bubble?"

"I'll get to that in a minute."

She took the card, and put it in her pocket, hoping she wouldn't mix them up with the ones she'd be using with her Nikon.

"Are there any credible threats against the President these days?"

"I treat it as ongoing."

"Must be hard for her."

"She doesn't have time to worry about it. That's *my* job. Now, when she moves about outside of the White House, there are hundreds of support personnel that travel with her in what we call the Bubble. It can seem a bit stifling to the uninitiated, but it frees her up to work without interruption."

"Will I ever be in the line of fire, like you guys?"

He thought about his answer silently for a few seconds. "Since you've qualified, you'll eventually be issued a firearm that you can carry. I don't expect you'll have to use it, but it doesn't hurt to have some insurance."

"That's...great. I guess."

"You're scoring in the low ninety percentile and clearly capable of handling a weapon. Is there a problem?"

She tried to speak, but something like a lump near her larynx impeded her words. She swallowed, then continued. "I know my accuracy's improved. But if push came to shove, I don't know if I could actually pull the trigger."

"You did when you had a gun pointed at Colson."

Her heart started jackhammering at the memory. "It wasn't loaded."

"You didn't know that when you pulled the trigger."

"That's just it. After going through that experience over and over in my mind, I just don't know if I could actually kill someone."

Concern laced his brow. "Not even if it was to protect someone you cared about?"

She considered the question, but couldn't quite answer. After a few more minutes reviewing protocols and processes, Wade checked his watch and stood. The meeting ended at the exact end of the scheduled twenty minutes.

He reached over to shake her hand. "Thanks for stopping by."

His grip was warm, protective.

In that very instant, a vision flashed through her like the sharp crack of static electricity. A shiny red tag, a name, black and white fur, a boy about seven years old. Not much, but it might just do the trick.

Pumping his hand once more, then taking hers back, she smiled and said, "Mister Jeeves."

"Pardon?"

"Your childhood pet. Black and white tuxedo cat, red tag?"

"Wait, how did you—?"

She gave him a grin and stepped out of his office. "Guess the switch got flipped."

# NINE

THE WHITE HOUSE
THE OUTER OVAL
10:31 AM EST

ADRIFT IN THOUGHT, Xandra managed to make her way into the Outer Oval, the office space with triune arched windows which afforded a generous view of the Rose Garden. According to David Scott, the President's personal secretary by whose desk Xandra now stood, this was the "holding pen" where people scheduled to speak with the Commander in Chief waited.

"You'll be spending a lot of time here between her appointments," David said, clicking his mouse as he stared at his computer monitor. "Each morning, we'll go over the schedule so you can be ready for whatever event might be on her docket for the day. As soon as her next meeting begins, you'll go in, get your shots, then slip out when you're done."

"How does it look today?" Xandra stepped away from the chair upon which she rested her camera and gear, and leaned over to the door that enclosed the Oval Office. She peered through a peephole and saw that Bradley's desk was unoccupied.

"She's been spending some extra time with her son every morning since the assassination attempt. But the day starts with the PDB, the President's Daily Brief, and a briefing with the Joint

Chiefs. After lunch, she's got a meeting with the Russian ambassador." He pointed to the credenza against the wall. "Top drawer. Keep whatever you need in there. Maya used to keep extra lenses, camera bodies, and SD cards as backups in there."

She pulled the drawer open and lifted out a bag with half a dozen Snickers bars. "Backup gear?"

David nodded over to a Secret Service agent at the other side of the Outer Oval. "That's their stash."

The agent nodded at the candy.

Grateful, Xandra pocketed a bar just in case she got too busy for menial things like lunch.

The intercom on David's desk beeped.

He picked it up, nodded, then said, "I'll send her in now."

When the door finally opened, it wasn't the president who came to greet her, but a sandy haired boy, his eyes bright and blue, peeking out from behind the edges of the door frame. He looked right up to Xandra, sat and regarded her with concern.

"Are you the new photographer?" he said, eyeing her skeptically.

"I'm Xandra Carrick. And you must be Mister Bradley." She extended her hand.

Rather than shake it, he frowned and walked back into the room.

"You're too young to work here."

Her surprise ebbed as she stepped into the Oval Office, eyes drawn to the pair of flags that stretched up the length of the pale blue silk curtains adorning the three south-facing windows. Before them, a pair of Louis XVI-style gilded chairs flanked the desk. Awestruck, she floated toward it.

*Oh my...*

Before her sat the world famous *Resolute* desk, a gift from Queen Victoria to President Rutherford B. Hayes in 1880, and constructed from the timbers of the British Arctic Exploration ship for which it was named.

Xandra resisted the urge to gawk and take pictures of the

morning rays casting a golden aura about it. For just a moment, the thought of terrorist attacks and assassination attempts evaporated.

"Good morning," President Bradley said, from behind her. She was seated at one of the two sofas facing each other and flanking the presidential seal in the center of a large circular rug.

Jolted from her reverie, Xandra turned to greet her.

"Madam President."

Jennifer Bradley came over and extended her hand. Despite what Xandra had always thought, the President was not much taller than her, perhaps five-seven without heels.

"It's an honor, Ma'am."

"Sorry about Mikey." She glanced down to her son with a sympathetic look. "He's still upset about Maya."

Standing somewhere behind her, the boy cleared his throat. "Mom...?"

"My apologies, Ms. Carrick. My son prefers to be addressed as Michael." She bent down and mussed his hair, then kissed the top of his head. "But to me, you'll always be my wittle Mikey-Wikey!"

"Mo-om!"

"Sorry, kiddo."

"You said we could go to the ranch today."

The President countenance dropped suddenly.

"I'm afraid we're going to have to do that another day."

"That's what you said last week."

"I know, I'm sorry."

He rolled his eyes and let out a dramatic sigh. "It's okay, I'm getting used to it."

"I'll let you play on my iPad," she said, with a hopeful look.

"Okay..."

"Just don't go hacking into Mr. Wade's files. He doesn't like that."

"I know."

With a light pat on his rump, she motioned for him to go over to her desk.

He glared at her, then scurried over to it. Pulling the tablet from under a pile of papers, his scowl gave way to a grin as he sat and swiped away on the tablet in quiet bliss.

"Crisis averted...for now." Bradley returned her attention to Xandra and gestured to the sofa facing hers. "Please, have a seat."

"Thank you." It was surreal sitting here where countless heads of state had met, where historic decisions of had been forged. Xandra had to keep reminding herself that she was a professional on duty, and not a gawking tourist.

"First off," President Bradley began, "I want to thank you for accepting the position of Chief White House Photographer on such short notice. These have been challenging times to say the least."

"I'm honored."

"You came highly recommended."

"Yes, well, I was briefed by Wade Masterson earlier."

"He thought highly of you. Are you okay with the dual roles?"

If Wade had been truthful, the President already had an idea about her clairvoyance. "I am."

"I won't order you to do this," the President said, looking surprised that Xandra had taken it that way. "The official position of Chief Photographer is yours, either way—with or without the investigative duties."

"Thank you."

"I take it you've already met with the press secretary."

"First thing this morning."

"And he's briefed you on your photography-related responsibilities?"

"It's a lot to cover, but I've got the basics. There is something I'd like to ask you, though, regarding his policies."

Seated at the *Resolute* desk, Mikey hummed a familiar song, remarkably in tune and well-metered. It was faint, but when he quietly sang the words, it was enough to draw both of their attention.

Poignant memories emerged from the recesses of Xandra's

mind: Sitting in the pews with Mom as a child, the kaleidoscope of morning light shining through stained-glass windows casting colorful hues onto the floor. And the words of that same hymn they had so often sung:

*Sweet hour of prayer, sweet hour of prayer*
*That calls me from a world of care,*
*And bids me at my Father's throne*
*Make all my wants and wishes known.*
*In seasons of distress and grief,*
*My soul has often found relief...*

Bradley's eyes glistened with tears. Quickly, she wiped them, turned back to Xandra, and put on a brave smile. "That was his father's favorite. They used to sing it together in his hospital room before he lost his battle with cancer."

"I'm so sorry for your loss."

She lowered her voice to just above a whisper. "It's been especially hard on Mikey. First his dad, then Maya."

"He still has you."

"You know...As President, you have to be strong for so many people. But mostly for your family." Bradley chewed her lip. "That bullet at the inaugural parade was meant for me."

"I can't imagine how difficult it must be. You face so much hatred."

"No more than the presidents before me." She lowered her voice so as to keep what she was saying from Mikey's ears. "They were disgruntled Americans."

"Thank God you and Mikey are okay."

"For now." Bradley shut her eyes for a brief moment, then drew a deep breath. Her dignified bearing returned. "We've got situations boiling in Tariqistan as well as threats to the U.S. which need to be dealt with. That's going to be occupying most of my time."

"Of course."

"Anyway, you'll just have to hit the ground running...Now,

you had a question about Adam's policies."

"Right. Well, he told me that all my photos must be cleared by him before release. Seems unusual. Could you explain why?"

A puzzled look crossed Bradley's features. "I've never given it much thought. Just an artifact of Colson's internal policies, I suppose. After all, Rick had a lot to hide and didn't trust anyone. Not even Jim Filmore, his photographer and friend who had worked for him before and all through his campaign."

"Guess I'm going to have to earn your trust before—"

"Consider the policy revoked."

Xandra blinked. "Ma'am?"

"I'm not Nixon, and I'm certainly not Rick Colson—though I supposed the questionable blessing of having been his running mate is what put me here in my first term—but no, there's no need for that kind of censure."

"You can overturn a policy, just like that?"

"It's not a Federal matter." She winked. "And last I checked, you were the President's photographer, and I was the president."

"I'll earn that trust, I promise."

Just then, the intercom on the desk beeped.

"Excuse me," Bradley said, and picked up the handset. After half a minute of nods and short questions, she hung up and regarded Xandra with an animated look.

"You can start earning that trust really soon."

"Ma'am?"

"I've just received a message from President Aamaal's office in Tariqistan. With the recent threats and demands for us to withdraw, there's been an increase in insurgent activity. Her generals and officials are getting cold feet. I'm going to move up next month's visit to show her our resolve and support."

"When are you going?"

"Don't you mean, when are *we* going?"

The thought raced through her like a jolt of electricity. "Yes, Ma'am."

"We leave a week from today."

Speechless, Xandra just stood there looking at Bradley. She couldn't believe it— traveling internationally with the President. In just a couple of days, she'd be flying with her aboard *Air Force One.*

*And shadowing a high profile target.*

"I'll take that stunned look as enthusiasm," Bradley said. "This being your first big assignment, do you feel up to it?"

"Absolutely."

"There is one thing I wanted to ask—not presuming—but based on your unique abilities, are you able to tell me if flying over to Tariqistan would be a mistake?"

A wave of tingly heat flushed Xandra's face.

"With all due respect, Ma'am. I don't know if I could discern future events like that."

"Well, the Reagans had Joan Quigley."

"Who?"

"Joan Quigley, their astrologer with whom they'd consult on the good or ill alignment of the stars. Nobody knew it at the time, but Nancy Reagan began calling upon her services after the assassination attempt on her husband in 1981 for practically every decision. She pretty much controlled the flight schedule of *Air Force One* during his administration."

Caught somewhere between a surprised laugh, and a nervous chuckle, Xandra drew a short breath, a false start, then shook her head. "I—I don't think I could do anything like that for you. I mean—"

Bradley shook her head and patted her shoulder. "I'm kidding, relax. You have a unique talent which might prove helpful, but I don't expect you to be my personal psychic."

"If I get anything, I'll be sure to let you know."

"Better to let Wade Masterson know first."

The President stood up.

Xandra did as well.

"Forgive me for cutting our meeting short, but I've got to talk with the National Security Advisor before our next meeting where

he'll undoubtedly rake me over the coals for my decision to go."
She extended a hand. "See you in the Situation Room in ten
minutes. There will be some very unhappy faces to record for the
archives."

Xandra reached out to shake the proffered hand. "Yes
Ma'am."

"Great to have you here," the President said, gazing straight
into her eyes. "I have a feeling we're going to get along just fine."

And with that, she went over to Mikey, took his hand and led
him to the door.

"Sweetie, I promise, we'll go to the ranch really soon."

His eyes were no longer on the iPad, but turned down to the
carpet. "You're going away again?"

"I have to fly out for another trip next week, but Grandpa will
come to stay with you at the White House until I get back. Then
we'll all go to the ranch."

With suddenly brightened eyes, he looked up and smiled. "For
real?"

"For real."

"Do I have your word?"

"Now you sound like your Daddy."

His smile grew wider and he stood tall with his chest puffing
out. "Well?"

"Yes, you have my word."

A female Secret Service agent entered and nodded to the President who then bent down, kissed Mikey, and exited, leaving him
in her care.

Xandra caught several shots of the affectionate exchange.

Through the viewfinder, she saw him wave her over.

The closer she got, the more she could see that his smile had
vanished, the corners of his mouth pulling down, his lips pressed
together and quivering.

Xandra knelt close to meet his gaze. All the loss and trauma
he'd recently suffered rose to the surface. No child should carry
such emotional burdens, on top of being the son of the busiest

woman in the world.

"What's the matter, Michael?"

"Are you going with my mother on that trip?"

Xandra nodded.

"I'm scared," he said.

"Of what?"

"I know it wasn't Maya's fault, but..." He recomposed himself, sniffed, then wiped his eyes with his sleeve. "Please, don't let my mom get killed."

# TEN

THREE YEARS EARLIER

UNDISCLOSED LOCATION
Outside the Border of Tariqistan

THE VOID YIELDED NOTHING but the sound of a slow drip somewhere in the darkness. He had no idea how long he'd been here, or where he was. For all he knew, this could be Hell.

*Hell wouldn't be this cold...*

Lying on his back, he forced his eyes open. But it afforded him nothing more than when they'd been shut. From his gut radiating to his extremities, pain shot through his entire body as he attempted to sit up.

He strained.

Even his throat ached.

Finally, managing to negotiate turning over onto his hands and knees, he wheezed, coughed, spat out what must have been the largest, foulest plug of phlegm he'd ever produced. He exhaled with enough force to let out an anguished moan.

The memories bled back into his mind's eye.

*Odin...*

*Aiza.*

The explosions, the flames.

A sob escaped his lungs. It thrust a dagger of pain into his side. Instinctively, he reached over, but the touch only caused it to ignite, sending him reeling back on the cold ground.

The trickle of images became a deluge. He fought to hold them off.

*Molten shrapnel*

*limbs,*

*burning flesh,*

*blood spattering onto his face.*

Tears burned his eyes.

*That last missile should have killed me as well.*

He slapped his hand against the ground. Slicing through the skin and carving its way up through his arm, shoulder, and neck, the ache was palpable.

Worse than Hell.

His wife and son were gone.

He'd survived.

"I should be dead too!"

His words resounded endlessly in what sounded like a series of cavernous halls. Eventually fading, they once again gave way to that hollow stillness.

He puled, "I should be dead..."

"Ironic, but I agree."

That unmistakable twang, the heavy Kishwari dialect, followed by a blinding white light drew Ishmael's arm up to shield his eyes. Despite the stitching aches and open wounds, he rolled over and backed away from the sound of Massoud Haashir's voice.

"Imagine my delight when I learned I might have the opportunity to repay your hospitality," Haashir said, his tone as cold as the stone floor from which Ishmael tried to stand up.

"How did you escape?" Ishmael grunted.

The light went out. But Ishmael's vision went from white, to red and began fading to black again.

"Did you really think you could contain me? I have many *loyal* friends." Haashir huffed. "Unlike you."

Ishmael let out a threatening growl. "What did you do?"

"I see...that's right. Sorry about your wife and son...and all your friends." A sardonic laugh. "But that wasn't my doing."

Unless he'd somehow gotten access to American drones, he was telling the truth.

"Oh, Ishmael, my little brother. If I've told you once, I've told you a thousand times. You can't trust the Americans any more than you can the British. They'll promise you a kingdom, wealth, and fame, then use you and when they're done with you, dispose of you like old trash."

"No, I don't believe—!"

"They did it to my father, why not you? What makes you think you're so special?"

The only thing that surpassed his confusion was the anger that raged within him. He couldn't make sense of it. All he knew was that Odin and Aiza had been blown to pieces by American Hellfire missiles launched from an unmanned drone.

How simple for them to extinguish the lives of innocent people, their own assets, at the mere push of a button—like it was some kind of video game?

"Come now, little brother—"

"I am *not* your brother!"

"You ought to be grateful, considering how you betrayed me. Even while you were about to hand me over, I came and pulled your worthless carcass from the burning remains of your family."

Ishmael launched himself with all his might in the direction of Haashir's voice.

"You should have killed me while you had the opportunity!"

The white light blasted his eyes, a pair of hands grasp his wrists, then swung him sideways into a wall. The pain was so exquisite, flecks of blue light swam before his eyes.

"Oh, I will, my brother…" Haashir said, with morbid repose.

Ishmael let out a snarl, hands blindly seeking purchase around Haashir's throat.

"But you haven't suffered enough yet." Haashir released his grip and shoved Ishmael back into the darkness. "I want you to feel the pain of how you failed your little boy, your lovely wife. How you made them pay for your arrogance."

Ishmael clambered to his feet rushed at the opening of the cell where stood the silhouette of Haashir's frame, and that of a guard holding what looked like a Kalashnikov. It earned him a blow to the ribs with the end of the guard's AK-47.

Ishmael fell to his knees, searing pain spreading upwards. He wanted to cough and retch, but even that hurt too much. Through his fury, confusion, and despair, it was that last glimpse of his family that drove the tears back to his eyes—Odin, holding his prized action figure, Aiza smiling in relief that soon, as Ishmael had promised, he would be done with that dark line of work.

If the balance of his life was sufficient, he would spend it seeking their justice. He owed them nothing less.

"Don't be in such a rush to leave, Ishmael," Haashir said. "Like they say in America: Today is the first day of the rest of your life."

# ELEVEN

*Because you want to know...*
                *...need to know...*
*Whispers, words of dubious sincerity, of nebulous intent*
*I can tell you....*
*His eyes gaze intently into hers, into her very soul.*
*Sorrow, despair, desperation*
*And a longing for absolution.*
*Tears...*
*Penitent tears...*
*I can tell you...show you*
      *...what you want to know...*
      *...need to know...*
*Her heart rent, pain pushes tears to her eyes.*
*Leaning her forehead against his, eyes squeezed shut with empathy, she wants to know.*
*Who are you?*
*What is it I need to know?*
*She knows him.*
*And yet she doesn't.*
*The fog around him dissipates.*
*The eyes, the face...somewhere in the unseen distance a low-pitched growl of a fierce dog or a wolf rumbles.*
*A friend? An enemy?*
*As he comes closer, he steps away and another person she doesn't know comes to her.*

*Who...?*

*His eyes...one blue, the other green.*

*She sees herself as a little girl about three or four years old, standing next to him.*

*Who is he?*

*In a paternal voice like Dad's, he says to her,* Trust me, *and holds her hand.*

*And then, as that comforting image evanesces, the penitent man reemerges.*

Oh, God. Not him!

A DAMP CHILL ENVELOPED HER like a burial shroud. Jarred awake, Xandra glanced at the sanguine LED numbers on the clock on her nightstand...

4:29 AM

Again.

For the second time since coming to Washington, a grotesque dream about the man who had tried to murder her and then ended up saving her, haunted her slumber.

But it had been so much more than a dream.

Though lacking the clarity of a full precognitive vision, this one shared that same sense of temporal transcendence, that momentary awareness of the connection, overlap, and intersection of past, present, and future.

A bead of cold sweat rolled down her spine eliciting a shudder. Nevertheless, she felt an overwhelming need to peel away the damp sheets which had entangled her during her sleep.

Sleep, of which the hideous specter of Ian Mortimer had robbed her.

With an exasperated sigh, Xandra shed the linen and sat up.

Day Two as the President's Photographer, and once again she'd been denied the two last precious hours of sleep by the image of...

*Strange.*

Why hadn't it filled her with dread?

Instead, a pang impaled the center of her heart, the way it had when Mom passed away. Not anger, not fear, but a curious wonder. As though she'd caught a glimpse of the future, of eternity.

But why of all people, Ian Mortimer?

Could that murderous assassin possibly know something about an impending threat to President Bradley?

With a shudder, she recalled his icy fingers crushing her throat.

The muzzle of his gun pointed at her.

And then it returned.

The utter sense of isolation of living alone here in Georgetown.

This new job encumbered her with responsibility as well as access to the President, but Xandra had yet to find that pervading sense of purpose in her life. She wasn't seeking fame, nor did she harbor any political aspirations. It had been the White House that reached out and offered her the job. She only accepted because it was ridiculous not to, and in truth, she had no better prospects.

*But why am I here?*

Mikey's frightened expression came to mind.

Wade's crumpled business card lay next to her watch on the nightstand.

For the first time since she began, she looked forward to the training sessions with Wade Masterson at zero-dark-thirty.

# TWELVE

JAMES J. ROWLEY TRAINING CENTER
SECRET SERVICE
BELTSVILLE, MD
Saturday, 7:48 AM EST

IN ALL HER YEARS AT JUILLIARD, PRINCETON, and at the *Times,* Xandra never imagined she'd find herself spending her predawn hours at a shooting range in the Secret Service's training facility—especially after a fairly successful first day on the job as the President's photographer. She'd made some great shots with Bradley addressing the Joint Chiefs in the White House Situation Room and had been permitted to stay longer than she would have expected. By the end of the day, she was so exhausted she fell asleep as soon as her head found her pillow.

But Rowley was precisely where she'd spent the past month-and-a-half training intensively. To her surprise—as well as Wade's—she was excelling in her physical fitness and self-defense, and could even fire a weapon reasonably well.

"You don't think I'll need advanced firearms training, do you?" Xandra said, leaving the range with him.

"You seem fairly competent, but no, I don't see the need. Not yet, anyway."

"Regular trainees undergo a lot more, right? I mean, this place is like a miniature city—in a Hollywood set kind of way."

"Simulated town, driving courses, caves/bunkers, helo pad with a chopper, obstacle course, 12 miles of roads, an airport apron sim, *Air Force One* and *Marine One* sims, a protective driver training course, K-9 training area, and outdoor training and tactical response areas..."

"How much of that will I go through?"

"Not nearly as much as an actual agent. But I have to warn you, the exam you're taking today is fairly tough. One trainee got a rib broken, but kept it to himself because he was afraid he'd get discharged from the program."

"Ouch."

"Another one had her leg all bruised by training bullets while chasing 'assassins' through the woods. An instructor got a broken jaw during a Remedial Control Tactics exam..." A faint smile surfaced along with a thoughtful glance at the ceiling. "Not sure which was tougher, BUDS or Secret Service training. My team trains here two out of every eight weeks and trust me, it's not for the faint of heart."

"You don't think I can't handle it?"

"I'm just saying..."

She smirked, eyed him with a razor sharp stare. "So, I'm just some helpless damsel in distress."

"I was just—"

"How did I do with that...that..." she made a gun out of her thumb and forefinger, "what's it called?"

"Sig Sauer P229."

"I thought you said I was pretty competent."

"I did. But we aim for center mass, the heart. No warning shots."

They stopped at a room with a sign that read: MAT ROOM - Dixon

Wade tilted his head towards the open door. "You ready?"

"Yeah. I got this." Xandra said, straightening the black baseball cap on her head, and slinging her backpack full of the gear she'd need for this exam. Pushing past him, she entered the room quietly. After settling down, she stood with the other trainees, palms growing cold and moist. Why would any sane person subject themselves to anything like this?

*No one ever accused me of being sane.*

Dixon, the instructor, stood about 6'4 and paced about with a frame that could make anyone cower. His chest stood high and his biceps were about to rip through his black T-shirt like Dr. Bruce Banner's "after" photo. Glaring at a room full of trainees—some male, some female—he spoke in an ominous tone.

"The whole world will spin and you'll feel like puking..." Dixon glanced over to Xandra, "Don't do it in my mat room. I get trainees passing out in the bathroom, so you're going to want to use the buddy system in this class."

After a few more words of instruction, Dixon paired off the trainees and the entire mat room went dark. Heavy metal music blasted in the room, now acting as a pub with flashing red and blue lights.

Xandra glanced out to the door, where Wade stood watching through its window.

*Good luck,* he mouthed.

"Carl McFee has made threats against POTUS," Dixon said. "You've got an arrest warrant for him, and your informant has tipped you off that he's in this bar." He opened the prop-door and the first pair of trainees entered. "Bring him in."

With astounding ferocity, the instructors attacked the trainees with sticks and knives. The ensuing chaos made Xandra wince. This was not play-acting, they were seriously trying to hurt the trainees. She remembered the agent with the broken rib Wade had mentioned.

"Are those real?" she whispered to her partner.

"Training knives," he said. "But we treat everything like it's the real thing here."

In less than five seconds one of the trainees got 'shot' three times, and the other ended up on the floor, his face cut and bleeding.

"Carrick, Orman!" Dixon barked. "You're up!"

This was where she'd see if any of what she'd learned had kept. After seeing the beating the last team took she wanted to slip out of the room and go back to her office. But quitting now, before her first real challenge? What kind of message would that send to Wade, to the President?

*That I value a fully intact body.*

"Quit stalling, Carrick!" Dixon shouted. "Go in and get your man."

She went in behind Orman, as the instructor shook his head. "She was a newspaper photographer," Dixon huffed. "Can you believe that?"

As soon as she and Orman entered, the role-players struck Orman in the face, knocking him to the ground, and then 'stabbed' him with his training knife.

The second instructor shoved Xandra on to her back, pinned her down with his knee and elbow, then raised his fist to punch her in the face.

"That's McFee." Dixon said. "This is your only chance, Carrick!"

Xandra's limbs tensed. For an instance, time stopped. She was back under that cold pond where Ian Mortimer had tried to drown her. Struggling to free herself, she opened her eyes.

'McFee's fist came down.

Xandra blocked it with her forearm.

She grunted, strained and grabbed his arm, trying to push it away.

But McFee pushed it down over her throat.

Her eyes felt as though they would explode. She couldn't draw the slightest breath, much less call out for help.

Amidst the flashing lights, the heavy metal blasting over the speakers, Xandra was about to pass out.

"Don't give up, Carrick!" Dixon yelled. "You never quit! You always win. Everything else is negotiable!"

She reached up, and dug her thumb into his jawline at the highest point, just under the ear, where it connected to the base of his skull. With whatever strength she had left, she pressed inward and upward.

McFee grunted, and backed away, releasing his arm from Xandra's neck.

But only for a moment.

He bent down, dragged her to her feet, re-establishing a new choke hold.

She sputtered out the last bit of air in her mouth while trying in vain to pry his sinewy arm from her neck.

And then, just as it seemed she would collapse, Xandra took the last visceral measure she could think of.

She turned her head, sunk her teeth into McFee's hand and bit down so hard, she felt his skin break.

In the split second it took for him to release her, she grabbed his arm to steady herself, lifted both of her feet off the floor, and kicked the heel of her boots into his groin.

Dixon cringed.

McFee rolled onto the ground in silent agony. Xandra went on to cuff him. Her cap had fallen off and her hair which had been tied up now covered her face like that of a mad-woman's. Nevertheless, she pulled McFee to his feet and managed a triumphant snarl.

"And that," Dixon said, grinning at Xandra, then facing the class, "is a passing grade in *Remedial* Control Tactics."

# THIRTEEN

AS THEY LEFT THE BUILDING, Xandra's neck and shoulders were so overwhelmingly sore she had to knead them with her fingers in order to stave off facial contortions.

Wade set a pair of dark sunglasses over his eyes as the morning sun fell right onto his face. "I can't believe you kicked him in the junk."

Xandra groaned. "Was that off limits? You think I'm going to play by some stupid male honor code and preserve the family jewels of a terrorist?"

He laughed. "You kicked some serious ass, anyway."

"That's not what I kicked."

Across the pavement where her car and driver waited, a uniformed officer stepped out of the adjacent car—a black SUV—and opened the rear door. A dog resembling a German Shepherd with a tawny coat climbed out and sat like a statue as the officer hooked a lead to its collar.

Xandra stopped, her entire body growing cold. "Could we just...go around that?"

"Don't worry, he's fine."

Wade kept walking.

But Xandra couldn't move. The last thing she wanted him to know was that she'd had a phobia of dogs since she was nine, when a Saint Bernard she'd since referred to as "Cujo" attacked her while she was taking a walk in Prospect Park with Mom and Dad back in Brooklyn.

"Wade?"

He stopped, turned around with amusement creasing his features. "Aw, come on, I'll introduce you." While Xandra stood petrified about a yard away, Wade stepped right up to the dog's handler. "Reed."

"Morning, Sir. Guest?"

Wade turned around smiling at Xandra's proximity, or lack thereof. "Assistant Operative in training." Increasing the volume of his voice, slightly: "She can take down a thug twice her size, but is afraid of dogs."

"Don't tell me," Reed said, "ex-kindergarten teacher?"

"Photojournalist. Used to work for the *New York Times*."

They could have been making all kinds of crude remarks about her, for all Xandra knew. The only thing she was aware of was the vicious dog, whose eyes fixed upon hers unrelentingly. All at once, she was back in Brooklyn, drowning in a sea of fur and dog drool, pinned down and immobilized. Her fear had been compounded with anger when Mom's laughter broke through Dad's panicked shouts. It turned out Cujo had been an overly-friendly dog that loved children, and the worst thing that had happened to her that day was a small scrape on her elbow and a face full of happy dog drool. Nevertheless, she'd inherited a life-long apprehension as a result and now, the canine phobia-incarnate stared her down, daring her to move, to breathe.

"It's okay," Wade called out, shattering her reverie. "He won't bite."

Nodding vacuously, because her eyes were still locked onto the dog's, Xandra somehow managed to drift over to Wade's side.

He made the introductions, which barely registered.

"This is Max," Reed said. "Lovingly referred to as 'The General.'"

"Max?" As soon as she said his name, the dog snapped to attention. Its eyes which had just been locked onto Reed's shot over to hers. "Why does he do that?"

Reed rubbed Max's ears. "Do what?"

"He just…stares."

"Max is a Belgian Malinois, recently retired from the K9 Explosives Detection Unit. Before that, he was an active duty Navy Seal. This guy used to jump out of choppers with his handler and hit the ground running, literally. So yeah, he's an extremely focused laser guided furball."

Xandra forced a smile, but Max didn't move his gaze. "That's…nice?"

"Plus," Wade said, "I think he likes you."

"Oh, no…" she took a step back. "No, Wade. Don't."

"Go on, Max, give her a hug!"

A sharp squeal worthy of a girl a tenth her age flew out of her mouth. "No!"

Max reared up on his hindquarters and his forepaws reached out.

"Down!" she cried. "Bad dog!"

But Max continued standing with his paws out. It would have been comical, had the need for Depends not become imminent.

"Down, Max." Reed said, in a firm voice.

The dog complied, and now sat like the Sphinx, his head erect, and all four paws on the ground. His mouth was open displaying brilliant fangs and a pink tongue casually draped over the edge of his lower jaw.

Xandra could swear the beast was smiling.

Laughing.

"Good boy," she said, but it came out as an embarrassing squeak.

More staring.

"The General's getting along in years," Reed said, "But he's a great dog. A lot more disciplined than most, and probably smarter than any other I've seen come through here."

"Smarter than some of our agents," Wade said, rolling his eyes to the sky.

Reed laughed in agreement.

Then Wade knelt down and ran his hand over Max's head,

massaging the scruff of his neck. He waved Xandra over but she didn't move.

"He's really nice. You can't be scared of him."

If there was one button Wade knew to press, it was her ego button. He knew she would never afford him the opportunity to gloat, or the excuse to drop her from the training program because she was too weak.

"Fine." Slowly, she approached and bent down. Once again, pride won out over discretion. One day, it would really get her into deep water. *Oh, right...as if* that *hasn't already happened.*

Stretching her hand as though over a boiling pot of sulfuric acid, she put a quivering palm before Max's nose, then rubbed the fur under his chin. "Hi Max," she whispered.

Right away, he lowered his head into her hand and looked right up at her with earnestly large eyes. Startled by his sudden display of affection, Xandra smiled. "Aw." She got closer as he leaned his face into her hand. A tingling warmth rushed through her.

In her mind's eye, she was seeing through the eyes of the dog, standing over a gravestone, his heart-aching. These vision flashes were the most powerful when seeing from within a subject's perspective. This was the first time she'd ever seen through that of an animal—and of all animals, a dog. But right away, she felt the profound love, loyalty, and pain Max had once felt. It might however be something he was currently feeling, or going to feel in the future, there was no way to be certain right now.

When she opened her eyes, Max was looking right into hers. It was as if they had been life-long friends, the kind you only need look at, and the other knows exactly what you are thinking and feeling."

"So what's he doing back here?" Wade asked Reed. "Aren't retired K9's supposed to live with their handlers?"

At that, Reed frowned and lowered his gaze. "Yeah, well that's just the thing. Max's handler died last month. Daniels was one of the best."

A look of surprise and uncharacteristic sympathy came over Wade. "Lee Daniels?"

Max let out a melancholy whine, turned his head to the side, leaned heavily into Xandra's lap, shut his eyes and did something she never knew dogs could do—took a deep breath and sighed. Instinctively, she cradled him and rubbed his fur. "I'm sorry, Boy...there...there..."

Wade straightened up. "Damned shame. Lee and all his dogs were the stuff of legends."

If a dog could cry, Xandra thought Max surely would. She had sensed, and now saw the loss he felt. It was in his eyes, the way this mighty animal seemed to deflate at the very mention of his departed handler. She knew it all too well, not just the signs, but the actual pain of bereavement.

His face resting in her lap, Max's eyes opened.

*Poor thing...*

"He's been going from handler to handler since Daniels' died," Reed said, "but they've all got their hands full."

"So what's going to happen to him?" Xandra said. "They're not going to..."

"Oh, no. Max is a veteran. We'll find a place for him eventually." He patted his thigh. "C'mon, boy."

But Max didn't move. He just looked up at Xandra.

"Max...come."

Finally, he got up and went over to Reed. But as he walked, there was a slight limp in his right front leg.

"What's wrong?" Xandra pointed at the leg.

"Injury in Afghanistan back in 2009. That's why he got transferred to K9 EDU—Explosives Detection Unit. His combat days were over by the time he came to us, but I'll tell you what: he'll tear a damned haji's arm right off."

Though she now felt more sorry than afraid, Xandra put a tiny bit of distance between her and the dog.

Wade patted Max. "I'll make some calls."

"Hope someone steps up soon," Reed said. "Max has been

howling at night—crying, more like it. Hate to see the old boy like that. If he has to spend another night in the kennel…"

"I'll adopt him," Xandra said.

At that, both Wade and Reed turned and for a moment remained speechless.

Fighting her life-long fear, she stepped over to Max, who stood perfectly still, eyes fixed on her, and offered him her hand.

"I don't know," Reed said. "His best days are behind him. I don't know how many years he's got left."

Max nuzzled Xandra's hand and at the very moment, something stirred within her. It was as though a connection had been made between their hearts. Big and fierce as he was, he sensed her sympathy.

"You sure?" Wade said, even as Max leaned his massive head against her leg, his tail thumping rhythmically on the ground.

"How hard can it be? I mean, he's already trained, right?"

"Yes, but—"

"And I could use the company, living all by myself."

"You're just settling in—new job, new place. Better think it through."

"Not to mention, he'd make a great body guard. I'd love to explore the capital, take some night time shots of the monuments, but with that Midnight Stalker sicko still out there, I can't. No one would dare attack me with Max by my side, though."

Reed leaned over to Wade. "She seems nice enough. And The General really needs a home."

Wade cast her a doubtful look. "I don't know…"


FIFTEEN MINUTES LATER, Xandra was riding in the back of the Secret Service limo with Max, and for once, she wasn't second-guessing herself. Of course there'd be adjustments to be made, but how could she possibly leave him there alone, and without a home? It was only 7:35 AM. Maybe she'd bring him home, settle him in, and then go to her first full day of work at the White House. There were countless details to figure out, but she'd have to take it on faith that it would work out and not over-think it.

After all, the best laid plans of mice and men...

# FOURTEEN

GEORGETOWN
9:55 AM EST

NATURE CALLS.

After a quick stop at Wag Mart for dog food and other supplies, then stopping by the apartment to drop them off, Max was
signaling his need to answer the call by pawing at the door.

Xandra had watched others walking dogs, but could she pull it
off, armed with only a few basic commands Reed had told her—
sit, stay, heel, down, and down-stay? And would Max obey or rip
her arm out of its socket with the lead still in her hand at the first
sight of a squirrel?

Either way, it was best not to get in the way of a dog and his
need to express himself urologically.

A couple of times around the block should do. Plenty of trees
and places Max—The General—could do his thing with discretion. With a plastic bag in hand, Xandra was ready. She snickered
recalling a t-shirt she once saw on the father of an infant which
read: Parenthood. It's not just a job, it's a doody.

Half a dozen trees and a couple of hydrant sniffs later, Max had
done nothing more than investigate.

"Come on, boy," Xandra said, as he sniffed another tree. "You
can do it. Make a potty."

He just stared at her as though she'd lost her mind—which she just might do if he made a mess all over her apartment. "Go on…"

He turned back to the tree, sniffed it, then looked back as if to say, "Nah."

"Fine. Let's go."

The General never strayed from her left side, never lagged nor pulled the lead. She hadn't even given the "heel" command. Were all dogs this easy to walk?

Just then, outside of Honest Abe's Coffee Depot, he stopped. Xandra would have continued, but Max was so perfectly still she too had to pause to see what he had so affixed his attention upon.

About a yard away from where his nose and eyes pointed, through the open door sat a chrome-plated bowl in a wire-framed stand. It contained a pile of bone-shaped raw hide treats. Above it hung a sign which read: All Four Legged Friends Welcome.

Max sat gazing at the treats, his ears and chest up like the military dog he was—or had once been. But when he turned around and regarded Xandra with those large and earnest eyes, she could almost hear him say, "Please, may I?"

"Really, Max?" She stole a glance at her watch. Rubbed her aching shoulder and neck finding a few bruises and abrasions from her RCT exam earlier. A sharp pain tweaked her left temple, probably from her insomnia.

Eyes still trained on hers, Max continued to wait for her answer.

"Fine. I could use some coffee."

After finding a seat where Max could gnaw away to his heart's delight, Xandra settled down with her Sumatran Dark Roast, and watched the morning rays backlighting Max's fur, creating a nice halo about his outline.

Unfortunately, her Nikon along with the rest of her gear was still at home. So she took out her smartphone and snapped off a few shots as he tore happily at his dog treat. Her first dog-selfie.

As the preview image came up on her screen, everything around her started to fade into darkness. The voices of customers and baristas diminuendoed, echoing as they dissipated into the void.

No dizziness, but it was definitely happening.

Another vision.

The images grew out from the screen of her phone and enveloped everything around her.

*Rows and aisles of seats.*

*Their occupants all completely still, not talking, not even breathing.*

*Their faces are either bruised or covered in...*

Blood.

*She sees clearly now—not on her phone, but in her mind's eye.*

*As though her body were across the room, she hears herself breathing shallow breaths. The relentless pounding of her heart fills the shop like a battery of tympani and bass drums.*

Must breathe...

*But the images sap her power to do so.*

*Blue, red, and black blood vessels protrude from each victim's face like a subway map.*

*Blood drips from eyes, noses, mouths, ears.*

*And then the voice of a child.*

*Please, don't let my mom get killed.*

# FIFTEEN

BEFORE SHE COULD FULLY GRASP it, the darkness swallowed everything around her in a swirling torrent of unintelligible voices, cries of agony, and images flashing about too rapidly to distinguish.

She needed to snap out of this vision, now.

No telling how long she'd been in this state.

She couldn't move, breathe, or even call out for help.

Until a single bark shattered the clamor.

Xandra blinked.

All at once, she was back in the moment at Honest Abe's.

A sturdy paw rested on her lap. Max looked up at her with concern.

Customers were talking, reading, and generally going about their business as if nothing unusual had happened. The vision hadn't taken any time at all, and of course, the customers at this pet friendly coffee shop were accustomed to dogs barking.

Xandra reached down and gave Max a hug. "Good boy."

Had she known dogs could be this caring, she might not have spent the better part of her life avoiding them. As her pulse settled back into a more reasonable tempo, she took mental notes about what she'd just discerned in her vision.

*Bodies.*

*Grotesquely strewn about.*

*Blood.*

*Mikey's plea for his mother, the President.*

Letting out a long breath, Xandra sat back and rubbed her eyes. She'd forgotten how draining these visions could be. Best not to have them in public.

*...Not something you can just turn on and off like a light switch.*

The breakfast scene in *When Harry Met Sally* came to mind where Meg Ryan's character Sally demonstrated to Billy Crystal's Harry in a diner how easy women could "fake it". Xandra let out an ironic chuckle, just as someone behind her said something.

It took another attempt before she realized that the man was talking to her.

"I said, is this seat taken?"

Still reeling, she turned around and spoke before seeing his face. "I'm sorry, were you—?"

The familiar voice matched with the distinct thirty-something caught her by surprise. Just as she'd remembered, albeit masked slightly in a whiskery mug which she'd never seen before.

"Jake?"

"I tried tapping your shoulder."

"Oh my gosh!" She got up and threw her arms around him. The last time she'd seen Jake Rittenhouse was during her tribunal in San Diego for which she had been exonerated. Before that, Jake harbored both her and Kyle Matthews, the FBI agent who helped her escape the murderous attempts of Ian Mortimer. There in the Mennonite colony in which Jake had been the pastor, they hid from the assassin and others working to cover up the newly elected President Colson's Vietnam War atrocities.

As the colony's young pastor, Jake dared challenge Mennonite traditions and comfort levels when he took in Xandra and Kyle. Members of their community treated Kyle's gunshot wounds while keeping them both "under the radar" until they could continue with the investigation.

Kyle had been the first and last man to whom she'd given her heart, and he died protecting her. After Kyle's murder at the hands of Colson's collaborators, Xandra had been framed, arrested, and put on trial for an attempt on the President's life and a bogus domestic terrorism charge. While she'd been held at Navconbrig, she requested to see Pastor Jake for spiritual direction, because she was certain she would be convicted and sentenced to death.

Jake had been the only person who could ever make sense of her preternatural abilities. But she hadn't seen him since her exoneration. The ongoing pang over Kyle's death spiked when she finally recognized his face right here, a few years later.

"So good to see you, Xandra."

She'd been holding onto him for longer than normal. When she let go, her ears were unusually warm. Slowly returning to her seat, she brushed a lock of hair from her face and twirled it between her fingers.

Max sat up and gave her guest an appraising look.

"Who's your friend?" Jake said, offering his hand for The General to sniff.

Max looked at the open palm, then back up to its owner as if saying, *Go sniff your own hand.*

"This is Max," Xandra said, rubbing his ears. "I just adopted him. He's a former military and bomb detection dog."

Jake crouched down. "Hey buddy."

"They nicknamed him The General."

Max didn't so much as blink.

Jake straightened up. "I can see why."

"I'm still getting to know him myself," Xandra said as she sat down with Jake. "So, what are you doing all the way out here?"

"If you'd answered my emails, voicemails, or accepted my friend requests, you might have known." He pulled over a chair from a different table and sat facing her. "I've been here for the past year."

"Yeah, sorry. Life has been complicated since…" she reached down to rub Max's scruff. "So, you've been here for a year? Doing what, exactly?"

"Professor of ancient history at Georgetown."

"But what about…what happened with the colony?"

He shrugged and gave her a sheepish grin. "It was best I moved on, seeing as how I was becoming such a trouble maker."

"You *did* break a lot of their rules."

"They're not bad traditions, don't get me wrong. But if I'd stayed, I would have upset a very delicate balance they've maintained for so many years. I'll miss them, but it's for the best." A wistful smile. "I'm involved with a campus ministry, though, *and* I've been scheduled to give a few sermons over the next year at the National Cathedral."

Xandra drew a deep breath and sighed. Since she'd moved here, his was the first familiar face from her past she'd encountered. Somehow, seeing him brought a deeper comfort than she would have imagined. "You've done well for yourself."

Jake shrugged. "I suppose. So what brings *you* here? Visiting? A gig with the Smithsonian?"

"Nothing that interesting."

Jake narrowed an eye at her.

She wasn't authorized to talk to anyone about her work with the Secret Service, and she was still recovering from her vision of bloody bodies strewn across rows of seats. Best not discuss it. "It's nothing, really."

But his penetrating gaze drew her out. "When a woman says, 'it's nothing,' it never is."

Fine. At least tell him part of it.

"You're going to laugh."

He folded his arms over his chest and leaned back in to his chair. At least he wasn't just being polite.

She cleared her throat, then whispered. "I've been hired as the Chief White House photographer. The President's photographer."

He arched an eyebrow. "I'm impressed."

"I'm still getting used to the idea. Didn't want to sound...I don't know, boastful, you know?"

"Not at all."

Xandra drained the last of her coffee and set the cup down.

"Can I ask you something?"

"You just did."

"Seriously."

The smile remained, but his eyes grew intense.

"Of course. Please, go on."

The mirth burned away like the Pacific marine layer by mid-day which always brought clear skies, and the familiar warmth that so characterized life in Dad's hometown. She searched her empty cup.

"That ability we have?"

"The visions."

"Do you still get those?"

"Once in a while." He leaned in closer. "You?"

She nodded. "Though sometimes I wish I didn't."

"Xandra..." He gave her an empathetic look reminiscent of when they'd first met. She had confided in him about how unbelievable it was that she'd been experiencing these visions, and he quoted Charles Spurgeon: *'We must take care that we do not neglect heavenly monitions through fear of being considered visionary; we must not be staggered even by the dread of being styled fanatical, or out of our minds. For to stifle a thought from God is no small sin.'*

"This gift is meant for helping people, I know." She thought of Mikey's frightened eyes. "But look what it's cost me: Dad, Kyle... I mean, what kind of gift robs you of the ones you love, in order to help others?"

He gave her an empathetic smile.

"Kyle was a good man. I know how much he meant to you."

The memories were a branding iron. Perhaps the best way she could honor Kyle's sacrifice was to continue using the very gifts that had helped bring his killers to justice. Working with the Secret Service equipped her better for this job, but she couldn't tell Jake about that part, regardless of how much she trusted him.

At that moment, Max stood up, looked out the door, back at Xandra, at the door, and back again.

"What is it boy?"

He gave a low-pitched growl and leaned forward.

"I'm sorry, Jake. I think he senses something." She stood and put her jacket on.

"A bomb?" Jake got up as well.

"I don't know. But one way or another I should see what's up."

"Might be another dog outside."

She gave Jake a hug and said, "It was great seeing you again. Maybe I'll see you around."

As Max leaned toward the door a bit more, Jake scribbled something on a napkin. "That's my cell and office phone. "You can reach me at either. Walk you home?"

"It's just around the corner."

"Really? I live just a few minutes from here."

"I don't want to put you out."

"Come on, Xandra. I insist."

With a smile, she conceded. Nodding at Max, she said, "Better go now, he's getting restless."

A minute later as she and Jake ambled down the street, Max eyed every dog around with suspicion, then proceeded with his tree-sniffing mission. They were only half a block from her apartment, and there was no hurry.

"You know?" she said, as Max finally chose a tree, "Colson killed himself, Kyle's dead, and Dad's in federal prison…did my gifts actually do anyone any good?"

He looked intently into her eyes. "For the relatives of the *Binh Son* massacre victims it did—not to mention those Colson secretly murdered. If you hadn't embraced your gift, none of them would have gotten the justice or closure they needed. And besides, what kind of sick world would we be living in with a monster like Colson in the White House?"

She let it sink in.

Jake's deep set eyes never left hers.

Seeing him for the first time in four years, all these questions just floated to the surface. She was already committed to her new job as photographer and assistant operative, why was she second guessing herself all of a sudden?

Max was done and they resumed their walk.

Xandra's apartment building came into view.

"What happens when you try to suppress your gift?" she asked.

"Why would I do that?"

"Rhetorical question."

His eyes narrowed as he pondered it.

"I imagine that like a muscle, it would atrophy."

"Not all muscles are critical to life," Xandra said.

"The heart's a muscle."

They arrived at the apartment building. She stopped to ask him something she knew he couldn't answer.

"I know this ability was meant to benefit others, but what about its cost to me?" She needed to resolve this within herself, because if that vision she had back at Honest Abe's was any indication, she was about to face something more terrifying than ever before.

"When the time comes, I know you'll make the right choice."

"You give me too much credit."

"You give yourself too little."

"Thanks, Jake."

Without thinking, she reached up and kissed him on the cheek.

# SIXTEEN

### THIRTY FOUR MONTHS EARLIER

AL SHARIF DETENTION CELL
UNDISCLOSED LOCATION
Outside the Border of Tariqistan

HE KNEW THIS DAY WOULD COME. Time had held little significance here within the dark cell in which Ishmael had spent the
past two months struggling not only to stay alive, but to keep
from losing his mind. None of the guards who came by each day
would tell him the date, or disclose whether it was day or night.
There were no windows through which sun or moonlight could
enter, no way he could tell otherwise.

"Fifty-eight...fifty-eight...fifty-eight."

Assuming the interval was twenty-four hours in which they
gave him each meal—a piece of stale bread and some kind of
broth, he began to chant the number of days that had passed since
he awoke in this prison cell.

Massoud Haashir rarely came down to taunt him anymore.
He'd stopped doing so somewhere around day twelve.

Ishmael had spent his days in pitch black isolation, hearing nothing more than the faint sound of someone listening to an iPod or some other electronic device capable of playing American pop music through earbuds.

Each day, the person who sat just around the corner for about an hour—judging by the number of songs he listened to—would occasionally snicker or laugh while listening to or watching some kind of comedy routine, and then poke his head around the corner and say, "Still alive?" before leaving.

Ishmael had learned that if he didn't answer, and they found out he was in fact alive, the person sent to verify this—not the young guard, but someone older and much larger, would punish him by beating him severely.

But it was in those few instances that he was able to see light, albeit the meager beam of a flashlight, and the eyes of another human being.

During one such beating, Ishmael spied the face of the young man that must be his daily guard. He was frowning almost with regret as the other guard administered his consequence. But Ishmael had noticed that the young man carried the very keys used to open his cell to let his tormentor in.

Since then, he knew this day would come. The day this young man would be the means to his freedom, his sacrificial lamb.

*Today.*

For weeks, Ishmael had been talking with Mohamed, appealing to his youthful lust for all things American. *I have hundreds of gigabytes of bootlegged MP3s and videos on my private cloud storage on the internet,* Ishmael would tell him, tempting him to ask more.

Mohamed set his flashlight on his chair to illuminate the narrow hallway. "Still alive?"

"Barely," Ishmael said, truthfully, but with calm levity.

"I will try to bring you an extra piece of bread tomorrow."

"May Allah bless you, my brother."

"See you tomor—"

"Mohamed, I'm curious. Was that Justin Timberlake you were just listening to?"

"You have better ears than a dog's!"

"I spent enough time in America to know. But there's nothing like the internet. That's where I've got my treasure trove."

"It must be amazing. Do you really have half a million songs?"

"More."

Mohamed dropped his voice to a murmur and drew closer.

"And those videos? How many did you say?"

"Months' worth. All kinds."

"Blonds?"

"Oh yes." Ishmael had taken his socks off and tied them together making them into a rope. Behind his back, he pulled it taut to test the knot. "Such a pity no one gets to enjoy them. All you'd need is the URL, username and password, and you could have complete access."

"Really?"

"You've been good to me. I wish to repay your kindness."

Mohamed was now standing right at the bars of the cell. The flashlight behind him cast just enough light to show his eyes wide with anticipation. "So you are going to give me your password?"

"Download as much as you like. Oh, but be careful not to get caught. Massoud will kill you if he finds out."

He clicked his tongue. "The old man doesn't know about these things. He'll never know." They were now face to face, so close he could smell the minty gum Mohamed was chewing.

"Well, then. Do you have something to write with?"

"I'll type it into my iPad and save it there."

"What iPad?"

He grinned, held up a finger, "Shhh..." and then stepped back down the hall. "See what I have found? We came here only a few days before Haashir found you. No one knows about it but me."

Crouching, he slid his fingers beneath some kind of rug on the ground. As he lifted it, it became apparent that it was fastened to the top of a trap door.

"Mohamed, be careful," Ishmael hissed. "You'll get caught."

"Do not worry," he said, descending into the opening. "I never get caught."

A few moments later, he climbed back up and shuffled over to the bars, the pale light of his iPad illuminating his face. "I am ready."

Just then, the sound of shouting came in the distance.

"What's that?" Ishmael said.

Reacting to the sound of automatic gunfire that erupted outside, Mohamed turned around to look down the hallway.

In that split second, Ishmael stuck his right hand out with one knotted end of his sock cord, pulled it around Mohamed's throat, and grabbed the other end with his left.

Pulling back with all his might and the full weight of his body, Ishmael tightened the cord then began to twist the ends, tightening the noose around Mohamed's neck.

Writhing, Mohamed dropped his iPad.

His boot came down and smashed the screen.

The staccato of gunfire grew closer.

As did the pounding of feet running about above the ceiling.

But Mohamed continued to struggle, clawing at the sock cord.

"Forgive me, my friend," Ishmael said. "I do you wrong, who only showed me kindness."

After he let out a bit of slack, Ishmael gave the cord a violent jerk.

The snapping bones in Mohamed's neck caused Ishmael deep regret.

*He's somebody's son.*

Ishmael gently helped him as he slumped down, back against the bars, into a seated position. A tear rolled down his face, knowing all too well how it would hurt the heart of Mohamed's father to lose his boy.

"I'm sorry," he whispered, and reached into the pocket of Mohamed's vest and found the keys.

Now the shouts became cries of fear.

The eruption of gun fire, and explosions rocked the entire building above him.

He slipped one of the many keys into the lock.

It didn't work.

Someone was pounding the door at the end of the hallway.

Whoever they were, if they found him, having killed the guard....

He tried another key.

The door blasted open.

"Go, go, go!" Someone shouted down the hallway.

*Americans?*

He tried another key.

Another wrong one!

Lights were coming on down the hallway.

"Clear!"

A third key—how many damned keys did Mohamed have!

Shuffling feet.

Clicking of weapons.

Voices of men growing closer.

"CLEAR!"

Finally, the lock clicked.

Ishmael almost laughed with relief.

He turned the handle and pulled on the bars to open the door.

The lights in the hallway of his cell came on.

It stung his eyes, almost blinding him.

The white veil faded and gave way to Mohamed's lifeless body, which had fallen back into the doorway of the cell, his mouth agape, his eyes wide with surprise.

Ishmael averted his gaze, lest regret hinder him from doing what he must to survive.

"Down here!" An American, probably a soldier or a marine, shouted.

Ishmael stepped over the body and ran to the trap door.

Only yards away from the corner, the sound of urgent steps approached.

Quickly, he found his footing, climbed down the ladder, and shut the trap door, shutting out the light of his entire world.

Once again, he'd been plunged into darkness.

# SEVENTEEN

*I can tell you....*

> *...what you want to know...*

> *...need to know...*

*He sits there, facing President Richard Colson at the Resolute desk, a dark shroud of secrecy blocking out any sunlight from entering the Oval Office.*

*I can tell you...*

XANDRA LET OUT A STARTLED GASP, and opened her eyes. Never in her life had she awoke to find a pair of eyes staring right at her.

"Oh my God, Max!"

4:29 AM.

Again.

Would she ever be able to sleep through the night? These

dreams and visions simply would not relent. If for no other reason but to stop them from intruding upon her much needed rest, she had to find some resolution for them.

And she knew with whom she must ultimately speak.

It was obscenely early, but he did say he didn't really sleep much. And thanks to these nightmares and premonitions, neither did she.

Xandra reached for her phone and found Wade's contact icon.

*It's time to do something about these visions.*

# EIGHTEEN

PRESENT DAY

FDC PHILADELPHIA
FEDERAL DETENTION CENTER
SPECIAL HOUSING UNIT
Sunday, March
11:04 AM EST

"YOU SURE YOU WANT TO DO THIS?" Wade Masterson said as he, Xandra, and a FDC staff member walked down the hall, their footsteps resounding with its vast emptiness.

"A little late to be changing my mind," Xandra whispered, her throat dry from anxiety. "How much did that helicopter ride just cost the taxpayers?"

"You might be onto something, so I'll spare no cost."

"Might not have anything to do with those video threats."

"Or it could be a connection to something else you saw in your visions," Wade said. "With your track record, I'd be a fool to ignore it."

"Not a psychic, remember?"

"Don't care what it's called, as long as it helps us."

She stopped at a heavy door with a small glass window.

The staff person knocked on the door signaling the visitation officer through the window. He then gave Wade a quick nod and walked off, leaving them alone outside the small meeting area.

Like the opening tympani strokes of *Brahms' First Symphony*, her heart began to pound. It had never occurred to her how she might feel confronting the man who once tried to murder her with his bare hands. This was the true reason for her hesitation, though she'd never show this vulnerability to anyone, especially not Wade.

"Okay..." Xandra turned, leaned her back up against the cold wall, and rubbed her temples.

Wade put his hand gently on her shoulder. "Ready?"

Hiding behind a façade of indifference, she shrugged. "Do or die." She was looking forward to this as much as she would removing the rancid carcass of a rat from the back of a closet.

*With your bare hands.*

Wade didn't open the door or hurry her. He just waited for her signal. It was clear he knew she was trying—in vain, most likely—to hide her apprehension.

She took a deep breath, fixed her hair, stood tall, and stepped up. "Ready."

He opened the door.

The door slammed shut, its thunderous sound reverberating back outside in the halls. It all but died, however, when Xandra caught a glimpse of the prisoner in a green jumpsuit sitting at a table, his wrists and ankles bound. He kept his shaved head bowed until she slid out the chair, and stood at the other side of the table. Off to the side, a stern female African-American visitation officer kept a watchful eye.

Slowly, the inmate lifted his eyes to meet Xandra's.

"Hello, my dear. Never thought I'd see you again." He smiled weakly, as though it hurt to do so, "Imagine my surprise...and delight."

She checked his eyes to see if by any chance one was blue, and the other green, though she would have remembered something that unusual. It was more to exclude the possibility that he was the man in her vision holding her hand, saying, *Trust me*.

The eyes were both brown.

And weary.

"Prison time hasn't been very kind to you," Xandra said.

"I've killed more people than Ted Bundy." He frowned, shrugged. "So they've kept me in segregation for my protection. Free meals, protection—who could ask for anything more?" His face crinkled in fatigue as he craned his neck to smile at the V.O. "Some Tea *would* be nice."

If Xandra had been covered in a blanket of leeches, it would be comforting compared to the revulsion she felt for Ian Mortimer right now. Yet there he sat, defeated, demoralized, nothing like the unstoppable monster that he had once been.

Still, this needed to be over with.

As quickly as possible.

Maybe he'd prove her wrong about those dreams.

That would be all. She'd be done.

"Mister Mortimer—"

"Ian, please. No one ever calls me Mister Mortimer anymore."

She cleared her throat. "I came to ask you some questions. Now, if you'll—"

"No questions." His chains rattled as he ran his hands over his face. "I'm sorry."

"Listen, Mortimer," Wade said, his voice low and threatening. "I had to jump through hoops to bring Ms. Carrick here, so you'd best cooperate—"

"Or what?" He scoffed. "You'll arrest me? Put me in prison, sentence me to death? Too late, Laddy. Doesn't get any worse than this. Now, if you'll excuse me, I've got a cozy six-by-six calling my name."

"Ian," Xandra said, trying to conceal her revulsion. "This won't take much of your time." At least she hoped it wouldn't.

Resting his hands in his lap, Mortimer leaned back in his chair, shut his eyes, and let out a tired breath. "Oh, all right." He opened his eyes and glared at Wade. "On one condition."

"Name it," Xandra said, unsure if she was glad or not of the progress.

Mortimer hiked a thumb at Wade.

"Secret Agent Man, leaves."

Wade bristled at the suggestion. "Not a chance."

"Oh, come on," Mortimer said, looking over to Xandra. "It's not like I'm going to try to kill her...again."

She glared at him, wanted to turn around and leave, but she'd already put Wade through so much to get here.

"Sorry," Mortimer said, grinning sheepishly. "That *was* rather tasteless, wasn't it? I'll be a perfect gentleman, I swear. Besides, we've got this formidable V.O. standing within striking distance should I fail to conduct myself properly. Isn't that right?"

"Damned straight," she said, rolling her eyes. "I'll whup you so bad, you gon' be cryin' for your momma."

"There. It's all perfectly arranged."

Wade came over to whisper to Xandra. "I don't like it."

"We've come this far."

"Your call."

Xandra shut her eyes for an indefinite stretch of time. The horrid memories seemed to be returning. But she forced them back.

"I'll be all right, Wade," she said.

"You sure?"

She nodded.

"I'll be right outside." He started for the door. "Anything happens..."

"Don't you worry, Sir," the V.O. said. "I got Morty under control."

"Of course you do," Mortimer said, a feeble smile emerging from his brooding countenance.

Wade stepped outside.

"Well, Lassie," Mortimer said, looking straight at Xandra with eyes that seemed to come to life for the first time in years. "Of what shall we speak?"

# NINETEEN

FAIR IS FOUL, AND FOUL IS FAIR: HOVER THROUGH THE FOG AND FILTHY AIR.

The witches who prophesied that Macbeth would take King Duncan's throne couldn't have described Xandra's conflicting thoughts better, had they been there with her in the visitation room. She tried to keep her eyes on Ian Mortimer, but found it difficult to maintain her gaze.

Like the great Scottish general, she grappled with the choice: walk away from the future, or face the evil through which it might come to pass. Either way, it left her feeling ill.

*Double, double, toil and trouble; fire burn and cauldron bubble...*

Ian glanced down to the chair before the table at which he sat.

"Won't you please have a seat?" An expectant and disturbingly genial smile emerged.

Xandra pulled the chair back, not too close, and sat.

"I'm here on official business."

"Of course you are."

The last thing she would ever do was tell him she'd been having dreams about him rescuing her. But at the same time, she had to know why she'd seen him sitting in the Oval Office. Could his maleficent dealings with President Colson shed any light on the current danger to Jennifer Bradley?

Unlikely, but if her second sight had gone through such pains to reveal him in her dreams, while showing her visions of a possible terror strike earlier, it must all be for a reason, right?

"First of all, Ian. What do you know about the assassination attempt on President Bradley at her inaugural parade?"

Right away, the smile faded.

The eyes drooped.

Ian let out a sigh.

"Such a dreary topic."

"What did you think we'd be talking about?"

"Oh I don't know...the weather outside, the price of petrol, books you've read...anything besides bothersome politics."

"This isn't a social visit. You've got your family for that."

"Right, well..." His lips pulled taut. The corner of his mouth twitched, and he lowered his head. "Won't be seeing *them* anymore, will I?"

"What do you mean?"

"Though I really must give Nicole credit for trying." He looked back up. "And try she did...but coming here with Robert? Well, he was starting to ask more and more questions about his father being a man who murdered people for money. In the end, she could no longer take it. Robert deserved a better life, a better father. Who can blame her?"

He deserved not an ounce of sympathy. Considering all the people he'd ripped from the lives of loved ones, he could rot in Hell for all she cared. But for some reason she couldn't bring herself to say it.

Couldn't even bring herself to feel it.

And it bothered her that she was being denied the satisfaction of abject contempt for this pathetic monster, defanged and declawed as he was.

It bothered her even more that empathy for him had wormed its way into her heart, where it had no business.

"Three years...a worthy stint..." his voice broke, "Wouldn't you agree?"

Xandra held her tongue. The revulsion never completely left her, but she almost wanted to reach out and touch his hand.

Almost.

But not quite.

"I'm sure it's not easy," she said, trying to avoid direct eye contact. She wasn't about to allow her own emotions to mingle in the same space as his. "But as I said, I need to ask you some questions—potentially matters of national security."

"Assuming I'm able to," he wiped his nose on his sleeve and composed himself, "I'll answer them if you make me a promise."

"What's that?"

"That you'll visit me again in the future."

"I can't do that."

"Well then," He stood up and regarded her smugly, then started walking away. "Good day, Ms. Carrick."

"Wait."

Ian stopped and turned around, a curious look in his eye.

"Give me some answers, something useful...and..."

"Hmm?"

"I'll come to visit you again."

He returned to the table and sat.

"Splendid."

"But only to ask you other questions, if it turns out you have the information I'm looking for."

"Fair enough." A curt nod. "Ask away."

# TWENTY

THIRTY FOUR MONTHS EARLIER

AL SHARIF DETENTION CELL
UNDISCLOSED LOCATION
Outside the Western Border of Tariqistan

IF THERE HAD BEEN ANY BENEFIT DERIVED from the countless days spent in pitch black solitary confinement, it was that compared to waiting in this underground cellar, or dungeon, or whatever this place was, nothing else seemed too unbearable.

For a long while after the gunfire and commotion quieted, Ishmael waited. Now, confident everyone had left, he climbed up the ladder, nudged the trap door open just a crack, and scanned the dusty floor.

The Americans were gone.

As was Mohamed's body.

Ishmael was so attuned to the environment down here that what struck him most wasn't the absence of shuffling feet, Mohamed's breathing or quiet chuckling—the only evidence of human existence or contact since Haashir brought him here—it was the absence of rats scurrying about, their claws scratching through the dust on the concrete floor.

Carefully, he opened the hatch and climbed out.

Hidden in the shadows, he turned his ear toward the corridor whence came the Americans.

Not a sound.

He didn't know the layout of this place beyond what he glimpsed every now and then when Mohamed had turned the corner either coming or going. There was no other way to go, so he turned the corner, his left hand feeling the wall in the darkness, and went on until he came to an alcove of sorts, flooded with pure white moonlight.

It nearly overwhelmed him.

Who knew that after so long, natural light—albeit nocturnal—could evoke such emotion?

Quickly, he wiped his eyes, turned to the source, and discovered a window near the top of a wooden staircase. It appeared to go up several flights.

*Freedom lies in being bold*, Robert Frost had said. A western education afforded countless nuggets of wisdom and platitudes to inspire him. And now, emboldened by this sudden turn of fortune, Ishmael scaled the steps past the ground floor as on the velvet paws of a cat. Just as he passed the second floor hallway, an unexpected sound arrested his breath.

He froze in place, his heart stampeding within.

Someone outside was talking, his words traveling through the opening of the skylight above.

Ishmael found his way into a crawl space near the top of the building. Slithering on his belly toward the singular beam of moonlight invading the darkness, he came upon a hole the size of a tennis ball and put his eyes up to it.

What he saw outside on the ground confirmed his fears.

From the plated body armor, flipped up night vision goggles, rifles with suppressors, he could tell.

Navy Seals.

Several bodies on the ground were covered with sheets, but

one in particular had its face exposed as one Seal took a photo.

*Haashir.*

They'd used Ishmael's intelligence reports after all, and found him. In the days leading up to the drone attack that killed Ishmael's family, they must have latched onto the trail that led to Haashir. The world's most wanted terrorist since Bin Laden, Massoud Haashir had been their primary target ever since his plot to deliver a chemical weapons attack on the Superbowl had been thwarted just twelve hours before its execution.

*And how did they repay me?*

By trying to simply delete him from their database of operatives? That was the American way, wasn't it? Exploit people, make *you* pay the price for their agenda, and when they were done, toss you away like yesterday's trash.

The Seals covered Haashir's face with the white sheet and hoisted his body onto a gurney. They carried it out of the compound's concrete walls and into the large helicopter—a Chinook, from the look of its twin rotors—in which they'd arrived.

A flash of light from below shot straight into his eyes.

Ishmael swiftly rolled his body away from the opening in the wall.

A Seal called out, "Got something?"

The light from below swiped around the opening.

"Thought I saw something move up there," the flashlight wielder said.

"The building's clear."

"Just making sure."

Ishmael's chest rose and fell repeatedly.

If they found him, they'd surely complete the original mission.

*You certainly succeeded in murdering my wife and son!*

As soon as the light went away he went back and glared down at the Americans, becoming palpably aware of the change taking place within him.

Anxiety morphed into a dark fury, voracious and inexorable as the event horizon of a black hole.

He'd come to a critical juncture.

This was indeed the point of no return.

Fight or flight.

Either spend the rest of his life evading the treacherous American thugs, or devote whatever life remained in him to ensure that President Jennifer Bradley's atrocities were redressed.

Eye for eye.

Blood for blood.

"Well?" One of the Seals called out to the flashlight wielder. "Anything?"

"Negative. Probably a rat."

"All right, move out!"

Two minutes later, the compound picked clean by the American vultures, the Chinook roared into the night leaving Ishmael simmering in his thoughts.

Like a Phoenix from the ashes, a newfound purpose emerged from within him.

*For you, Aiza, and you, Odin.*

A purpose which he must for the sake of honor and justice fulfill...

...or die in the attempt.

# TWENTY ONE

PRESENT DAY

FDC PHILADELPHIA
FEDERAL DETENTION CENTER
SPECIAL HOUSING UNIT
11:15 AM EST

HE COULD HAVE BEEN AN ELEMENTARY SCHOOL TEACHER, or an accountant, or even a dentist. Sitting there as peacefully as he was, Xandra could not reconcile the fact that this man had been hired by Richard Colson, and God only knew how many others, to kill people and hide their bodies. The only boundary between this serial killer and say, Hannibal Lechter, was the thin line between sanity and psychopathy.

And Ian Mortimer had all but erased that line

"So, lassie, what's on your mind?"

She pulled her chair closer. "First of all, what do you know about the assassination attempt on the President?"

"Ah yes. News of that traveled remarkably fast," he said, with a pensive stare. "Right, well…Either they were amateurs, or it happened exactly as it was meant to."

"What do you mean?"

Ian shifted in his seat and blinked as though he didn't know or care to expound further. "Heard from your father, lately?"

"That's none of your business. What did you mean by amateurs, or exactly as it was meant?"

"He's a brave man, he is. You really should respect all he's done, taking on so much to protect you and your mother. We're not all that different, he and I."

"You're not half the man—!"

*He's testing you. Don't fall for it.*

Ian answered in an appeasing tone. "I'm merely stating the fact that Peter Carrick and I share a common trait...or flaw, as it were: Everything we did, we did to protect our families." His eyes wandered to the overhead lights. "In those last days, anyway."

"If you want to perpetuate such delusions, I can't stop you. But you still haven't answered my question."

Eyes rolling, his chest heaved with exasperation.

"How you *do* harp on that."

"It's why I'm here."

"You sought me out. Not the other way around."

Enough.

Clearly he had no interest in anything but playing mind games.

Xandra stood up and glanced over to the V.O.

"All right, we're done here."

She took another look at Ian, who folded his arms over his chest and sat back into his chair defiantly.

Nothing.

She leaned over the table, looked him straight into his unblinking eyes.

"Have a nice life—what's left of it."

"Hm."

Her heels rapped against the floor as she strode to the door.

After all it took for her to come here, he'd proven nothing more than an enigmatic jester whose court hadn't found him criminally insane. No, he'd been deemed fit for trial. But she was beginning to wonder.

*Why did I ever subject myself to this?* Visions or not, it just wasn't worth it. The moment she walked out of that door, it would be forever shut.

The cold metal of the door knob sent a chill through her entire being.

She grasped it.

Twisted.

"Fine!" Ian said.

Fighting the temptation to simply walk out and let the door slam behind her, Xandra stood still, her lips pressed tight. She didn't turn around as he spoke.

"I'm sorry," he said, his penitence sounding almost human. "Please, don't go."

"It's all a big joke to you."

"I struggle with my own cynicism constantly. I suppose it's become a part of my nature."

She turned to face him, but kept her hand on the door knob. "If you're just going to jerk me around…"

His shackled hands came up in surrender.

"No…you have my word."

"Which doesn't hold much stock at this point, as you well know."

"Quite."

"So if you're just going to waste my time…"

"I promise, I won't. Please," his eyes bade her return to the table.

"You'll tell me everything?"

"I'll tell you what I can."

Cautiously, Xandra returned to the chair, leaned close and said *sotto voce,* "Why would you withhold anything?"

"Secrets…a gentleman's got to keep some, no?"

"Is that what you fancy yourself?"

He smiled. "Hm."

It took a while for him to finally speak, but when he did, he spoke so quietly she could barely make out his words. "No assassin trying to take out the President of the United States would miss by so miserable a margin. Trust me, I know."

"Amateurs?"

"Perhaps..."

With her eyes, she issued him a warning. "Ian..."

"Look, it just doesn't add up, the way it happened. Amateurs are not nearly so organized that they would think of a coordinated diversionary strike—the bomb—to take all eyes from the primary target. That's more like *Al Qaeda* or..." he drifted into thought.

"So it might have been more than just a failed homegrown attempt?"

"What do you think?"

"*I'm* asking the questions here," she said, barely containing her irritation.

He gave it some more thought. "I can't be certain, but my instincts tell me it's more than what it appears on the surface."

The inadvertent rattling of his chains drew her attention to his fist resting on the edge of the table. From the corner of her eye, she noticed the veins bulging, his wizened skin, the sparse hairs on his left wrist not quite covering what looked like a small faint marking—a tattoo perhaps. As if sensing she was looking at it, Ian withdrew his hands and stretched his right fingers to pull the cuff of his sleeve down to cover it.

"Was that all, Xandra?" He smiled calmly, but the twitching in the corner of his mouth betrayed him.

She must have made some kind of expression of disgust, because a wounded look etched itself all over his face.

"You know, I didn't really want to hurt you," Ian said. "It was Colson who—"

"You worked for him." She could never bring herself to refer to him as *President* Colson, not because his term had been so short, but because in her mind he was never worthy of the office.

"I was blackmailed. He held the lives of my wife and son as leverage. My orders to kill you were never meant to be personal.

Can't we just kiss and make up?"

"Not even in your dreams." Stifling her disgust, she ignored his twisted attempts at humor. "Now just listen for a minute and try to answer my questions. Think you can do that?"

"Maybe."

"Good." She cleared her throat because it was about to erupt with the tickle of a dry itch. How could she actually be here seeking help from this high-paid serial killer? And yet, it was completely consistent with her past experience that her visions would lead her into the depths of darkness. Gathering herself, Xandra sat tall and looked straight into his eyes. "Do you have any knowledge or suspicions as to the recent terror threat by the FTM?

"Ah, the Free Tariqistan Movement. I've read about that in the paper. Most intriguing."

"I have a feeling you might know a lot more than what we've all read."

"Perhaps."

"Is there a connection…between FTM and the assassination attempt on President Bradley?"

His gaze wandered to the ceiling. "A second term…most remarkable."

"Ian."

"Hmmm?"

"Focus."

"Right. Well, there very well could be. But conjecture abounds, doesn't it? Can't you be a bit more specific?"

This was the part she dreaded. It was like inviting a murderer into your bedroom, and giving him a detailed tour of all your personal belongings. But if she held any hope of finding a connection between her recent visions, she had to do this.

Images of the blood covered bodies flashed in her mind.

A shudder crawled up her spine.

"What about the threats against the US, if Bradley refuses to meet FTM's demands?"

"How should I know?"

Unconvinced, Xandra discerned his evasiveness immediately. She was onto something. The next question was a bit of a stretch, but her visions had been reliable enough to trust where they led. He might actually know why she had seen dozens of dead bodies in her vision.

"Is it possible they might have access to WMDs, and have the ability to deploy them here in the States?"

His face lost its complexion. Though his other features remained static, his eyes darted from side to side. He blinked rapidly, sucked in a terse breath.

"I've said too much."

"You've barely said a thing."

"You don't understand."

"Help me, then. Were you ever in the White House discussing—?"

"No, not that."

"What are you saying?"

"Look, Xandra," he said, his voice bloated with exasperation. "Me? I'm a dead man. Just a matter of time. But Nicole and Bobby are still out there, and I have to think about their safety." The sincerity in his eyes was undeniable. "I can't say any more, I'm sorry."

She hadn't gotten any real answers, though in truth, she didn't quite know what to ask. She'd come here hoping that her visions of him were indicative of him having something of importance to reveal.

But he didn't.

"Just what are you looking for, anyway?" he asked, with a puzzled expression.

"Clues, answers...truth."

"Ah, that inquisitive nature of yours again. It's what put you in Colson's crosshairs in the first place, you know. Best be circumspect."

"If you have any knowledge about a coming terrorist attack, you have to tell me."

"Have to? There's an entire agency dedicated to that, my dear. If they haven't come to me for answers, why have you? And besides, there are worse things than terrorism. But you probably already know that, don't you?"

"Let me just remind you. That *inquisitive nature* of mine put an end to Colson's machinations," Xandra said, not unaware of the frost in her tone. "And it put you here as well."

"*I* put myself here," he said. "Your father and I came forward to exonerate you from a conviction of treason, which in this country is still punishable by death!"

It was true. Because she had threatened to expose Colson's war atrocities and the entire murderous cover-up, he'd framed her as a traitor and domestic terrorist.

But she was not about to back off.

"The truth is, Ian, when you realized Colson had turned on you and was about to have you killed, your only choice was to team up with my father—even though you were sent to kill him. It was the only way to stop Colson from threatening your family. So let's be real here, it was self-interest."

"Your father had no other reason to throw himself at the mercy of the tribunal than to clear *your* name. I don't expect you to trust my motives, but trust me on this—You'd best keep your nose out of things into which you have no business snooping."

So there was a connection.

And Ian knew something about it but was too frightened to discuss it.

It was time to try a different approach.

Softening her voice and demeanor, Xandra retired the iron fists, and put on the kid gloves.

"I know you're afraid," she said, pushing past the repugnance. "But think of the people who you could save. Think of your wife and son."

At this, he became pensive and tugged restlessly on the cuff of his sleeve. "I could tell you...show you...what you need to know..."

An arctic chill rushed through her.

Snapping back to the moment, Mortimer shook his head and blinked repeatedly. "But that would put us all in far greater danger than you can imagine. It would only hasten Nicole and Bobby's death."

"I might be able to help—get them protection."

He huffed bitterly. "Once you become their target, no one can save you."

"From whom? The FTM, al Saif?"

Ian lowered his eyes and shook his head slowly from side to side. "Least of our worries."

"Come on, Ian. Give me something."

Shimmering beads dotted his forehead. His brow furrowed in an expression completely foreign to this man who she'd always known to have Freon for blood.

"Let it go, Xandra."

"You know I can't do that."

"I haven't got the complete picture, but I know enough to stay clear. And the less you know, the safer you'll be."

Xandra glared at him. "As if you care."

"I care about my family. Hell, I'm putting them in danger telling you as much as I already have. I'm sorry, but we are finished here." Abruptly, he stood, turned, and started for the door.

"Ian!"

He stopped, hesitated, but kept his back to her.

Xandra got up and walked around to meet his anxious, yet distant eyes. He was so close to talking, she could feel it. She softened her gaze to project kindness, vulnerability…anything to make him drop his guard.

"Oh, you'll be the death of me, won't you?" He slowly exhaled. Flexing his fingers repeatedly, he stared at the ceiling.

*Come on, come on.* She tapped her toe within her shoe and chewed her lip. He had something for her, she just knew it.

Returning to his seat at the table, he shut his eyes and let out a tremulous breath. "Don't ask me how I know, all right?"

He had been in league with President Colson. There was no way other than full disclosure to know what kind of collusions he'd been privy to, nor the scope of their impact. "Okay."

He remained still, eyes sweeping all over the room. Then he spoke in a cautious murmur. "I'm not convinced the whole issue is about ridding Tariqistan of American influence. After all, everyone knows Bradley will never agree to those demands. No president would."

"Then why bother issuing them?"

"Why did they need a bomb on Pennsylvania Avenue, when a single bullet would have sufficed to take out the President?"

Though the shooter failed to kill Jennifer Bradley, it was clear that the coordinated strikes shared the same methodology. Every agency had been on that case like flies on molasses on a hot summer day. But there had been more to the assassination attempt than met the eye.

"A distraction?"

"Precisely." Mortimer glanced over to the door and back a couple of times. "And do you find it as interesting as I that the shooter's accomplice suddenly died while recovering in the hospital?"

She hadn't thought of that until he mentioned it.

"Ian, does this mean—?"

"From what I remember, you're quite well-read. If I were you, I'd brush up on the classics, like—oh, I don't know—Melville, perhaps."

Was he playing games now? Had he been playing her all this time?

Mortimer nodded to the V.O., and then to the door.

"What do you mean brush up on Melville?"

He stood. "Don't believe everything seen by the naked eye, Xandra. That in which you place the deepest trust can turn out to be your worst enemy. You've the best chance of survival if you view everyone and everything with suspicion."

She stood up, wanted to grab him by the collar and shake the information out of him.  "That can't be all."

"I'm afraid it is." Signaling to the V.O. that the visit was over, Ian rose wearily and stepped over for inspection.

Xandra went to the exit door, stopped and said, "You can't possibly expect me to visit you again."

"That's just the price I'll have to pay. Much as I covet your company, there's a line that must not be crossed at any cost. I believe we may have just done so."

# TWENTY TWO

## TWELVE MONTHS EARLIER

## ST. NICHOLAS' CATHEDRAL
## PRINCIPAUTÉ DE MONACO, FRANCE

YOU SHOULD BE GRATEFUL, his handler had always said.

*To whom, exactly?* Ishmael stood with a sardonic grin as he gazed blankly at the image of the crucified Christ hanging at the front of the cathedral. He bowed his head as the afternoon sun cast a rainbow through the stained glass windows across the pews, candles, and marble floor.

In order to blend in, he knelt on the padded kneeler and lowered his head as if praying with the other visitors scattered throughout the sanctuary. Yes, he ought to be grateful that after all that had happened, he was still alive. Yes, he should be grateful that he'd been rescued from Tariqistan and given another chance to live, to right the wrongs inflicted upon him by those treacherous Americans to whom nothing mattered but their own self-interest. And yes, he should be grateful that his new handlers had seen the potential in working with him.

But none of that did a thing to mitigate the perpetual thorn in his flesh over the heinous murder of his family.

"I didn't think you'd show up," a woman's voice said in French. Her tone matched her demeanor—calm, in a sensual way.

"I too had my doubts."

She crossed herself and knelt at his left, bowing her head and speaking softly. "I am pleasantly surprised, and selfishly disappointed. You are ready then, no?"

Ishmael turned slightly to face her. "*Oui.*"

The emerald eyes, the crimson lips, and flirtatious lashes made her look more like a fashion magazine cover model than a covert operations handler, codenamed Hemlock.

She reached out, touched his clean-shaven face with icy fingertips, and examined him. "*Passablement.* The doctor has done a decent job. I would have preferred a more Roman nose, though."

"It will do." The truth was, six months since the organization had arranged to have the plastic surgeon alter his appearance, Ishmael still found the man in the mirror a disturbing intruder. But perhaps it was for the best that the face of the Ishmael Al Shihab he'd once been was gone.

This new face, so completely alien to him and anyone who might possibly know him, afforded him that extra degree of psychological separation and anonymity needed to accomplish his own mission.

Hemlock handed him a small black pouch. "It's all here—passports, credit cards, documents. You fly at 2300 tonight."

He took the pouch and nodded. "I trust all the arrangements have been made?"

"I personally saw to it."

"Because if I find you have deceived me, your people will never even lay eyes upon the—"

She put her finger on his lips, then kissed him gently on the forehead. "Why always the threats, hmm? Have I ever lied to you, broken a promise?" A tear fell from her eye.

"You must understand how difficult it is for me to trust anyone."

"Even me?"

Their relationship had gone well beyond professional months ago. He was fully aware that it was in order for her superiors to ensure they got what they wanted out of this mutually beneficial arrangement. But he didn't mind. He would exploit her warmth, her companionship, even her love, regardless of whether or not it had been genuine. "I'm sorry, even you."

She sniffed, wiped her eye, then placed her hand over his. "I know you'll never completely believe me. But I will miss you."

Ishmael turned and regarded her with tenderness. He brushed the auburn hair from her eye and caressed her face. "I have chosen to believe you from the start. And I will take your kindness with me to the grave."

At that, she put her arms around him and wept quietly into his chest. "Don't talk like that, *Chéri*. You can live a long, happy life as long as you do as they say. Maybe one day..."

"You know better than that." He stroked her head and spoke in as soothing a tone as he could. "I will do whatever I can to accomplish my goals. If that fails to align with their agenda, then so be it. You understand this, no?"

Resigned to the fact that nothing could change him, not even God, she looked up at him and nodded.

"Good." He took her hand and stood, helping her to her feet. Lifting her chin, he gave her a poignant smile. "You will always have a special place in my heart, Marie."

Her eyes widened with fleeting joy.

For the first time in all the months he'd known her, from the first time he saw her as he arrived in Istanbul in the back of a smuggler's truck, to these final moments before his transition back to where it all began, he called her by her true name...

...and kissed her on the lips.

# TWENTY THREE

PRESENT DAY

OVAL OFFICE
THE WHITE HOUSE
9:02 AM EST

AFTER HER MEETING WITH IAN MORTIMER, it was almost jarring to return to the elegance of the Oval what with its pristine lines, classic furniture, opulent curtains framing the triune bow window looking out to the lush green South Lawn. But today, Xandra had been asked to accompany the President in her photographic capacities.

At Bradley's request, she had brought Max along, as the very mention of the veteran K9 seemed to bring life into her son's eyes. Following the swath of sunlight flowing in from the Rose Garden through the East Door to which it opened, her lens found Mikey Bradley sitting behind a sofa, an iPad in his lap, and white ear buds plugged in. Max was down on the rug right next to him, and seemed at peace with his role as the boy's companion.

Bradley sat at the *Resolute* desk, her phone call lasting longer than anticipated. Xandra faded into the background and made as many pictures as she could without obtrusion, a technique she'd learned from Pete Souza, President Obama's photographer.

She captured some candids of the President talking on the phone, and her son hiding unseen behind the furniture with The General. Quietly, she approached the two. Mikey had become so accustomed to the Chief White House photographer's presence, he showed no sign of acknowledging it.

Though she stood right next to him, he didn't react by pulling away. So she took the liberty of looking down at the screen to see what he was doing.

Her heart sank with sympathy.

On the iPad screen, a YouTube video she recognized was playing. It was that same one that had gone viral a few months ago where a Marine had returned from a deployment and had surprised his son by showing up at school. In slow motion, the overjoyed boy ran with all his might, leapt up into his daddy's arms and cried for joy.

Mikey kept replaying that part of the video.

Emotion lodged itself in her throat.

His eyes red, Mikey glanced up to her. But he didn't turn away, just held her gaze for a while.

"You really miss him, don't you?" Xandra said, empathetic.

"I still can't believe he's gone. Sometimes, I dream that he's gonna walk through that door in his uniform, and I'm gonna just run up to him like the kid in that video."

"Well," Xandra said, struggling to keep her voice from breaking, "maybe one day, many years from now, after you've lived a long and fulfilling life, you will." After about four years, the sting of Mom's passing had somewhat diminished. But at least Xandra had her in her life for her entire childhood all the way through landing her first big break with the *New York Times*. Mikey had not even turned ten, and already he'd lost his father. It rent her heart.

"Sorry to keep you waiting," Bradley said to Xandra. She hung up the phone and rose from her seat. "Ready to go?"

"Yes, Ma'am." Xandra patted her leg and Max came over. Then, regarding Mikey warmly, she offered her hand. He took it and pulled himself to his feet. To her surprise, he didn't let go when they started for the door.

ARLINGTON NATIONAL CEMETERY
10:50 AM EST

SHE TRIED NOT TO SAY A WORD when they arrived at the late Ben Bradley's grave, but something just didn't seem right. It wasn't her place to ask, but Xandra really thought there ought to be at least some kind of explanation.

Nevertheless, she held her tongue and faded into the background with her Nikon, affording the President and her son a private moment. Secret Service Agents did the same, though they focused more on the surroundings.

Grey overcast skies diffused the light nicely over the faces of the remnant of the First Family, no harsh shadows with which to contend. Rows of white headstones stood uniform and straight as a company of Marines before their Commander in Chief. A bird sang a mournful song in the branches above them.

After kneeling at her husband's grave, her head bowed for a while, she set a wreath by the headstone, then got up and walked back to the tree under which Xandra stood.

With Max in tow, Mikey slowly approached the grave, which Xandra still wanted know about. It looked no different from all the other surrounding ones.

"I hope you'll forgive my impudence," she said, as Bradley

came to her side. "But I would have expected a much more distinct memorial for the late husband of the President of the United States."

"As would I," she said, while far off in the distance, a soldier in fatigues knelt by one of many such graves, and set a small American flag before it.

Before she could continue, Xandra caught a quick glimpse of Mikey standing before his father's grave, his back straight as a post. She lifted the camera and started taking photos in quick succession. "Forgive me."

"Of course." Bradley took a couple of steps back.

Through the viewfinder, Xandra watched and captured Mikey forming a perfect salute, his upper arm horizontal, and forearm inclined at a forty-five degree angle. Max sat completely still facing the same direction. She zoomed in to find his eyes brimming with tears but bravely trying to keep himself together.

*He's only nine.*

Behind her, Bradley sniffed.

Then Mikey knelt down before the headstone. Xandra was too far to hear what he was saying, but she could see his lips moving, the pained expression in his face. She had to put the camera down.

"It's been so difficult for him," Bradley said, returning to her side.

"I can only imagine."

"Ben was his absolute hero, and his best friend. No one could ever take his place."

Xandra lowered her head, trying to push away the feeling of having intruded upon a sacred place of which she had no business being. "I know."

"It was what he wanted."

"Ma'am?"

"The grave site. No fancy memorial, no monument. Ben was never into the glamor or glory of anything he did. He hated the limelight that my career forced him into. So he made me promise that he would be buried like any other Marine, no special treatment.

"Sounds like an amazing person."

"Amazing doesn't even begin to describe him." Bradley dabbed her eyes with a tissue. "Which is what makes his departure all the more difficult to deal with, for both Mikey and me. But you know what? He wouldn't want me lamenting his death. I can just hear him say—she dropped her voice half an octave—'*Don't waste your time crying over me, you've got a nation to mind.*'"

In the periphery, Xandra caught a glimpse of movement. She didn't want to intrude but was duty bound to make pictures of what she saw.

Kneeling, Mikey rested the side of his head on his father's gravestone, and wrapped his arms around it as he wept.

# TWENTY FOUR

OVAL OFFICE
THE WHITE HOUSE
1:18 PM EST

A LIFE OF REGRET WAS NOT what Ben would have wanted for her. And yet, after her visit to his grave in Arlington, Jenna (that's what he had always called her) could not help but wish she'd spent just a few more days with her husband, and a few less on the campaign trail.

Seated at the *Resolute* desk, she'd just finished taking a second look over the PDB which Douglas Kendall the director of the CIA prepared in a coordinated effort with other members of the intelligence community with meticulous care. The reports of increased security of US embassies, and plans to strike at the secret locations of al Saif and the FTM around the outskirts of Tariqistan were all SOP, surreal though it seemed.

In the precious few minutes she spent alone processing and preparing for the rest of the day, she wrestled with her emotions, confining them to that prison cell in her mind which threatened to burst open if she were to be caught off guard.

The afternoon sun had finally broken through the haze. Through the windows facing the Rose Garden, warm diffused light entered the Oval Office. Outside, a tiny hummingbird hovered about the trellis. Not something she saw, or at least noticed every day. A deep-rooted pain impaled her heart as she remembered that it was there in the Rose Garden that Ben had confessed.

SHE HAD JUST ANNOUNCED her decision to run for a second term the night before. As they strolled in the hush of sunrise, Ben plucked a red rose, broke the thorns from the stem, and handed it to her with a sheepish grin.

She took in the sweet fragrance, but then noticed something rare; a thinly veiled sadness over his countenance. "What's wrong, Ben? You have this look."

"Honey," he said, his complexion unusually pale, not bronzed from running every day on the track President Clinton had installed back in '93 around the south drive because his jogging habit disrupted Washington traffic. "I should have told you sooner, but the last thing I wanted to do was sidetrack you."

She didn't know how to respond, but something in his tone turned her stomach into a cinder block plummeting into the depths of the Atlantic.

"You would have made a terrible mistake if I'd said anything earlier."

"Ben..."

A brave smile, a gentle touch on her face. "It wouldn't have made a difference, anyway."

"No..." Deep down, she knew. But she'd never permitted the intuition to form into words, or even a possible thought. Tears filled her eyes, but she tried to reciprocate the courage in his.

He took her hands and kissed them. "It's Stage IV, and it's metastasized."

Without even knowing when it started, she broke down and collapsed onto his shoulder which seemed frail, now that he'd confirmed her worst suspicions. His entire body felt lighter, but because of how he'd worn his clothes, and how little time of late they'd spent together in bed at night, this truth had eluded her.

"Ben, I don't know if I can—"

"Shhh…" He gave her a strong hug and held her as she wept. "Don't you worry. I'm going to fight this and win. You know me."

He'd served in both Gulf Wars, and was no stranger to battle. He'd watch his marines die with honor, and he'd saved from death more than a few under his command. A lifetime of victory, only to be taken down by cancer?

"It's crucial that we keep this between us," he said. "If the public gets wind…"

"We can't hide it forever."

"It's strictly need-to-know. For now, anyway. You have to project strength and resolve. I don't want anyone accusing you of going for the sympathy vote. You're going to be elected President on the merits of your work, your character, and I'm not going to let anything or anyone stand in the way of that." He kissed her forehead. "Especially me."

Ben went on and kept up the appearances until a month after she became the first elected female American president. Having held the disease at bay as long as he could, his health suddenly declined. In a sense, he had been successful. No one knew he'd been fighting cancer, or that he'd declined radiation and chemo because A) he knew it would weaken him physically and B) despite several heated arguments, he simply didn't believe it would help. *The treatment is worse than the disease*, he kept saying.

In a matter of months, Ben was bed-ridden, the cancer raging with a vengeance.

The whole world could not help but know.

It was time to inform Mikey that Daddy was soon going on his final deployment.

THE HUMMINGBIRD seemed to be staring into the window straight at her. Through the aching memories Bradley found the ability to channel Ben's strength and smile at it. But as she stood and walked over to the window, it zipped away.

A fleeting moment of beauty.

Like Ben's life.

How could she go on without him?

And yet, she must.

*Live your life without any regrets,* he'd said on his death bed that evening. *I know I have...*

After reading the PDB today, only one regret remained.

Operation Nighthawk.

Ben had counseled her to wait until there was more definitive evidence.

But they'd barely dodged the proverbial bullet just months before and stopped a Superbowl terrorist attack in Texas by Massoud Haashir, the world none the wiser. Furthermore, after the PDB that came across 42's desk on August 6, 2001 (*"Bin Laden Determined to Strike in US"*), no president could ever afford the luxury of taking intelligence reports of this type for granted.

There was no way she could agree to the demands of the FTM, now. But the possibility that the most recent intelligence gathered might have underestimated the scope of the coming terror strikes, only compounded her regrets over Nighthawk.

It had boiled down to the taking of one life, that of an operative suspected to have turned, or saving the lives of countless innocent Tariqistanis and Americans.

One life versus thousands.

To this day, she could never be sure if the operative had in fact located Haashir's WMD's, or if he had actually acquired them and turned against the United States.

And she might never know.

But this she did know: Tariqistan had been liberated from the clutches of an extremist dictator—the perpetrator of countless crimes against humanity. Ensuring the country's security and peace was the right thing to do. And whether or not that operative had truly turned, he'd served his purpose, and cleared a path for Seal Team 6 to take out the worst terror leader since Bin Laden.

Regrets?

The only one about Operation Nighthawk was that it had been the one time she directly opposed Ben's counsel, while not being absolutely sure she was right.

A knock came on the door.

David Scott peeked into the door frame.

"MacArthur's here, Ma'am."

She shook her head, didn't need this. Not today.

The best thing about being an Independent was that people on both sides of the partisan divide loved you. The worst thing about it was that people on both sides hated you.

House Speaker Kenneth MacArthur was of the latter camp.

Today, the old vulture was here most likely to take her to task over her current policy on revoking financial assistance to countries suspected of human rights violations.

She really didn't see the need to persuade him, or assuage his misgivings. But brushing him off as he deserved, would only widen the gap between parties, which more and more she found herself struggling to bridge. Necessary as it was, at times it felt as if they were walking—no, driving tanks over her.

Bradley smoothed out her jacket, dabbed her cheeks, and turned to David.

"Have him wait two minutes, then send him in."

# TWENTY FIVE

HE WAS THE LAST PERSON SHE WANTED TO SEE right now. Jennifer Bradley was not in the best of moods to meet with the Speaker of the House, but from his message, it sounded too important to re-schedule.

"Madam President, I'll be completely frank with you." MacArthur leaned forward and placed his elbows on her desk, all his usual mirth drained from his face. "You've made some enemies."

"You said important, not obvious."

"Not talking about those petty rednecks who tried to take you out in February. I've learned of a report that will put a big, ugly stain not only on your record, but your good name."

"I'm touched by your concern for my 'good name.'" Bradley shifted in her chair and leaned forward. "And yet I can't help being surprised."

"Cynicism was never your *forte*, my dear," he frowned paternally, "Doesn't suit you."

"Meanwhile, hypocrisy suits you like Spandex."

MacArthur let out a hearty laugh. "*Touché*. But the fact that it's come to light on the cusp of the FTM's terror threats..."

Bradley knew better than to allow the old croc to lull her into letting down her guard. He maintained that affable façade behind which many a trap had been set. But this time she found herself at a disadvantage. The Speaker had never kept his feelings about her presidency a secret. To him, she was nothing more than eye candy for a media driven public. That's why Colson had chosen her as a running mate. She was the X-factor making his administration not only relevant but, in Rick Colson's own words, *sexy*.

MacArthur had on several occasions pressed the issue after Colson's demise: the void in the office had never meant to be filled by a woman. Certainly not this one. Despite her experience running a successful e-commerce corporation that, at its height, was on its way to becoming Amazon's top competitor, MacArthur had all but demanded she step down and yield the presidency to him—a man with actual political experience.

Of course, he'd implied this demand with the same charm he did with every maneuver and setup. Never raised his voice, never out right threatened, always spoke with courtesy, but behind it all lurked a man who she could no more trust than she could part the waters of the Potomac.

"Cut the bull, Ken. What do you want?"

"Is that how little you think of me? Always coming to you with ulterior motives?"

"In a word...yes."

"Fine. You can thank me later, Madam President. Just re-member, it was I who advised you to distance yourself from Col-son's unofficial arms deals with Russia. Just imagine if you'd gone ahead and honored it when you took office, like you so naively thought you should?"

MacArthur was right.

It would have ended disastrously. And because she'd heeded his advice, she garnered the reputation as a president with—what did he call it?—*really big cajones.* Ironically, though it had per-turbed Putin, in the end, it saved both countries from descending that slippery slope which Colson had meant to forge under the table.

"I'll admit," she said, "that's true."

"You see? I'm not the enemy after all. You've got to learn who your friends are, who you can trust."

"Weren't you the one who said that there are no friends in Washington, only allies?"

"Then maybe you should think of me as one...for a change."
She crossed her arms. "I'm listening."

# TWENTY SIX

"MADAM PRESIDENT, IT'S ALL GOING TO HIT THE FAN," the House Speaker said without a trace of the levity upon which he'd floated into the Oval Office. "The bottom line? We were wrong."

"You're going to have to be more specific," Bradley said, though her chest tightened at the thought of the most significant secret she'd kept for the past few years. Could it really be coming back to haunt her?

"I'm not sure how it happened," he said, shaking his head slowly and pressed his lips together, "but it seems there's been an intelligence report that's been leaked."

"Nighthawk?"

He nodded gravely.

"I thought we'd covered all the bases."

"The intelligence we got was solid. There was no question about it: Ishmael Al Shihab *had* access to Haashir's WMD's and would likely have used them against us. Especially after..."

"He was our operative." Bradley said, her jaw clenching.

"He went dark for too long, we could only assume the worst."

"But he wasn't supposed to be there that night."

"You had no choice." The Speaker gave her a sympathetic look. "The threat was credible. And don't forget, it did eventually lead us to Haashir."

"Ken, listen to me. We've paid too high a price for so small a return." It wasn't thoughts of how she would explain this to the people of the United States, or the World, that troubled her most. It was the fact that she'd given the order, thinking it was the only way to protect the United States as well as a newly liberated Tariqistan against deadly terrorist threats, only to learn that the stockpile of chemical and biological weapons had either never been there, or had been moved.

It could have been Iraq all over again, but the plan which she'd executed under extreme pressure was to take out Al Shihab's terrorist contacts to whom he'd reportedly turned after being removed from interim leadership in Tariqistan.

The Predator Drone strikes were supposed to have destroyed the reported cache of bioweapons as a means of deterring Ishmael from joining forces with the very extremists he'd helped the United States oust from power.

Bradley's stomach wrenched a bitter reflux upward.

Why hadn't she taken Ben's counsel and steered clear from the operation, or at least delayed until she'd gotten definitive confirmation? She'd since learned not to cave into pressure from those who trumpeted their years of experience as a means to gain leverage for their own agendas. And she'd learned firsthand how lonely the Capital truly was.

Now, all those years of regret were exacerbated by the fear that she may have repeated Bush's WMD debacle.

Though liberating Tariqistan hadn't become a protracted war like Iraq, mistakes had been made. And in her inexperience and naiveté, she had erred greatly by hiding her eyes from the details, the ugly truth of what she'd done.

Every day since, she'd second guessed herself.

"May want to get with the Joint Chiefs, Sec Def—anyone else you regard as related—and explore your options." He pondered it for a while. "If there's any plausible deniability..."

"It was my decision, Ken. I gave the order."

"Oh, come now. You were young, wet behind the ears. With what you were facing? You had no choice. Given what we knew, Al Shihab would most likely have turned and joined with Haashir.

Anyway, look—you took out a potential Al Saif compound."

"But we found nothing. No chemical weapons, no bio-weapons."

MacArthur shrugged. "You couldn't chance it. He had to be stopped. That's all there is to it."

Her jaw clenched.

"His wife and son were also killed in the strike."

MacArthur's mouth opened, but no words came out.

"The boy was Michael's age, Ken." She took a breath, ready to turn away if the tears standing in her eyes spilled out.

"Oh my..."

"I've never considered myself a murderer—"

"Stop it, Jennifer. Just...stop. It wasn't your fault, you had no choice."

Even if Andrew Bingham, upon whose intelligence reports she acted, were still alive today, she would not throw him under the bus. As Commander in Chief she would have to take full responsibility. She had often tossed and turned in the subsequent nights, wondering if Bingham ever had trouble sleeping before the heart attack took him in his sleep, last year. A decorated general, he never seemed one given to regret or self-doubt. But behind his public persona, it must have plagued his conscience as well.

"I need to come clean."

"A preemptive disclosure might be best, before the media crucifies you."

Was that a grin at the corner of his mouth?

One thought pushed to the surface in the cauldron. Bradley steeled her emotions. "We know Haashir had WMDs."

"Do we, really?" Judging by his expression, the tides of his concern were changing.

"The evidence was irrefutable," Bradley said, her mind fading in and out of the moment.

"We thought so, anyway," he said, somewhat ironically.

"So if the WMDs weren't found after Nighthawk, where are they today?"

The Speaker inclined his head ever so slightly and went to the door. Knowing him, nothing would please him more than to see her disgraced and forced to resign. After all, next to the vice president, he was next in the line of succession.

He narrowed his eyes and smiled wickedly as he turned the knob. "That *is* the question, isn't it?"

As he left, David came in with a rather urgent expression. "You're needed in the Sit Room."

"This wasn't scheduled, was it?"

"No, Ma'am. But there's been an attack in Kishwar."

# TWENTY SEVEN

PHOTO OFFICE
THE WHITE HOUSE,
WASHINGTON DC
9:00 AM EST

CALL ME ISHMAEL.

Xandra stared vacuously at the opening words of Melville's timeless classic *Moby Dick* displayed on the Kindle App on her smartphone. It was the only clue to which Ian Mortimer had alluded and she couldn't divine any meaning from it as she scrolled through the pages.

Taking mental notes, she noted certain keywords that might form a better picture.

*White Whale, Ishmael, Pequod, Queequeg, Ahab...*

Nothing stood out.

It could well have been Mortimer's idea of a joke, in order to appease her, while sending her on a wild goose chase. But he seemed genuinely concerned afterwards that he'd disclosed something important that might have endangered him or his family.

After forty minutes of reading and searching the text, she tossed her phone onto her desk, leaned back in her chair. Clicking through the archives on her monitor, she came across a photo with President Bradley boarding *Air Force One,* taken by Xandra's predecessor Maya Flores.

And then it started.

*Standing atop the steps before the blue band that stretches across the plane's fuselage, Bradley waves as the wind blows her hair back in a dramatic effect.*

*The sun strikes her countenance from the east casting a faint shadow over the right side of her face.*

*But the light seems to increase in intensity until it washes over Xandra's perception in a blinding white.*

*Time stands in place as the vision unfolds.*

*For Xandra, the recognition of what is about to happen gives her the resolve to remain in the moment, despite the tingling extremities and subtle nausea.*

*The white flash dissipates.*

*Once again, scores of bodies lie deathly still.*

*This time, the details are clear.*

*They're in rows and aisles.*

*Inside an airplane.*

*But they're all dead, dark veins forming macabre lattices over their faces, making their identities too difficult to discern*

*Blood oozing from their noses, mouths, and ears, some from swollen patches in their skin.*

*Xandra walks through the bloody scene thankful that at least this time, she cannot smell the unimaginable stench of corrupted flesh.*

*And then, in one of the seats, a sight that makes her heart sink*

*A dead child...*

*Xandra turns her head quickly and instantly finds herself transported to another locale.*

*The old wood boarded floor creaking beneath her feels buoyant*

*Up and down, up and down, her body seems to be bobbing in the water*

*She looks up and before her are three wooden masts*

*The physical sensations are ethereal, like seeing, hearing, and feeling everything through a diaphanous veil*

*Her olfactory senses have returned, though*

*The briny fragrance of the sea wafts past her as she walks the empty decks in the dark*

*The only light she's afforded finds its source in the stars and moon above her, but she is alone.*

*Utterly*

*Adrift at sea*

*It's only a vision,* she tells herself, striving not to succumb to a rising sense of panic

*Ivory pendants adorn the antique decks of this nineteenth century ship like the finger bone necklace of a savage cannibal, rows of harpoons are mounted on the walls.*

*White teeth of some large creature line the railing making it resemble the jaw of a whale*

*A whale...*

With a jolt, Xandra blinked and sucked in a breath.

At the top of a glass case, Dad's vintage Graflex camera stood like a sentinel, scrutinizing her every move.

Vivid as the revelation had been, she still could not piece it together.

Nor could she form any kind of opinion on them to share with Wade or Bradley.

But of this puzzle, unmistakable pieces had been bestowed unto her. If she could just concentrate and think about it for a while.

*Think.*

A text message alert chimed on her phone.

It was from David Scott.

**REPORT TO POTUS
OVAL OFFICE IN 5**

# TWENTY EIGHT

**INSURGENT ATTACK ON AMERICAN MILITARY BASE
FOLLOWED BY SUICIDE BOMBING IN CROWDED SQUARE**

By Harold Jordan
Kishwar, Tariqistan

(Reuters) At about 9:00 AM local time, a small group of local insurgents believed to be associated with al Saif launched an assault on a US Army Base near Kishwar. Armed with automatic weapons and RPGs, the insurgents managed to damage property and injure about six soldiers before they were stopped by American Soldiers.

While it seemed an ill-planned attack which cost all six insurgents their lives, it appears that the objective had been to distract the military and local police from the more deadly attack that took place just half a mile away in downtown Kishwar, minutes later.

In a crowded square where street vendors and hundreds of residents gathered to purchase food, gifts, and other supplies, three young girls ages ten through sixteen dressed in typical western clothing—jeans, walked into the middle of the crowded marketplace.

Eyewitnesses report that the girls began to cry and hold hands. Before anyone could react, a massive explosion sent shrapnel, nails, and glass through the crowds.

Al Saif has claimed responsibility for the suicide bombing, and has reiterated its demands for the withdrawal of all US presence from Tariqistan, and the resignation of President Nasra Aaamaal.

# TWENTY NINE

THE OVAL OFFICE
THE WHITE HOUSE
WASHINGTON, DC

AIDS AND STAFF AWAITED THE PRESIDENT as she sat at her desk, pondering the situation.

She had left David clear instructions: Do Not Disturb - Ten minutes.

Still reeling from the report of the insurgent attack in Kishwar and the suicide bombing by three girls about Mikey's age, her head ached.

With just a few days left in their deadline, would they dare carry out a strike in the US? Could they possibly slip past all our surveillance and intel?

In just nine minutes and thirty seconds, she'd have to face these questions in the Situation Room.

But now, she sat with a clenched fist and mounting frustration. Before she could stop it, it slammed down onto the desk.

The impact shook everything on it, but she only took note when the framed picture of her with Ben holding Mikey as a toddler in the Rose Garden fell off the edge and onto the floor.

Her fingers trembled with a mixture of anger, anxiety, and ultimately sadness that this treasured photo taken by Maya Flores had for the first time since she'd set it there, fallen from its place.

And now the glass was shattered.

Amidst the concerns for an elevated terror threat, security issues, and decisions that must be made, a singular thought surfaced.

*How do I keep Mikey safe?*

Turning the picture frame over, she couldn't make out the faces because the cracks in the glass had spider-webbed so elaborately they obscured them.

Ignoring the blood it drew as she pulled a shard off to reveal Ben's face, defensive numbness radiated through her mind.

*What have I done?*

Ben had all but sacrificed himself so that she could pursue her dream—though according to him, running for her second term had been so much bigger than an individual's dream. She was running for posterity, the future hope of the world that anyone, regardless of your race or gender, could make it to the top, if they were worthy. He had built her up, shown her that she was in fact, more than that. And when she'd won, he could only gloat there in the Master Bedroom with a faint smile saying, *I told you so.*

Now, had she put their son's future in danger by stubbornly refusing to yield to opposing voices that protested not only against a female president, but her policies as well? If she were to die today, leaving Mikey an orphan, would it have been worth it?

She was furious, troubled, and profoundly concerned for her son. But in just a few minutes, she'd have to rise up as the leader of the free world, meet with her principles in the White House Situation Room, and assess the situation—past, present, and to come.

Seven minutes before David opened the gates.

If only Ben were here. He'd know how to calm her.

He'd probably pray, read her something from the book of Psalms.

She remembered it like it was just last night. The very words he recited the night before she gave the order to deploy troops into Tariqistan to drive Haashir out. As a new mother, she'd identified with the parents of the young marines and soldiers ready to give their lives for the freedom of the people oppressed under that extremist regime.

Ben read the Ninety-First Psalm to her as a prayer, which she later quoted in her address to the troops and their families:

> *Surely He shall deliver you from the snare of the fowler*
> *And from the perilous pestilence.*
> *He shall cover you with His feathers,*
> *And under His wings you shall take refuge;*
> *His truth shall be your shield and buckler.*
>
> *You shall not be afraid of the terror by night,*
> *Nor of the arrow that flies by day,*
> *Nor of the pestilence that walks in darkness,*
> *Nor of the destruction that lays waste at noonday.*
>
> *A thousand may fall at your side,*
> *And ten thousand at your right hand;*
> *But it shall not come near you.*
> *Only with your eyes shall you look,*
> *And see the reward of the wicked.*

"Oh, Ben." She had never been particularly religious, but his faith had always been enough to cover them both. The nation never knew how much they owed this beautiful man who had given their president the resolve and fortitude to get them through some of its darkest days.

Eyes shut and head bowed over the shattered picture frame, Jenna let out a barbed breath and swiped away the last of her tears.

One and a half minutes until show time.

Just then, a muffled commotion outside of the Oval Office caught her attention.

The door swung open.

"Leave me alone!"

In ran Mikey, flustered and winded.

Agent Kelly Davis came right in behind him but seemed a bit out of her element.

Jenna stood up and came around to the desk to see what was wrong.

Mikey glowered at Davis, his chest heaving from all the running. "I just want to be alone."

"I'm sorry, Ma'am," Agent Davis said to the president, "He was so fast, he slipped right past me."

She waved her off and mouthed, *It's all right, thank you.*

Davis shut the door and waited outside.

Holding Mikey's gaze with a sympathetic smile, Jenna took a step back

He folded his arms over his chest. "You missed breakfast."

"I'm sorry. Something's come up."

"Was it balsamic terrorists again?"

She stifled a laugh. "You're too young to be worrying about things like that. Come on, I'll always be here for you."

He held her gaze as though examining her eyes.   "Well, okay."

"That's my big little man."

"So when do we leave?"

"Leave?"

He put his fists on his hips. "Mom, you promised."

"Oh, right, the ranch? I'm so looking forward to that."

"That's what you've been saying forever. C'mon, let's go—you said we were leaving today."

"That's right," she said, but it had completely slipped her mind.

He grabbed her hand and pulled on it as he started for the door. "Let's go, we're already an hour late. Grandpa's gonna get worried."

"Oh, sweetie." She didn't budge. But he kept pulling, body leaning forward, shoes slipping on the carpet as though he was walking on a treadmill.

"C'mon, Mom. We should go now."

"Mikey, listen."

He stopped and let her hand go.

Turned around slowly. "You're going to do it again, aren't you?"

Taken aback, she forced herself to stem the flood of thoughts about what the principles of the NSC, the CIA, State, and Defense Departments would have to say about the attack in Tariqistan. In just seven minutes, she would have to make some important decisions. "Michael, just what am I going to do again?"

"Break your promise, I *knew* it!"

A full scale international incident which could forever change relations in that region threatened, and right now she stood eyeball to eyeball with the one person she didn't want to disappoint.

"Mikey, I'm sorry but—"

"You said we were going, Mom!" His lower lip quivered. "It's...it's not fair!"

How could she explain to him that the terror threat was growing, that the world as we knew it might forever change, if she didn't get a handle on the situation in Tariqistan?

"Listen, Son. We're still going, just a little later." She reached down and took his hand.

But Mikey yanked it away.

"Hey...come on, kiddo. Give your mom a break, will you?"

At that, he turned and ran out of the Oval.

Through the opening of the door, Agent Davis stuck her head in. "I'll get him, Madam President."

She nodded her appreciation. "Thanks."

Davis went after Mikey, leaving the door ajar.

Before Jenna could fully gather her thoughts and process her emotions, David Scott called on the intercom.

"She's here."

# THIRTY

THE OVAL OFFICE
THE WHITE HOUSE,
WASHINGTON DC
9:15 AM EST

MICHAEL BRADLEY BURST OUT of the Oval Office and ran down the hall. Half a second later, Agent Kelly Davis went after him. The relationship between this protector and protectee didn't seem particularly warm, but Xandra never expected to see a Secret Service agent chasing after a nine year old boy. She caught a few pictures of it, in case later on they might prove more humorous than it looked today. She might have found it completely amusing, had it involved anyone but the President of the United States.

David Scott shook his head and punched a button on the intercom alerting Bradley to her arrival.

Though it had festered in her mind on her way up to the Oval, Xandra just wasn't sure what to make of her vision back in the Photo Office. Best run it by Wade before sharing it with the President. Until then, she'd just have to shelve it and focus on the matters at hand.

"She's ready for you." David opened the door and Xandra entered.

Looking well-composed, Bradley gestured to the sofas on the circular rug before the presidential seal.

Xandra went over to take a seat facing the President.

"I hope you'll forgive the drama," Bradley said. "He's upset with me because of some promises I've had to break."

"I'm sure one day he'll understand the sacrifices you have to make."

Bradley pressed her lips together, looked out the window, then said, "So, I wanted to let you know before we meet in the Situation Room—Evan's going to have a cow, but—I'm flying into Kishwar tomorrow."

"Tomorrow?" If blood could slowly freeze within one's veins, this is how it must surely feel. "After what just happened, are you sure that's such a good idea?"

With a wry grin, Bradley leaned forward and said conspiratorially, "What does it say when my National Security Advisor thinks I'm reckless?"

"I'm sure your reasons are sound..." This might be a good time to tell her about the vision she'd just experienced. "But, things are volatile over there right now."

"Our advance team has been there for the past couple of weeks, coordinating with local authorities, US intel, and military. If we do this right, I can appear in an unscheduled visit, get filmed making a statement and shaking Aamaal's hand, then slip out and be home before the rest of the world gets wind of it. Minimal risk."

"I'm sure you've deliberated extensively, but—"

"Now more than ever, President Aamaal needs a show of support from us, from me. Her own constituents are skeptical and it does our interests no good if the situation destabilizes over there. That's just what al Saif is hoping for."

"I see."

"You don't seem convinced," Bradley said, with a polite smile.

"I'm sorry. I just..." Xandra must have been failing at concealing her apprehension. "You don't need my approval." She should just speak up and tell her about the visions. But she'd never spoken about them in an official manner, certainly not before someone as powerful as the President of the United States.

Bradley glanced at the clock on the wall, then back to Xandra. "Well then, it's settled. We fly from Andrews..." she fumbled through some papers, "..oh, something like Zero-Dark-Thirty. Now, for this trip I want you there both as my photographer—"

"And your psychic?" Xandra smiled, hopefully not overstepping. But the irony of that remark must have betrayed her. Because Jennifer Bradley's demeanor became grave.

"Ms. Carrick, if you have something to say..."

She sat up and cleared her throat. "I'm concerned that the trip to Tariqistan could prove dangerous, if not fatal."

Features galvanized, Bradley looked directly into her eyes. "A vision?"

"I'm afraid so."

"Are you certain?"

"It's never definitive, at least not initially. But I did see you boarding *Air Force One*, and then the image of a lot of people dead."

That came out rather crudely.

After a thoughtful pause, during which time the space between her eyebrows crinkled, Bradley blinked and said, "Anything else?"

"Nothing that made any sense." Xandra was loathe to mention the rest. The vision being aboard the whaling ship from *Moby Dick* might hold some esoteric meaning, but she had no idea to what it pertained. What did she expect the president to make of that?

Bradley stood. "All right, we'll proceed as scheduled. I'm going to have a hell of a time calming Evan down about this trip, much less Wade."

"Yes, Madam President."

On one hand, it was a relief to unload the burden of that vision. On the other, however, the plans to fly into Tariqistan under the proverbial radar filled Xandra with dread.

Should she press the issue? Did it matter, really? The President's mind was made up.

And Xandra was going to be on that flight with her.

# THIRTY ONE

GEORGETOWN
WASHINGTON DC
9:24 PM EST

SHE HADN'T EXPECTED TO SEE HIM AGAIN so soon, certainly not under such circumstances. But there he was, waiting at the door of his home—a charming rowhouse on Cambridge Place. Jake Rittenhouse stood there looking rather suave in a pair of Levis, a pale blue dress shirt, and a navy sport jacket. He was peering down the steps bemused.

"Xandra Carrick, you never fail to astound."

"Good evening, Jake." Xandra lugging a tote bag full of supplies slung over her shoulder.

"I know you're new in town," he said, as she climbed the steps with Max, "but surely you could meet someone here in DC of the bipedal persuasion."

"They're *all* dogs," she said, trying to maintain the façade. "Max just happens to be among the better ones."

They reached the top of the steps and Max sat on his haunches.

"Evening, General," Jake said, as the Belgian Malinois stared unflinching into his eyes. "All business, isn't he?"

"Looking for weapons, drugs, bombs? He's your man—or dog,

rather."

Grinning, Jake glanced down at Max. "Hey buddy."

In true professional form, The General didn't move a muscle. He just sat there, awaiting a command.

"Max," Xandra said, "Give Jake a high-five."

Jake bent down, lifted his palm and received a dutiful paw.

"Love it." He straightened up, and held the front door open, gesturing inside. "Won't you come in?"

The door made a solemn groan as it swung shut behind her.

Admiring the antiques, the high vaulted ceilings, the hard-wood floor upon which lay a dark Afghan rug, she couldn't help but notice. "This is incredibly rude of me, but how does a college professor afford a place like this?"

"Oh, it's not mine. A friend of a friend's took a three year position in Leipzig and was looking for someone to house sit. I just have to keep the place in one piece and I get to live here rent free."

"That's luck for you."

"No such thing," he said, "Coffee?"

"Can't stay, sorry. I've got to get ready for an early flight in the morning."

He leaned an elbow onto the polished banister of the staircase that led to the second floor.

"Oh, is that the trip you texted me about?"

"I really can't talk about it," she said, though deep down she wished otherwise. It would be great having his perspective and counsel, about what her visions were trying to tell her. She couldn't say no to this trip when it was her duty to the president. However, those visions about the aircraft would not give her peace. "Thank you so much for agreeing to look after Max."

"Well, unlike this really great person I know, I grew up with dogs and happen to like them a lot."

"I'm not afraid any more. Not of Max, anyway." She handed Jake the lead and a tote bag. "That's dog food, chew toys, and plastic bags for picking up his little campaign contributions."

"Max and I are going to have a great time together, aren't we, buddy?" The General sat there, the only sign of life being the yawn he just let out. "Right."

"I should be going." It had only been a few days, but in that time, Xandra had grown attached to Max. Must be what parents feel like when their kids go off to school or camp for the first time.

"Have a great trip, and don't you worry about a thing." Jake gave her that same reassuring smile she'd seen back in the Mennonite Colony when they first met. Four years and nearly three thousand miles later, it felt like a tiny bit of home. She started for the door, Jake and Max following.

Still, a few things weighed heavily on her.

She really couldn't get into it, not when she planned on going straight home and packing for the flight to Tariqistan. But what if her visions had been a warning sign for her to quit before it was too late?

She didn't have time to get into a deep conversation with him right now.

There might not be a better opportunity though.

*This is the only today you get,* Mom used to say.

She stopped and turned around.

"Can I ask you something, Jake?"

"Anything."

"When was your last vision?"

"A few weeks ago."

"Do you still get them often?"

"They come and go, why?"

"Mine seem to be increasing in frequency."

"What are they about?"

"I can't really talk about it right now, but let me ask you this. What would you do if you were able to help save someone from harm, but in the process might suffer harm yourself?" Though he was the one person who could truly understand, she couldn't disclose that she was referring to President Bradley.

Jake's brow tensed.

"Tough choice. I'm not sure I'd know until the moment I'd have to decide."

"And what if one of your visions led you to a dark place you never wanted to revisit, and all you got were bits and pieces of cryptic and useless information? What would you do with it?"

Rubbing the whiskers of his five o-clock shadow, he thought about it. "I'd pray...I mean, even more than usual."

"You still pray?"

"Just because I'm no longer a pastor doesn't mean I stopped believing. I've just got a different job now. Thing is, this gift is from above, so we have to trust that the revelations we get matter—regardless of how incomprehensible they may seem at the moment. In faith, I treat them like they *do* matter."

"How?"

"By not ignoring them, by continuing to seek the truth in prayer and the confirmation of scriptures. Think about it: Your visions have led to important discoveries which helped set people free, and stop the atrocities of those whom they revealed, right?"

"Yeah, but—"

"Mine never led to anything that significant," he said. *"Your* gifts are far too important to ignore."

Holding his gaze, she let out a sigh. Like a salve, a sense of resolution soothed her mind. She didn't know why her visions had driven her to visit Ian Mortimer any more than she understood the significance of all those dead people in the vision she'd seen at Honest Abe's. All she knew was they had portended to a deadly danger. Jake's quiet confidence however, made its way into her mind and for now, it was enough.

"Figured out what you're going to do?" he said.

"Not exactly. Maybe I'll know after this trip."

"Takes a lot of faith to embrace a supernatural gift. Even more to use it."

Xandra laid her hand on his and gave it a warm squeeze. Why had she waited so long to talk with him? His was a powerful mind and deep spirit. And the truth was, no one else could understand her the way he did. Part of her wished she didn't have to fly out to Tariqistan so early tomorrow. "I can't thank you enough."

"You can thank me when you get back," Jake said, an expectant grin spreading over his face.

"Oh?"

"Have dinner with me some time," he said. "I hate eating alone, which is all I've done since I got here."

"Pastor Jacob Rittenhouse, are you asking me out?"

"I'm not a pastor anymore," he winked. "And it's just dinner."

She patted his hand, then bent down to rub Max's ears. "Better keep an eye on this one, General." And with that, she stepped out the door, turning only once to look back over her shoulder to find Jake standing there with Max, and waving good-bye.

# THIRTY TWO

PRESIDENTIAL PALACE
KISHWAR, TARIQISTAN
10:00 AM Local Time

INTERNATIONAL ASSIGNMENTS WERE NOTHING NEW
for Xandra, whose career as a *New York Times* photographer had
taken her to Iraq, Vietnam, Germany, and other exotic locales.

Miles from home in the recently democratized capital of Tariqistan, she had come to record for posterity President Bradley's
endorsement of this nation's first elected president, Nasra Aamaal. Like Bradley, Aamaal also held the distinction of being her
country's first female president.

The crowds cheered as Sayid Khuda, the Tariqistani Foreign
Minister addressed the media crowding around the steps of the
Presidential Palace. Xandra kept her camera focused on President
Bradley standing next to her counterpart just two yards away with
an aristocratic bearing.

"You okay there?" Wade said, his expression unreadable from
behind his dark Ray-Ban Wayfarers. "You seem tense."

"Baptism by fire," Xandra replied. If he took her visions seriously, he would be tense as well. He hadn't dismissed them, nor
had he acted as though they concerned him. What exactly did he
think of them, anyway?

Still as a monument, his eyes behind dark shades scanned the crowd like the infrared optical sensors of a cyborg, Wade's lips barely moved when he spoke to her. "Worried?"

"Other than the fact that this region is filled with armed malcontents who hate the concept of a female president? Other than the fact that insurgents have recently killed dozens not far from here?" She snapped off a series of shots in rapid succession, the shutter's mechanical percussion beating like moth wings. "Nope. Are *you* worried?"

"I exist in a state of perpetual concern," he said, then touched his coiled earpiece. "It's my job."

She was about to make a wisecrack when he turned and started speaking into his mic. When focused, Wade exuded all the warmth of a granite slab in the snow. He couldn't be more than a few years her senior, but he took himself as seriously as he did his job.

It didn't matter, she wasn't about to waste either of their time bantering and running the risk of missing an important shot.

Khuda made the introduction first in his native tongue, then in English. "Please welcome the President of the United States, Jennifer Bradley."

At the thunderous applause, Bradley turned to acknowledge President Nasra Aamaal, grasped both of her hands warmly, then approached the podium.

Xandra positioned herself so that in the shot, President Bradley stood against the backdrop of the columns that framed her perfectly. Clouds above had just broken, the sun casting a golden veil behind her. A gentle breeze blew her brown hair, making it unfurl and fly like a banner.

As the speech commenced, Xandra made a series of shots which would surely capture the essence of this historic moment. Tariqistan had been liberated from the oppression of extremists, a provisional government had been set up with the help of the United States. It had taken four years of fighting insurgents and taking out splinter terrorist groups, but now, the civil rights of

Tariqistanis were upheld. Among other important matters, for the first time ever women could work, get an education, walk unescorted, and even vote. There was no way Bradley would let terrorists and insurgents take back the ground that everyone—Americans and Tariqistanis had shed blood to liberate. Her presence here sent a powerful message to the World. The United States would stand by Aamaal, by Tariqistan.

Bradley turned and motioned for Aamaal to join her at the podium.

They shook hands and embraced.

Turning to face the cheering crowd and news cameras, they waved.

The serendipity of this day was not lost on anyone, the least of whom, Xandra: Two first time elected female presidents side-by-side, championing many a common cause and taking a stand against terrorism.

Xandra caught it all, not missing a frame.

But as she panned to the left, and zoomed in for a tight shot, that dreadful and familiar nausea assailed her. For a second she blacked out, a mild sense of vertigo overtaking her.

*Oh God, not now.*

Glancing down at the LED monitor of her Nikon, she noticed a male figure at the edge of the police lines. Unlike everyone else, his eyes were not fixed on the two presidents, they were looking out into the crowd.

In that instant, the still image in the monitor shimmered into a monochromatic haze. Then the form of...something...began to come into focus.

A sudden pain behind her eyes forced them shut.

"Xandra?" Wade came to her side and grasped her arm to steady her.

She strained, and struggled to concentrate on the alternating images that went from her camera's monitor into her mind:

A man's forearm.

Beneath the patch of dark hairs, infused beneath the surface of deep mocha skin, a tattoo of three small concentric circles.

Familiar.

Where had she seen it?

More details came up as the vision became clear.

A hand...

And a finger coiled around some sort of trigger.

# THIRTY THREE

THE IMAGE RESOLVED fully in her mind's eye. Not just the tattoo on the gunman's arm, but the eyes, the goatee, the nose. Xandra nearly lost her balance, but Wade held her up by the arm and called for assistance.

Her throat went dry. "Gun…"

"You sure?"

She blinked hard, trying to regain the use of her physical sight. "Male, dark complexion…goatee."

"That could be any number of people out there." He let go of her arm as she braced herself against a rail. Stepping ahead to a better vantage point, he spoke the description into his mic, and alerted all the agents in the area.

Another agent came to Xandra's side.

"Take her back inside," Wade said and pointed to the entrance to the palace behind the columns. A second later, he was converging on Presidents Bradley and Aamaal's position even as two other agents did the same.

SHE MIGHT HAVE BEEN SEEING THINGS, Wade thought, but there was no way he could risk it. Especially after the inaugural assassination attempt and the likelihood of an attack here being so high. Bradley had just concluded her speech and was about to leave, which helped him handle the situation like the proverbial duck—calm above the surface, and paddling like hell beneath.

"Madam President," he said, urging them back to the palace doors, "We've got a situation." Agents Lee and Wynton flanked and closed the space behind them. Two more from his team and a pair from Aamaal's formed a "meat shield" around them.

"What is it?"

Rushing past her, he called for additional assistance. "I'm sorry, Ma'am, you need to get inside." Something caught the corner of his eye. He stopped and motioned for Lee and Wynton, who rushed over. A team of several more agents took hold of both presidents by their arms and legs, and carried them into the safety of the palace.

A man fitting Xandra's description saw Wade approaching, turned to the left and right, eyes large with surprise and started pushing through the crowd to get away.

"I don't think so," Wade muttered, and went from a jog to a run. He signaled the team on the ground. "Suspect is afoot and headed for the west gate."

"Confirmed," Strickland, one of his plain-clothes agents answered.

It all happened in a matter of seconds. Before Wade reached the suspect, Strickland, Conner, and Moss tackled him. Like oil in water, the crowd dispersed in an ever-widening radius, gasps, screams and shouts rising into the air.

Over the radio, Strickland reported, "We've got him."

Keeping his gun down and as inconspicuous as possible, Wade slowed to a casual stride, directing people out of the way and clear of the scene. But there were so many of them it took him a while to get to his men. Most of the onlookers faced the commotion with their backs to him, so he had to get their attention as he pressed through.

"*Ismahli,*" he said, "Excuse me. Official business. Coming through." When he finally arrived, the subject was kneeling with his hands behind his head, his jacket removed as Strickland's men patted him down. No sign of a struggle, just a very nervous looking man with a goatee and a black t-shirt.

"That's all he had on him," Strickland reported and nodded to a bruised tomato on the ground in a Ziploc bag his men had sealed for evidence. "Looks like a common heckler. Otherwise unarmed."

Wade gave the suspect a head-to-toe once over. "Make sure. Never know where these guys hide their stuff, 'specially if they're going to blow themselves up."

A moment later, local law enforcement arrived, acknowledged Strickland whose men signaled them, and spoke brusquely to the subject as they cuffed him.

"Thirty-five seconds," Strickland said, nodding to the subject and the Kishwari police officers. "Not too shabby, all things considered."

"I want *our* people on this."

"I'll see to it."

Before they cuffed the suspect's hands behind his back, Wade noticed a peculiar tattoo just above his wrist, evocative of the Olympic rings, minus one or two. He made a mental note, in case the suspect turned out to be more than just a heckler. For now, he had some explaining to do to POTUS.

Cameras and mobile phones aloft, members of the crowd snapped off photos as the police marched the suspect away. Wade shook his head at the impending headlines: *U.S. President's Security Detail Apprehend Suspect Armed with Rotten Tomato.*

Xandra had been mistaken.

But it was always better safe than sorry.

Wade smirked and regarded Strickland with annoyance, and then nodded to the police officers escorting the tomato-terrorist into a squad car. Local agents would oversee the interrogation, but it wouldn't be declared resolved until he said so. "I want their report before we touchdown at Andrews."

# THIRTY FOUR

AIR FORCE ONE
KISHWAR AIRBASE
TARIQISTAN
12:03 PM Local Time

THE PRESIDENT WAS NOT DEAD.

Xandra, let out a long breath and shifted in her assigned seat in the staff cabin section of the Boeing VC-25 better known by its callsign *Air Force One*. Her seat—indicated by a place card that read, "Ms. Carrick. Welcome Aboard Air Force One," was one of fourteen, eight of them facing each other across a table. Emblazoned on the napkins, boxes of M&Ms, mugs, glasses, playing cards, and the blue and white notepads was the plane's call sign. There was no way you could ever forget where you were. The seating was first class style, something Xandra had never experienced until becoming the President's photographer.

"Attention on the aircraft," a voice announced over the PA, "the President is five minutes out."

"Yeah, right," Adam Finley, the press secretary said with a huff. "Three minutes ago, they said she was ten minutes out."

Xandra looked over to him across the cabin and over the table. "Are you keeping track?"

"You'd think they'd be more precise." He shook his head and

gazed out his window. "Can't wait till we're back stateside. Flying over Tariqistani airspace gives me the chills—especially these days."

Xandra smiled politely, "You seemed a lot more at ease on the way here."

Without even turning to face her, he waved a dismissive hand and blew raspberries. "Wasn't as much a chance of getting shot at by shoulder mounted rockets, leaving DC."

"You think—?" She swallowed a dry lump. "Isn't the National Security Adviser on this flight too?"

"I'm just saying…" Finley turned to her slowly, and a mischievous grin twisted his mouth, as though to say, 'just kidding.'

"Yeah." She rolled her eyes when he looked away.

The flight to Tariqistan had been Xandra's first ever on *Air Force One*. An hour after they'd taken off from Andrews Air Force Base, President Bradley called her for a briefing. Xandra hadn't fully understood the envious looks from all the other passengers, VIPS, and press members until Wade introduced the phrase 'Access Itch"—something that quietly afflicted everyone aboard from reporters to dignitaries, and even other heads of state. *"Everyone wants facetime with the President."*

Now, just a couple of days later, she felt considerably more comfortable with her role even here on what some referred to as The Mobile White House.

Pensive, she stared out onto the tarmac at the meticulously orchestrated logistics of the presidential entourage loading up for take-off. Part of the advance team had already taken off half an hour ago. How much longer it would be before President Bradley boarded for the long flight home?

With frustration, she recalled the vision she'd experienced at the Presidential Palace. And those she'd had before taking this trip.

But she'd been wrong at the Presidential Palace.

*Thank God no one got hurt.*

She hadn't expected Wade to act on her vision so decisively.

Hopefully, she wouldn't have to file a written report explaining how exactly she spotted the suspect. Unlike Wade, the rest of the Secret Service wasn't likely to believe in her precognitive abilities. She prayed he wouldn't have to report what precipitated his actions.

"This seat taken?" The deep voice said, with a demonic sense of timing. Wade sat down in the vacant chair next to her, not even bothering to wait for an answer.

"Shouldn't you be with POTUS, right now?" Xandra said.

He gave her a wry smirk. "Just because I head the detail doesn't mean I'm the only one assigned to her. Shouldn't *you*—?"

"As long as she's safe."

"Turns out your shooter was armed with a deadly vegetable." Wade's eyes were dead calm, without a trace of mirth to be found on his countenance.

"What?"

"We responded to and apprehended the suspect fitting your description. He was packing a 78 millimeter tomato."

Xandra didn't look away or even blink.

"That's where you're wrong."

"Excuse me?" Wade narrowed his eyes.

No matter what, she wasn't going to back down from his piercing gaze. A lesser woman might have found his sea-green, deep set eyes attractive. Not Xandra. She hadn't the time nor inclination for anything like that.

"Tomatoes aren't vegetables," she said, "they're fruit." And with that, she picked up a copy of the Washington Times and erected a barrier between them.

Wade let out a subtle groan.

Silence filled the microcosmic bubble they occupied. His fatigue and frustration were palpable. This was the point that awkwardness ordinarily ensued, but she wouldn't be the first to blink. Actually, she rather enjoyed the fact that Wade wasn't speaking.

Until he let out an ironic breath. "Should've seen the look on Bradley's face, when I told her about it."

At that Xandra lowered the newspaper and allowed a smirk to tug the corner of her mouth. "That you rushed her and Aamaal inside because of the threat of a tomato?" Though technically, it had been Xandra's fault, not his. "What did she—?"

"Wait, Xandra," he craned his neck towards the front of the plane. "Aren't you supposed to be out at the main door getting pictures of the President boarding?"

As if jabbed with an electric cattle prod, she bolted up, grabbed her camera and gear, and raced out of the cabin to the main door, chiding herself. But before she got anywhere near, she heard it.

President Bradley was already standing at the entrance, her back to the plane's fuselage and waving out to the press photographers on the ground.

Xandra snapped off a few shots, but she'd missed the most important ones. Her heart sank as the voice came over the PA.

"Attention on board the aircraft. The President has arrived, we are now on *Air Force One*."

# THIRTY FIVE

THE FEW PICTURES XANDRA HAD MADE would probably not cut it. It was a key moment for President Bradley—boarding *Air Force One.* A shot the Chief White House Photographer should not miss.

As Bradley stepped into the plane along with her security detail, Xandra took a few more pictures before stepping out of the way for the rest of the aids and security detail to pass her in the hallway.

Just then, Erica Gordon stepped out from the stream of people and leaned over. "Don't worry," she whispered, sounding as haughty as she looked. "I made some good ones."

"Good."

"Had a feeling you might miss it, being so new."

She gave her a courteous smile. "Thanks."

"Of course. That's why I'm here." Erica sauntered down the hall in her high heels, all the way to the aft where the press cabin was situated.

TEN MINUTES LATER, *AIR FORCE ONE* WAS IN FLIGHT. Xandra sat in the staff cabin debating whether or not to take Advil for the ache carving its way up her shoulder blade through her neck and all the way into her right eye socket. She'd been on edge, exhausted from jet lag, and stressed over her recent blunders. Thankfully, Wade had been called into the conference room and wasn't around to harp on them.

Some of the passengers were up and about. With the exception of a handful of aides trying to nap, the staff cabin was devoid of anyone but Xandra and her gear. The shade for her window had been down, and only now did she think to lift it. Rather than a blanket of clouds stretching across the horizon, she saw something that caused her to gasp with a start.

Off in the distance, a pewter colored fighter jet loomed off *Air Force One's* starboard wing, matching her speed perfectly.

But the image of a frightened Michael Bradley appeared in her mind and distracted her.

*Please don't let my mom get killed.*

Pins and needles ran along her arm, up her neck and through her scalp. The visions were fraying her nerves. Trying her best to ignore the tingling, Xandra shut her eyes and let out a slow breath.

Relax.

*You missed an important shot, you're stressed—it's not the end of the world.*

*Yet.*

Someone bumped into her shoulder.

Startled, she spun around.

Adam Finley had returned to the staff cabin. "I didn't mean to startle you."

"No, no…it's all right." Once again, her eyes wandered out the window. "What's that?" Xandra said, hiking a thumb at the fighter jet out the window.

Finley smirked. "That, my dear, is a McDonnell Douglas F-15 Eagle."

"Those aren't American markings on it." She could tell that much. "Should we be concerned?"

"Of course not. They're Tariqistani. Over the years, among other things, we've given them a modest fleet of fighters." He pointed at the jet. "That Eagle and its wingman on our port side are official escorts, compliments of President Aamaal and her government."

"Do we really need them? I mean, are there any concerns—?"

"Never mind them," he said, letting out an impatient breath. "Listen, if you hope to keep your job as the Chief Photographer, you're going to have to be proactive."

"I *am* proactive, I just—"

"Why aren't you in the conference room with the President?" He motioned for her to get up.

Not hesitating, she stood, though she cringed at the thought of having erred yet again. As far as excuses were concerned, being new would not cut it. "Wouldn't she have sent for me if she needed me?"

"You think the president of the United States has time to micromanage you?" He reached out, took her hand, and gently led her to the hallway. "You're her shadow, remember?"

Xandra nodded and increased her stride.

"Won't I be intruding?"

"It's just like the White House—only, in the sky. Look, she's accustomed to having her photographer around practically all the time. When she goes to her private cabin? That's when you give her space—unless she calls upon you. Got it?"

She gave him a terse nod just as they arrived at the conference room door.

Finley opened it and stepped inside first.

Donning a navy blue jacket with the presidential seal, Jennifer Bradley sat in a leather chair, her ear pressed into the handset of a phone. Still speaking, she gestured to Wade Masterson, then caught Finley's eye, and waved him and Xandra into the room. Despite the frenetic activity, Bradley exuded a deep-running calm that put Xandra's mind at ease.

Xandra took a seat on a couch by the starboard side of the plane's fuselage and switched to a 20mm-90mm lens in order to capture as much of the conference room as possible, and the various expressions of those present.

Zooming in on Bradley, she could see that the president was

used to tuning out anything and everything upon which she was not currently focused. Xandra caught it all, the earnest expression in her eyes, the forehead cradled in her left hand, the phone pressed into her ear, and the words that became audibly intelligible as the words formed on her lips.

"Please don't talk like that....Yes, as soon as I come home we'll go to Grandpa's ranch...No, this time it's really going to happen, I promise...Love you, Mikey," Bradley said in a maternal tone. "I'm sorry...*Michael*." She lifted her eyes, looked straight into the camera, and motioned for Xandra to come over. "Yes, sweetie. She's here."

Xandra went over and sat in the chair next to her.

Bradley offered her the handset. "My son would like a word."

Xandra came over and took it. "Hello?"

"Ms. Carrick?" Mikey said, in a valiant attempt to overcome the childish sound of his voice by lowering its pitch as far as a young boy could.

"You can call me Xandi, it's okay."

"He cleared his throat, sounding upset but in control of it. "You're gonna hafta be careful, okay? More careful than Maya was." A chilling reminder of how her position had suddenly and tragically become vacant.

"I'll be careful, Michael, I promise."

His voice returned to normal—what one might expect of a boy his age. "And um...Xandi?"

"Hmm?"

"Can you bring Max to visit when you get back?"

"If it's okay with your Mom, sure."

"It should be," he said, his tone lightening with delight. "I can't wait to see you again."

"Well, Max and I are looking forward to seeing you too."

"I have to go now."

"All right, nice talking to you."

"Oh, and Xandi?"

"Yes, Sir?"

"Promise you'll always listen to Mister Wade, okay?" He made an adorable attempt at sounding manly. "He and his men will keep you all safe."

Xandra suppressed a giggle and glanced over to Masterson who, if he looked any more austere, might be mistaken for a gargoyle. "I'll do my best."

"Thanks. Could you put my Mom back on the phone?"

"Here she is." Xandra smiled and returned the phone to Bradley, who warmly returned a grateful smile of her own. *Thank you*, she mouthed, then said her good-byes to her son, and hung up.

"Thank you for being so kind to my son. I keep promising to take him out to the ranch, but keep having to postpone. His patience is going to run out any day, I'm sure of it. I'm bracing for the nine-year-old-boy-version of Chernobyl."

"He's such a good kid."

"He really is. But things haven't been the same since Maya's death."

"She must have been really special to him."

Bradley nodded. "Mikey really liked her."

"Guess that explains why he made me promise I'd listen to Wade."

"Wade?"

Xandra rolled her eyes.

"He's a little stiff I'll admit," Bradley said, "but he's the best there is."

"Indeed." The scare back at the Presidential Palace had been on account of her vision. It might be best if she came clean and saved Wade the trouble. "Madam President?"

"We're somewhat private now," she said. "Call me Jenna."

"Right, Jenna." Still, it felt odd to address the most powerful person in the free world by the diminutive form of her given name. "I don't know what Wade has told you about the whole scare back at the palace square, but…well, it was my fault."

Her eyes brightened with curiosity.

"How so?"

"I thought I saw an armed man. At first it seemed to be one of my premonitions. I had no idea Wade would act so quickly on it."

A thoughtful pause.

Jenna glanced out the window for a few seconds without a word, her expression unreadable. Finally, she chuckled and shook her head.

"President Aamaal was not accustomed to being picked up, and carried around like a rolled up rug. I think she was the most surprised of us all."

"I hope it wasn't too embarrassing."

"Don't worry," Bradley said. "She's just glad our people responded so quickly. Especially in light of recent events. In any case, I'm sure Adam will find a way to make it look good in the press."

"All the same, please don't fault Wade. It was my mistake."

She patted Xandra's hand.

"Given the choice, I'd always err on the side of caution. You very well could have saved my life."

"Thank you, Madam—"

She lifted a finger to cut her off. "Informal."

"I mean Jenna."

"Much better." Bradley gave her hand a gentle squeeze. "So, we have a few minutes. I'd like to ask you a question?"

Xandra relaxed into her chair and smiled. "Absolutely."

"With the frenzied pace of the White House, you and I don't get many opportunities to speak. Being on *Air Force One* affords us the rare luxury to kick back and let our hair down, without the constant pressure of the press and staff."

"I noticed."

"So, tell me more about yourself—and for this discussion, forget about the Secret Service part of what you'll be doing." She leaned in closer. "What do you hope to accomplish as the Chief White House Photographer?"

"Glad you started with something easy," Xandra said, her brow lifting in surprise at the directness of the question.

Bradley grinned, but her eyes were unrelenting.

"Well, it's hard to top Oke's aspirations."

"I'm sorry...Oke?"

Xandra nodded. "Yoichi Okamoto, LBJ's photographer."

"Oh, right."

"Among the greats—Kennerly with Ford, McNeely with Clinton, Draper with George W. Bush, Oke is legendary. He wanted to take ageless photos that people five hundred years in the future could appreciate. I guess, I'd like to contribute to the archives in a distinctive way that honors Oke's ideals as well. And for me, it's a particular honor to be doing so at this important milestone in history—The United States' first elected female president."

Bradley smiled. "I have every confidence you'll do just fine. Now, do you have any questions for me?"

"As a matter of fact, I do." Xandra sat tall, regarded her Nikon sitting on the conference room table. "How much do you know about me, my involvement with the Colson Conspir—"

"I've been briefed on everything."

"By everything, you mean—?"

"*Everything.*"

She cleared her parched throat. "So, knowing that I brought down your former running mate, why would you even consider hiring me?"

"Simple. You're great at what you do," Jenna said, without hesitation. "I've seen your work as a photojournalist, your work in Iraq, your pieces for The *Times.* I like your style, your honesty."

"What about Colson?"

"We were friends. However, he deceived not only me, but the entire nation. The whole world was shocked and outraged at what he'd done. I can only hope these past four years have been evidence enough that I had nothing to do with all that."

Before Xandra spoke another word, the curtain over the starboard windows swayed in her periphery. It sent a disturbing chill through her. She tried her best not to let it show, but it was probably too late. The president's words faded into a dark void, a cloud of images resolving into Xandra's mind.

*Once again, a man's hand.*

*The tattoo on his wrist—triune intersected rings…*

*Gripping a device, with a trigger…*

But now she could tell exactly what it was, no mistaking it this time.

# THIRTY SIX

"ARE YOU ALL RIGHT?" President Bradley said, reaching out to grasp Xandra's shoulder.

"I'm sorry, would you please excuse me?" Xandra stood up so abruptly, Wade took note and walked over to meet her as she went to the window with her camera.

"What's the matter?" he asked, even as she threw open the curtain and pressed her lens against the glass. Without even thinking, she zoomed in as tight as she could on the pilot in the cockpit of the F-15 escort. The pilot gave a quick thumbs up, then waved.

"Wade, something's wrong." Xandra took a shot. Right away she checked out the image on the DSLR's monitor and zoomed in on it as much it could. "Damn."

He hiked a thumb at the Eagle. "Don't worry, those fighters are just for show. And last I heard, Tariqistani law enforcement confiscated all shoulder mounted tomato launchers."

He wasn't going to let her live that false alarm down any time soon, why would he take her seriously now?

"Do we have any other air support?" She panned around the image of the pilot's hand—the one doing the thumbs up—and looking for a confirmation of her vision.

"Everything okay?" President Bradley said, her face a juxtaposition of curiosity and concern.

Then Xandra found it.

The urge to let out a vindicated whoop was overridden by dread.

"Xandra," Wade said, impatience seeping through.

"Look," she put the camera's LCD monitor up for him to see. "See that?"

"What are we looking at?"

"That tattoo on his hand, it's right there."

Wade's brow pinched together. "No, it's just his hand."

"It's clear as day. The three circles—Wait..." in that moment, the symbol which she'd seen somewhere before vanished. "I think I just had a vision."

"Did you say it was a tattoo, three circles?"

"Yes, but—"

Before she could explain that it must have been the pilot whom her initial vision had been about back at the Presidential Palace in Kishwar and not the tomato guy in the crowd, Wade pressed in his ear piece, spoke into his mic, and went straight to Bradley. He whispered something into her ear.

A look of surprise came over Bradley's eyes as she listened. *Are you sure?* she mouthed silently.

"Not absolutely, but we need to take every precaution."

Bradley nodded and went over to one of her aids. "Get me President Aamaal on the phone."

With great purpose, Wade rushed to the door, about to pass by Xandra.

"Wait a second," she said, "Do you even know what I—?"

"Give me a minute," He stepped around her, not missing a step, and left the cabin.

"But..."

Gone.

"Xandra?" The President gestured for her to return.

She did, but the friendly fighter escort on *Air Force One's* wing kept drawing her eyes and thoughts.

"Did you just have a vision?" Bradley whispered.

"I'm not sure." Xandra sank in her chair uncertain how much she should say. Best not to put herself out there if she wasn't a hundred percent certain. "I...I was just surprised, concerned...I don't know. Last time I heard of a fighter escort for *Air Force One* was when Bush was returning to Washington right after the September 11 attacks."

"I'm sure everything will be all right. That escort wing out there was handpicked by President Aamaal's most trusted generals. We're safe."

Xandra acknowledged it with a tight nod.

But it didn't ease her apprehension.

She kept that escort in the corner of her eye.

"In any case, I'll double-check with Aamaal. And for an added security measure, Wade's consulting with Evan Cromwell. I'm sure if there was any cause for concern, the National Security Advisor would have mentioned it."

*Cause for concern?* Xandra thought, struggling with the fact that her cryptic visions were about to drive her mad. What if she was wrong?

*What if I'm right?*

# THIRTY SEVEN

THE SINKING FEELING IN HIS GUT was almost enough to send Masterson banging his head against the wall repeatedly, as he left the conference room. She'd caused him to overreact back at the Presidential Palace, why should he react to this? There was nothing on the image of the pilot's hand, but how did she know to describe what he'd seen on the suspect's hand back in Kishwar?

It took less than a second to recall.

The tattoo on the suspect's wrist.

Three intersecting circles.

*Can't be a coincidence.*

Double timing, he turned right and stepped directly into the senior staff cabin.

Four chairs in an X formation, only one occupied.

In it sat National Security Advisor Evan Cromwell, reclined and fast asleep, his bushy white eyebrows twitching atop the black eye mask.

"Sorry to bother you, Sir."

Cromwell grunted. "Then don't."

"It's important."

The older man lifted the eye mask, slowly sat up, and regarded Wade with a perturbed look. "Just fell asleep, son," he said in a gruff voice. "What is it?"

"I need you to put in a call to the Sec Def."

"We at war?"

"I don't think so, Sir." He glanced out at the window at the F-

15 steadily maintaining its escort position. "Not yet, anyway."

"What is it, then?"

"Security concerns." He pointed at the F-15.

Cromwell grumbled. "That's what the damned escort's for."

"Sir, I have reason to believe…" *What, that a blurry image of the pilot's hand that Xandra showed him was a matter for the Secretary of Defense?* "I'm concerned the Tariqistani escort may not be adequate."

"Hell of an assumption."

"Still, I'd feel better about the President's safety if we had some American pilots nearby."

"Closest base is Al-Dhafra."

"Can you see what they've got?"

"I'll make an inquiry, but only if you really—"

"Thank you, Sir. Now if you'll excuse me, I have another lead to follow up on."

"Yeah, don't mention—"

Wade stepped out and entered the cabin aft of the conference room. There he found Special Agent Strickland speaking on the phone. Strickland glanced up and acknowledged his presence.

"Kishwar?" Wade murmured.

Strickland nodded.

Wade held out his hand, and Strickland gave him the handset.

"Inspector Qadir, here." The voice on the other end of the line spoke with a subtle accent.

"This is Wade Masterson of the United States Secret Service, what have you got on the suspect?"

"He was completely unarmed—just a heckler. He said he planned on throwing a tomato at President Aamaal. He and a few other locals had planned this, but nothing more."

"Did you get their names?"

"Yes, sir."

"And the evidence?"

"I'm sorry, the what?"

"The tomato. Have you had it checked?"

The Kishwar Inspector snorted. "It has been stepped on by many people by now."

"You mean, you didn't retrieve it?" Wade clenched his jaw.

"Mister Masterson...it's a tomato."

"Where is it?"

"Probably distributed under the soles of a hundred people who walked all over it."

"Listen very carefully," Wade took a deep breath. "You're to recover whatever remains of that damned tomato there are and have it analyzed. Under no circumstance is the suspect to be re-leased—"

"But...we've already released him."

Wade let out a frustrated grunt and pinched his temples. "Get. Him. BACK!"

"Sir, I do not appreciate the tone you are taking with me. I don't work for you, you know."

"Your boss reports to a member of the United States Secret Service, who reports to me. So you'd best get your ass in gear."

A dead silence.

Then, a tight breath from Qadir. "Right away, Mister Masterson. We'll have an update for you within the hour."

"I want it in half an hour." He hung up.

PRESIDENTIAL PALACE
KISHWAR, TARIQISTAN
1:08 PM Local Time

IN THE PUBLIC SQUARE directly outside the Presidential Palace, the crowd had thinned to a few pedestrians and tourists taking pictures of the long steps leading up to the pale marble columns behind the gates. Media crews had all left. The only evidence of the historic speech delivered by the American President were the discarded flyers and souvenir buttons scattered on the pavement.

The plastic bag containing the tomato from the thwarted heckler had been trampled, kicked, ripped open and smeared over into the gutter where a black crow diligently pecked away at its remains for a few minutes.

The bird had been so fixated that even as people stepped right over its ebony frame, it didn't so much as flap its wings in an attempt to avoid them. Eventually, half a dozen flea-infested rats crawled out of the sewer drain and partook of the tomato remains as well.

Without warning, the crow squawked. With a ferocious jab, it impaled one of the rats with the point of its beak. The rat screeched in pain, wriggled itself free, and ran behind the other two that were still tearing away at the tomato.

The crow cocked its head for about half a second, then proceeded to rip into the remains, scarlet shreds and liquid dripping from its mouth like blood. Every now and then, it would stop, ruffle its feathers, stamp its feet wildly, then resume eating. This persisted for about ten minutes, until the bird rolled over on its side and began breathing heavily.

It barely reacted to the rats—the injured one particularly fierce—as they swarmed over its body.

Before the crow could fully right itself, the rats began gnawing at the hapless bird at a heated pace. Feathers, blood, and flesh flew until scarcely anything remained but some of its skin, feathers and the viscous remains that the rats had missed.

With a collective feral shriek, the rats dispersed into the street and nearby alleyways, a few of them keeling over and convulsing as their flesh dissolved from the inside and oozed out of their mouth, eyes, ears, and eventually through their skin.

No one in Kishwar seemed to have noticed but a stray dog that began licking at the pools of blood in the curb.

# THIRTY EIGHT

AIR FORCE ONE
FLYING OVER THE BLACK SEA
2:31 PM

SHE TRIED HER BEST to ignore the jitters in her stomach. Despite Bradley's confidence, experience had taught Xandra that there was always more to situations than met the eye.

"What did Wade say?" Xandra glanced back at the fighter jet, still flying perfectly in sync.

Bradley gave her a reassuring smile. "He wanted to follow up on something pertaining to the incident back at the Presidential Palace."

Xandra still couldn't shake the anxiety coursing through her like arctic water.

A few minutes went by, and an impromptu meeting in the conference room became light-hearted and animated. The topic: Nasra Aamaal. Though she was rather young to be the President of any country, Bradley felt she embodied that same dauntless spirit as so many young women of Tariqistan who'd dared stand against Haashir's extremist dictates. His regime had denied them the right to vote, to an education, and the freedom even to walk the streets without male supervision.

Tariqistan was now a democratic nation on the bleeding edge

of rapid modernization in every respect—economically, socially, politically, and technologically. That their elected president just happened to be an attractive woman in her mid-thirties, Harvard educated, with the appeal of a western pop singer, only added to this impression. The general population loved her enough to vote her into office.

But the ousted extremists were still bitter. Especially so, since the killing of Haashir. For such extremists, Tariqistan had deteriorated into a sacrilegious cesspool of Western vice. Thanks to the support the United States had provided, however, the insurgency had been kept under control. In fact, in just a few short years, Tariqistan had stabilized—and in record time. A textbook success story, unlike the questionable attempts of previous administrations.

And a glorious feather in President Bradley's cap.

*You need to relax and see this moment for what it is,* Xandra thought, *or you'll compromise the quality of your photographic work. You still don't know enough to protect the President. Leave that to Wade.*

Bradley must have told a joke, because the entire staff seated at the table erupted into roaring laughter. Xandra caught a shot of the President throwing her head back laughing while her personal assistant Joanna Croft fanned herself with both hands. Candids like these were priceless. Xandra had captured a moment worthy of the walls of this airborne White House, or the Oval Office itself.

*It's going to be all right.*

Allowing herself a moment to smile and even laugh along with the rest of those in the cabin, Xandra lowered her camera and eased herself into a seat by the window. Her misgiving about the fighter escort had all but evaporated.

She relaxed, choosing to believe that all would be well.

Until she pulled the curtain open to take a look.

In that instant, the F-15 dropped out of formation and vanished from sight.

A second later, an alarm sounded.

In a steady, yet urgent voice, the pilot instructed everyone over the PA to secure their seat belts.

The President, and everyone seated in the bolted down chairs around the conference table managed to do so, just as the plane lurched violently.

Xandra fell.

Her Nikon slipped from her hands, its strap over her head.

It went flying to the forward section of the cabin.

*Air Force One* was taking a nose dive.

# THIRTY NINE

AIR FORCE ONE
OVER THE BLACK SEA
2:38 PM

NO TURBULENCE SHE'D EVER EXPERIENCED could compare. Xandra rolled and hit the forward bulkhead of the cabin, which was now beneath her like the floor. President Bradley's hair dangled sideways towards the front of the plane, which was now diving at a near vertical angle.

Abruptly, the plane righted itself.

Xandra fell to the ground, groped at anything she could hold onto as *Air Force One* thrust violently ahead, then banked sharp to the left. She let out a gasp and slid on the floor flailing about.

The next thing she knew, Wade Masterson entered the cabin, gripped the door frame, took a quick glance at President Bradley strapped in, then went over to position near her.

In the short moment the plane was level and straight, Xandra got into a secured chair at the table opposite Bradley, and strapped herself in.

The President called out, "What's happening, Wade?"

He stepped forward and threw the curtains open to reveal that they were deep inside the white cover of a cloud formation. "We're under attack."

"By whom?"

"I'm not sure. But we just deployed flares." He glared out the window. "I think it's the escort wing."

"Tariqistan's jets?" The President turned sharply, motioned to her aide, and he picked up the phone. A moment later, he was talking frantically into the handset trying to get Aamaal on the phone again. Finally, he gave the handset to Bradley.

Once again, *Air Force One* banked sharply to the left, then to the right.

Every unsecured object flew through the cabin, coffee mugs, pens, books, Xandra's camera.

The distant thunder of an explosion turned the heads of just about everyone in the conference room.

"Was that a missile?" Xandra said, gripping the arms of her chair.

"Countermeasures and radar jamming can only do so much," Wade said, "the cloud cover, even less."

Bradley slammed the handset down. "Those are *Tariqistani* pilots. Why are they doing this? Kishwar's scrambling more fighters to assists, but they're at least five minutes out."

"We'll be dead by then!" Adam Finley said.

Another nose dive followed by a sharp roll to the right.

The protective cloud cover peeled away.

Rays of sunlight cut through the windows.

Somewhere outside of the airframe, a rattling noise resembling a frantic knocking on a door rang out.

The F-15's guns.

Wade gripped the door frame as the plane rolled sharply. "Good thing he's a lousy shot."

The entire cabin rolled sideways.

Like an enormous roller coaster, *Air Force One* began accelerating in a circular downward pattern.

"Have we been hit?" Bradley said, her features tense.

Xandra pressed her back up against the chair and gripped the armrests. *Oh my God, we're going down!*

TEARS CLOUDED HIS VIEW within the cockpit of the F-15, as Lieutenant Sarab rapidly depleted the ammunition of the M61 Vulcan. Within seconds he'd fired off several hundred rounds and wondered if he'd subconsciously meant to miss the target.

*Air Force One* was surprisingly agile for a plane its size. As it went into a defensive spiral dive, Sarab took his eyes from the HUD for a moment and glanced down to the photo of his wife and eight year old daughter taped to the console. From this day forth they would hate him, remember him only as a traitor, not a man without a choice. If he failed to successfully execute this mission, they would be tortured for days before being allowed to die.

"I am sorry."

The regret did not extend to his family alone, but to the American president he admired, and all the innocent people aboard *Air Force One* as well. He signaled to Lieutenant Taseen, his wingman—another poor soul who had also been blackmailed.

Taseen's Eagle roared just outside of the engagement area as a backup in case Sarab failed. Meanwhile Sarab worked to keep in phase with the mammoth plane in its "rolling scissor" maneuver.

It was growing increasingly difficult to get a lock.

Especially when he had no desire to murder these people.

But he must.

*For Ranya and Zerina.*

Sarab glanced down to his hand on the flight stick, noticing the accursed tattoo on his wrist. Why had he ever agreed to join them? He should have known that people who promise just what you want, will do so to extract from you just what *they* want. And now, he was going to Hell for this lapse in judgment.

Finally, the weapons lock chimed.

He squeezed his eyes shut.
Let out an agonized cry.
And fired the missile.

# FORTY

*AIR FORCE ONE* DESCENDED at a steep angle and pulled up horizontal over the water. Sarab swore in frustration as the missile he'd fired went straight into the sea. The American pilot was obviously well-trained and took his plane back up in an evasive pattern.

He breathed a sigh of relief, but at the same time wished it could be over with. Firing upon practice drones was one thing, but this went beyond anything he could imagine. He pulled the stick back and gradually increased his throttle, his instincts deterring him from overshooting his target.

Sarab signaled for his wingman to get in position while he performed a Low Speed Yo-Yo maneuver. As *Air Force One* began its climb to a safe altitude, Taseen would attack from above and Sarab from below. There were only a few seconds in which either of them could get in phase with their target. Taseen hadn't fired his weapons yet, and Sarab had only one sidewinder left, thanks to the meager resources afforded the Tariqistani Air Force.

"Stand ready," he radioed to Taseen in the Kishwari dialect.

"I don't know if I can do this."

"You must!" Sarab barked. Then his voice softened, sympathizing with the turmoil of his friend—a kind man, loyal husband, and loving father. "*We* must. For our families."

Taseen drew a trembling breath. "I understand."

The veins in Sarab's hand bulged as he strangled the flight stick. "Don't cross the Tigris until I say so." Which was code for, *hold your fire until my command.* If he could spare Taseen the guilt, he would. It was all he could do to appease his conscience. And to complete the mission, they must crash their planes into the sea and kill themselves. No absolute guarantee their families wouldn't be killed anyway, but this was their only hope.

"Allah forgive us," Taseen said, his voice detached and cold.

"Indeed." Sarab snorted quietly. If there even was a God, He would never condone their actions today; they had been damned from the moment he got involved. All that mattered now was that he had done everything to protect his family. Nevertheless, history would forever see him as a traitor and terrorist.

Within the tiny window of opportunity, he saw the right moment to fire his last sidewinder.

Clenching his teeth, he launched the missile.

Hopefully its infrared missile guidance (heat seeker) system would not fail.

He sent two short bursts of static over his radio to Taseen indicated the equivalent of "Fox Two," the brevity code he would have called out, had he been flying with a squadron of NATO pilots.

The heat seeker screamed out from under his wing.

Almost immediately, the target released a stream of flares that resembled fireworks. Three lines of bright countermeasures shot out from its aft, down, left, and right.

Sarab let out a frustrated grunt and punched the throttle.

"It is with you now, Taseen."

"Understood."

PRESIDENT BRADLEY was on the phone speaking urgently. The plane had turned, climbed, rolled and centrifuged Xandra's innards, but she was determined not to sit idly.

If these were their final moments, Xandra would do her best to record them. Perhaps among the wreckage pulled from the depths of the Black Sea, they'd find her camera's SD card and learn what happened to them.

Despite the chaos and violent flight patterns, she unbuckled herself just long enough to get out of her seat and grab her Nikon.

Still working, thankfully.

Without hesitation, she pointed it to the window.

The complete absence of any attacking fighter jets caused her even greater concern.

"*If there's a wasp in the room*—she remembered reading somewhere a long time ago—*I like to be able to see it.*"

Only, these wasps were capable of blowing a jumbo jet out of the skies, and all those aboard it.

"Wade!" Bradley called out. "Where are they?"

He climbed over to the sofa next to Xandra, looked out the window first down, then up.

He swore and slapped the bulkhead.

Xandra went to the window and looked out. High above their position, the second F-15 seemed to be lining itself up for an attack run.

"If he's a better shot than the first one..." Wade said, dryly, "We're—"

All at once, the attacking jet dove straight down. Like a lethal sparkler, lights flashed from its guns.

"Get down!" Wade grabbed at Xandra's arm, but missed.

*Air Force One* banked hard out of the incoming fire. Both she and Wade fell against the window and wall of the fuselage, Xandra's face pressed against the glass with all the force of the turn. The rounds had just missed the wing.

The F-15 sped down past them, pulled up sharp.

Now its weapons were pointed right up at *Air Force One's* belly.

It didn't take clairvoyance to know what was coming next.

At this close range, the Eagle would eviscerate the plane like a piñata. A horrific shudder worked its way through Xandra's body. Nevertheless, she aimed her camera at the steel bird of prey coldly eyeing its quarry.

There was something eerie, yet compelling about the way it glared up at them, waves of the Black Sea shimmering with golden light as its backdrop.

Xandra took a long burst of shots, expecting to capture the stream of rounds, or one of its missiles flying straight at the viewfinder. Though they'd be the last pictures she made, they would be spectacular.

*If anyone ever retrieves it.*

"Xandra!" Wade called out. The plane had leveled itself, and he was now shielding the President with his body, arms draped over her. "Get away from that window!"

In that split second, as she stared though the viewfinder, a strange calm came over her like the refreshing breeze off the shores of Del Mar, where Dad's house overlooked. She'd lived a short, but meaningful life, and chose to banish any regret from her final moments.

# FORTY ONE

IT COULD HAVE BEEN THE MISSILE'S IMPACT, or the sun going supernova for all she knew. Brilliant light from the explosion made Xandra recoil and squeeze her eyes shut.

Momentarily blinded, she blinked repeatedly trying to see.

She felt it all over, within her chest cavity.

The profound detonation.

It rocked the cabin.

Shook the entire plane.

Bewildered, she continued pressing the shutter button, but lowered the camera.

Outside, the attacking F-15 expanded into a huge fireball.

Flaming shrapnel flew out in all directions.

"What just happened?"

Wade rushed over, but all that was left out there was a trail of smoke and burning debris plummeting into the sea. "Was that—?"

"It just…" Xandra's throat went dry, uncertain whether to cheer or scream. "It's gone."

LIEUTENANT SARAB WATCHED IN DISMAY as Taseen's jet exploded, amber flames licking through dark plumes. Aamaal must have scrambled another pair of fighters to intercept them, though he couldn't tell where exactly they were, thanks to *Air Force One's* radar jamming.

No time to mourn.

Sarab steeled up his emotions for his family's sake. This was the end. With or without his wingman, there was no turning back.

As Taseen's jet disintegrated, the target flew into a heavy patch of clouds. Would Sarab suffer the same fate as his friend?

No. At all costs, he had to destroy that aircraft.

But in his haste, he'd expended all his rounds and hardpoints.

Pushing his throttle as far as he could, he pursued *Air Force One* with the one weapon he had left at his disposal.

*Only a few seconds.*

Racing above the cloud cover, he made out its faint outline.

Though the President's aircraft jammed his radar, he could tell where it would soon become visible. Before they could get a visual on him, he would attack.

Blinking tears from his eyes, Sarab cursed the day he took that pamphlet from that protester at the outskirts of the capital. The meetings were supposed to be a civilized discourse about the restoration of conservative Tariqistani values. But it had quickly revealed itself as nothing of the sort. They had merely employed Islam as the bait on their hooks which only dug deeper the more you tried to pull away.

The people from whom they took orders were neither religious, nor even Tariqistani. Their agendas were nothing like those of the religious extremists, and they—their superiors, at least—seemed much more effective at exerting absolute control over anyone they wished.

Sarab had only wished to express concern over the rapid westernization of his country. But now, he was being used as a pawn to assassinate the president of the most feared nation in the world.

*And probably start a war.*

All he had wanted was to retire, write poetry, watch his daughter grow up and get married, hold his grandchildren, and grow old with the wife of his youth.

*What kind of monster have I become?*

The target emerged from the clouds.

Closer than he could have hoped for.

With perverse joy, a smile twisted his lips.

Before he could second guess himself, he thrust the flightstick forward...

...and launched his jet straight into *Air Force One*.

# FORTY TWO

AIR FORCE ONE
OVER THE BLACK SEA
2:41 PM

SECONDS AFTER the first F-15 went down, *Air Force One* flew into a thick layer of clouds. Barely catching her breath, Xandra turned away from the window and slid down into the couch.

During the short interval of level flight, President Bradley remained on the phone, which was about all Xandra noticed as her attention was fixed on the situation unfolding before her eyes.

"Where are they?" Bradley demanded. Though Aamaal had scrambled backup fighters, they were nowhere in sight.

Her aide who was on the other phone shook his head and frowned. "Less than two minutes out."

"Two minutes?" Xandra craned her neck to the window and looked back to where one of the attacking fighter jets had been destroyed. "Then who just...?" She scanned the area, yet saw nothing but white around, beneath, and above them.

"Whoever they are, we'll thank them later." Wade came to the window. "There's still another Eagle out there."

A flash of sunlight struck Xandra's eyes.

Momentarily blinded, she rubbed them.

Her vision cleared.

Xandra gasped, almost fell off the couch.

Wade reached out and caught her.

The oncoming F-15 hadn't fired any of its weapons, but judging by its proximity and rapid descent, it was on a collision course. Just seconds after surviving the first attack, they were facing death all over again.

Only this time the fighter jet itself was the weapon.

The Eagle lurched forward abruptly.

Staring out the window, Wade swore. "He's going Kamikaze."

Xandra wanted to scream, *This can't be happening!*

No, it was far too ironic. How could the President's plane be knocked out of the sky by "friendly" aircraft *we* supplied to our allies?

Once again, *Air Force One* pitched into a steep nosedive.

Xandra fell.

But she kept her focus on the F-15 careening toward them, and beheld another spectacle.

It must have been about three hundred yards away, but she saw it.

Even as it closed in.

Something flew straight into the attacking fighter jet.

It erupted into a brilliant sphere of fire and smoke, large pieces of its airframe shooting out in every direction. Xandra heard herself shouting in—she didn't know what exactly—excitement, terror, joy?

When it resolved and all became tangible, she found herself in Wade's arms, having fallen into them without realizing. But they were both too embroiled in the moment to think anything of it.

*Air Force One* leveled out and the ride grew strangely smooth.

"What just happened?" she asked, pushing away from Wade absently and walking back to the window.

"It's over," President Bradley said, now at her side.

Xandra turned and noticed the moisture on her brow as she held the curtain back and searched the sky. As subtly as she could, she stepped back and grabbed her camera.

Bradley was clearly shaken, but exuded a constancy that could only be described as "presidential." The pictures Xandra made of her staring out the window would surely grace the walls here on the plane, or in the halls of the White House.

She motioned to Wade. "Speaker phone."

He went over and hit the button.

Still searching the airspace over the Black Sea, Bradley cleared her throat. "Still there, Tony?"

Over the speaker: "Yes, Madam President." It was Anthony Berg, the Secretary of Defense.

Leaning against the window frame, she lowered her forehead into her hand and let out a relieved sigh. "Raptors from Guardian Wing have arrived."

"Thank God."

"And not a second too late." The edge of Bradley's lips twitched with emotion, though her voice exuded the strength she'd shown throughout the ordeal. "Thank you, Tony. But for the record, I'm flying with my own escorts next time."

"No doubt you'll take that up with Evan, Ma'am."

Just then, another fighter jet appeared on *Air Force One's* wing. It looked much more technologically advanced and intimidating. Xandra gasped with a start, but then realized these were the jets the Defense Secretary had sent. American jets.

Exhaling in relief, she found just the right angle to capture a shot with the President gazing out the window and returning the American pilot's salute.

Evan Cromwell stepped into the conference room, wiping his brow with a handkerchief. He and Wade exchanged incredulous looks. The president's Chief of Staff made eye contact with her, then with Wade. He pointed out at the new escort fighter jet flying off the starboard wing.

"Damned Raptors," Wade growled with admiration. "Bandits never saw them coming."

Xandra would learn later that the F-22s were the apex of air superiority. Thanks to their stealth and ability to fly well over twice the speed of sound, they'd been scrambled from Al-Dhafra as soon as the National Security Advisor had requested them. Which, of course, happened as a result of Wade Masterson's hunch that the President might need their assistance.

"Are you all right, Madam President?" Wade said quietly.

"I am now."

"Is that Wade Masterson?" Berg said, over the speakerphone.

He turned to the phone to address the Defense Secretary. "Yes, Sir."

"Good call, Son."

"Thank you, Sir."

"Make it earlier next time."

Wade grinned. "Yes, Sir."

"Need anything else?"

"Assuming the Raptors are all they're cracked up to be, we don't anticipate any issues with Angel's return to Andrews."

"We'll have another escort take over as you get closer."

"Again, thanks." Wade turned to President Bradley.

She came over, lifted the handset, put it to her ear, and spoke in a softer voice. "We're in good hands now, Tony. Tons to investigate. Not a word about any of this until you hear from my office, understood? Great. Thank you."

During the entire call, Xandra had taken so many shots of the President in different expressions she didn't realize until she came right up to the camera.

"Xandra?"

She lowered the camera. "Madam President?"

She leaned close and spoke quietly. "I'm going to ask that you not release any of the photos of this incident."

"Ma'am?"

"Not until we get to the bottom of it. Neither President Aamaal nor I have any idea how their pilots could have done this. Considering the ongoing terror threat, I don't want to incite public panic."

"Of course."

"Not to mention the blow it would strike to the alliance between our countries. Until we determine what just happened, we've got to contain this."

"Understood." But how would Adam control the press corps in the aft section? Would he confiscate their SD cards, have them placed under some kind of gag order? They'd witnessed it all and would undoubtedly seek answers as to why they'd nearly been killed by fighter jets from our allies.

"Glad I can count on you," Bradley said.

"I'm just relieved it's over." Xandra took a long breath.

For the next few hours, now that they were being escorted by American F-22s, Xandra allowed herself to rest at ease, knowing they were safe.

The fulfillment of her visions of death might have just been averted.

Or maybe not.

For the rest of the flight, ominous thoughts afflicted her without mercy.

Could the worst be yet to come?

# FORTY THREE

NATIONAL AIRLINES FLIGHT 1306
EN ROUTE TO WASHINGTON DC FROM SHANGHAI, CHINA
SOMEWHERE OVER THE PACIFIC OCEAN

FOURTEEN AND A HALF HOURS wasn't all that bad, considering the flight would take him clear across the Pacific Ocean, and the entire North American Continent. But Lawrence Collins, CEO of GENTEC, the hottest new biotech firm that just went public could think of a million better ways to spend the time.

"Seat belts please," the pretty red head flight attendant said, and patted the back of his headrest. "We're anticipating a bit of turbulence up ahead."

"Are we going to be on time?" He said, giving her a friendly smile, as he faked having trouble with the buckle. "You would think things worked better in business class."

"Allow me." She leaned over, letting her sweet smelling hair fall into his face, grasped the buckle and tab, then pushed the tongue inside joining the two parts with a crisp click. "We'll probably arrive in Washington a few minutes earlier, if everything goes smoothly."

"Music to my ears."

She leaned slightly to one side, pointing her left hip out, then held out a stack of magazines, TIME and Fortune at the top.

"Something to read?"

"I'm going to try and sleep," Collins said, glad she seemed to be enjoying his flirtations. "Do you have a blindfold?"

"Let me get one for you."

As she left, another flight attendant came by. She was petite with raven hair, olive skin and a sweet demeanor. Going around to each passenger, she was taking orders for drinks. When she spoke to the other passengers, her voice laced with a slight British accent was so soothing, Collins started making a list of things for which to call on her during the flight—pillows, drinks, blankets...massage? He laughed at himself inwardly.

*Old coot. Flirting in your mind is still flirting.*

At least that's what Linda would say.

He raised his hand and waved at her.

Lifting one finger, she mouthed, "Be right there."

That was the worst thing about being in the last row. Even though you were in business class, you still had to wait your turn. He never liked being anything but first. Anyway, it was still going to be a pleasant trip. Nothing like pretty flight attendants to take the sting out of long international flights.

When the brunette finally arrived, she took his drink order and started talking to him about his work, and then shared that she had aspired to become an actress, but couldn't make ends meet.

The blond flight attendant returned and quietly placed a blindfold with National Airlines embroidered in gold thread on his tray.

"Thanks, sweetheart."

He thought better of patting her on the rear. Times had changed over the years and he could get sued, or worse, someone might Instagram it and it would become bad press for his company.

Linda wouldn't think too highly of it either.

The blond walked away, but he was too engrossed in the brunette's story.

"So, in addition to working here," she said, looking a little sheepish, "I've decided to try running a business of my own."

At that, his eyes widened. "An entrepreneur, eh?"

She looked to the floor, her fair features blushing. "I've been working on it for some time now." She pulled out a tiny spray bottle.

"What is it, perfume?"

Gently grasping his wrist, she misted his open hand.

He took a whiff of it. "Smells like roses."

"It's actually a hand sanitizer. Most smell like medicine. I say, you can be germ-free and smell pretty. You think it'll sell?"

He took her hands into his. "I think you'll sell."

With a bashful grin, she turned away. "You're just flirting with me."

"I'm old enough to be your father, and yes, I am flirting. But the truth is, you've got a great concept, and every product needs a human face behind it. Yours is perfect."

"You really think so?"

"I know so."

"Well, then. Maybe I'll give everyone on this flight a sample of it and see if I can't get a few new customers to my website. Thank you so much." She took a step back and turned to the front of the plane.

"That's the spirit. Go get 'em." Collins leaned back into his seat and put his blindfold on. Drifting off into oblivion, he faintly heard the sound of her spray bottle, and a few people sounding a bit surprised.

The girl was a go getter, that was for sure.

She was going to achieve something big, if she kept it up.

As he fell asleep behind the blindfold, the hissing sound above him sounded like a malfunction of the air condition nozzle. But the lingering fragrance from the flight attendant's spray bottle lulled him into a deep sleep.

From which he would never awaken.

# FORTY FOUR

ANDREWS AIRFORCE BASE
JOINT BASE ANDREWS, MD
09:46

"I WANT YOU TO DO SOMETHING FOR ME," President Bradley said to Xandra as Wade's team urged them across the tarmac, after touching down at Andrews. "Take the rest of the day off and visit your father at Petersburg. Wade's already made the arrangements and cleared your visit."

"Ma'am?"

"Family first." The President pushed through a few Secret Service Agents flanking her as they scanned the area. "After what nearly happened over the Black Sea? We're lucky to be alive. Never take that for granted. Whenever possible, we should always make time to be with our loved ones."

"That's kind of you, Ma'am. But really, I can handle it. I've got a lot of work to do and things to discuss with Wade regarding—"

"There will be time for that." The Beast pulled up along with several other black cars in the motorcade. "Go see your father. Today."

It made sense—the increased scrutiny, the heightened security about POTUS who had almost been shot out of the sky. Amazing that amidst all that, Jennifer Bradley still had the capacity to address Xandra's personal concerns. "Ma'am, I can finish my work for the day, and then visit him on the weekend."

Bradley looked her straight in her eyes. "That's an order." With a smile, she put her hand on her shoulder. "We only get so many chances."

Grateful, Xandra assented. "Thank you. I'll be back bright and early tomorrow morning." The truth was, she was starting to wonder if she should even continue in this line of work. As photographer/operative—neither of which she was doing such a stellar job—was this really something she could give her life for?

"One more thing, Xandra."

"Yes?"

"I had planned to go directly to the ranch in Cabotstown with Mikey and his grandfather today and spend the rest of the week."

"He's been looking forward to that."

"But I don't think I can. Not yet. We've got to get to the bottom of the attack before we can consider any kind of response. Aamaal's people are investigating this too, but we need more information."

"I'll be ready for you first thing in the morning."

"I won't be able to make it out to the ranch for the next couple of days. So I want you to go there ahead of me. Tomorrow."

"Ma'am?"

Wade came over and stood ready with a team to escort Bradley into The Beast.

"Mikey made a special request that you visit, and that you bring Max. We've got fifteen acres out there. They'll have a blast together."

"Sounds great."

"Thanks," Bradley said and climbed into the limo.

The idea of relaxing in an open field with Max was appealing, but the threat of a terrorist attack weighed on her. She nearly got killed today. Wade may have sworn an oath to protect Bradley with his own life, but that wasn't what Xandra had signed on for.

For now, however, with some trepidation, she anticipated visiting Dad whom she hadn't seen for longer than she was willing to admit.

Today of all days, she would put aside her personal discomfort.

*Nothing like a near death experience to bring things into focus.*

# FORTY FIVE

OVAL OFFICE
THE WHITE HOUSE
WASHINGTON, DC
10:55 AM

SHE'D NEVER BEFORE BEEN THIS RUSHED after returning to the White House from an overseas trip. Ordinarily, Jennifer Bradley would make a stop by the residence, check in with Ben and Mikey, and spend a good few hours catching up.

Today was entirely different.

The Black Sea Incident wasn't just another assassination attempt; it had been a deliberate attack on the office of the President, which constituted an attack on the United States itself.

She marched through the halls, past aids and staff, into the Oval and straight to the *Resolute* desk. As she normally did under stressful circumstances, she instructed:

Do Not Disturb - five minutes.

But the order was not upheld.

The door opened and Mikey entered.

Right behind him, Agent Kelly Davis cautiously followed with an unspoken apology on her face.

Taking a deep breath, Bradley smiled, stood up, came around to receive her son into a tight embrace.

"Ma'am," Davis said, "Do you want me to bring him to—?"

She shook her head and walked over to her son, knelt down and wrapped her arms around her. "Thank you, Agent Davis. I've got this." Mikey returned the embrace while Bradley did her best not to break down in front of him. If she'd been killed today, leaving him orphaned…No, she must remain strong for him.

After holding him for a while, she felt him let go and begin to squirm. Finally, realizing that it would be best not to deprive her heir of breath, she relented.

He took a step back, and rather than smile, gave her a frown. "You're late."

"I'm sorry. Something came up on the way back."

"Were you in danger?"

Hating herself for lying, she straightened up and touched his face. "It was a rough flight, that's all. Everyone's fine."

At first, he didn't seem to buy it. But judging by his expression, he'd decided not to pursue the matter. A hopeful smile emerged.

"So, are you ready to go?"

"Go—?" As soon as she realized he was talking about going to the ranch, she cut her words short. With the attack on *Air Force One,* and the looming al Saif terror threat, it had been the last thing on her mind.

She reached out and took his hand.

But Mikey rolled his eyes, pulled away, and blew out an exasperated breath. "Oh, don't tell me…"

"The trip to the ranch is still on."

"You said as soon as you got back from Ta…Ti.. Ritakistan—"

"Tariqistan."

"You're bailing again!"

"Oh, sweetie." She stepped over and took his hand again.

"You gave your word! Dad always said, 'You're only worth as much as your word.'"

"I know, but something's come up. I need you to understand."

"I always have to understand. Why don't *you* understand?"

The meeting was coming up soon. The last thing she needed was to show up emotionally shaken, which would telegraph the very weakness her detractors cited as the reason a woman should not be president.

"I do understand how you feel," she said. "Here's the deal. You'll leave with Grandpa to the ranch today, and I'll—"

"So, you're not coming!" He was about to burst into tears but was holding it back as best he could.

"I am, just a little later after—"

"No you're not. You're breaking your promise. Again!"

"Hey…come on, kiddo. Give your mom a break, will you?"

He turned angry and hurt eyes on her.

"Daddy would never break his promises!"

"Now, Michael."

"How can you be a good president, if you can't keep your promises to your own son?"

"That's hardly fair." He was starting to hurt her, but she didn't want to show it.

"You never keep your promises to me!" He wiped his eyes, then looked up at her, his face so twisted with anger she almost couldn't recognize him.

"All right, Michael. We're going to have to talk about this later. Mommy's got an important meeting—"

"I'M IMPORTANT TOO!"

Before she could respond, David and Agent Davis entered.

David pointed to his watch indicating that she was overdue in the situation room and left. Davis was ready to escort Mikey to meet up with his grandfather and depart to the ranch.

She tried to give Mikey a hug, but he pulled away.

"I wish Daddy were here!"

"So do I, Sweetie."

"No, I mean I wish *he* wasn't the one to go. Daddy never broke his promises."

*Nothing cuts quite so deep as the wounds inflicted by those we love.* And this wound Mikey inflicted ran as deep as any she'd ever suffered.

"That was very hurtful, Michael Bradley!" She grabbed his arm, not realizing just how firmly.

"Ow!" He rubbed his arm and glared at her, his lower jaw quivering.

Surprised at herself, she let go. In a more controlled tone, though not entirely concealing her aggravation, she said, "You and I are going to have a talk later."

"I hate you!" Mikey stomped off and then ran out of the Oval.

"I've got him, Ma'am." Agent Davis followed after him.

The ensuing moment was interminable. Never in a million years could she imagine her sweet baby uttering those words. Nor could she believe she'd ever hurt him—physically or otherwise.

Ben's words came to her.

*Was it worth it?*

Absently, she shook her head, sighed.

She didn't realize she'd been staring out the window into the Rose Garden until a hummingbird hovering about the window—perhaps the same one she'd been seeing recently—flew off.

A gentle touch on her shoulder.

Just like Ben's in the worst of times.

But it was David Scott's.

Her secretary took a step back as she got to her feet.

"I'm sorry, Ma'am. But they're waiting for you in the Sit Room."

# FORTY SIX

FEDERAL CORRECTIONAL INSTITUTION PETERSBURG
(FCI PETERSBURG - MEDIUM)
Hopewell, Virginia
12:46 PM

THE POUNDING IN HER CHEST evoked teenage memories of those pimped out rides back in Brooklyn with their monstrous subwoofers shaking the walls as they passed by and pumped out reggae, hip-hop, or whatever else it was their drivers played.

Over the past few years, she'd spoken on the phone and written Dad. But she'd only visited on Holidays. This would be her first since moving back to the East Coast. Part of the jitters came from the judgment, or worse, disappointment he'd surely express because she'd waited this long to visit.

It didn't matter. He could judge her all he wanted. Having gotten that from him for her entire life, it'd be nothing new. What mattered was that he knew she still cared, despite how it may have seemed. All this time, she found it difficult to see him in prison. But the longer she'd put it off, the more ashamed she felt.

She'd given it a great deal of thought, now that she'd spent some time on the ground. After the attack on *Air Force One,* she now wondered if it was time to give up on this whole assistant operative idea.

Hadn't she given up enough already? Was it her job to save the President, the world?

A dull ache shot from the back of her neck. Wincing, Xandra shut her eyes and massaged her temples.

How could she throw herself into a situation like this again?

After Colson's death, life was supposed to return to normal—as normal as it could be, having your only surviving family member incarcerated while you lived like a fugitive from the public eye.

Apparently, four years had not been sufficient.

*It's your gift, Xandi,* she could hear Mom say. *Our gift. We were meant to use it to help all God's children.*

"What if I don't want to?" she murmured. "What if I just want a normal quiet life?"

"You wouldn't know normal if it bit you in the rear."

She lifted her head to find a face she barely recognized.

He stood there not bound with handcuffs but a gaunt pallor that made him look like a stranger. His gray hair was cropped to the scalp, scars lined his cheekbones, and his left arm hung in a sling.

"Dad?"

The visitation officer seemed remarkably relaxed as Xandra got up and put her arms around her father. "Oh my gosh, Dad!"

"Hello, Xandi."

It was as though she was standing on quicksand. How could he have changed so drastically? How could she have allowed so much time to pass?

"Oh Dad, I'm so sorry it's taken me this long." Burying her face into his shoulder, she said, "Will you forgive me?"

"Not even an issue." He kissed the top of her head. "And I did get your emails. Congratulations on the White House gig. Good for you."

She stepped back, gave him another once over. "Have you been in a fight?"

"What are you talking about?" He took a seat at the table, but every move caused him to wince in pain.

Slowly, she sat at the round table next to him.

"You've been hurt. Are you okay? Did someone try to—?"

"You should see the other guy." A strained smile and shake of the head. "The clown tried to steal my Jello."

"I've never seen you hit anyone in my life. How did you...?"

He leaned over and whispered.

"I got a heads up. From a friend. Preparation is everything, when it comes to winning a prison fight. Or a shanking."

He had always been a gentle soul, an intellectual. How could he possibly be sitting here with bruises and cuts, like some kind of common ruffian?

"This is insane. It's not like you were a violent criminal. You shouldn't be in here."

"Of course I should. I kept silent, helped him cover up the *Binh Son* Massacre—"

"Colson threatened to kill me and Mom, you had no choice!"

"Should have stood up to him."

"There was nothing you could have done."

He sat back, rubbed his eyes slowly. "You don't know what it's like—living a lie, keeping a secret like that—all that blood on our hands."

"*His* hands."

Dad blew out a terse breath, opened his eyes and looked straight into Xandra's.

"The sin of omission is still a sin. I've come to accept responsibility for my part."

"But Dad—"

"You didn't come here to argue with me, did you?"

Exhausted as she might be after a sparring session at Rowley, Xandra let a breath out slowly. In some ways, a conflict with Dad was more draining.

"I came to check up on you."

"Don't worry," he said, looking over his injuries. "I can take care of myself."

"You need protection. I'm going to see about getting you transferred."

He let out one of those laughs he always did when she was a child talking about how she'd one day fly Wonder Woman's invisible jet, and other such foolishness,

"Nothing anyone can do. But don't worry, the SHU's nice and quiet."

"SHU?"

"Special Housing Unit. They've got me under protective custody, separated from the general population."

"Is it really safe, though?"

A puzzled look came over him.

"What's going on, Xandi? Something you want to tell me?"

*Other than* Air Force One *nearly getting blown out of the sky?* "Nothing in particular, I just... I wanted to see you. It's been long overdue."

He reached out, put his large hands over hers, warming them. His palms had grown leathery.

"You're trying hard to not tell me something," he said with a reassuring look, "I know you."

"Thought *I* was the precog."

"Photographic memory." He pointed at his head and winked. It put her at ease, but only slightly. "You've always had that look whenever you were trying to hide something."

"I don't have a look."

"Sure you do." He aped her, grossly exaggerating.

That elicited a laugh, first from Xandra, and then Dad joined in.

"Seriously, what's the matter?" His smile remained, though Xandra felt hers melting away.

"C'mon, Dad. A girl has to keep some secrets." *Sometimes to keep their loved ones safe, and far removed from trouble. You of all people should understand that.*

"Fine. Then let me tell you something, based on—oh, let's call it a hunch."

"What?"

"I can see it in your eyes, Xandi. You need to do something, but you're worried that doing the right thing might bring harm to someone you love." He pointed to himself. "I'm assuming that's me."

"Wait, Dad—" She never realized it until he said it, but it was true. She wasn't so much afraid of dying, as breaking her father's heart as he fought to survive in federal prison. Losing both his wife and his daughter might very well sap his will to go on.

"I can tell because I lived it for forty years," he said. "No one knows better what that feels like, what it looks like." He touched her face tenderly, fingers caressing her cheek the way he did during those thunderstorms that kept her awake in terror back in New York when she was in grade school. "Don't repeat my mistakes, Sweetie. You have to do what's right, no matter the cost. If Mom were still alive today, you know what she'd say: "Do what's right, do your best—"

They said it together: "And then trust God with the rest."

For a moment, they just sat there remembering her. It was as if she'd come for a visit. Like the sweet fragrance of her Honeysuckle Rose candles, a bittersweet nostalgia infused their presence. For just a moment, Xandra forgot the White House, the assassination attempts, the ominous visions.

None of it mattered.

But the moment didn't last.

There was still an unseen danger out there which seemed only she could help uncover.

"If I dig deeper, using my gifts?" Xandra said, "There's no telling what might happen. I'm just not sure I should be doing this."

"Well, you're working for the White House. Whatever you're investigating, it's got to be important." To her surprise, Dad sounded intrigued.

She looked up at him. "I think it is."

"Lives at stake?"

"Hard to tell just how many."

Giving her hands a squeeze, he smiled poignantly.

"I need to tell you something, Xandi. Something I should have told you a while ago. Better late than never, right?"

"What is it?"

"Last year, I went to the infirmary because of headaches and numbness. And after a CT scan, they found a large cranial aneurysm."

Her thoughts resounded in a hollowed out chasm formed by shock. A sudden evacuation of sensation and emotion ensued. "Can anything be done?"

"Because of its location, no. Any surgery would be much too risky and could kill me, or cause permanent brain damage."

*Don't start crying, not here with the guards and other inmates around.* But it was too much. Even thought it had been four years since, she still hadn't completely come to terms with Mom's death."

"How long?"

"I could live the rest of my natural life without a problem," he said, "As long as it doesn't rupture. On the other hand, no one can tell when or if it will."

That was almost worse. At least with Mom, they had an idea of when the end might come. This was like living in a constant state of anxiety.

"What I'm saying," he said, being strong for her because he knew her so well, "is that I'm living on borrowed time."

"Don't say that, Dad. We're going to pull through this."

"I didn't tell you this to make you all sentimental." His demeanor became grave. "Now, you've got a chance to make a difference, with your abilities. I know there are voices trying to talk you out of it, to keep your head down and mouth shut. But take if from a man who did just that. If you let them silence you, you may regret it your whole life."

"It's not me I'm worried about."

"I refuse to be your stumbling block."

"Don't you see, Dad? I need to be here for you. If anything

happens—your aneurysm, dangerous inmates...”

“Nothing, and no one, can take my life,” he said, his eyes intense. “I’ve already put it in God’s hands.”

She was at a loss. Unlike Mom, though Dad had always respected her faith, he had always been an atheist.

“Wait. Did you just say—?”

“Remember how you told me that the truth would set me free?”

“Not my words. I was quoting.”

“When I learned of my aneurysm, it changed everything. I saw just how finite my very existence is. I’m finally understanding what Mom had always tried to show me—what did she call it? An eternal perspective.”

“Daddy,” Xandra’s voice broke. “You’re *not* going to die, okay?”

“We’re all going to die. Could be years from now, could be tomorrow. All I know is that I’ve given my life to God, and no one can take it from me without His authorization. And, one day, I’ll be completely free.”

She wanted to be strong right now, show him he could be proud of her. But it was no use. She drew a shaky breath. “I’m working on getting you a pardon from the President—I won’t give up.”

The juxtaposition of his placid countenance against what should be a morbid conversation was strange and yet, inevitable. “Listen. However it happens, whenever it happens, I’m ready. Now, you have to do what you’re meant to do, understand?”

She nodded, unable to keep from breaking down and falling onto his shoulder.

His arms engulfed her in warmth—a security she hadn’t felt for a long time. “Shhh....Don’t be afraid, Babygirl. If I can embolden you to do what you’re called to do with your gift, then maybe—just maybe, it’ll make up a little for how I failed you and Mom.”

“You don’t need to do anything, Daddy.”

After a long pause in his arms, Xandra found her strength

again. She sat back, wiped her eyes again. "Stupid ability...it's always getting me in trouble."

"Glass half full," he said, remarkably upbeat for a man who was basically walking around with a gun perpetually pointed at his head.

"But if anything happens to you, while I'm out there..."

"Xandi, you have to follow your calling."

"I thought I was supposed to follow my heart."

"The heart is deceitful, volatile. Hitler followed his heart, right? You need to do what's right, what you're destined for, regardless of how you feel."

The visitation officer came over.

"Sorry, Pete. Time's up."

Dad sighed, gave Xandra an encouraging smile, then stood. "I know you'll do the right thing."

"I'm not so sure." She got up as well.

"You will." He opened his good arm and drew her close to his heart. "I have faith in you."

"I love you, Daddy."

"Love you too." He kissed the top of her head, released her, and turned to the exit where the visitation officer awaited. "Don't be a stranger, kiddo."

He left...

...and didn't look back.

# FORTY SEVEN

## PRESENT DAY

### UNDISCLOSED LOCATION
### 10:26 PM

IT HAD TAKEN A TOLL, but there was no other way. Ishmael knew this day would come, he just didn't know exactly how, and what it would cost him. Nevertheless, he'd come this far, there was no way he would allow anyone or anything to jeopardize the primary reason for his existence.

The moon hung in the sky like a panther, patiently awaiting its prey. It reminded him of an oil painting he'd once seen in the Louvre in Paris. He'd since forgotten the work and its artist, but the same portentous sensation ran though his blood.

Puffs of vapor rose from his fists as he blew hot breath into them.

The only leverage he had at this point was the formula for which they'd waited since the start. And tonight's deciding action might very well render their whole arrangement void. But it didn't matter. No fear for his life because it was worthless unless he could accomplish his goal.

A black truck pulled up, crunching pebbles on the dirt path about a hundred meters away. He'd given clear instructions to his contact, with whom he'd struck a good rapport since his return. Peregrine had always treated him with respect and provided whatever he needed and promptly. Ishmael sincerely hoped he wouldn't have to end the night by putting an end to their professional relationship.

In the distance, Peregrine flashed his high beams twice—the signal that he had arrived alone and without incident.

With his remote control, Ishmael caused the lights in the shed to blink three times.

From that point, Peregrine followed the GPS coordinates to the woods where he would find the shed and wait there for him.

It wouldn't hurt to have him wait an extra five minutes and sweat a bit.

Six minutes later, Ishmael entered the pitch black shed, sealed the blinds, and switched on the lamp.

Seated on a crate, Peregrine squinted.

He was wearing a pair of black jeans, a brown leather jacket and a ridiculous hat that made him look more like an American redneck than a spy.

"Sorry to have kept you waiting," Ishmael said, and extended his hand to shake Peregrine's.

"You said you had some concerns," he said, speaking in a perfect Kishwari dialect. "As always, I am here to help."

Ishmael pulled up another crate and sat before him. With a smile, he said, "I don't know how much you're able to do, but I appreciate your taking the trouble to come all the way out here."

"If not for the coordinates, I doubt anyone could find it."

Which is why this place was miles from his actual base. As much as he admired Peregrine, he worked for the very organization that operated in the shadows. He couldn't be trusted any more than anyone else in this wretched world. "That is by design. And you're the only person on the planet who knows of this place's existence, right?"

"Of course."

*Liar.*

"So, what did you want to talk about?"

Ishmael leaned forward. "The attack on *Air Force One*, yesterday."

"What attack?"

"Don't insult me," Ishmael said, laughing outwardly, but ready to slit Peregrine's throat. "We've known each other too long."

He raised his hands and laughed along. "Yes, yes. You are right. But first, I wanted to talk to you about our test case."

"You are here to address *my* concerns."

"Of course. But give me something to bring back to my people, all right? Now, we've tests B89 Delta on live subjects in a real world setting, but it didn't result in the expected scope. Are you sure that was the correct strain?"

Ordinarily, Ishmael wouldn't have given Peregrine's diversionary tactics a second thought. But because he had a vested interest, he had to ask. "Where did you test it?"

"I cannot tell you."

"Then I can't help you."

"I can say this much: It was inadvertently tested on common street animals, rats, birds, dogs..."

"I guess you'll need my help more than you thought." In fact, Ishmael had given them a limited version of the virus for more than just job security. As long as he held the genetic marker codes for the full blown virus, its cure and vaccine, he would be in control. They would need him alive and well.

"Let me be perfectly honest with you, old friend. My superiors are losing patience. They don't particularly like this game you are playing."

"That's just the price they'll have to pay."

"Not if they decide to look elsewhere," Peregrine said with an aspect of concern. He looked straight into Ishmael's eyes. "Come now. Let us work this out."

For a moment, Ishmael almost fell for the bluff. He genuinely panicked for a couple of seconds at the thought of his becoming irrelevant. Not so much that he would die suddenly at the hand of one of their assassins—maybe even Peregrine himself—but because he would fail to complete his mission.

"Send me their data and I will look at it," Ishmael said. "But first, we must talk about what happened with *Air Force One* yesterday."

"How do you know about that?"

"I too have my sources." Ishmael's smile grew more plastic by the second. He didn't care, though. It was good for Peregrine to know that he was upset. "So, your people were behind it, weren't they?"

Peregrine thought about it for a few seconds before relenting. "Yes. But for some reason, we failed. Those accursed pilots probably lost their nerve. Anyway, we've got it contained, cover story in place—"

"President Bradley is off-limits! We had an agreement."

"I told them you wouldn't like that move—"

"It was *the* absolute non-negotiable. If your people ever want the codes, they had better not try anything like that against the President again, as long as I'm alive."

"Be careful what you demand, old friend."

"If they take me out, they lose the codes forever." But what if Peregrine wasn't bluffing? What if they were prepared to look elsewhere? They were now eyeball to eyeball. And Ishmael could not blink.

Peregrine nodded. "I hear you, I hear you." He rubbed a spot on his chest and said, "But I'm wondering, why does it matter to you so much? You hate President Bradley. Don't you want to see her dead?"

"But it must be by my hand! You understood this from the very beginning."

This was it.

Decision point.

How Peregrine responded next would determine how everything would go from this point on.

"Of course I understand," he said. "But the organization doesn't find this particular parameter—your personal vendetta—efficient, in the context of its primary objectives."

Ishmael slammed the crate with his hand and stood. "Efficient?"

"I am just the messenger."

"I thought you were my 'old friend.'"

Peregrine stood, and let his hands fall to his side. "Come now, Ishmael..."

Without warning, Peregrine reached behind his back and pulled a gun out. "Sorry, old friend."

But Ishmael had prepared for this.

He kicked the lamp over, crushed its light bulb under his shoe, and rolled to the ground.

"Come now, Ishmael. Let us discuss your terms."

In one swift move, he completed the roll, pulled out a knife, got to his feet behind Peregrine, pressing the blade right against his throat, even as he struggled to point the gun back at Ishmael.

"You're wearing a wire, *old friend*," Ishmael snarled, pulling it from Peregrine's shirt. "So let this message be heard loud and clear, you filthy sons of dogs: This arrangement is finished!"

"Don't be foolish, Ishmael. Please—!"

A blinding muzzle flash shattered the darkness of the shed.

But not before Ishmael sliced Peregrine's throat and carotid artery open.

# FORTY EIGHT

RITTENHOUSE RESIDENCE
GEORGETOWN
WASHINGTON, DC
9:17 PM

"I DIDN'T THINK YOU HAD IT IN YOU to take advantage of a woman in her time of need," Xandra said, seated across from Jake at the candlelit table in the brownstone in which he lived. "Brilliant strategy making dinner, though. You knew I couldn't refuse."

"Actually, it was you who took advantage of me." Jake glanced down to Max lying on the ground at her feet. "You knew I couldn't say no to watching a dog like The General, and now you're going to just take him away."

She pushed her plate away, and sat back in her chair enjoying the warmth of the fireplace beside them. "I'm sorry, but like me, Max has duties to the President."

"Speaking of which," he put his glass down and narrowed his eyes at her. "I don't want to pry, but I'm wondering why you haven't said anything about your trip."

She couldn't say a word about the Black Sea incident. She'd been asked to keep it confidential, and the facts were still uncertain. But with all the threats and cryptic visions she'd be experiencing, Xandra felt the need to confide in the one person who understood the pressure she was facing.

And she could really use his advice. Should she go forward with her investigative work, or call it quits, for safety's sake? "I can't get into specifics..."

He laughed. "In other words, you could tell me, but then you'd have to kill me."

"Something like that."

Max groaned, stretched and rolled lazily onto his other side.

"The General doesn't appreciate your humor," Jake said.

"It's yours he doesn't care for."

"I don't know." He reached down and rubbed him behind the ears. "Max and I? We're tight."

"Jake, I've got a dilemma."

The smile remained on his face, but his eyes became thoughtful.

"Yes, I know."

"You do? Have you been having visions about me?"

"Nothing that distinct," Jake said, "but I've sensed that you're going to be facing a greater challenge than ever before."

"Lucky guess. Anyone could have—" She realized how cynical she sounded and regretted it. "I'm sorry, that was unkind."

He waved it off. "I'll admit, my visions have never been as clear or frequent as yours."

"Or as potentially dangerous."

"True." He rubbed the cleft of his chin with this thumb. "I'll tell you what's come to me while you were away. Then you can let me know if it makes any sense, okay?"

She nodded, chagrined at her rudeness. He hadn't deserved that. Thankfully, unlike many men she'd met, Jake wasn't easily offended.

Looking over to the hearth, he said, "I saw you standing on a high wire above the opening of a volcano about to erupt. You were trying to keep your balance but struggling. In your right hand, you were holding something fragile—maybe glass or something, I couldn't tell because it was clenched in your fist close to your heart. But the way you regarded it—with such tenderness and concern—led me to believe it was something precious to you.

"In your left hand, as you struggled to maintain your balance, you held what looked like a hand grenade. You couldn't let either of them go because doing so would cause you to lose that balance and fall.

"The line on which you walked was starting to fray and unravel at two points—behind and in front of you. I tried to tell you that you needed to let both objects go and leap off of the wire, because if you did, you would be able to fly away from the danger."

"Fly?"

"In this vision, for some reason, I knew you could."

"But how—?"

"It's metaphorical. Most of my visions are."

"So what did I do?"

"Didn't see that far, sorry."

She sat there for a while, the hairs on the back of her neck prickling. He didn't know what his vision had meant, but it was clear to her.

"Jake, I've got to make some choices and commitments, and there's no guarantee of success or even safety for any of them."

"Sounds like your M.O."

"I don't seek these situations, they just stalk me and force themselves on me."

"If my vision holds any truth, Xandra, then you're going to have to step out in faith, whatever you do...or don't do."

She didn't want to admit it, but his vision corroborated Dad's words. For all her evasive maneuvers, her help was clearly needed in the crisis dawning over the horizon.

"I just don't know if I can go through with it." She turned away. "Especially when I can't tell how it will all work out in the end."

Jake touched her hand. It was like the touch of a friend or a brother. "May I share a word that's given me strength in uncertain times?"

She nodded. Opened her mouth to say, "Yes," but only a silent version of the word came forth.

"It's from the quote from Saint Paul: '*All things work together for good, for those who are called according to His purpose.*'"

"That was one of Mom's favorites. She used to say it to me before I went on stage for my recitals in Juilliard. Despite hours of practice and rehearsal, I never felt adequately prepared."

"For truly great things, Xandra, no one ever does."

She let it sink in, then turned her palm over to squeeze his hand. "I know what I have to do."

"Really?"

"Mmm-hmm." She stood up.

Right away, Max got up as well.

"Leaving already?" He stood and regarded the tall grandfather clock across the room. "It's not even ten."

"I'm sorry. Long day tomorrow and I'm fighting jetlag."

"Of course. Let me walk you home, though. It's dark outside."

"I'll be fine," she said. "It's not like I'm going to run into that Midnight Stalker."

"That's not funny. They still haven't caught him."

She had been joking, but the fact that Jake didn't share her amusement gave her pause. Still, the last thing she wanted was to appear like a frail damsel in distress. "Besides, I've got The General with me. He was a Navy Seal, you know." She patted the back of Max's neck. "We're a formidable team, we are."

"You sure?"

"Like Batman and Robin." She picked up her bag, and coat which Jake helped her put on. Her mind raced with thoughts and had been doing so from the moment she decided to embrace what she had been avoiding.

As they reached the door, Xandra reached up and touched his face.

"Thank you so much." Without thinking, she shut her eyes and stretched up to kiss his cheek. But it ended up being the corner of his lips. Ears burning, she opened her eyes and smiled timidly.

Jake blinked in surprise and absently handed Max's lead to her. "Oh, uh...so...The pleasure's all mine."

She took the lead, her back tingling, but only a bit embarrassed. "I've been living in fear way too long." The General came right to her side, but stared up at them both. "I've got to take this ability I've been entrusted with, and use it—whatever the risk."

"Sounds good."

She smiled, wrapped an arm around him and pulled him close for a hug. "Okay."

As she left, a galvanized sense of purpose mixed with irrational courage came over her. Walking down the sidewalk, she looked down to meet The General's dignified gaze, and drew a deep breath.

"We can do this, Max. We're *going* to do this."

Still tingling from that accidental kiss, Xandra was completely oblivious to the man watching her from within the shadows.

# FORTY NINE

GEORGETOWN
WASHINGTON, DC
9:49 PM

SHE SHOULD HAVE FELT NERVOUS, walking after dark where the streets were quiet and poorly lit, but she didn't. Even with the Midnight Stalker still at large, her mind floated between the weighty matters that had burdened her for so long. Jake's musky scent and the tingle she still felt from kissing him still lingered in her mind. Safety hadn't crossed her mind as an issue.

Anyway, she had Max with her. *No one's going to mess with us.*

It would have been nice if she'd had a gun on her as well, but that was another issue altogether with which to come to terms. Wade had offered to get her a CCP/CCL (Concealed Carry Permit/License), but she'd balked. It might make a good deterrent, but she'd already learned that if she was going to point it, she'd better be ready to fire a lethal shot. And that wasn't something she felt ready to do yet.

Walking at her typically brisk pace, she caught a glimpse of a figure across the street beneath the shadow of the trees. As she passed him, she noticed that he'd turned around and started walking in the same direction.

"Don't be paranoid," she murmured.

She quickened her stride, just in case.

The stranger across the street did the same, maintaining his distance behind her.

Relax, it's nothing.

Wouldn't she have gotten a vision about this?

They're usually about someone else.

Great.

If only there was a car or two driving down the sleepy streets.

She decided to make a right turn, even though it would add a few extra blocks to her walk home.

But when she crossed the street, the shady stranger did likewise.

Max's lead felt cold and slick in her hand.

The man was now on her side of the street, about a dozen paces behind.

Why hadn't she learned Max's command for "Attack?"

Don't show fear...

"Max?" she whispered, "Now would be a great time to snarl."

The Belgian Malinois only looked up and back at the pavement as she broke into a power walk.

The stranger's footfalls matched hers.

In her haste, she'd lost her direction.

Without thinking, she made another turn.

This time into an even darker street—an alley.

If things weren't bad enough, another figure turned the corner following both her and her pursuer.

She found herself at a dead end, of all places. The alley was surrounded by the windowless brick walls of buildings under reconstruction. No one to hear her scream.

No choice but to turn back, and run.

She turned around, and let out a gasp.

The silhouetted outline of the man who'd followed her was standing right before her.

For all her training at Rowley, she hadn't been prepared for this.

She took a step back. "Back off, or I swear, my dog'll rip your throat out!"

"Cute." He lifted the long blade of a knife up so that it glinted in the scant light bleeding into the gloom of the alleyway. This creep might or might not be the Midnight Stalker, or some other serial killer, but there was something decidedly wrong about him.

Back pressed against the cold brick wall, Xandra shouted, "I said, back off!"

With alarming speed and force, he drew the knife and lunged at her.

# FIFTY

GEORGETOWN
WASHINGTON, DC
9:55 PM

"MAX! KILL!"

Max barked so loudly it reverberated against the walls.

But in all the excitement, her body tensing up and preparing to employ the hand to hand combat skills she'd acquired at Rowley, Xandra neglected to release the lead—didn't realize she was holding Max back.

The creep lurched forward, launched his knife at her.

Xandra ducked.

Light flashed behind him.

She barely heard that distinct *crack!*, the sound of which she'd never forgotten since Kyle's murder.

The attacker's back arched.

His body fell with a thud.

The knife clattered to the pavement.

In the time it took for her to process it all, the acrid smell of a discharged round wafted by, reminiscent of the firing range at Rowley.

Max continued to bark.

Blinking in disbelief, she stood a few feet from where the attacker fell.

"Quiet, Max," she said, her own voice sounding hollow.

He stopped, as another figure—this one significantly taller than the first—approached, sliding what had to be a gun with a suppressor into his jacket.

"Come with me," the man in a black jacket stepped over, knelt, turned the attacker's body over, and touched its neck. "Unless you want the police to waste your time with incessant questions."

Xandra could barely catch her breath, but managed to speak nevertheless.

"What did you do?"

The man regarded her through the dark lenses of a pair of Gargoyles. "It is traditional to thank the person who just saved you from an unpleasant death." He looked around furtively, all the while exuding cool poise, then straightened up. "Let's go."

Max growled.

Xandra took a sideways step from him. "You expect me to just trust you?"

The man clicked his tongue. "I could use my gun to persuade you, but that would defeat the whole purpose."

"Of what?"

In the distance, a police car's siren wailed, growing louder as it approached.

"Fine," he said with a shake of the head, though she still couldn't see his expression behind the dark glasses. "Figure it out yourself."

With that, he walked off.

Which was probably for the best.

"Hey!" She called out.

Back already turned, he waved dismissively, rounded the corner, and was out of sight.

Despite the resistance in Max's leash, Xandra stepped around her attacker's corpse and out of the alley to follow him. "Hello?"

His departure was as spectral as his arrival.

Xandra exhaled slowly and scanned the area.

Behind her, the night obscured all but the dead man's feet.

The police siren faded.

Taking a moment to recalibrate, she figured that she had to turn right in order to get home.

So she did.

A cold hand covered her mouth before she could scream.

It was the man in the black jacket and dark sunglasses again.

Her eyes bulged in surprise.

"Promise you won't scream."

If he'd meant to harm her, he would have by now. She nodded. "Mmm-hmm."

"All right." He released her and adjusted the dark glasses which had been knocked ajar from her sudden reaction. The streaks of silver in his cropped hair belied what looked to be a very fit stature beneath his jacket—probably retired military. "I'm here to help you."

"You don't even know me."

He arched an eyebrow, released her, then began walking down the sidewalk as though taking a leisurely stroll. "I know you better than you might imagine, Xandra. I know all about you."

"Of course you do," she said, rolling her eyes, not even realizing that she was following him. Donning dark sunglasses at night like the Terminator, he *would* at least know her name, wouldn't he? She was just waiting for the part where he'd say, 'I'll be bahck.'

"I have something you need," he said.

"Oh really?" Halfway down the block, the interior lights of a midnight blue Mercedes lit up. When they reached it, he opened both the front and rear passenger doors. She let out a tentative laugh. "And just what do you think I need?"

"Answers."

Despite her shock at nearly getting stabbed, and then watching that same attacker killed, Xandra let Max climb into the back seat and she herself took the front.

SHE STOOD WITH THE MAN in the black jacket behind two of the thirty-six Doric columns of the Lincoln Memorial below the enormous image of the president it enshrined. They paced the cavernous space which gazed philosophically out into the night over the reflecting pool from which shone the Washington Monument's reflection.

Xandra had come here on a school trip when she was a student at Stuyvesant High School, but it had been crowded, hot and humid then, not religiously sepulchral. Tonight, the place was devoid of life save for herself and the enigmatic man in black.

He'd been silent for the entire drive, but since he had promised, she decided that her compliance earned her the right to ask. "Who are you?" she said, staring out over the water with Max sitting dutifully at her side.

The man came right up to her, and removed the Gargoyles.

Xandra's entire body went cold.

His left eye was green, and his right, blue.

*The man in the vision.*

In that very moment, against all reason, she felt that same sense of comfort little Xandi did in her vision, when the man with the different colored eyes held her hand. For just that moment, it curbed her objections.

"Consider me a friend," he said, slipping the shades into the breast pocket of his jacket.

She wasn't frightened but relieved rather, to finally meet him. It confirmed that her clairvoyance was intact and gaining in strength. "What's your name?"

"I can't tell you that," he said flatly.

"So how should I address you? She held up a halting hand. "Wait, don't tell me. You've got an enigmatic code name, like The Jackal or Deep Throat."

With a subtle grin, he shook his head. "Why don't you just invent one for me? And please, nothing so cliché."

He was considerably more patient than she would have been, had the roles been reversed. Xandra regarded Max, whose eyes shone with concern. "Oh, I don't know. How about Tempest?"

"Dark, brooding."

"Shakespeare."

"I was just about to say."

Beguiling as he was handsome—for a guy his age, anyway—this banter was not what she'd come for. Someone had just tried to attack her, and Tempest just happens to show up to intervene. It couldn't have been a coincidence that he just happened to be in the vicinity. He'd been watching her for God only knows how long. And those eyes, those mismatched eyes. They did seem to do as they'd done in that vision: beckon her to trust him.

"What do you want from me?" she asked.

"Not much." He came to her side, hands clasped behind his back and stared out in the same direction as did she. "Just that you stay alive and continue to do what you're supposed to."

"What's your idea of what I'm *supposed* to do?"

"Utilize the tools with which you've been entrusted."

She let out an exasperated breath. Of course he would know about her gift of second sight. Who didn't by now?

"Listen, Tempest—"

"I like that. Tempest." He turned to Max, who seemed to take to him well. "Rather suits me, wouldn't you agree, General?"

*Yet another thing he knew.*

"We'll be here till the dawn's early light, unless you start speaking plainly," Xandra said. "You said you had answers."

"Only the ones you need." He pulled out a cigarette, cupped it in his hand and lit it. "Ask the right questions, and you'll get the right answers."

Waving away the toxic fumes, she side-stepped them, covering her nose and mouth.

"Do you mind?"

"Not at all. Care for one?"

"You can commit slow suicide on your own time."

A curt smile, another sickening cloud. He checked his watch. "Five minutes and I'm out of here."

"All right, all right." How was she supposed to know what the right questions were, anyway? "Let's see…Okay. Was that creep in the alley The Midnight Stalker?"

"Maybe he was, maybe he wasn't. I don't really care."

"You killed him."

"He was getting in the way." He plucked the cigarette, snuffed it with his bare fingertips, and slipped it into his jacket pocket.

Rummaging through everything in her mind that might pertain, she stopped upon one thought. "Do you know anything about the recent terrorist threat?"

"I might."

"Not helpful."

"Ask me another question."

"Someone I know might have some information about the assassination attempt on President Bradley, and its possible connection to the FTM and al Saif. But he won't talk. Who's he so scared of, and why?"

Tempest grinned. "You always were sharp."

"What?"

"The people you're talking about, the ones he fears so much? They've had a recent change of heart and have decided they want you alive."

She had to exert a great deal of restraint not to show her dismay. Until now, she never saw herself as a target. It had always been the high profile people, like President Bradley that needed round the clock protection. "Wait, they want me alive? When did they want me de—?"

"They want me to recruit you…"

"For what?"

"…but they *really* want you off the case."

"What case?" She was testing him now.

He gave her an incredulous look. "Suffice it to say, they want you to stay away from Ian Mortimer."

She could swear her heart skipped a beat or two.

Tempest really *did* know all about her.

Her legs started to feel weak, the way they did after her first ever 5 mile run at Rowley. Xandra settled herself on one of the monument's numerous steps. This dizziness wasn't from a vision, it was because of the alarming realization that this world with which she'd become embroiled was unfathomably more complex than she could have imagined.

"I don't have time for games," she said, holding her head as if doing so would stave the spinning. "Just tell me what I need to know."

He sat down beside her.

Pulled out another cigarette.

"No, don't." Xandra said, as firm as she could in her weakened state.

A low-pitched growl emitted from Max's throat.

Tempest put it away and shrugged.

"I don't usually allow this kind of information to transfer without receiving a large payment in return, or killing the person to whom I've given it…"

"You came to me, remember?"

"…but because you're my niece, I'm going to tell you."

# FIFTY ONE

LINCOLN MEMORIAL
WASHINGTON, DC
10:13 PM

NIECE?

That other players were involved was confusing enough, but if this man whom she'd given the moniker "Tempest" was really her uncle? That was sufficient cause for her to take a flying leap into the reflecting pool and splash wildly until someone came to lock her away in a padded room.

Xandra bit her lip until she felt her repose returning. This was the man in her vision, the man with different colored eyes. He must be trustworthy, right?

"You'll have to walk me through this."

"Indeed." He stood up, lit up, and took a few courteous steps aside, taking care to exhale away from her. "Forgive me, I'm going to need this."

"Knock yourself out." She covered her mouth and nose.

Max sneezed in protest as the fumes wafted by.

"I'm your father's half-brother," Tempest said. "Of course, he's never mentioned me because I had vanished and was considered dead while he was still young. He's never seen me—or rather, has never been aware of me.

"Anyway," he said, taking another puff, "What you need to know is this: I work for an organization of extraordinary power and influence that has existed for nearly two millennia."

"Very Dan Brown."

"Oh, are you a fan?"

"I'm more partial to Dean Koontz, actually."

A patient smile. "Xandra, it will be far more expeditious if you would refrain from these digressions."

Feigning apathy, she shrugged. However, if there was even a remote chance he might be speaking truthfully, she had to hear him out.

"This clandestine body has through the ages operated in various incarnations. However, since World War One it's referred to itself as Cerberus."

Doubtful, she turned and looked at him with an arched eyebrow.

"Are you serious? The Three-Headed dog from Hades?"

He puffed a cloud and glared at her.

"Do I look like the sort who'd joke about something like this?"

Good point.

"Fine, go on."

"If you were to attribute the rise and fall of kings, nations, and empires to natural selection, you couldn't be more mistaken. It has, and always will be the result of the Cerberus's manipulation. Global balances, economic tides, military, and political power—they've always been under our control."

"What country does Cerb—"?

"No, no, no." He waved her idea off as though it were a gnat hovering around his face. "You're going about it all wrong. Think of the world as a chess board, the nations as its pieces. Until now, there has always only been one player—that player being Cerberus."

"Until now?"

"With virtually unlimited power and resources at its disposal, the council has always strove for unity. So you can imagine the ensuing chaos if a schism of any magnitude were to occur."

"Until now?"

"Through the ages dissension has always loomed, but it wasn't until recently that this schism actually began."

Whether or not she believed him, she had to know more. "How recent?"

"It's been a credible threat since Richard Colson ran for office. The majority favored him because of his decisiveness and ability to wield the power Cerberus granted him. But the faction that objected was quickly silenced."

The very mention of Colson's name made her uneasy. "Are you saying that he wasn't—? That he was..."

"I can see how it would be difficult for an ordinary person to fathom, but yes. Colson was merely a pawn—Cerberus's pawn."

The more he spoke, the broader the scope of it all grew.

"How did this split happen?"

"It had already begun by then, though in secret—as secret as one can theoretically be within Cerberus. There's hardly anything that can be truly hidden from them, so it's going to be a quiet revolution. But by the time they discover Aegis, our merry band of rebels, it will be too late. As for the actual split, upon which Cerberus' internal intel has only theorized, it occurred sometime the end of last year. "

A cold gust blew through the columns and seemed to pass straight through her bones.

"Dare I ask what the split was over?"

"I'm certain you can guess."

"Don't make me."

"The first female American president."

She turned to him slowly, thoughts spinning out of control. "Wait, you mean Cerberus was behind the assassination attempt in January?"

"Yes, but—"

"Then why in the world am I even here talking with you?" She considered running away, but wouldn't that just get her a bullet in the back of her head?

"Calm down, Xandra. If *Aegis* had wanted her dead, she would be. Though we're a secret minority, we're all key players in Cerberus. And we in Aegis still believe Bradley has what it takes to set and maintain the course for the correct global balance through the next decade."

"The sniper, the pipe bombs...people died."

"At the risk of exposure, we did everything possible to prevent the President's assassination. In doing so, we saw an opportunity and seized it."

Trying to make the connections, she only got more flustered. "I don't understand."

"We found a way to stop Bradley's assassination, and at the same time deal with another issue, all the while not alerting Cerberus to Aegis's existence."

"What other issue?"

"Aegis's target was Maya Flores."

It took a second for her to internalize that.

Her brow tightened. "Why would anyone want to kill the President's photographer?"

"Flores had been working for Cerberus, but she proved a threat both to Bradley and the Rebellion. She was about to expose Aegis operatives. Quite simply, she had to go."

"But how did you manage it?"

Tempest leaned against a column and stared out over the reflecting pool. With another pull from his cigarette, he blew out a noxious cloud. "Cerberus had contracted the shooter and bomber to take out the President. I secretly altered the gunman's orders. As planned and expected, the Secret Service Counter Assault team killed him on the spot. As far as Cerberus knows, their shooter was incompetent."

"What about the bomb? Couldn't you have stopped that?"

He frowned and shook his head slowly. "Not without raising undue suspicion."

"Still...you killed Maya Flores, allowed the bomber to strike."

"Don't be so sentimental. They were all necessary sacrifices. We had to get her out of the White House, and you in. That's all there was to it."

Shaking her head slowly, she felt as though her heart might leap out of her throat. This was the man she was supposed to trust? "I don't care how you try to rationalize it, you're murderers."

"Can't blame you for not understanding," he sighed. "It takes a much higher level view of things—"

"Spare me the sanctimonious crap! A thug is a thug, no matter how you spin it."

"I never said we were—oh, what would you call it?—the good guys. We do what it takes to reach our objectives. And right now, whether or not you approve of our methods, our agenda is for the most part aligned with yours."

"I don't have an agenda."

"Oh, you do, trust me." He put out his cigarette and slipped its remains into his pocket again. "Everyone does."

"My only agenda is to get as far away from you as I can. Preferably alive."

"My dear Xandra. We paved the way for you, placed you in the White House."

Her grasp of reality was quickly unraveling. It was too much to process all at once.

"What about Wade Masterson? Is he with Cerberus or Aegis?"

"Neither. But we have operatives—doubles like me—who act as assets to Masterson's investigative team. When we learned that he was interested in getting you to work with him, I simply put you on his radar."

"Why?"

"Because I know of your abilities, your character."

"You don't know me from Eve," she bluffed, in an attempt to make him show his hand.

"On the contrary, I've known you since you were born. And your mother entrusted your future to me."

"Now I know you're lying."

"I assure you, I'm not."

"How can I possibly believe you?"

A faint smile broke through his icy demeanor. "Ah, that's the thing about faith, isn't it? Your mother used to say that there are some things you just can't know, you can only choose to believe or not. I didn't put much stock into her religion, but I did like that one phrase she often said: Do what's right, do your best, and then trust God with the rest."

That brought her to her feet. She didn't want to believe he was who he said—it was overwhelming enough to have just escaped death at the hands of a psychopath—but to learn of a long-lost relative who for her entire life heretofore, she knew nothing of? The implications of all he claimed was enough to make her want to run.

His next sentence, however, thwarted that impulse.

"Decades ago, your mother sensed the trouble your father had gotten entangled in, and asked me to look out for you, in case anything happened to him. That's why I'm here tonight, risking exposure. I intend to honor my word."

"Wait, you mean Dad...?"

Tempest shook his head again. "He knows nothing about Cerberus."

She sighed in relief. "Aren't you worried they'll find you out?"

"At this point they don't suspect I'm with Aegis, or that we actually exist—that won't last, but..." He scanned into the distance, then continued. "No, they believe I'm trying to recruit you to join Cerberus."

Inadvertently, she held her breath. After a while, when she realized it, she released it slowly. "It's all so confusing."

"It *is* a bit much to grasp all at once." Tempest checked his watch again. He scanned the area and took a few steps back into the memorial. "But I don't have much time. Here's what you need to know: Cerberus wanted President Bradley dead, and to replace her with someone better aligned."

"A man, no doubt?"

"That's beside the point." He came right up to her side. "In any case, *they* were the ones behind the attack on *Air Force One.*"

That made no sense—and at the same time, it made perfect sense. "How did they manage that?"

"We've been operating in that region long before Tariqistan's new borders were carved out. Cerberus contracted local operatives who supported the Haashir regime and even recruited extremists for that side of the equation. In the case of the rogue pilots, it was simple blackmail."

Tempest made another visual sweep of the surrounding area, then pulled his sleeve up to check his watch.

Xandra just happened to catch a glimpse—enough to see it, even in the cover of the night.

Without thinking, she grabbed his wrist, and yanked the sleeve up.

"What—?" Tempest tried to pull away.

But Xandra only gripped it harder. "You've got one too!"

With the slightest pressure, he pressed his thumb into the fleshy spot between her forefinger and thumb. The sudden pain made he release her grip instantly.

"Ow!"

Max turned and growled. But she calmed him when he released her.

"You always were impetuous," Tempest said.

"What's with the tattoo?"

"Haven't you already figured that out?"

Annoyed that he'd subdued her so effortlessly, she rubbed her hand. "The three intersecting circles. I saw it on..." She wanted to say she'd seen it on the rogue fighter pilot's hand, but had it really been there, or was it a vision?

"It's the mark of Cerberus," Tempest said. "A most anachronistic practice, if you ask me. But what can I say? It's tradition. We all have it. If I were to have it removed, I'd be putting myself and Aegis on their radar."

She was still considering the tattoo's symbol.

Then it came to her. The first time she'd seen it. "Ian Morti-mer."

"And we're back to the assassin." He sighed. "The only reason he's still alive is that he's got information they need. He dies, he takes those secrets with him. Could be disastrous."

"What secrets?"

"None that concern you."

"I want to know."

Fixing a stern look upon her, he said, "Curiosity killed the cat."

"Cats have nine lives."

"You're no cat, Xandra." He reached down to pat Max on the head. "Besides—quite surprisingly—it's apparent you're a dog person, now."

"Leave Max out of this."

He smiled smugly.

"Let me get this straight," Xandra said. "Cerberus wants President Bradly dead, but Aegis doesn't, right?"

"Aegis doesn't think she needs to die. That's not the same as not wanting her dead. Though it's my understanding that Cerberus has since changed its priorities and is no longer targeting her—for now, at least."

That should have come as a relief, but it didn't. "What's changed?"

"They've got a bigger concern."

"Bigger than killing the President of the United States?"

Tempest pulled out his cigarettes, turned it over to find the pack empty, then clicked his tongue in annoyance as he slipped it back into his pocket. "We managed to convince them to stop targeting her because of a greater threat. This is where I need your help."

"Is the President still at risk?"

"The primary risk might be over in Tariqistan. But yes, she might be."

"So what do you need from me?"

"Come on." He scanned the area, took her by the elbow, and started walking in the direction of where he'd parked the car. "We need to go now."

She went along without resisting, and Max followed at her side.

"I need your help locating a rogue operative, someone who poses a threat not only to Cerberus and Aegis, but to President Bradly and the entire world.

"How is it that a sophisticated double-agent like you, working for an all-powerful organization can't locate this one person?"

"I can. With the help of talented people—like you."

Max pulled the lead slightly and turned back to give her a quick look. Then he continued walking at a brisk pace.

"That's putting a lot of faith in someone you just met," Xandra said.

He stopped at the corner, checked all sides of the street, then regarded her gravely. "You toppled one of Cerberus' rooks. Colson was one of their best. He kept the *Binh Son* Massacre buried for forty years. But in a matter of days, you unearthed it all." He continued down the steps. "I act on evidence, not faith."

They arrived at the sidewalk and approached the car.

"Whatever the case," he said, opening the door, "I need to know if you're willing to help."

"How, exactly?"

"Use everything at your disposal to find the rogue operative."

"Right. Just like that." She shook her head and let out an ironic huff. "Who is this person?"

"Al Shihab. The actual name doesn't matter, he's probably assumed so many aliases, we'll never know what he goes by today."

"What does Cerberus call him?"

He hesitated, the grinned. "Judas."

"Fitting, I suppose. Is he in Tariqistan right now?"

"I believe so, but there's no way to be certain, he's gone dark for three years now. However, our intel indicates a likely connection with al Saif, and the FTM demands."

"So you want me to help you find him," she said, guiding Max into the backseat of the car.

"It will help us, yes. But you'll also be helping the President with the current crisis."

She deliberated as they got inside and shut the doors.

*I'm in way over my head.* But then she thought of everything Mom and Jake had said about her gifts, thought about Jennifer and Michael Bradley. And she reflected on how working with the Secret Service was a way of honoring Kyle's sacrifice.

"So, what do you say?" Tempest started the engine, put the car in gear, and drove. As the monuments and reflecting pool shrank into the passenger side mirror, she considered it. The more she saw, the more it became clear that the world was not as nearly as clearly delineated as most would like to believe. Grey areas abounded. Whose word could she take?

The man with the blue and green eyes was supposed to be someone she could trust, and the truth was, she was starting to believe him.

But was it just a gut feeling, or an intentional act of faith?

"All right, I'm in."

"Good." The car accelerated. Judging by the route, he was taking her back to Georgetown.

"What first?" Xandra asked.

"For now, work as you typically do."

"How do I contact you?"

"You don't. I'll contact you. Don't discuss any of this with anyone else."

"Not even Masterson, or the President?"

"Not a word to them or anyone about me, Aegis, or Cerberus—it would only put them in danger. In addition to your extraordinary abilities, do try to utilize the Secret Service's and any other agency's help in locating Judas."

"Who comes up with these code names?"

"A Cerberus deputy director whose cover is a bestselling author."

"Anyone famous?"

"Focus, please. I'll be doing the same work as you, in my own way. But our goals are mutual, we must find and stop him. Countless lives are at stake."

"What's in it for you, then?"

"Cerberus wants him contained, they've assigned his case to my division. If we can stop him, Cerberus will have mitigated a major risk of exposure—and, it'll buy Aegis some breathing room. As dangerous as Judas is, he's just one part of a far greater threat."

Xandra checked the back seat to make sure Max was all right. "What could be worse than a presidential assassination or a terrorist attack?"

"A global power shift, the scope of which extends way beyond the President and this nation. We're all at risk. Not just you, your father, or me—and not just Aegis, but the future of the entire world. If Cerberus discovers us before we can get into position and effect the necessary changes, we could be facing cataclysmic global power shifts."

"Isn't that just a bit dramatic?"

He gave a derisive sneer. "If you had any idea..."

"Give me a hint."

The car stopped.

They'd arrived at her apartment.

"Good night, Xandra. And good luck."

# FIFTY TWO

BRADLEY RANCH
CABOTSTOWN, MD
6:48 AM

OVER THE EASTERN HILLS the Sun's mantel prowled the peaks, its amber hues bleeding into the ever-brightening sky. The only sounds Thomas Bradley heard were the waves softly lapping against the rowboat, and Mikey's quiet breathing.

"Look, Grandpa," the boy whispered, holding his fishing rod in one hand and pointing with the other. "It's almost here."

Ben had been about his age when Tom had started taking him fishing here at the lake, which was just a five minute hike from the ranch. It had been a tradition of theirs at many a significant juncture—the morning before Ben left for Annapolis, the evening before he shipped out for his first tour of Iraq, the day before he married Jenna, and in the last days before cancer so cruelly tore him from those who loved him.

"If you're really quiet, the fish might come up and watch the sunrise with us," Tom said, smiling at Mikey with poignant echoes of Ben's boyhood laughter, his deep-chested voice as a decorated Marine, and eventually, his quiet sighs during that one last fishing trip he requested before his passing.

"Really?" Mikey turned to look up at him, completely taking

his grandpa at his word.

"Uh huh." Tom looked into Ben's blue eyes, full of wonder and trust. He wanted so much to tell Mikey how much he reminded him of his son, but in the boy's fragile emotional state, it would only make him miss his father more. "When your dad was your age, he used to wait and wait, until he saw them jump out of the water."

"Did he ever catch any?"

"Oh sure.' Exaggerating, Tom spread his hands about a yard wide. "Caught one this big once."

"Wow..." Mikey said, almost inaudibly. "Hope I catch one that big."

"You will. You're just like him."

And he was. If ever there'd been a carbon copy—or as Ben used to call him, a "mini-me," it was Mikey Bradley, the beautiful doppelganger of his father, displaced in time. Like a dagger, a pang impaled his heart. Ben had always been fiercely independent and stubborn, locking antlers with him on more than a few occasions. But by the time he left for his first deployment to Iraq, he had come around and more than made his peace with Tom. From that point on, their relationship had changed. Yes, Tom would always be Ben's father, but for the first time, they were like friends. Ben had told him that it was because he finally learned to honor and respect his father. But in truth, it had been a mutual effort. They had finally found that rare equilibrium of which fathers and sons only dreamed.

What kind of man would Michael become, now that his father was gone?

Tom leaned over, kissed the top of his head, his downy hair brushing his face. *I will do everything to raise you in a way that would make Ben proud.*

Mikey turned around, wrapped his arms around him and buried his face into Tom's jacket.

"I love you, Grandpa."

"Love you too, Kiddo."

"I'm gonna catch a big fish in honor of Dad."

A lump caught in his throat. "You bet."

Still holding his grandson, Tom noticed that the first rays of the morning were cutting through the Pines and stretching down into the water. "Have a look, Mikey."

"Awesome..." He leaned against his chest. "My first sunrise fishing trip."

"The first of many, Kiddo."

Just then, something rose over the hills. At first, Tom thought it was a Pelican, but he'd never seen them this far inland before. Then the beating and whirring sound reminded him. It was something he'd been seeing more and more of in the past month or so.

Its silhouette rose up into the blaze of the rising sun.

"What's that?" Mikey said, shielding his eyes.

"Looks like one of those remote control crop dusters."

"Nah, that's a helicopter."

"You're right, Mikey. It *is* a helicopter. But look at it. It's probably about four or five feet long, too small for anyone to sit in. Someone's been flying them around down there. Maybe someone's bought that land by Broughman's Mine after all these years."

Somehow, the sight of a helicopter evoked memories of when Ben had nearly gotten killed getting his injured men airlifted out of Fallujah during a surprise insurgent attack. When he'd learned about what Ben had done, he couldn't remember having ever been so angry at him.

Or so proud.

"What's a cop-buster, Grandpa?"

Tom chuckled. "*Crop* duster. They use them to fly over farmland to spray for bugs."

"Not in choppers they don't."

"Well, they used to only use airplanes. But from what I read, too many people were getting hurt flying those. So that's why they've been experimenting with these remote control helis." On second thought, he'd heard nothing recently about anyone buying up Broughman's Mine, it had been abandoned for over sixty years. The place was as dead as a cemetery.

The crop duster turned south and flew off with a loud, flatulent buzz.

Which was odd, because that was out towards town, the opposite direction of Broughman's.

"Aw shoot." Mikey folded his arms, and pouted. "That chop-duster just farted so loud it probably scared away all the fish!"

Tom laughed. "Not to worry, Kiddo. If we don't catch anything, we'll just swing by town and bring home some bagels and lox."

"That's just not the same."

Was it the helicopter-prompted memory of his son, the war hero, or was it the way Mikey sounded frightfully identical to Ben, using the same exact phrase in the same exact situation—*that's just not the same*? Tom couldn't say.

But it was important not to simply avoid talking about Ben with Mikey, not when his father had been such a great man. To do so would cut short the lineage of greatness that was his heritage.

"Mikey, did your daddy ever talk to you about what happened in Iraq? Why they sent him home?"

"Uh huh. Mom says he came home to see me get born."

"Oh, really?"

A sharp look came over the boy. "Yeah, but I know the truth. Dad told me. He got hurt in Fallujah, and they said he had to come home to get better."

"Is that all he told you?"

"No." His demeanor became solemn. "I know what happened. He almost got killed making sure all his men were safe. Even the guys who were gonna die for sure anyway. He carried one of them onto the helicopter and made himself into a meat shield."

Tom laughed. "A what?"

"That's what Wade calls it when you put yourself in front of the bullets to protect someone else."

Tom took Mikey's cold little hands into his.

"Your father was a great man. Someone I am proud to call my son. He didn't have to risk his life like that, but because he did, everyone one of those boys came home to their families in one piece. Some of them would have died right there, if he hadn't done what he did. That's courage, Mikey. And do you know why he would do such a thing?"

"Dad said that a good man will do what he can to help others, but won't let bad stuff happen to himself. But a *great* man..." He sat tall, his chest puffing out slightly. "A great man will do everything to help his people, even if it means losing his own life."

If Tom had ever worried about that heritage, he now need not. It was alive and well, clearly manifest in Michael's heart.

"That was your Daddy, all right."

"Yup. He used to always say, 'Greater love has no man than this, that a man lay down his life for his friends.'" The morning light haloed Mikey's fair head, transforming him into a young Prince Caspian. "Maybe one day, I'll be as great as him."

"You've got all his greatness," he put his hand on his grandson's heart. "Right here."

# FIFTY THREE

SITUATION ROOM
THE WHITE HOUSE
WASHINGTON, DC
9:02 AM

AS MUCH AS SHE WANTED TO KNOW what intel they'd gathered regarding the Black Sea incident—and whatever other crises lurked in the Morning Book—President Bradley couldn't help thinking about how she'd left things with Mikey yesterday. When she'd finally gotten the opportunity last night, she called the ranch to check on him. But he'd already fallen asleep.

With today's schedule, her chances were equally dismal.

*I should be there for him more.*

There was never enough time, however. She had a nation to run, a world to hold together. The ranch was probably the best place from him at this time. Of course, they'd forgive each other with hugs, kisses and snuggles the next time they were together, but when this whole terror threat was over, she'd make it her business to live each day with him as though it were their last.

A morbid thought afflicted her, though. What if that blowup in the Oval turned out to be the last time she saw him?

*Enough.*

Seated at the head of the conference table in the black leather executive chair, the weight of the presidential seal on the wall behind her encumbered her shoulders. She must act decisively and provide an appropriate response to the entire press corps regarding what had happened over the Black Sea yesterday.

Now, in addition to the video threats from al Saif, and the recent attacks on the Marine base and open market in Kishwar, she had to deal with something much more direct and volatile. All the good she might have done by visiting Tariqistan to show her support had been eclipsed.

CIA director Douglas Kendall was well into an intelligence brief regarding the possible suspects involved in the attack. The occasional impatient sigh belied the frustration lurking beneath his otherwise calm demeanor. But when he reiterated the fact that the suicide bombers were little girls, a sobering cloud fell upon the Situation Room enshrouding all in a momentary silence.

He continued. "We've had our hands full with potential insurgencies brewing at local universities. But our operatives haven't found any actionable intelligence about them. FTM seems to have dispersed, and most of our informants are reporting that their contacts on the other side have severed all communication since the FTM video threat. They're concerned for their safety."

Bradley folded her hands before her and rested them on the desk. "The embassy?"

"As per your orders, we've doubled security and are ready to evacuate at a moment's notice. They're standing by."

"And what's the exit plan for our local informants?"

"Gradual relocation. We don't want to lift our skirt with a sudden, comprehensive pullout—" He smirked, "Pardon the expression, Ma'am."

As soon as Bradley realized that she was resting her head in her hand, massaging her temple, she lifted it. As expected, all eyes were upon her. "As for the domestic threats and threats to our interests, is it someone from FTM, or al Saif? Any theories?"

"We're looking into all but the most...correction—*including* the far-fetched ones."

"List a few."

"A small group of conservative Tariqistani's who have only staged peaceful demonstrations against the cultural changes that have taken place in their country. Professors, writers, journalist— they've always employed passive means of getting the message across that the government under President Amaal has strayed too far from traditional values and religion.

"We've just obtained evidence that a handful of them used to work publicity—propaganda—for Massoud Haashir before he was driven from power."

But that had taken place a few years ago.

Bradley's head ached as she grappled with connecting any details she could recall.

Kendal went on.

After another half a minute, a Sit Room staffer approached Bradley's Chief of Staff Mitch Donovan and whispered something into his ear.

Immediately, Donovan cleared his throat. "I'm sorry to interrupt, but I've just been informed of a new issue."

One of Cromwell's NSC staff came over and handed him a printout. Immediately, a corroborative dread filled his eyes. He looked to the President, then to Donovan.

Turning to her Chief of Staff, Bradley said, "What is it?"

"Madam President, we've got a leak."

Cromwell looked to Donovan. "Nighthawk?"

The Chief of Staff nodded. "One of our classified documents got to the media through an anonymous source. Al Jazeera ran it first. It's all over the Internet now."

"What does it say?" Bradley demanded.

Donovan passed the printout to her, an al Jazeera article with a headline:

```
CIA Operative and Family Killed by White House Or-
            dered Drone Strike
```

"Bottom line it for me, Mitch."

Pointing and clicking on the laptop before him, Donovan said, "It's been syndicated over all major outlets. The report's gone viral and the bloggers and vloggers are having a feeding frenzy right now."

"We might not have found the WMDs, but at least we were successful in stabilizing the new government," Kendall said, defensive because it was the CIA which had compiled the reports and concluded that Al Shihab had gotten access to bioweapons, and had joined Haashir's terrorist group. "Unlike Iraq."

"Our problem, Doug," the President said, her innards knotting painfully, "is that I lied."

"With all due respect, Ma'am," Kendall said, "You never said anything untrue. We never disclosed that we were going after Al Shihab."

"Or that in the process, his wife and son were killed," she said.

"The credibility of your office—of the nation—was at stake." Kendall sounded less and less convincing. "We had no choice but to keep it classified. Imagine the fallout—"

"I don't have to imagine." She quietly beat the heel of her fist on the table in steady succession. "It's happening right now. I should have stated this up front before it came to light this way."

"How'd that work for Bush after they failed to locate Saddam's alleged WMD's?" Donovan said.

"*He* didn't hide that failure."

"He couldn't keep it classified," Kendall said.

As everyone else contended to be heard over each other, myriad thoughts swarmed her mind. Bradley had to decide on a response from the White House—the right response.

How could she have let this slip by without even considering the consequences? She remembered what Andy Bingham, then CIA director, had advised her early in her first term, '*You can't treat every scenario as the worst case; it'll cripple you.*'

She rapped her knuckles on the table. "I'm going to come clean."

Her chief of staff regarded her with consternation. "I suggest you hold off on a response until we've had a chance—"

"The longer we keep silent, the deeper this hole gets," she said, becoming more determined as she spoke. "It was a mistake."

"An intelligence mistake," Donovan said, aiming his gaze at the CIA director. "They should issue a statement first."

"It's never been my practice to throw anyone under the bus, and I'm not about to start now. It happened under my watch, it was my call, I'm going to own—"

But before she could continue, Cromwell put his hand on her shoulder. "I'm sorry Ma'am, but we've got *another* situation."

Just as she turned to respond, Wade Masterson and several of the PPD agents burst into the Sit Room.

Their eyes met. "We need to evacuate everyone to the PEOC now, Ma'am."

He would never interrupt like this unless it was absolutely necessary. Bradley got up, ready to go with them to the President's Emergency Operations Center beneath the East Wing, a facility designed to protect from threats as dire as an incoming ICBM.

From the corner of her eye, she saw Xandra taking photos. She'd almost forgot that she was there, which was the mark of a great Chief Photographer.

Bradley motioned to her. "Xandra, you're with me."

As everyone drained from the Sit Room, Bradley went ahead at the brisk pace Wade and his team set. She turned to Cromwell. "All right, Evan. Talk to me."

"Langley's just scrambled a pair of Raptors from the 27th to establish Guard Dog CAP over Washington."

*Combat Air Patrol?*

Bradley stopped, turned and grabbed his elbow. "Are we under attack?"

Wade urged her through the corridor while principles, cabinet members, and members of the joint chiefs got on their cell phones. "We have to keep moving, Madam President."

Running on autopilot, she continued to press the issue with

her National Security Advisor. "Why the CAP?"

"National Airlines Flight 1306 was scheduled to arrive at Dulles in ten minutes, but it's gone silent and hasn't responded to any calls from air traffic controllers for the past 50 minutes. Bottom Line: We've got a rogue airliner headed for Washington."

# FIFTY FOUR

AIRSPACE OVER ANNAPOLIS, MD
USAF 1st FIGHTER WING F-22

AT LEAST I WON'T HAVE TO RAM IT.

Lieutenant Sharon "Panther" Parsons didn't find the thought particularly comforting as she gripped the flight stick of her F-22, and flew in tight formation with the Boeing 747 known as National Airlines Flight 1306. En route from Shanghai to Dulles, it had not deviated from its flight plan. But about forty minutes back, Air Traffic Controllers reported the trouble.

Flying wingman to her C.O., Colonel Gary "Raptor" Marks on Guard Dog CAP, they had been on the intercept mission for the past half hour. Despite all efforts, neither military nor civilian ATCs could get a squawk out of the commercial airliner's pilot or crew members.

The situation was the first occurrence since September 11, 2001 when Lieutenant Heather "Lucky" Penney scrambled an F-16 with her C.O. to intercept the rogue United Airlines Flight 93, the fourth hijacked plane that was headed for the nation's capital. Only, Penney and her C.O. had flown without any ordinance or live rounds. They just hadn't been prepared for such attacks at that point in history.

But we'd learned since then, and Parsons, holding the throttle steady, had more than enough firepower to bring the airliner down before it reached D.C. airspace.

The 747 banked slightly, but was still on its scheduled course.

She matched it and whispered a mild rendition of the Fighter Pilot's prayer. *"God, don't let me screw this up."*

They were coming dangerously close to Washington. It was only a matter of time but at this rate, with no communication from the airliner, it really could only end one way. And they'd have to destroy it over an unpopulated landscape, so there wasn't much of a margin.

Close enough to the 747's airframe, Parson looked into its cockpit.

She made out what seemed to be an empty chair and at least one pilot who was either asleep, or otherwise immobile. From the looks of it, the airliner had been on autopilot. Gradually dropping back alongside the plane's fuselage, she observed through its windows, passengers slumped back in their seats, shades lowered, and one particularly troubling sight—a pair of bloody hand prints on the glass.

A parasitic chill worked its way through her body.

She strained to keep from reacting.

"This is Panther," she said as calmly as she could to Marks through her headset. "I have a visual indicating possible distress or hijacking. Are you seeing it, Sir?"

"Copy that," he replied. "I've got blood stains in the passenger windows."

The inevitable constricted her chest like a python, deprived her of breath. "Orders?"

"Awaiting confirmation. Fall back, get a lock, and standby."

She acknowledged and did so, even as the azure waves of the Chesapeake came into view. They would most likely down the 747 there before it got any closer to D.C.

What was its target? The White House?

Memories of the Pentagon in flames, her aunt Charlene who died in the crash, and the other attacks of that infamous September day helped her retain her focus as she targeted the area around the airliner's fuel supply. But the thought of innocent passengers dying with the push of a button threatened to overwhelm the objective of her mission.

With all that was happening, despite the cloudless sky and warm sunshine, she found one thing disturbing.

The deathly silence.

A clear indication something was wrong.

The window of opportunity would soon close.

"Cutting it close, Sir."

Marks responded. "We've been ordered to standby, straight from the White House, but I'm not getting anything else."

"We've just crossed—"

"Copy that." He paused for a beat. "If I hear nothing in the next ten seconds, we'll follow protocol."

Which meant taking out the commercial airliner.

Parson's throat went dry as she choked out her words. "Aye, Sir."

# FIFTY FIVE

PRESIDENTIAL EMERGENCY OPERATIONS CENTER
(PEOC)
THE WHITE HOUSE - EAST WING

THE LAST THING SHE WANTED to do was to take photos. But this part of her duties was all she could hold onto, amidst the cacophony. Any thoughts of her meeting with Tempest last night failed to resolve in her mind. Xandra's responsibilities as the President's Photographer required that she record events like these, capture character defining moment for the archives so that posterity could glimpse that of Jennifer Bradley, especially under duress. Xandra had to hold onto something familiar like her photography to keep from getting overwhelmed.

"F-22's are standing by for your orders, Ma'am," General Krieger said, a telephone handset pressed to his ear. Behind and above him, a CNN news report displayed footage of a reporter at Dulles International Airport, while a scrolling marquee read:

```
National Airlines Flight 1306 unresponsive, under
                  fighter escort.
```

The pictures of the President remained imprinted in her mind even after Xandra made them. A firm brow with eyes locked on Evan Cromwell, Bradley shook her head tightly.

"How many passengers on the manifest?" the President said.

"About two hundred and twenty."

"Damn." She bit her lower lip. "Where are they now?"

"So far, there's been no ADIZ breach. They're completely on schedule and haven't deviated from their flight path."

"But no communication on any chan—"

General Krieger pulled the handset away from his ear and addressed Bradley. "Our pilots have confirmed signs of distress aboard the plane."

"What signs?" Bradley said, her attention shifting across the table.

"One pilot missing, and co-pilot appears incapacitated, or dead. But most disturbing of all, large amounts of blood on the passenger windows."

"Blood?"

"Yes, Ma'am. I think it's safe to assume it's a terrorist strike."

At this Xandra's head spun. A tingling charge coursed through her limbs all the way to her fingertips and toes.

The vision.

She had to say something.

But it really wasn't her place, not now, not here. As far as everyone in the PEOC was concerned, she was just a civilian staff photographer meant to be seen, and not heard.

For that matter, not even seen.

They'd all grown accustomed to tuning out the very existence of the President's photographer and never noticed her slowly approaching.

"Ma'am?"

Despite what Xandra thought had been her stealth, all eyes turned to her. She swallowed, hyper-aware, her neck muscles tensing, and her pulse careening down the slippery slope upon which she had just ascended, from whose edge she now hung precariously.

But when President Bradley welcomed her presence with her eyes, Xandra leaned over and spoke into her ear.

"I've seen this."

Bradley matched her *sotto voce*. "A vision?"

Xandra nodded. "I thought it had been about *Air Force One*, but now it's becoming clear to me. If I'm right, they're all dead. The passengers on Flight 1306, that is."

"Madam President, you need to decide," Krieger said, his hand covering the mouthpiece of the phone. "Fighters are standing by, awaiting your orders."

"Is there a chance that they might just be having technical issues?"

"There are fail safes, and even under these conditions, there would be some way to convey that they weren't overtaken and about to fly into a building."

"Your recommendation?"

He paused, looked up at the television screen before him with images of Flight 1306 under fighter escort, then frowned. "We should take it out of the sky."

"And if it turns out we were wrong?" Bradley's Chief of Staff said. "You don't want to be the President that ordered the deaths of two hundred plus innocent men, women and children."

Rather than projecting indecisiveness, Bradley was in complete control. "Evan?"

The National Security Advisor's chest rose and fell. "I'm afraid I'm with General Krieger on this."

And finally, much to Xandra's surprise, the President turned to her. This time she spoke in full voice. "They may already be dead, Xandra. But whoever killed them might still be in control of that plane."

"I understand." She tried not to think about what was about to happen. Thankfully, such decisions didn't fall upon her.

"All right," Bradley said to General Krieger, her features determined, "Call your pilots."

# FIFTY SIX

EN ROUTE TO DULLES INT'L AIRPORT
USAF 1st FIGHTER WING F-22

PINS AND NEEDLES could not begin to describe what Lt. Parsons felt. Cruising to match speeds with National Flight 1306, which had gone eerily silent for the past hour, her eyes couldn't help but be drawn from her HUD (heads up display) to the blood-stained passenger windows. And yet, there was no motion within to indicate the slightest signs of life.

Flying aft of the 747, she and Colonel Marks' F-22's weapons were hot—ready and able to obliterate their target at the push of a button. They'd already waited a full two minutes past the outlined protocol at President Bradley's orders, but deep down it came as a relief because Parsons could not imagine having to live with the thought that they'd shot down a plane full of innocent passengers.

"Any word, Sir?"

"Negative. Still waiting."

"Sir, if the time comes..."

"Listen, Panther..." The pause only lasted about a second, but she could feel its weight. Gary "Raptor" Marks was a solid man who never flinched at doing the right thing, no matter how difficult. But this pressed as heavily upon him as it did her. "We don't make the decisions, we carry them out. That's the mission, and that's our duty. You keep reminding yourself of that from this day on, okay?"

She was just about to answer when a voice came over their headsets.

"...orders are from the President: Stand down and continue escort unless Flight 1306 deviates from her flight plan. I repeat, stand down and continue escort pattern."

Parsons let out a strained breath. "Copy that." Her smile probably broke through her professional coolness, though.

"Don't get too happy just yet, Panther," Marks said, his tone stoic. "If she veers off or does anything other than land safely, we'll still have to destroy her."

TWELVE AND A HALF MINUTES passed and felt many times longer than the previous forty-five. At any given moment, Flight 1306 might go off course or make a sudden dive. Parsons would then have to launch her AIM-9 Sidewinders, and transform it into an aerial ball of flames.

Based on all the civilian Air Traffic Control chatter, countless commercial flights were being routed away from Flight 1306's path to Dulles. The number of exchanges between Marks and Dulles increased as they got closer.

"Dulles Approach," Marks said to the ATC, "Raptor with you descending to one-one-thousand."

"Raptor, Dulles Approach, Dulles altimeter three-zero-zero-eight. Advise changes in course and altitude."

The minutes ticked away. Parson's hands grew clammy as she held the flight stick steady. From everything she could discern, the 747's behavior was routine. However, the uncertainty of what was going on, and how this would play out was what really put her heart in the cold jaws of a vise.

Was the plane rigged with explosives, set to detonate on the tarmac?

Would it suddenly veer off course and fly into the airport?

She hadn't realized it until now, but this was almost worse than having to shoot the plane down. At least then, there was a predictable outcome.

Still tailing Flight 1306, Marks once again spoke. "Raptor turning toward Dulles."

"Roger that. Exercise caution, we've got a SWAT team on the ground set to move in as soon as she touches down."

Parsons drew a deep breath. *Assuming we get that far.*

# FIFTY SEVEN

PRESIDENTIAL EMERGENCY OPERATIONS CENTER
(PEOC)
THE WHITE HOUSE - EAST WING

THOUGH THE AIRLINER HAD NOT BREACHED the no-fly zone, nor deviated from its flight path, the radio-silent 747 continued steadily towards Dulles International Airport without the slightest response to air traffic control communications.

As the President awaited updates, Xandra kept her focus on her photography duties. Could this situation have something to do with Al Shihab, as per Tempest's intel? She considered talking to Wade and mentioning Al Shihab, but could she trust him enough to mention Tempest? What would happen if she deviated from Tempest's instructions?

The chilling images of her vision flashed in her mind, interrupting her ruminations. If the plane wasn't about to be used as some kind of terrorist weapon, then perhaps her vision indicated a crash of some sort.

"Flight 1306 is making its approach," General Krieger said, his eyes locked on the live footage from a local news affiliate filming, from a distance, the jumbo jet with escort, approaching its destination. "ETA eleven minutes."

"If there's any connection with al Saif and FTM, I want to

know," Bradley said, her tone low and steady.

Disconnecting a call, Wade Masterson pocketed his cell phone and addressed Bradley. "We've got SWAT teams, FBI and Homeland out on the tarmac ready when it touches down, Ma'am."

"Anything that might shed some light on this?"

"No connections we know of. But we're prepared for multiple contingencies. Until this is resolved, we've cleared the airport and closed it off."

Xandra moved closer despite the confines of the crammed PEOC. "Madam President," she whispered, subtly getting both her and Wade's attention. "If you let me go in to investigate, I might be able to bring you some firsthand information."

"Press access is restricted," Wade said.

"I mean up close."

Wade shook his head and frowned. "There is no way."

The overwhelming need to resolve the images from that vision drove her persistence. "Ma'am, this is the reason you hired me. If I can go to the scene, take some pictures, I might be able to find something others miss." The rational part of her brain—locked away in a dungeon somewhere—didn't even bother protesting.

Her attention split between this discussion, those of the joint chiefs, and the ongoing CNN report, Bradley kept her eyes on the television screen. "Wade?"

"Wouldn't recommend it, Ma'am," Masterson said. "Not until—"

Xandra set her Nikon down and pulled over an empty seat so she could speak at Bradley's eye level. "I did nine months in Fallujah—"

"As a photographer," Wade said.

"I've been training at Rowley," Xandra continued, turning to Wade, "I think I can handle taking some photos when that airplane lands."

Bradley shot up a hand. "Hold it."

Several in the room who had been talking on the phone

dropped their handsets and let them dangle by the curled cords as they stood and faced the television.

The television showed the bright blue 747 airframe of Flight 1306, with its F-22 escort coming into view and approaching the airport. In a matter of seconds, all of Washington—perhaps the world—would witness its fate.

General Krieger stood and squinted at the monitor. "They're coming in."

# FIFTY EIGHT

DULLES INTERNATIONAL AIRPORT
RUNAWAY

A BLUNT PAIN SPREAD through Special Agent Edward Blake's clenched fist as the 747 made a flawless landing on the runway. Flight 1306's fighter escorts had followed it until the Jumbo Jet's landing gear screeched on the ground. They then flew off.

The roar of F-22 engines brought Blake's hands up in an instinctual attempt to shield his ears. He couldn't hear any of the chatter through his earpiece but it didn't matter. Nothing did, except what would happen next.

Personnel from all the agencies under whose jurisdiction this situation fell had gathered outside a hangar nearest to the landing strip. Armed SWAT team members, FBI, and Homeland Security agents stood ready, awaiting their orders. Heading up the Bureau's task force, Blake was on point for this operation.

What exactly they were supposed to do was yet to be determined. That would depend on how the crisis presented itself, once anyone could establish contact with the occupants of the plane.

Hijackers that had gone this far would ordinarily have made their demands known by now. The paranoia of a terrorist who still hoped to get away alive would have become obvious.

Which was what made this whole damned thing so odd. The entire flight and landing had a cadaverous calm to it that didn't fit the profile of a hijacking.

The airliner was taxiing now, but not turning toward any of the gates, likely the first sign of intent from those in control of the aircraft.

Blake spoke into his two-way. "All units stand by."

The plane slowed to a complete stop in the middle of the runway.

Blake turned to Lieutenant Foster, commander of the SWAT unit. "Any word from your men?"

Foster frowned, checked his watch, and put his binoculars back over his eyes. "Still nothing."

Sylvia Jameson, the lead from the Department of Homeland Security came over to join them. She had once reported to Blake when she still worked for the FBI. "Have you established a time frame? Exceeding that, we should move in."

"*After* I fully assess the situation. We don't know if it's a hostage situation, a bomb, or whatever. Once we have a handle on that, we can implement the appropriate plan."

"You of all people know that there's risk with inaction, Blake."

He narrowed his eyes at her. "You do your job, and I'll do mine."

Before walking off, she turned back and said, "Make sure you do."

Just his luck. Of all the people from Homeland to be stuck with, why'd it have to be Sylvia? It was bad enough that she'd broken up with him because of what she called his 'lack of initiative', and that she'd taken her move to DHS as a means of looking down her nose at him, but now she could challenge and scrutinize his every move with impunity since it was his career, not hers, riding on how everything went down today.

*Yet another reason not to date someone you work with.*

Forster lowered his binoculars. Quickly sweeping his gaze from Blake to Jameson, he shrugged nonchalantly. "Whenever you've made up your mind, give the word and I'll have my men in position."

Blake borrowed the binoculars and looked out to the runway.

Hard to imagine that there were upwards of three hundred people on such a dead looking plane.

It just sat there, like a massive coffin.

# FIFTY NINE

DULLES INTERNATIONAL AIRPORT
RUNAWAY

THE PRESSURE WAS RISING. Blake Edwards typically enjoyed the challenge of taking the lead in crisis situations, but this was different. The entire nation—maybe the whole world—was watching to see what would happen as soon as the ghost plane, as some of the people on the ground were calling it, landed.

As he spoke to the SWAT team leader over his walkie-talkie, a cold film of perspiration coated his back. "Murph, you and your men in position?"

"Yes, Sir."

Through his binoculars, Blake saw Lieutenant Murphy give a thumbs up. He and his team stood along the top of the stairs that had been rolled up to the door on the jumbo jet's fuselage.

"All right, let's do it."

In less than ten seconds, they'd opened the door.

With guns at the ready, they entered the plane.

The last thing Blake needed to do was to micromanage or sound less than completely confident and in control. But even after the first second went by with almost no sound over the walkie-talkie, he wanted to say, "Murph, what's going on in there?"

Nothing could prepare him for what happened next.

SHOUTING AS THEY ENTERED, each member of Murph's team rushed in ahead of him, ready to subdue anyone—criminal, hijacker, or terrorist—that came at them with a weapon.

Within seconds, silence fell over all the shouting and chatter over the channel.

Murph stepped inside the cabin and made his way through the rows.

He barely noticed that the cockpit door was forced open by someone on his team. The rest paced slowly up and down the aisles, staring at the most horrific sight he'd ever laid eyes on in his ten years with the Army, and seven in law enforcement.

There didn't appear to be an immediate threat in the form of armed terrorists.

But what he found in the belly of Flight 1306 caused him more distress.

"Special Agent Blake?" he said into the walkie-talkie.

"What've you got?"

"We're not equipped for this."

Within the next two seconds, he was shouting to his team. "Everyone off the plane! Now!"

# SIXTY

PHOTOGRAPHY OFFICE
THE WHITE HOUSE

SHE HAD SOMEHOW MANAGED IT. Convincing the President's Chief of Staff, and head of her Secret Service protective detail proved more difficult than convincing POTUS herself. But in the end, Xandra had gotten the green light to go and look into Flight 1306. Wade had even assented to her request for clearance to get as close as possible to the plane to take pictures.

Bradley's authorization was a clear indication that she believed Xandra could bring a unique perspective to the situation. Either that, or she was just trying to toss her a bone. Hopefully, Xandra hadn't oversold herself.

Wade was waiting out in the hallway as she packed her gear. She caught a glimpse of the old vintage Graflex. It had been repaired several times and still took decent pictures, but could it reveal anything extraordinary in the darkroom like it had before?

Just as she was about to open the door to leave, her cell phone rang.

It was from an unknown caller whose number had been blocked.

Ordinarily, she'd ignore such calls, but something told her she should pick up, this time.

"Hello?"

"Are you watching the news?"

"Who is this?" She thought the voice sounded familiar, but couldn't place it.

"Tempest. Are you paying attention?"

"What are you talking about?" Xandra tried to keep her voice down, but it was rising in intensity. She hadn't expected him ever to call her, especially not when she was at work.

"Flight 1306, are you up to speed on it?"

"As much as anyone in the White House Situation Room can be. Aren't you worried about getting traced?"

"Burner cell. Now, listen. We've already got some people there, but you need to be there too. This could be connected to Judas. If so, you might find something, a clue, a hint, as to his connection or whereabouts."

"Okay, I assume I won't be able to reach you at this number?"

"This phone will be destroyed the moment we disconnect."

"Fine. What am I looking for?"

He hesitated, then said, "I'm counting on your abilities to help you find a clue. I believe you'll know it when you see it."

That was all she needed to decide.

On her way out, she grabbed the Graflex.

# SIXTY ONE

DULLES INTERNATIONAL AIRPORT
TARMAC

HAVING PASSED THROUGH countless checkpoints and security screenings, Xandra wondered if she was ready to launch herself into such an investigation. Her stint in Fallujah had sharpened her instincts about terrorist and insurgent attacks, and despite being just about certain that her visions had portended to this very event, she wasn't prepared for how she felt looking out at the tarmac at Dulles.

The tingling in her extremities was not from an oncoming vision, she knew that sensation too well to mistake it for this. No, this came from the juxtaposition of anxiety and anticipation that fought for control of her mind.

Special Agent Quentin Parker, one of Wade's team members, stood with her as she stared out at the long white tunnel which encased the entire path from the 747's exit door, down the stairs, and into a white makeshift tent.

CDC workers in pale Hazmat suits bustled about the bottom of the plane, while others carrying black body bags could be seen through the transparent sheet plastic windows into the tent.

Parker turned to her, his expression obscured behind the dark sunglasses. "You sure about this?"

"I'm not sure about anything."

"What are you dragging us into?"

He hadn't been made privy to her extraordinary abilities and would certainly start asking about the vintage camera she'd have to strap over her neck, and later have irradiated. "We've been cleared, haven't we?"

"Yes, Ma'am."

She flashed him a crooked smile. "Then quit being such a girl. Let's go and suit up."

Five minutes later, Xandra felt like she would suffocate inside the Level B Hazmat suit, hood and face piece with SBCA (self-contained breathing apparatus). It bore a faint resemblance to a World War I gas mask, but connected to an air tank strapped to her back. The steel toed boots were chemical resistant, but made every step uncomfortably rigid. Her own hot breath fogged the transparent face piece and though its material was surprisingly light, it felt like her entire body was wrapped in the coils of steel.

"This is…" she sucked in a long breath, trying to stave off hyperventilation as she spoke to Parker through the two-way radio "…intolerable!"

"Who's being a girl now?" He said, as they both stood at the foot of the stairs, peering up to the plane's fuselage.

Catching her breath, she regarded him through the suit, and knocked on his face piece. "Did Wade ever tell you how I passed my RCT exam?"

"Remedial Control Tactics? No."

"Keep it up, and I'll give you a demonstration."

"Cute." Parker seemed to respond well to this kind of banter. He actually smiled this time. "Ready?"

"No." She slung the Graflex over her neck, but couldn't quite feel anything but its weight through the suit.

"Good, let's go."

They started up the stairs to the plane.

Strange, she'd always thought that going into the pit of Hell was a downward climb. Thankfully, Parker didn't say or ask anything about the old camera she held. Neither had the medical examiners in the tents, who were too engrossed in their work to notice.

As they got to the top, a sense of recognition—deja vu was too simple a term—came over her. Before she even stepped into the cabin, she knew what she would find. She'd seen this before.

"Initial reports don't indicate a chemical agent," Parker said, stepping in first. Though the entire plane had been secured, he stood, alert and vigilant.

And somewhat in the way.

But Wade insisted on sending someone to accompany her; it was the one condition to which she could not object.

Parker whispered some kind of expletive, but stopped himself.

"What is it?" Xandra said.

"It's fugly. Just giving you a heads up. You sure you want to see this?"

"I'm ready." She took a few steps in.

But when she stepped past him and looked into the cabin, it became acutely clear that she was not. With a gasp, she stumbled back, her oxygen tank bumping into Parker, then steadied herself against the bulkhead.

It was exactly what she'd seen in her vision, but so much more.

Even behind the protective screen of her face piece, this was significantly more horrifying to behold.

Bodies strewn across the blood-stained carpet, blood-stained seats, eyes oozing blood so dark it resembled India ink....men, women, and even children bent in painfully contorted positions—all of it punctuated by the fact that some of them appeared to have died violently. Some of them still had their hands clawing and clutching the throats of others.

"I'm going to hurl."

"Hold it together, Parker."

He nodded abruptly and turned away from her and from the scene. He was a relatively young man, maybe twenty-nine or thirty, and though he'd been trained for the Service, he probably hadn't seen this much blood and gore in his entire life.

Xandra, however, had seen victims of suicide bombers, IEDs, and insurgent gunfire, so blood wasn't all that shocking. What troubled her most were the children three rows ahead.

They couldn't have been older than ten—perhaps brother and sister—but it was clear they had died from the wounds they'd violently inflicted on each other.

If it had been murder, then each of them still held bloody murder weapons in their hands.

Xandra would never look at pencils the same way again.

"What do you think?" Parker's voice came weakly through the two-way.

"I think they killed each other."

"Mister Magoo could see that."

Her pity for the young agent prevented her from making a snide remark about his sarcasm. Instead, she lifted her Graflex, fumbled through her gloves to bring it to eye level and started taking pictures of everything she could.

"So you came here, risked both of our lives, just to take pictures with an ancient camera?" He was really pushing it now.

But Xandra went on and took some more pictures, ignoring the annoyance. "I came to find the truth."

She stepped a bit closer to the brother and sister sprawled across the row. The boy's hand had smeared a bloody hand print on the window. The girl clutched a broken pencil covered in blood in one hand, and the boy's throat in the other. Amongst several others, their remains had not yet been collected, thought it would only be a matter of time before the CDC workers came for them.

This was about the time she expected to receive a precognitive mind flash. A crucial clue, a hint linking to the perpetrator—Al Shihab?—perhaps his whereabouts? But nothing of the sort surfaced.

*Perhaps in the darkroom.*

Hopefully.

Or she'd prove herself unhelpful and never know for sure if her decision to trust Tempest had been right.

"Parker, think you can stand to take a look here and give me your opinion?"

He hadn't seen this particular set of bodies, but he would probably be able to confirm her suspicions about their deceased owners.

"Yeah..." A wet sniff followed by low-pitched groan over the two-way, and he came over and stood behind her.

While not everyone on the plane seemed to have been violently attacked, this poor boy most certainly had. She stepped aside to afford Parker an unobstructed view and pointed to the broken stump of the pencil protruding from the corpse's eye socket. "Do you think he died from the wound, or something else?"

First came the sound of retching, then the stumbling rush of a hazmat suit racing passed her.

"Parker?"

She turned around and watched in horror as he ran to the exit door, tore his face piece off, and began vomiting over the steps.

"Parker, you'll be exposed. Keep your mask on!"

He couldn't hear her because he'd removed everything from his face and head, including the two-way radio earpiece. No matter how loud she shouted, it would be muffled by her own mask.

As quickly as she could, Xandra made her way down the aisle, stepping over the same bodies she'd encountered on her way in, and grabbed Parker by the arm. Pulling him up tall, she ignored the residue on his face, took his face piece and tried to put it back over his head.

When their eyes met, through the airtight panel, a sudden look of distress washed over his already blanched countenance.

He understood.

Mouth opening and shutting like a fish on the hot wooden planks of a pier, he reset the face piece and SCBA over his face. The scratch of his mic rubbing against his skin came over the channel.

"Oh my God," Parker said, eyes wide in terror.

"You're going to be okay, just stay calm, all right?"

He nodded, but he looked as frightened as a child.

"We need help," she said over the two-way to the command center on the ground. "Agent Parker removed his SCBA and may have been exposed."

"Is he contained?"

"Yes."

"On our way."

She turned and put a gloved hand on his shoulder. "You're going to be okay, you hear?"

Shaking his head, he scoffed at himself. "I'm an idiot."

"I could've told you that." She had to keep him from panicking.

Parker let out a nervous laugh. "Yeah. I'll bet you would too."

"Other than stupid, are you feeling anything unusual?"

"My heart rate is elevated, but that could be from all the excitement."

"Anything else?"

"Do you think..." he arched his brow over to the cabin, "...you think what happened to them will happen to me?"

Footfalls pounded on the steps behind them.

The CDC people were coming for him.

Xandra gave him a reassuring smile. "You'll be fine."

But as they led him down the steps, she chided herself for lying. The truth was, she had no idea what had happened to those poor souls on the ghost plane.

CDC might find the cause of death for all the passengers, pilot and crew, but if she were to help stop whatever threat to which this might pertain, she had to find something beyond anything the labs could reveal.

And that just might require a visit to the darkroom.

# SIXTY TWO

PHOTOGRAPHY CLOSET
THE WHITE HOUSE

THE BODIES of the passengers and crew members that hadn't apparently died at the hands of the other passengers, looked grotesque enough for a scene in a horror movie. Under the amber safelight in the darkroom, Xandra examined the close-ups she'd taken with her Graflex of those fortunate enough not to have been bitten, bludgeoned or mutilated with pens, plastic utensils, or personal electronics.

The fact that she hadn't experienced an internal vision troubled her. But knowing how unreliable her ability was when she sought to exploit it, she'd brought the old medium format camera which had first revealed her second sight four years ago.

So far, none of the prints she'd exposed showed anything the naked eye couldn't easily discern. Her stomach didn't appreciate this, though, as she perused the victims' faces from whose eyes, noses, and ears blood oozed.

The CDC had not yet issued an official statement regarding the cause of death for Flight 1306's passengers, but the word on the ground in the emergency tents umbilically connected to the 747 was that it appeared to be the result of two things: 1. A biological agent, rather than chemical, which presented Ebola-like external manifestations, and 2. Extreme violence—meaning the passengers and crew seemed to have murdered each other in a widespread rage, as if they'd become rabid savages before they either died from hemorrhagic fever, or from a variety of causes such as blunt force trauma, mortal stab and even bite wounds.

Perhaps the black box would provide further clues, but Wade was doubtful. The authorities were still waiting to retrieve cockpit voice recordings which might give some kind of indication as to what actually happened before the pilots went silent.

"Come on," Xandra murmured as she immersed another contact sheet in the developer solution. Though she'd seen it countless times, it never ceased to give her the chills, as human subject's faces went from a skeletal inverted negative into a fully resolved monochrome likeness.

This particular photo was that of the boy whose sister had attacked him with a pencil. She hated to look at this one, but that was the very reason she must. She took the exposed sheet and held it in the developer tray.

It began.

Her hands grew cold and numb.

*Steady.*

The first time this happened to her in New York was when she developed a photo taken with the Graflex at a Central Park pond. The photo had been of ducks, but in the darkroom, she saw the spectral image of a dead girl floating face-down just beneath the surface of the water.

The image had vanished before she could place the contact sheet in the stop bath and fixer, but Xandra had been absolutely certain, and horrified about what she'd seen.

Of course, the body hadn't been there when she took the picture, but soon after she experienced the vision, she saw on the evening news that a girl who fit the description of the one she'd seen in her darkroom had been reported missing.

Xandra shook her head, remembering all the trouble she'd gotten into when she tried to make an anonymous call to the police, telling them to check the duck pond in Central Park. When they found the remains of Stacey Dellafina the missing Juilliard dance student, Xandra became a person of interest.

If she'd only known that first vision would have unraveled the entire Colson conspiracy, she might never have made the call.

Mom would have disagreed, had she been alive today.

*It was your destiny, Xandi,* she could just hear her say. *Every event in your life has been woven together to draw you to your destiny.*

But what if she found the answers to Flight 1306, its connection with Al Shihab, or with al Saif and the FTM, if there was any? Surely that knowledge would become the burden of Atlas on her own shoulders.

Xandra watched the submerged contact sheet even as the tingling sensation ran through her entire body.

As the unfortunate boy's image resolved, she thought she saw something completely different.

It was not a trick of the safelight, or faulty memory.

Something that hadn't been there when she took the photo was now visible.

Then it became clear.

Clearer than an ordinary photograph could ever be.

It was as if she was standing there in the cabin of the plane again.

And what she saw caused her heart to freeze.

# SIXTY THREE

OVAL OFFICE
THE WHITE HOUSE
7:43 PM EST

THOUGH THE CRISIS of Flight 1306's mysterious deaths loomed, Jenna Bradley could not help but think about Mikey. But in order to remain focused in the PEOC, from which she'd just emerged, she'd had to push those thoughts aside.

Several meals had been brought to her both at the PEOC, and here in the Oval. But she had neither the appetite nor the will to even look at the sandwich sitting on an elegant plate atop the *Resolute* Desk.

Just past the bowl of tomato bisque, from which aromatic tendrils stretched, she eyed the telephone. She'd have to call Mikey and let him know that once again, she could not make it over to the ranch. *He doesn't deserve this.*

All she had worked for to secure freedom and peace in Tariqistan was now threatening to unravel. All the people who died fighting radicals and insurgents, all the people who died helping to rebuild, how could she give into FTM's demands now?

And yet, they'd demonstrated their ability to strike, not just Kishwar, not just *Air Force One*, but at America, on its own soil. Flight 1306 could have ended much worse than it had, but it wasn't exactly over. The question of who exactly was responsible, and how they managed to do this still remained.

How could she keep Mikey safe if she couldn't even protect the United States from such a gruesome catastrophe?

"I could really use your help, Ben."

She slumped back into her chair and noticed that she'd not turned the lights on. The only illumination came from the beams cast from an ivory moon onto the wall. Her shadow against the wall regarded her with skepticism.

How long had she been sitting here?

"I'm calling him now," she said to herself. It didn't matter how Mikey would react to the bad news, she needed to hear his voice, angry or not.

She reached for the phone.

Just then, a knock came on the door.

"Yes?"

The door opened and Wade Masterson stuck his head in. "I'm sorry, Ma'am. I know you're trying to catch your breath, but it's important."

Bradley swore silently and put the handset down. "All right, come on in."

He entered, and to her surprise, he was not alone.

"Have a seat." Bradley motioned to the chairs facing her desk in which Wade and Xandra sat. As usual, her Protective Detail head appeared collected and severe. Xandra however seemed somewhat preoccupied. Her gaze trailed off into an unseen oblivion. Why had she even accompanied him? "All right, you've got my attention."

"Thank you, Ma'am." Wade sat forward in his seat. "We have some new information."

# SIXTY FOUR

OVAL OFFICE
THE WHITE HOUSE
7:50 PM EST

BARELY A WORD Wade said to the President registered in Xandra's mind. She vaguely heard him mention something about a weaponized biological agent, something that resembled both the Ebola virus and Rabies, but her thoughts kept floating back to the vision she'd just experienced.

"What we do know is that the plane landed via autopilot," Wade said, sounding incredulous, "but based on the M.E.'s reports, the pilots were already dead for at least two hours prior to touch down."

Bradley shifted in her chair. "How did they die?"

"The captain's body was found alone in the cabin. He died of massive cranial hemorrhage, and some self-inflicted wounds to the head. The co-pilot, found just outside the cabin, also exhibited signs of hemorrhagic fever, but was most likely beaten to death based on the trauma to his entire body."

"Xandra, did you find anything unusual?"

She heard the words, but didn't make the connection that they were addressed to her. "I'm sorry, what was that?"

Bradley let out an impatient breath. "I need you to focus."

"Of course, I was just…" Finally regaining her bearings, she re-engaged. "Everything I saw corroborates the reports. The degree of violence was staggering. It must have been mass hysteria, though some looked to have died from bleeding out of every part of their body." Just then, she remembered. "Any word on Agent Parker?"

Wade shook his head and frowned. "He's still under quarantine, but last I heard, he's show no signs of infection. Just annoyed that he has to stay in that plastic bubble until they know what we're dealing with."

Bradley and Wade continued, but their words faded once again into the recesses of Xandra's consciousness. Her eyes wandered over to the bowl of tomato soup sitting on the President's desk. It reminded her of all the blood. Whatever had happened to the victims of Flight 1306, it was clear that they'd died in a horrific manner.

If only the vision she just experienced could afford her some kind of insight rather than mere pieces of the puzzle. If second sight was indeed a God-given gift, then surely He understood this was not a game. Countless lives were at stake.

Instead, it only pointed her in a direction that both worried and puzzled her. She wanted to ask about Al Shihab (or Judas), if he could possibly be responsible for the biological attack on the plane. But Tempest had said that the ex-CIA asset was presumed dead. *Am I supposed to know otherwise?* Or that Cerberus and Aegis believed he was still alive?

Best bring this up when she could be more definitive. So far she hadn't been justifying the President's confidence in her abilities.

Which she might very well do, if she followed the clue that appeared in her darkroom. As the latent image had turned up under the developer solution, she saw for a distinct five seconds the image of Mikey Bradley, hugging Max. As usual it appeared superimposed over the actual subject, then vanished afterwards. But she couldn't forget what she saw.

Nor could she forget the poignant memory of Mikey at Arlington, hugging his father's headstone.

Before she could speculate or allow herself to assign an emotion to that vision, she spoke up. "How's Mikey, Ma'am?" Right away, Xandra bit her lip—she'd just interrupted the President of the United States.

But Bradley, though slightly taken aback, paused for a thoughtful moment. It was as though she'd just remembered something important. She looked over to her phone, made a false start, then retracted her hand.

To Xandra: "Thank you for asking. To be honest, I haven't had a chance to call him."

"He's at the ranch?"

Wade turned to confront her with his imposing gaze. "Ms. Carrick—"

"It's all right," Bradley said, her eyes still on Xandra's. "Yes, he's there with his grandfather. I'm afraid I'm going to have to break my promise to him again."

"If you like, I can go ahead of you as you requested, and bring Max to the ranch."

For the first time all day, she saw a hint of a smile on Bradley's face. "Great idea. He adores The General."

"I can return to duty at a moment's notice, and Max can stay on the ranch with them."

"If I were you, I'd take some time off. We've all had a rough couple of days."

"So have you," Xandra said, "You could use the respite."

"Want to trade jobs?"

Xandra turned to Wade who instead of laughing, scowled and shook his head. "Madam President," she said, "I couldn't handle a fraction of what you do."

"You'd be surprised at what you can rise to, when push comes to shove," Bradley said. "In any case, pack your things and be ready with Max tomorrow at 7:00 AM. It'll be a nice break for you"

"Yes, Ma'am." Xandra stood, thanked her, and then started for the door. But deep down, she had a feeling rest would be the last thing to which it would lead.

# SIXTY FIVE

BRADLEY RANCH
CABOTSTOWN, MD
8:05AM

IT SEEMED UNFAIR that amidst everything that was happening, Xandra could be here, deep in the countryside of Western Maryland surrounded by the birches, smooth alders, and magnolias. The sun rose over the hills green with trees budding, birds chittering and brooks babbling. Crisp morning air carried a piney essence that evoked memories of that one camping trip she, Mom and Dad had gone on in the Adirondacks, years ago.

"This way, Ms. Carrick." Special Agent Walker motioned for the door of the main cabin where another male Secret Service agent stood watch. Never pulling the lead, Max walked in perfect step with Xandra as they strode up onto the wooden porch.

"Walker," the male agent said in greeting.

"This is Special Agent Hayes," Walker said to Xandra. He and Special Agent Davis were on duty for the duration of Michael's stay here at the Bradley Ranch.

She greeted him, noting the gun slightly showing inside his open jacket. "Max is in great demand these days."

Hayes nodded. "Michael could use some cheering up." He opened the front door for her.

Upon entering, the aroma of bacon and eggs welcomed her.

Max licked his chops.

In a matter of seconds, preceded by an excited whoop, Mikey came running down the hall, his feet pounding on the polished hardwood floor. "You brought him!"

In a single move worthy of a Major League Baseball star, he dropped to his knees and slid right up to The General, who, sitting except for a slight tail wag, didn't even flinch.

"Max!" He wrapped his arms around him. "You're here!"

"Hi Michael," Xandra said, surprised at just how glad she felt seeing him.

Rubbing Max's fur and smiling so hard his eyes became joyful slits, he replied, "Hi."

Agent Kelly Davis came over. "There you are, Mikey."

He turned and gave her a perturbed look. "Michael." He rolled his eyes.

With a smile that seemed just a bit insincere, Davis regarded Xandra. "Was this authorized?"

"Max? Of course. By the POTUS herself."

"Right. Well, we can keep him in the kennel—"

"No way!" Michael turned to her, scowling. "You can't treat him that way. He's a war hero."

With a patronizing tone, Davis bent down and put her hand on his shoulder. "Sweetie, if that dog bites you, I'll lose my job."

"He won't." Facing the General, he rubbed his ears. "Isn't that right, Max? We promise."

"They'll be fine," Xandra said. "I'll keep an eye on them both."

Davis shrugged. The tension in her face ebbed. "I could use all the eyes I can get on this guy." She mussed his hair lovingly. "Just looking out for you, little man."

"Seriously? Little man?" He got up and turned to Xandra and held out his hand. "Can I?"

"Sure." She handed him the lead.

"See ya!" In a flash, he ran off with the General. "C'mon, Max!"

"Wait, Michael!" Agent Davis ran after him and passed his grandfather Thomas Bradley down the hall. He was a handsome man that time had treated well. With a full head of silver hair, his chiseled features were weathered but still strong, his military posture undiminished by age. When he arrived, he extended his hand. "Tom Bradley. Pleasure to meet you finally."

"I'm Xandra Carrick, the new Chief White House Official Photographer and Director of the White House Photography Office."

"I've never held a title with that many words," he said, a twinkle in his striking blue eyes. "Welcome to the ranch—we call it a ranch, but there aren't any horses."

"I see. Well, thank you, Mr. Bradley."

"Missy, I don't need anyone making me feel any older than I already do. Why don't you just call me Tom?"

Warmed by his charm, she acquiesced. "If you insist." In the tiny pause, her stomach let out a distinct growl. "Oh my—excuse me."

"Have you had breakfast yet?"

She peered over his shoulder. "Something smells delicious."

He took her bags and nodded down the hall. "I always make too much food. Come and join me, looks like I've lost my breakfast partner to The General."

# SIXTY SIX

THE ROSE GARDEN
THE WHITE HOUSE
8:11 AM EST

THE OVERNIGHT REPORTS were accumulating at an alarming rate. The FTM's deadline was fast approaching, and there was absolutely no way Jennifer Bradley could give in to their demands. Every department and agency was preparing for an attack, as well as trying to prevent it. David Scott had been trying to triage the incoming messages and constantly fluctuating priorities, but despite the dawn of a new day, Bradley didn't hold out much hope for one easier than the last.

Before the mad rush began, she took the only five minute slot of private time she could carve out, and stood leaning against one of the pillars of the West Colonnade. Teacup in hand, she gazed out over the Rose Garden. After a restless night, she kept replaying yesterday's events, trying to make sense of it. Flight 1306 had been perhaps the most bizarre incident since Malaysian Airlines Flight MH370, only this time, the plane landed itself, delivering a grotesque payload of corpses infected with some kind of biological agent of which neither the CDC, nor any other agency was familiar.

If al Saif or the Free Tariqistan Movement had been responsible, they would surely have claimed it by now. It would have served as considerable leverage for their demands. As it was, no one had come forward. While she had absolutely no intention of negotiating, much less considering their demands, there was still concern about what might happen once their deadline passed.

Judging by the way things had been looking, the threats had been presumed to be abroad—until Flight 1306 touched down yesterday, tossing the proverbial monkey wrench into the intel machine.

Today's PDB and conference in the Situation Room would have to shed some new light.

She took a sip of Oolong Tea, a gift from Zhongxi Wu, the Chinese ambassador. It was much more effective than black coffee in keeping her alert, though it had the tendency to make her heart race. Perhaps not the best state to be in, considering all that had transpired, all that was pending, and all that threatened to happen.

Every now and then, between thoughts, concerns for Mikey would surface.

Once again, he'd already fallen asleep by the time she called the ranch. But she'd alerted Tom of Xandra and Max's arrival this morning, asking him to keep it a secret. A nice surprise wouldn't make up for her absence, but it might soften the blow. Hopefully, spending time with The General would provide her son with some happiness, if only temporary.

*I'll be with you just as soon as I can, Mikey.*

How long that would take, however, was anyone's guess.

Another sip of tea.

Through the rising vapor she saw Wade Masterson about ten yards down the colonnade, speaking to another agent. Straight out ahead, a hummingbird hovered about the rosebushes.

Interesting.

In all her time living here at the White House, she'd never noticed any hummingbirds. But in the past few weeks, she'd seen them almost daily.

As if it realized she was watching, the hummingbird buzzed past her and out of sight. Perhaps this was a good omen. Certainly a better prospect than seeing a murder of crows first thing in the morning.

Wade came over.

"Ma'am, I'm sorry to interrupt your morning tea."

"Nothing lasts forever."

"I just got word that Special Agent Parker has been discharged."

"Oh, thank God."

"They've run a full battery of tests, kept him for observation, but he's showing no evidence of infection."

She set the teacup down in its saucer. "Maybe it's not all that contagious, after all. Do they know any more about what killed everyone on that plane?"

"Latest reports show some kind of pathogen—"

A sudden sharp pain below the ear made Bradley gasp in surprise.

"Ma'am?"

In less than a second, though it seemed to happen in slow motion, Bradley felt her legs give out as the trees, the sky, and the lawn melded into a blur of color and motion.

She faintly heard Wade calling out to her as she fell to the grass.

# SIXTY SEVEN

OFFICE OF THE NATIONAL SECURITY ADVISOR
THE WEST WING
THE WHITE HOUSE
8:17 AM EST

HE HATED MORNINGS like this. So much of Evan Cromwell's attention had been focused on the FTM and al Saif threats to Tariqistan, and working with State and Defense to increase security at the American embassy in Kishwar, that the scant intelligence blips had been marginal by comparison. It troubled him deeply, though, how the attack on *Air Force One* and the puzzling deaths on Flight 1306 could have happened on his watch. All within months of the assassination attempt on the President.

I'm getting too old for this.

By far, the worst part was that he'd have to set up shop in the Situation Room until the crisis was over. In just fifteen minutes, he would have to bring his recommendations to the President regarding the preparations for a domestic terror strike.

So far, everything pointed to threats abroad, with very little in the way of confirmed and actionable intelligence regarding a domestic terrorist threat—which as of this morning, Flight 1306 would be officially deemed.

He was still waiting on a report from Homeland when, a text

message alert on his Blackberry chimed. It was from Steve Chu, one of his sharpest staff members who routinely scanned the internet and other global media for anything noteworthy.

The only thing in the body of message was an abbreviated hyperlink.

Cromwell particularly hated these kinds of texts, they usually coincided with something urgent, the news of which was always bad.

He forwarded the URL to his email, went to his inbox on his Dell desktop, then clicked the link and waited for the browser to launch. Right away he noticed the familiar IP address for a secure server that hosted videos for Al Jazeera.

As the video buffered, another text from Chu came in:

**MY CONTACT AT AL JAZEERA SENT THIS AS A COURTESY.**
**THEY'RE GOING TO AIR IT IN ONE HOUR.**
**GOOD LUCK.**

It began with a still image as the buffering icon spun. An Islamic man seated on the ground with an AK47 in his hand. His turban, which wrapped around his head such that only his eyes and mouth were exposed through the ski mask, gave the impression of a common thug, his demeanor lethally frigid.

Cromwell tugged on his collar, which seemed to have shrunk an inch.

Finally, the video began streaming.

The gun-wielding terrorist spoke in near perfect English, his accent a mixture of Middle Eastern and British.

"This message is for President Jennifer Bradley and the people of the United States. The American occupation and colonization of Tariqistan is neither welcome, lawful, nor moral. Despite your rhetoric of bringing stability, freedom, and general welfare to the people of this region, your military strikes with aerial drones have murdered countless innocent people, including our women and children.

"Because of your government's duplicitous practices, the global community knows nothing of these atrocities and crimes against humanity here in our home. Instead you prop up puppet leaders in the name of democracy, when all along you destroy our culture with Westernized infidels you place in leadership." At that moment, still holding the Kalashnikov in one hand, he used the other to remove the ski mask and reveal a face the White House had all but forgotten.

"My name is Ishmael Al Shihab..."

Cromwell clicked the pause button. "I knew it!" He slammed the desk so hard, drops of coffee leapt out onto the papers next to his mug.

Ishmael Al Shihab—of course.

He was the operative presumed killed in Operation Nighthawk three years ago. He looked different, but that was to be expected, considering he was supposed to have been taken out by the predator drone which inadvertently killed his family. Ishmael was alive somewhere in the region of Tariqistan. It was clear that he was intent on seizing power and taking control.

Cromwell resumed the playback.

"As you know, the deadline for the unilateral withdrawal of American Presence from Tariqistan, and the removal of Nasra Aamaal from power is at hand. As we have seen negligible motion towards this, nor have we received any communication of intent to comply, we can only conclude that you have not taken our threats seriously.

"For this reason, I draw your attention to National Airlines Flight 1306."

"Bastard."

"The virus planted on that flight was of a strain with a limited effect. However, if you do not meet our demands by the time the sun rises on Kishwar tomorrow, we will systematically release a much more virulent strain in multiple international locations of American interest, starting with locations abroad and eventually striking you in the heart of your homeland.

"There is no cure, there is no vaccine. The projected impact of this bio-engineered pathogen is more than twice that of the *Yersinia pestis* bacterium, better known as the Black Death, which wiped out upwards of two hundred million of the world's population in the Fourteenth Century.

"If you chose to consider this an idle threat, then I welcome you to test our resolve. You have until 6:00 AM Kishwar time to evacuate the capital palace, all government buildings, and American Military bases."

The video went dark and concluded.

"Sonofa—"

A sudden commotion outside in the hall stirred Cromwell from his tirade. Walkie-talkie chatter, hurried footfalls rushing past his office, the Vice President's.

Cromwell got up, went to the door and opened it.

Secret Service agents ran through the lobby toward the Cabinet Room and the Oval. Double-timing to follow them, he asked one of them, "What's going on?"

The agent never slowed his pace. The expression in his eyes was clear, even for the split second it took for him to turn and answer. "The President is down."

# SIXTY EIGHT

MASTERSON COVERED THE PRESIDENT with his body. He called out over his mic for assistance, pulled out his gun and did a quick visual sweep of the area.

Clear.

As far as he could see.

"Madam President," he said, checking her neck for a pulse. "Can you hear me?"

She was breathing, but her eyes were rolled back into her head. Her hand cupped the spot under her ear on her neck.

As she labored to breathe, Wade moved her hand away to find a small red welt about a quarter of an inch in diameter.

Within seconds, an entire armed team came and spread out, scanning for hostiles behind shrubs and trees.

The other half of the team scooped her up and rushed her inside.

Wade followed until they brought her to the Diplomatic Reception Room in the Executive Residence, opposite the West Wing. They immediately set her down on a chaise where Dr. Greene, a staff physician came with an assistant to meet them.

Wade pointed to the spot on her neck and said to the doctor, "She was touching it when she fell."

The doctor knelt down and started taking her vitals.

President Bradley began to convulse.

"Help keep her still," Greene said.

Wade and Agent Moran held her down just long enough for the doctor to inject something into her arm. Gradually, the seizure subsided and Bradley seemed to relax, barely conscious.

"She's running a fever," Greene said. "It spiked a lot higher, but it's down to 103.5 now."

"Is it some kind of insect bite?" Wade said, speaking of the welt on her neck.

The doctor took a closer look, then with tweezers carefully pulled out what looked like a splinter from her skin, and placed it into a clear specimen jar. "That's no insect bite."

Just then, Moran, one of the agents who had come out to assist came jogging into the resident. "We found this near where she fell."

It was wrapped in a handkerchief. He set it on the coffee table and opened the folds.

"What the hell?" Wade took a second look.

"Looks like a toy," Moran said, pointing at its wings.

The green body, the long beak-like point, and wings gave Wade the impression, but the word took a moment to form. "It's a NAV."

"A what?"

"Nano Air Vehicle, just like the ones DARPA's Defense Science Office sponsored."

"Looks like a friggin' hummingbird." Moran squinted at it. "Was that what shot the President?"

Just then, its paper-like wings slapped the table repeatedly, causing Moran to jump back. Wade however grabbed it and ripped them off.

It made a mechanical beeping sound.

Out of sheer instinct, Wade dropped it onto the table.

Its body rolled over, something tiny shot out from its belly and onto the table top.

"What in the world?" He picked up the microSD card with his fingertips, then handed it to Moran. "Download everything on it, and report back immediately."

"On it." He rushed out into the hallway.

Bradley moaned and tried to say something. Drops of perspiration dotted her brow and upper lip. Her complexion had become gray and her eyes drooped.

Doctor Greene dabbed her forehead with a damp towel. "Ma'am, how are you feeling?"

"Like Hell." She attempted sitting up, then grimaced. "Aching all over."

"You're running a fever."

"So thirsty."

Greene told his assistant to bring water and ice chips.

For the next few minutes, Wade explained what had happened. When he reached the part about the hummingbird drone that spat out the microSD chip, Moran came back into the residence, an Android tablet in his hands.

All eyes turned to him.

"Well?" Wade said.

He handed it to him. Wade noticed that the video player app was up and paused. "You need to see this."

# SIXTY NINE

MAIN STREET, DOWNTOWN
CABOTSTOWN, MD
8:14 AM

GINNY DOLAN poured a second cup of coffee for Deputy Larry McBride of the Garrett County Sheriff's Office just like she'd done for the past fifteen years. Sitting at the same stool at the same spot by the counter in Darby's, McBride took a long whiff of the black magic and smiled as he sipped it.  The only other customer present was Old Man Keller, who never did anything but read his morning paper over a tall glass of milk and a bowl of applesauce. Besides good morning, and goodbye, the only words McBride ever heard him speak were to order the same two items he always did.

"Sure gonna be quiet without you, Larry." Ginny frowned playfully at McBride.

"Somehow, I think you'll manage." Years ago, he and his wife Mary had made some smart and fortuitous investments on the advice of her nephew, a hotshot broker up in New York City, and just sold enough shares of Amazon last month for them both to enjoy an early retirement.

That is, if you could call retirement at fifty-nine early.

"You and  Mare be sure to come back and visit sometime after you move out to sunny Cali-forn-I-A, you hear?" This was his last day with his job and come Monday, he'd be on vacation, then packing up to live temporarily in Seal Beach California with his daughter's family. From that point on, they'd be looking for a house by the water to live in for the rest of their lives.

"We'll send you guys lots of photos."

Old Man Keller harrumphed. "You kids got facebook, dontcha?"

Ginny put her hand on her hip. "You kidding me? My grand-son got me one of them iPad do-dads last Christmas. I can do Face Time, Skype, Google Hangouts..."

"Whoa," Larry said, hands up in surrender. "The point of re-tirement is to relax. Computers, cell phones, tablets, and all that stuff? They just make me slave all day trying to figure them out. Shoot, if I wanna talk, I just pick up this old fashioned gadget called the telephone. Ever heard of those?"

She swatted him playfully with her dish towel. "We're all gon-na miss you, Larry."

He set his mug down taking care not to spill any of the coffee. As he did, he noticed through the large glass window a crowd forming across the street looking up at something. In a town with a population of five hundred and seventeen, six people on a side-walk constituted a crowd.

He set a twenty on the counter and said, "Thanks for every-thing, Ginny. Keep the change."

Before she could thank him, he was already out the door, pull-ing his hat down over his head and walking over to the people gathered. They were talking and pointing up into the air. As he arrived, even more people had come out of the various stores and out of their stopped cars to gawk.

"All right folks, what's going on?" McBride said.

Lisa Winters, holding her mother's hand turned around with a big smile on her face. "It's a helicopter!"

"Where? I don't see anything." Of course, he was expecting to hear the air-beating percussion of its rotors, even if it was far away.

"It's right there, Larry." Jim Bains turned around and pointed up the street.

Rounding the corner in front of the post office, a small red and white vehicle whirred into view. It was too large to be a remote control toy, but too small—about five or six feet long—to be a manned aircraft. Its cheerful running lights flashed as it hovered about ten feet from the ground.

"I bet it's got a camera. You know, for some kind of reality TV show," Jim said. "Hey, y'all! Wave!"

There were about thirty people now gathered in the street jumping up and down, cheering and waving at the approaching helicopter. They whooped, and danced, trying to make a scene for the camera.

But something wasn't right.

McBride would have been informed if there was going to be a filming on Main Street today. There would at least have been a memo, if not a briefing and plan for security and crowd control.

He unclipped the walkie-talkie from his shoulder and called in to the office.

The helicopter stopped to hover right above them.

The crowd let out a jubilant cheer.

"This is Deputy McBride," he said into the mic. "We got anything on the books for a filming on Main Street today?"

"A what?"

As he explained, a subtle hissing sound came from the helicopter. McBride looked and saw a light mist spraying from a nozzle mounted to the bottom of the helicopter. A tube ran from it and connected to a container mounted onto the back of the vehicle. Sort of like a crop duster.

But the fragrance it sprayed was too sweet to be a pesticide.

"Mmm, smells like roses," little Lisa said to her mother. "So pretty."

Everyone around took a deep breath and had a similar reaction. "Maybe it's a perfume commercial," one man said.

McBride didn't care for it though. Something felt really wrong about this.

But he never got a chance to voice his concerns.

Within seconds, the screaming began.

# SEVENTY

DIPLOMATIC RECEPTION ROOM
EXECUTIVE RESIDENCE
THE WHITE HOUSE
8:16 AM EST

THE ROOM WAS STILL SPINNING. Except for Wade's report, Jennifer Bradley couldn't tell how long she'd been out. All she knew was that some kind of tiny remote controlled drone had injected her with something that was responsible for her present feverish state.

Every nerve ending in her body throbbed with pain. Every heart beat brought excruciating pressure behind her eyes. Every few minutes she went between burning up from the inside out, to uncontrollable trembling from chills.

The last cogent thought she recalled having was how strange it was that Agent Parker had been discharged with a clean bill of health, after being exposed.

Now, Wade Masterson held the screen of a tablet before her, a video extracted from the microSD card courtesy of the humming-bird drone that shot her.

Wade held his finger over the triangular play button. "Ready, Ma'am?"

She nodded.

He pressed play and the video began.

A man with a dark complexion was on the screen.

Though Bradley didn't recognize the face, there was something familiar about him. And then he spoke.

"Hello, Jennifer," he started, his demeanor chilling. "Though we've never met, I feel like we've known each other for years. In fact, we do. I realize that I don't look much like my pictures, and that's thanks to the cosmetic surgeon who rebuilt all this." He pointed and drew an invisible circled around his face. "But trust me. You know me. I am Ishmael Al Shihab."

During the pause, the man on the screen smiled.

Bradley blinked rapidly.

A bitter reflux pushed upwards.

*Ishmael?*

"I know…you're skeptical. After all, I'm supposed to be dead, aren't I? But no, in typical American arrogance and incompetence, you killed everyone, including my wife and my son. Everyone…but me. And for what?" Anger threatened to throw him off balance. Regaining his composure, he continued. "Well. Let's settle that matter later, shall we? For now, as a courtesy you never bothered to show me, I am here to inform you of a few important facts before I contact you again. First, you have been injected with a variant of the virus that killed the passengers on Flight 1306. I've spared you all the madness and violence that precedes the painful hemorrhagic death, not because you deserve any better, I just have a different plan for you. I mean for you to live your last hours fully coherent so you may witness all that is to come.

"For now, all you need to know is this: You have already murdered me along with my family three years ago. Since then, I have existed for only one thing: Retribution.

"To give you an idea of what you can expect in the next several hours, I want you to take a good look at what you forfeited when you turned your back on me. Had you kept your faith in me, I would have turned Haashir over to the United States, as well as the stockpile of chemical and biological weapons which Saddam

Hussein had given him to hide. I held in my fist Haashir's life, and the very WMDs you sought to recover."

His voiceover continued while the screen switched over to footage of a crowded rural food market. They were fighting, clawing, biting, and beating each other so viciously, it looked like something straight out of a zombie movie.

"These tribal members living in the outskirts of Tariqistan all died within hours of exposure. This is what happened to the passengers on Flight 1306 as well. The particular strain used in these cases are not contagious after the initial infection. However, the strain that I will release in the United States is exponentially more virulent, since you have not complied with the demands for unilateral withdrawal from Tariqistan.

"There is nothing you can do now. Every city will soon be laid waste by a pestilence of biblical proportion. And you, Madam President will have the death of a nation's population as your enduring legacy. As for me? I am the mere specter of a man. If President Aamaal's intelligence agents find me before the outbreak, they will only find what you created. A lifeless corpse, but one whose only remaining purpose has already been fulfilled...Oh, but we shall speak again...soon."

The video ended frozen on a frame of Ishmael's face smiling with satisfaction.

With barely enough strength to lift her head, Bradley realized that her Chief of Staff Mitch Donovan had been there the whole time—just the person she needed to see.

"Mitch, get Kate on the line with Aamaal..." Kathryn Landers, the Secretary of State had been in the loop for just about every meeting in the Situation Room regarding the FTM and Al Saif's threats. But it would surely shock her to know that Ishmael—if that really was him—was alive and behind all this.

"She's already been alerted."

"Get the joint chiefs, Sec Def..."

"They're all in the Sit Room now."

"And inform the Vice President that he may need to..." like an icepick into the eyes, an acute ache bore into her head. Bradley could barely speak because of the sudden onslaught and chills. "Never mind...not yet..." Though it was probably most prudent, she was not quite ready to enact Article II, Section 1 of the Constitution. She was still able to discharge the powers and duties of her office.

Continuing to delegate, Bradley struggled to stay alert.

While speaking with Donovan, Wade Masterson stepped aside and spoke through his two-way. Within moments, he strode over with purpose and said, "Ma'am, White House bio hazard detectors have gone off."

She shut her eyes and slumped back, fending off the overwhelming fever and stress from the ever-mounting crises. "Dear God."

"Several staff members have been struck like you have. We're not certain of how much exposure or how contagious, but we can't risk spreading the virus."

"What's the protocol?"

"We're going to have to quarantine and lock down the White House."

# SEVENTY ONE

MAIN STREET, DOWNTOWN
CABOTSTOWN, MD
8:18 AM

THE FIRST SCREAM had been one of terror. Deputy McBride's mic dropped from his hand and dangled from his shoulder as he swung around. Mrs. Winters, Lisa's mother stood over Jim Bains, who had fallen on the ground.

"He needs help!"

McBride rushed over to find him sprawled on the pavement, convulsing and holding his hands over his face. "Jim, what's the matter?"

Nothing but a gurgling sound and a strained groan.

Jim reached up, his hand blackened with what looked like bruises.

McBride took the hand.

He regretted it instantly.

As soon as Jim established a grip, blood burst through his skin all over his hand. His nails dug into McBride's hand ripping through his flesh.

McBride pulled his hand away, but it was already torn badly, a searing pain spreading across it. "You hang in there, Jim. I'm calling for an ambulance."

All around him, people were either dropping to the ground, or flailing wildly. But he couldn't quite focus on what was happening because the burning pain now coursed through his arm, into his chest, and then began radiating to his extremities.

Jim eyes were now bleeding. Dark red blood oozed from his ears. His teeth were stained in red as he snarled. Then something truly unexpected happened.

It was as if he'd been injected with a quart of adrenaline.

Jim lunged upwards, grabbed McBride by the neck and wrestled him to the concrete. "Damned...terrorist!" In a crazed frenzy, he clawed at McBride's face, his eyes, as if he could rip the flesh off his bones.

"What? Jim, what are you doing!" McBride reached for his gun.

But Jim was too fierce and quick. He grabbed McBride's right hand and bit into it.

The gun fell to the ground.

Before the pain and the snap of bones registered, McBride watched in horror as this savage creature with whom he used to play poker every Friday night spat his severed fingers from its mouth.

With inhuman strength, the shell of Jim Bains pinned him down, his eyes feral, and bared his teeth, grotesquely adorned with blood and flesh.

McBride cried out for help, only to find bodies strewn across the street, blood running from every one of them like crushed tomatoes. Those still on their feet were brutally attacking each other like sharks in a feeding frenzy.

He squinted as he heard the sound of a gun chambering a round.

When McBride opened his eyes, the muzzle of his own firearm stared him in the face.

"Jim...please..."

In a flash, everything went red, then black.

# SEVENTY TWO

BRADLEY RANCH
CABOTSTOWN, MD
9:14 AM

RUNNING THROUGH THE TALL GRASS with Max, Mikey laughed and leapt about. Max gave chase, and then became the chased in an energetic romp through the fields just outside the ranch house.

With her Nikon, Xandra made some delightful pictures of the two, with just the right light spilling through the tree branches and tall grass as the backdrop. The boy and dog even stopped long enough for her to capture a pensive moment of the two of them looking over the placid waters of the lake.

"I haven't seen him this happy since…" Tom Bradley walked up to Xandra and stood at her side. "It's amazing what a dog can do."

"Max is really special," Xandra said, letting the camera hang on its strap and smiling at the two besties as the boy turned around and waved. "Glad they struck up a friendship."

"Couldn't have come at a better time," Tom said, folding his arms. "He's been having a hard time."

"Tough being the son of the President. I can imagine."

"It's not just that. He's really been struggling since his father died. Hell, Ben was my son, and *I* still have trouble dealing with it. An old man like me is supposed to have his son bury him, not the other way around. And a boy like Mikey? Well, he shouldn't have to bury his daddy till he's a much older man himself, you know?"

"Come on, Max!" Mikey said in the distance. "Race you to the lake!"

Just then, Agent Kelly Davis came over with concern etched into her brow. She gave Tom a puzzled look. "Sir, I'll go with them."

"Ah, they'll be fine."

"All the same, Sir, the closest hospital's twenty miles away, and down that unmarked dirt path, it'd take more than an hour to get to the main road. I'd be remiss."

"Go on, then." He shook his head as she radioed the other agent and went after them. After a few seconds, the boy, the dog, and the Secret Service agent vanished behind the tall grass.

Tom shook his head. "A boy comes out here to get away from all that structure and protocol. But that's just the thing about being a member of the First Family, isn't it? The constant watch, the constant protection. I don't blame him for being unhappy."

"He's a great kid," Xandra said, empathy welling up. "I don't think I'd handle it so well." She wasn't sure what the vision of Max and Mikey had meant, but if it had meant nothing more than bringing the boy a couple of days of joy, that was more than good enough. "I'm just glad we could help."

"You have. More than you know."

Xandra picked up her camera again and did a slow three-sixty, proactively seeking potential shots: the Ranch house, the sunlit field, the driveway with two dark Secret Service SUVs parked, Special Agent Hayes scanning the area with a pair of binoculars, and the other agents standing by the cars they were in charge of driving—nothing all that interesting.

The sound of Mikey's disappointed voice approached. "Aw man! That stinks!"

"I'm sorry, but we've got to hurry," Agent Davis said holding his hand and double timing back. As she, Mikey and Max returned, she lifted her dark sunglasses and glanced at her watch. She put her finger in her ear and spoke into her cell phone. It must have had a signal booster, or operated on a special frequency, as Xandra's had only one bar of signal strength.

"Are you absolutely certain?" Davis said. "Right...all right, I'll confirm with Hayes."

"Problem?" Tom said.

"I'm afraid so," Davis said, her demeanor urgent. "We need you to be ready to leave in two minutes."

"I trust you'll explain as we go?"

Davis nodded and started speaking to Hayes on her two-way.

"We're leaving?" Mikey said, with a sigh. "But..."

Tom crouched down to meet the boy's eyes. "If Agent Davis says we have to go, it's got to be important. Don't worry, kiddo," he mussed his hair, "I'll make sure you get a nice, big Chocolate milkshake out of this."

He cast his gaze to the ground. "Oh, all right." Just as quickly, his countenance lit up and he grabbed Xandra's hand excitedly. "Max and Xandi are coming too, right?"

"We go where you go," Xandra said.

"Okay then!"

Tom patted the boy on the back. "Go in and get your stuff, I'll be right there."

Mikey dashed into the house.

Tom followed him, turned back and mouthed "thank you" to Xandra and went inside the house.

"What's going on, Kelly?" Xandra took Max's lead, a prickling tingle running through her fingertips.

"We've got to get out of Cabotstown, immediately." At a brisk pace, Davis started for the driveway where Agent Hayes was already prepping his car.

Xandra fell in behind her with Max in tow. "What's going on?"

"There's no time. Get in the lead car with the Bradleys. I'll explain as we drive."

# SEVENTY THREE

THE COLD PROFESSIONALISM of the Secret Service never ceased to impress her. By the time Xandra reached the pair of black Chevy Suburbans, the entire team was ready to roll.

"I've got some belongings and equipment back inside that—"

Davis shook her head. "We'll come back for it. Please, Ms. Carrick, get inside."

Xandra opened the door to the rear bench for Max who was pacing around the second car which Agent Hayes had just boarded with the rest of the Protective Detail. "Come on, boy. Time to go."

He jogged over, but kept staring back at the second Suburban, "Max?"

He looked into the door which Xandra held open, looked back, and whined softly.

"It's okay, boy. Look! Mikey's in here." She tapped on the back of Mikey's seat and he turned around.

"Come here, Boy," Mikey said, patting the upholstery. "Let's go."

But Max leaned toward the second SUV, pulling slightly on the lead.

Davis finished typing something on her phone and came over. "I'm sorry, but we really have to go."

With a slightly firmer pull, Xandra managed to get Max into the back seat. "Good boy." She climbed in and sat with him, but he kept staring out the rear window.

Davis climbed into the front passenger seat, and shut the door. "Let's go."

The Chevy rolled forward.

"Wait!" Mikey shouted.

The driver turned to Davis, but she shook her head indicating that he should keep driving. She turned around. "What is it, Michael?"

"Your cell phone, you dropped it back there."

"Really?" She checked herself but couldn't find it. "It's okay, I still have the radio to communicate with Agent Hayes." She pointed at her ear piece. "We have to hurry."

Thomas Bradley handed Mikey his iPhone, which he gladly took and became engrossed in a game. Tom then leaned forward and tapped Davis on her wrist. "I assume this is a matter of life and death?"

That caught Xandra's attention. She too leaned forward.

Davis lowered her tone almost to a whisper. "I didn't want to make him anxious," she said, pointing her chin to Mikey. "But there's been an outbreak in town." She looked to Xandra. "It's reported to be the same one as on Flight 1306."

"Outbreak?"

"How do they know?" Xandra said.

Trying to keep the details from Tom and the boy, Davis said, "Same manifestations. We were just alerted and given the order to evacuate to a secure location where we'll be airlifted away from Cabotstown, and any risk of exposure."

Max let out a bark, followed by a low-pitched growl. He kept staring at Agent Hayes' Suburban which was tailing their vehicle about fifteen feet back.

Within the confines of the vehicle, it was as loud as it was alarming.

"Quiet, Max." Xandra gave his lead a light tug, then turned back to Davis. "How bad?"

"What about that Flight?" Tom said, "What happened, was it in the news?"

"No, Sir," Davis said, then turned to Xandra. "CDC still isn't sure what to make of it."

The thought of the dead passengers on the plane, the violent deaths they'd suffered, returned. But then, Xandra remembered the clearest vision she'd seen in the darkroom—Max and Mikey. "I thought he was back in Tariqistan and targeting Kishwar."

Davis gave her a puzzled look. "Who?"

Xandra had almost slipped—shouldn't have let on that she knew about Al Shihab (Judas). Tempest had been strict regarding the secrecy over what they had spoken of. "Oh, never mind. I'm confusing names. I was thinking about that other person...what was his name? Haashir?"

"I don't know what you're talking about. But my primary objective right now is to get you to the dropoff."

The car sped down the marginally paved road kicking up clouds of copper dust. Davis glanced out the rear window, around the side windows, and to the front.

"Ms. Davis," Tom said, with a hint of irritation. "Why are we going off road? This doesn't take us anywhere. You need to tell me exactly what's going on before—"

A thunderous detonation severed his words.

It rocked the entire Suburban.

Mikey let out a startled shout.

Max kept barking urgently at the rear window.

Pushing him aside, Xandra saw what had happened.

On the dirt road, a huge explosion had rolled Agent Hayes' SUV over, roaring flames and black smoke spewing from the windows and undercarriage.

# SEVENTY FOUR

PRESIDENTIAL EMERGENCY OPERATIONS CENTER
(PEOC)
THE WHITE HOUSE - EAST WING
9:30 AM EST

SHE INSISTED ON BEING KEPT IN THE PEOC, despite Dr. Greene's recommendation otherwise. If she was going to die, Jennifer Bradley would spend her last coherent moments doing all she could to stop Ishmael Al Shihab.

Your sin will find you out.

She'd read that somewhere when thumbing through Ben's Bible weeks after he passed on. Whatever the context, the essence of that text was coming true today. But it was the people of Tari-qistan, the American citizens stationed and working there that were paying for her mistakes, her sins.

Bradley had her hospital style bed propped up so she could communicate with the Situation Room via videoconference equipment set up behind the transparent sheets of the isolation tent. The medical crew monitoring and attending wore the same kind of hazmat suits used by the CDC personnel tasked with the gruesome job of collecting the bodies from Flight 1306.

One of the uniformed Secret Service security agents had al-ready died, a grounds keeper, and an intern were in critical condition. Bradley had asked for regular updates with the CDC regarding their analysis of the virus and a possible cure.

Ishmael had been telling the truth. Her symptoms did not progress nearly as rapidly as the other staff members who'd been infected. But since it was yet to be determined if any of them were contagious, no one under White House quarantine was permitted to leave.

All they knew was that once infected, nothing could stop, much less slow the effects of hemorrhagic fever, followed by delusional paranoia and savage violence. For that reason, she had ordered that she be confined to a room which could be locked from the outside if she began exhibiting such symptoms.

The IV in her arm was attached not only to a saline drip for the dehydration from which she was now suffering, but a sedative that could put down a horse, as well.

"Jenna," Vice President Philip Marsden said over the video conference in the Situation Room. Just about everyone she was supposed to have been with was there, quarantined, though not showing signs of infection. "How're you holding up?"

"Please convey my apologies to Gwen. I'm afraid you're going to miss your anniversary dinner tonight."

Marsden gave her an encouraging smile. "She told me that if I didn't stop this outbreak, she'd kill me herself."

"Doug," she said, addressing the director of the CIA, "Anything on Ishmael?"

"Running all of Tariqistan through a strainer. We're looking into a promising lead."

"Is the intel good?"

"Yes. If that really was him on the video, we'll find him. Nothing new has happened in Kishwar...yet."

Her neck was too sore and stiff even to nod. "Curious." The National Security Advisor sat near the front of the long table, his head in his hand. "Evan, are you all right?"

"Just a headache," Cromwell said, "Stress induced, I'm sure."

"Mitch?" She searched for her chief of staff at the table. It could have been the effects of her infection but the video conference image looked unusually grainy.

"Ma'am."

"If there's even one of you there who might not have been exposed…"

General Mark Fuller, chairman of the joint chiefs spoke up. "Ma'am, with all due respect, we've all put aside personal safety to remain focused on the crisis at hand. We're with you until we drop. Now, we've mobilized all resources in Tariqistan in preparation for a biological terror strike. Domestically, we're going to need to activate the reserves, and every possible law enforcement agency."

"NTAS has bumped the alert from elevated to imminent," Cromwell added. "DHS made the announcement via all channels and all agencies have been alerted."

"General," Bradley said, trying to stay alert. "How confident are you that we can contain a domestic outbreak?"

"We've got multiple contingency plans, however—"

Bradley felt herself slipping out of consciousness when Cromwell interrupted. "I'm sorry General, Ma'am—I've just gotten word of a local outbreak."

That jarred her back to the video conference. "Local? Where?"

"The report is from the Garrett County Commissioner's Office. They've declared a state of emergency. Local authorities reporting thirty dead, all exhibiting symptoms identical to those on National Airlines Flight 1306. And their hospital's filling up."

"Where in Garrett?"

The hesitation couldn't have been longer than a second, but it felt like an eternity.

"Jenna, it's Cabotstown," Evan said, solemnly.

"Oh my God." Whatever blood was still remaining in her face drained away. She reached over to activate the intercom that connected to the speaker outside her room. "Wade!"

# SEVENTY FIVE

9:33 AM

BRAKES SCREECHING, the Suburban stopped abruptly by a tree. Xandra could barely hear Agent Kelly Davis over the din of Max's barking, and all the simultaneous chatter.

"Everyone out of the car!" Davis shouted.

As soon as Xandra stepped out, another blast from Hayes's SUV rocked the ground beneath her. A wave of heat hit her square in the face forcing her to shut her eyes and shield herself. Max was pulling on his lead and barking frantically.

"Take cover, behind this tree!" Davis said, directing everyone away from the conflagration that raged behind them.

Black smoke filled the air around them stinging Xandra's eyes and wringing painful tears out of them. She made the mistake of inhaling while running to the tree where Davis stood. She couldn't control the coughing.

As soon as she came to the tree where the rest of them were standing, she fell on its trunk to steady herself.

"Stay here," Davis said, scanning the area with her gun ready.

Mikey was hiding in Tom's arms, his terrified cries muffled.

"We have to help them!" Xandra said.

"I said stay here!"

Cooper, the agent who had been sitting in the driver's seat

next to Davis came around. He opened his mouth to speak and before a word came out, Davis pointed her gun into the center of his chest and fired two quick shots.

Xandra flinched, the shock of it cutting off any breath or sound.

Cooper dropped to the ground.

Tom gripped Mikey and turned so that his back shielded him. "What the hell!"

Davis spun around and aimed the gun at both of them. "Don't move! You're going to do exactly as I say, is that clear?"

Xandra didn't realize until it was too late—she'd let go of Max's lead.

Growling and baring his fangs, the Belgian Malinois charged at Davis.

His hind legs crouched, he launched himself at her, going for the throat.

"Max, no!"

Davis turned away.

Fired another shot.

Max let out a pained whine, fell to the ground, even as Davis stumbled back landing on her rear.

"Max!" Mikey cried out.

Next to Agent Cooper's body, Max lay on the dirt, his chest rising and falling in tiny breaths.

Xandra tried to go over to him, but Davis got up and pointed the gun at her. "You should've left him home."

Anger, outrage, and anguish raged within Xandra. She had just watched Cooper get gunned down before her eyes, and now she couldn't do anything but watch Max die a slow and painful death.

"Dammit, Kelly!" Tom said. "What are you doing?"

"Bring the boy to me," she said with cold detachment, though her gun shook in her grip.

"Are you insane?" Tom pushed Mikey behind him and stood tall, his fists clenched. "Do you have any idea—?"

She fired another shot, this one hitting Tom in the stomach.

He grunted, dropped to his knees, then fell into a fetal position holding his belly as blood oozed out.

Mikey stood there, his mouth silently agape. Eyes equally wide, his entire body trembled as Davis stepped over to him. Part of the way there, Davis turned and put the muzzle of her gun right in Xandra's face, then went over to where Tom was. With both hands on the gun she waved him over deeper into the trees. "Move."

"Either of you so much as breathe..." she aimed the gun straight at Mikey.

He wasn't capable of resisting when Davis grabbed him by the arm, and yanked him over. Now, with the gun pointed at his head, she reached into her pocket, and swore when it came out empty.

"Carrick," she tilted her head to the open driver's side door of the Suburban. "Get me the keys."

The ostinato of Xandra's pulse would not relent. It kept pounding like the tympani in a Shostakovich symphony. But she refused to let her anxiety show. "Get it yourself!"

She cocked the hammer of her gun and pressed it into the side of Mikey's head. "Let's try that again...Get..me...the KEYS!"

Xandra was actually trying to buy some time. Her hand felt as if she'd just struck her funny bone, the tingling so numbing the entire side of her hands were cold.

Then, in her mind's eye, she saw it.

Lying on the floor of the car, right under the driver's seat.

Cooper's gun, perhaps a spare, strapped into a velcro/ballasitic pouch. Apparently Davis had either forgotten about it, or never knew.

"All right," Xandra said, moving slowly to the Suburban. "Just don't do anything rash, okay?"

"I'll issue the warnings and orders, all right?" Davis came around behind her with her left arm wrapped around Mikey's neck, and right hand pressing her gun into the back of Xandra's head. "Keep your hands where I can see them."

Davis had not been privy to Xandra's secret work with Wade

Masterson, where she'd gotten enough training to be more than just a victim at gunpoint. So Xandra went along, and put her hands up where they could be seen.

Xandra got to the open door and slowly turned her head back to face her. "What did they promise you? Money?"

Davis' expression twisted in disgust, she almost seemed insulted. "You think I'd sell out my family, the President and family I'm sworn to protect for money?"

"Everyone has their price."

Davis lowered the gun slightly so she could look her in the eye. "I'm doing this so my family will live! I saw what that virus could do months ago. He promised me access to the vaccine and antivirus." The gun came right back up to the center of Xandra's forehead.

Xandra almost gasped. "Who?"

"Doesn't matter, I had no choice!"

"You *always* have a choice," Tom said, straining.

"Shut up, you self-righteous ass!" Davis shouted over her shoulder. "You have no idea what you're talking about, or what's coming."

"Hey, you can't talk to my grandpa like that!" Mikey said, courage overtaking his nerves.

Davis ignored them both. To Xandra: "Before you judge me, ask yourself what you'd do if you were in my shoes. He found me, threatened my husband and kids. This is their only chance of survival when..."

"When what?"

Davis' expression turned glacial again. She glanced down at the watch on her wrist, then back to Xandra. "Get me those keys, now."

"Right." She leaned in, rooted around under the seat while feigning a search for the keys. Sure enough, the Velcro pouch was there. Without looking down, she spoke loudly to mask the ripping sound of the flap opening. "I think he might have dropped them!"

"Watch it..."

She wrapped her hand around the familiar grip of a Sig Sauer P229. Must have been an old spare—and slowly straightened up. "Found them!"

She wrapped her finger around the trigger and began her slow turn.

# SEVENTY SIX

PRESIDENTIAL EMERGENCY OPERATIONS CENTER
(PEOC)
THE WHITE HOUSE - EAST WING
9:32 AM EST

THE URGENT CALL from President Bradley had a much greater effect than Wade Masterson could have imagined. In all his time working the detail, he'd never seen her so frail, and yet so focused.

"I'm here, Ma'am."

She was sitting up in her bed, IV's in her arm, tubes in her nose. "We need to get Mikey and Thomas Bradley away from the ranch. They're just a few miles from Cabotstown."

"I've already contacted Agents Davis and Cooper, they're the agents assigned to that detail." He pulled out his mobile phone.

"It's the same virus on that plane, Wade. Dozens have already been infected and died on the streets downtown."

"We'll get them out of there," Wade said as he waited for the call to connect with Agent Cooper's phone.

It rolled over to voicemail.

So did Davis's.

"What's going on?" Bradley asked, concern creasing her brow. She tried to get up, but winced in pain, holding her knee, and returned to a lying down position.

"We've lost contact with every agent on duty out there. No one's responding, not even on the sat phones."

"Get a chopper out there. I don't care if we have to have you fly in hazmat suits, you need to find them!"

Wade nodded to the agents standing on either side of the sealed doorway. "I'll be in contact. Keep an eye on POTUS and have emergency medical personnel ready."

"Yes, Sir," Special Agent Duncan said.

"Ma'am, I'm going out there and will personally see to their return." He pressed a hand against the Plexiglas barrier and pointed to the handset by her bed. "I'll report back to you on that phone."

"Thank you."


FIVE MINUTES LATER, Wade was sitting next to the pilot of a Sikorsky S-92 SAR (Search and Rescue) helicopter flying to the hills of Western Maryland.

All of the agents' cellphones' GPS locators placed them right there on the ranch, which of course would be the first stop. Thankfully, there was an open field out back which would make an acceptable landing zone.

But what if they weren't there?

What if they didn't know about the outbreak in Cabotstown and were heading toward the epicenter?

The GPS transponders on both of the Secret Service vehicles didn't appear to be transmitting either.

"Keep a visual as we get close to Garrett County," Wade said to one of the two agents in the back of the chopper. But because the Bradley Ranch was situated in a region with such dense forestry, that would be challenging unless they happened to be out in the open, or driving on one of the few paved roads that led to town.

"Needle in a damned haystack," he muttered, trying Agent

Davis' number again.

"What was that?" the pilot said, increasing the aircraft's speed noticeably.

"Never mind."

What he needed now was Xandra's help. A vision, a clue, anything that could help locate them before it was too late.

But in that "haystack," she was one of those needles.

# SEVENTY SEVEN

9:33 AM

ONE SHOT, ONE KILL.

That's what Wade had drilled into her every time they'd trained at the firing range at Rowley. Xandra had gotten fairly confident in hitting those targets, but this was entirely different. Kelly Davis was desperate and had Mikey at gunpoint. If Xandra somehow missed that one shot, it could end really badly.

Did she actually have the nerve to do it?

"Show me the keys!" Davis said.

Xandra drew a breath.

Held it.

Then spun around with the Sig Sauer, pointed it straight at Davis' face...

*Where's Mikey?* She saw the top of his head just above the agent's arm.

...then squeezed the trigger.

Davis shoved Mikey aside and ducked just before Xandra fired off the round. Because she'd hesitated, Davis had a chance to roll out of the way and started firing back.

Drawing fire away from the boy and his injured grandfather, Xandra leaped behind the front of the car and crouched low. A quick glance beneath the undercarriage revealed that Davis was coming around the back and toward the passenger side.

With only a second or two to do it, Xandra aimed the gun, leading her target. Just as it reached the mark, she squeezed off one round, hitting Davis in the ankle.

Davis let out a grunt and fell forward.

Xandra dashed over to find the agent rolled over on her side, holding her bleeding ankle and writhing in pain.

Davis heard her arrive.

Her arm stiffened as she tried to point her weapon at Xandra.

But Xandra stomped her foot down pinning her wrist and the gun into the dust.

Letting out a pained cry, Davis released her grip and dropped her weapon.

Never lifting her foot, Xandra kept her Sig pointed at Davis' head and knelt down. She swept the turncoat agent's gun aside and leaned on her trachea with her elbow. "You of all people know how easy it is for me to crush your windpipe right now."

Davis' body went soft.

"You don't understand." Tears streamed down her face and her shoulders made tiny tremors as she wept. "My kids...they're just toddlers."

"I'm sure they'd be really proud of you," Xandra said, not buying it. With great haste, she ran her hand over Davis' body and found a case with a pair of handcuffs strapped to her belt. Xandra popped open the case, took the cuffs, and slipped them into her jacket's pocket.

In one quick sequence of moves, Xandra grabbed Davis' arm, stood and pulled her up, and forcefully twisted her arm behind her back as she shoved her face-first against the Suburban's window.

She grimaced as she raised her injured ankle off the ground, while using her shoulder to steady herself against the vehicle.

"Here's the deal," Xandra said. "I'm going to cuff you, then call for medical assistance for Mr. Bradley back there. While we wait for them, you and I are going to have a talk." She pressed the gun into the base of her skull. "Heart-to-heart."

Davis sniffed wetly and nodded. "Okay."

As Xandra reached with one hand into her pocket to get the handcuffs, Davis began sobbing and losing her balance, which must have been difficult to maintain with a gunshot wound to one foot, and standing on the other.

Xandra tried to steady her but missed.

Knees locked, Davis let out a yelp and fell hard to the ground on her back. She lay there shaking her head from side to side, tears streaming from her eyes, and blubbering apologies to Joey and Krista. "I'm sorry...Mommy's so sorry..."

"Oh for heaven's sake!" Xandra said. "Get up!"

She didn't seem to hear.

Xandra kept the Sig Sauer aimed at her and bent down to grab her arm.

Without warning, Davis grabbed her wrist and twisted so hard Xandra dropped the gun. The agent swung a knee into Xandra's gut and with a heavy blow, drove the wind out of her. In less than the time it took for Xandra to blink and open her eyes, Davis was now on top of her, a knife she'd been hiding in her grip.

Davis drove the point of the blade straight at Xandra's throat.

But Xandra simultaneously caught her forearm, and kicked the agent's wounded ankle, the shattered bones crunching under the heel of her shoe.

Mikey was shouting in the background.

Still wrestling for control of the knife, Davis and Xandra rolled around in the dirt. A swift strike at Xandra's jaw nearly made contact, but she moved away just in time. When she found another opportunity, she dug the point of her shoe into the same wound in Davis' ankle.

Though she screamed in pain, Davis didn't let go of the knife.

Neither did Xandra.

With one final thrust, Davis launched all of her weight down onto Xandra.

Rather than push back, however, Xandra pulled her attacker's knife plunging arm down, using her own momentum and rolled Davis over, throwing her down onto her own blade.

Davis let out an abrupt gasp, and coughed.

All at once the struggle ended.

Xandra turned Kelly Davis over to find the handle of her knife protruding from her chest, her eyes frozen open and red. Before she removed her hand from Davis' which still clutched the weapon, an image flashed before her.

*Hanging on a wood panel*

*A rusted plaque*

*An iconic symbol: An Eagle etched over a large capital B*

"Xandi!" Mikey's voice brought her back to the moment. Leaving Davis' expired form on the ground, she ran over to the boy who was kneeling by his grandfather.

"I think he's dying!"

# SEVENTY EIGHT

PRESIDENTIAL EMERGENCY OPERATIONS CENTER
(PEOC)
THE WHITE HOUSE - EAST WING
9:48 AM EST

PERHAPS IT WAS BETTER TO DIE. The *seppuku*-like pain impaled Jennifer Bradley's innards, an experience far worse than any she'd ever experienced. Ironically, *seppuku, or harikari* was a practice that samurai warriors employed to avoid falling into enemy hands, mitigate disgrace, and avoid possible torture.

Death would be preferable to the protracted torment of this virus Ishmael Al Shihab had customized just for her. But if she succumbed, how could she ensure Mikey's safety, and that of the nation?

*Come on, Jenna. Fight it!*

She'd faded in and out of consciousness, awakened by the agent on duty when a call came from the Sit Room.

More reports of outbreaks were coming in from other small towns across the country. Cromwell had tried to spare her the ugly details, but she insisted on knowing. In the states of Louisiana, Georgia, Oregon, and New Hampshire, local authorities were dealing with mass hysteria as people were viciously attacking each other like rabid animals. Those who weren't already dead, were dying or incapacitated.

Based on the collected data, CDC had determined it to be an airborne pathogen. They were still trying to devise a safe means of entering the infected areas to investigate its initial method of delivery.

Al Shihab was now attacking on both fronts: In Tariqistan, and by some remote means of deployment, here in the United States. Every possible agency was on this like ants on a watermelon rind, but that bastard had somehow managed to elude them.

Amidst the countless thoughts and concerns, if Jenna were to simply follow her heart, she would be out there on that helicopter with Wade Masterson looking for her son and father in law. But even if she could tear herself from this prison, she was too weak physically.

Seemed like it had all been going on for hours, but a quick check at the clock revealed that less than half an hour had actually passed. In that time, she'd declared a national state of emergency. Citizens were ordered to remain in their homes and keep away from public places.

Managing the information flow proved difficult because of social media. A teenager from Cabotstown posted a short video clip on Instagram of the carnage on Main Street which had gone viral. Within minutes, the NSA had it taken offline. But when other such videos went up, as well as the public outcry that ensued from their shutting down all video streaming social network sites, Bradley knew The White House had to issue a statement.

Unfortunately, with her periodic violent blood-filled coughing fits, she was in no condition to appear before the nation. As much as they needed to see her face at this time, she would have to issue a statement through Phil Marsden.

The video conference alert chimed.

Bradley sat up and clicked the remote to activate the screen before her bed.

"General Fuller, talk to me."

"Ma'am we've got a new development," The Joint Chiefs

Chairman stood before the camera beside CIA director Douglas Kendall. "With the cooperation of Al Jazeera's IT department, we've determined the origination of the videos made by Ishmael Al Shihab."

"Where is he?"

"Nemidan," Kendall said.

Bradley squinted, an ache in her neck spread through her head to a spot just behind her eyes. "Nemidan? Sounds familiar."

"A village about twenty miles outside of Kishwar," General Fuller said, "It's been abandoned since we kicked Haashir to the curb."

"Recommendations?"

"Direct Action, Ma'am. We've got Force Recon Marines from 1st FORECON Company ready to deploy." These were the elite Special Operations Marines that worked with the CIA in Black Operations, of which the general public knew little to nothing. In some ways they were like the Seal Team 6, minus all the spectacle and glamour.

Kendall stepped forward. "Madam President, we're going to get him."

"Are your sources reliable?"

He nodded gravely. "Rock solid."

She drew a raspy breath and began coughing. Turning from the camera, she cringed at the blood in the tissue. When she felt able to speak again, she returned to the video conference. "General, do what you can to bring Ishmael in alive. But the priority of the mission is to prevent the attacks in Tariqistan and here in the States. You do whatever it takes."

"Understood, Ma'am."

"All right," Bradley said, sitting up in her bed. "Send them in."

# SEVENTY NINE

UNDISCLOSED LOCATION

IF HE DIED TODAY, he could leave this miserable existence a happy man. Or satisfied, at least. But only if he accomplished his final objective.

Ishmael ran integrity checks on the remote controlled valves which he activated over the obsolete analog cellular band AMPS (Advanced Mobile Phone System) first used in the United States during the early 1980s. From miles away, he would release an apocalyptic pestilence with just one tap of his iPad on which he could enter the command codes, even from thousands of miles away.

First, however, President Jennifer Bradley must feel the pain of the injustice and cruelty she'd inflicted upon him and his family.

Ensconced safely in what he called his lair, just above the multitude of computer monitors, he considered the framed replica of *Four Horsemen of the Apocalypse*, an 1887 painting by Victor Vasnetsov. He smiled, fancying himself the Pale Rider, the Fourth Horseman who, on his ashen mount and with Hades on his heels, bore neither sword, nor shield—but a scythe.

*"... They were given power over a fourth of the earth..."*

With a chirp, all systems reported back, functioning within

normal parameters. Train stations, shopping centers, churches, mosques, restaurants, theaters, anywhere where for the past seventeen months he'd jury rigged their ventilation systems, would soon be breeding grounds for the genetically engineered bioweapon he'd helped Cerberus manufacture.

It had been a marriage of convenience—their advanced biotech technology and his access to the WMD's Haashir had hidden for Saddam Hussein before the Iraqi despot's capture and execution. In the end, Ishmael's part of the agreement would not be upheld. But he didn't care. For all intents and purposes, his life had ended three years ago. All that remained was his mission—a fool's errand, the charge of the damned.

The beauty of this virus was that it really didn't require many to be initially infected. It was an airborne pathogen more virulent than the bubonic plague, so it only needed to be deployed once in the center of a populated area, and within a couple of days, hundreds of thousands would be dead, the numbers skyrocketing exponentially, with no practical way of stopping it.

The very laboratory in which he presently sat was fitted with a similar deployment system, but it would seal itself off from the outside world, trapping any intruder and exposing them to the lethal doses of any number of neurotoxins and chemical agents. An added measure toward safeguarding his base of operations.

Ishmael glanced over his computer monitor to his bookshelf. In this Spartan place, he kept very little in the way of objects with sentimental value. He always had to be ready to mobilize at a moment's notice. The three items of importance he kept could easily be tossed into a backpack: A pair of wallet sized photos of his beloved Aiza and Odin inside a clear Lucite picture frame, the worn hardback edition of Melville's *Moby Dick* which he'd kept since his Harvard days, and a gold cross which Marie had given him before he left Monaco. Such was the extent of his earthly possessions.

It was actually quite a lot, for a man who had lost everything except for the determination to bring President Bradley, that haughty political harlot, to justice.

An alarm chimed on his iPad.

They were late.

He pounded his fist on the desk. Why hadn't his contact checked in yet? All he'd worked for in the past three years hinged upon this one piece. Missing a check point could spell failure. Ishmael Al Shihab held the power of world-wide death and destruction in his hands, he would not be thwarted by the incompetence of those with whom he'd entrusted this component of the plan.

If forced to step in, he'd see to it that they too would pay.

# EIGHTY

9:58 AM

COVERING THE WOUND in Thomas Bradley's abdomen with her jacket, Xandra struggled not to lose her nerve. She'd never before beheld human viscera, but she had to keep his internal organs covered. The bullet had probably hit his spine—he managed to tell her that he couldn't feel his legs. She had tried to call for help, but there was no cell phone signal, and none of the walkie-talkies seemed to be working. If he didn't receive medical assistance soon, he'd bleed out and die.

Over on the other side of the tree, Max lay still in the dirt. Back about six yards, Agent Cooper's car continued to burn. And on top of all that, Xandra had barely survived an attack by a trained Secret Service agent who had betrayed them all.

That sensation, reminiscent of Ian Mortimer forcibly holding her under water, his cold fingers around her throat, returned. Everything happened so quickly, never affording her a moment to speculate on the one question that mattered:

*Why?*

Thomas Bradley groaned in pain.

"You're going to make it, Tom. Just hang on." He kept holding her hand with his own icy hand, squeezing it now and then, as she spoke.

Each breath he drew made his brow crinkle. It had to have been a great deal more painful than he let on, but Tom forced a smile as he looked to Mikey. "Hey, Kiddo...quit worrying. I'll be fine...You just be strong, okay? Don't be scared."

"I'm not scared, Grandpa." He sniffed, and quickly wiped his eye. "I'm just...concerned."

Shivering from the blood loss, Tom shifted his gaze back to Xandra and whispered, "Whatever happens, stay with him...I don't know if I..." his eyes began to close.

"Stay with me," she said. "Come on, stay with me."

But he could barely open his eyes.

"Tom," she said, trying to keep his mind active but grasping at the wind. "Have you ever seen something like a rusted plaque with the shape of an eagle over a large letter B?"

"A what?" A grin started to form. He laughed, but the pain cut him off.

"Never mind." Why she'd seen that when she'd stood over Agent Kelly Davis' expiring body was lost on her. "Just trying to keep you awake."

"No...I mean...Yes." Tom's breathing grew shallow and increased in frequency. "I know what you're talking about..." His voice faded, eyelids flickered like dying embers.

"What is it?"

"Grandpa." Mikey dropped to his knees, put his face on his chest and wrapped his arms around his neck. "Don't go, please."

"It's okay, Kiddo," he whispered, "...going to...be...with...your daddy...soon."

Mikey buried his face into his bosom and wept softly.

Tom's head dropped to the side, facing Xandra with his eyes half open.

He squeezed her hand weakly, and with his final breath said, "It's old...nothing's left of it...

"Yes?"

"Old...mine." One final breath, then Tom's gaze went a thousand miles away—just like Kyle's final dying breaths.

How had it come to this? So many deaths in just a few days. Worst of all, Michael Bradley, a boy not even ten years of age, had witnessed more violence and loss than most would in a lifetime.

She released Tom's hand and reached over to put her arm around Mikey.

Weeping, Mikey dissolved into her arms.

It took a great deal of strength not to break down in front of him. She needed to be strong for him.

Holding him close, the warmth of his sobs rose up and touched her face like a poignant caress.

She stroked the back of his head gently. "I'm so sorry, Michael." Rocking back and forth in a subtle arc, she let him know without words that she would not leave him, nor allow anything else to happen to him.

As she held him, she shut her eyes, silently wrenching out tears of her own. Rather than darkness, however, the lowering of her eyelids brought forth imagery she had nearly forgotten.

*A ship*

*Rows of harpoons mounted on the wall.*

*White teeth of a large creature line the railing.*

It all came together, illuminated in a flash of light and cognizance.

A ship: *The Pequod*

*Call me* Ishmael.

Xandra snapped back into the moment, barely noticing the sound of tires rolling over rocks and twigs behind her. Before she even realized it, something rigid and cold pressed into the back of her head and clicked.

The voice that spoke behind her was colder still. "Get up slowly."

# EIGHTY ONE

IT WOULD HAVE BEEN BEAUTIFUL, had circumstances been anything but the nightmare that began this day. Through the verdant fields, and miles of red spruce, balsam fir, and mountain ash, Wade Masterson searched the paths and dirt roads through the binoculars he held, from within the cockpit of the Sikorsky SAR chopper.

They'd just left the Bradley Ranch, which was empty and devoid of any evidence that might have implied foul play. The only thing that struck him as unusual was the mobile phone—like the one Agent Davis used—on the driveway, apparently crushed by the tires of a vehicle. May very well have been hers, which explained why she hadn't answered his calls.

But the cellular coverage out here was so spotty, which could also have been the reason. Why neither she nor any of the other agents hadn't responded on the sat phone was not as easily addressed.

Wade called out to the agents searching from the sides of the helicopter windows. "Anything?"

"Just a lot of trees," one of them called out.

"The paved road's ending in a half a mile," the other said.

So did Wade's hopes of finding them quickly. "Damn..."

He had hoped to contact the President with a status update five minutes ago, but he preferred to call her with good news, rather than empty hands.

Taking another look down onto the coppery dirt road, something caught his eye.

A black car coming on the eastbound side swerved erratically, kicking up clouds of dust. It spun out, stopped short of hitting a tree, and blocked the narrow road.

Wade turned to the pilot and pointed down to the road. "We've got some motion down there. Bring us in closer—could be them."

The helo hovered, then began a slow descent.

As it did, another car came skidding, but struck the first one before coming to a full stop.

Neither of the vehicles were Secret Service issue, but that wasn't what surprised Wade most. It was what happened next that caught him off guard.

The driver of the second car leapt out. His face looked like it was covered with bruises and blood. Enraged, he rushed over to the first car with such ferocity the ensuing violence was bizarrely inevitable.

The man tried to open the other driver's door but it was locked.

With his bare fists, he pounded repeatedly on the driver's side window until blood from his hands filled the fissures in the tempered glass like a DC metro map. Before the crazed man could break a hole large enough to reach inside, the driver within opened the door with such force it knocked the attacker back onto the ground.

The agents in the aft came forward to the cockpit to get a better look. "What are they doing?"

Wade could hear the detachment in his own voice. "They're infected."

A female driver burst out of the first car and leapt upon the man who had been pounding on her window. With demonic ferocity, she thrust her fingers into his nose, eyes, and mouth, tearing flesh away as though it were crepe paper.

"What should we do?" The pilot asked.

Suppressing revulsion, Wade glanced to the agent directly behind him. "Get some video of this, call it in, and make sure CDC knows."

Blood covering his face, the man on the ground got up with what had to be adrenalin-induced rage, then lifted her into the air with both hands.

But the feral woman bit his wrist.

He lost his grip as she grabbed onto his neck and pulled him down with her. The two rolled around like feral cats, leaving streaks of blood on the ground.

A steady stream of expletives flowed from the back of the chopper.

There was no hope for the two infected victims. Their paranoid aggression would result in death at the hands of the other, or by the rapid organ failure and massive internal hemorrhage, whichever came first.

Masterson considered putting them out of their misery with a round in each of their skulls, but decided against it.

He had to stay on mission. They'd already lost two minutes in the search for Michael and Thomas Bradley, as well as Xandra Carrick and the protective detail who had hopefully gotten away from the outbreak in time.

Masterson needed to keep himself and everyone aboard the Sikorsky clear of the virus as well. Slowly shaking his head as the hapless creatures below continued to slaughter each other, he let out a barbed breath. "Let's get out of here."

# EIGHTY TWO

10:03 AM

HER FIRST INSTINCT was to shield the boy. But when the muzzle of another gun came to rest on the side of Mikey's head, all Xandra could do was comply. Rising to her feet, she spotted one of the Sig Sauers well beyond her reach. The men in earthen colored fatigues had come out of nowhere.

Another man, somewhat shorter than the others knelt to examine the body of Kelly Davis. "She's dead," he reported to the one holding a gun to Mikey's head. "I told him not to trust a woman."

"Shut up," he said in some kind of middle-eastern accent. "Get the bodies out of sight."

The short man gave him a one-fingered salute, grabbed Davis's arms, then dragged her past the burning wreckage and into the bush.

The man holding Mikey at gunpoint holstered his gun and yanked him away from Xandra.

He struggled, kicking and swinging fists at the man. "Let go of me!"

Xandra spun around only to find the muzzle of an M-16 pointed at her forehead. She flinched, then froze. "Why are you doing this?"

From the corner of her eye, she watched helplessly as Mikey's captor pulled his hands behind his back and restrained them with plastic tie-wraps. He then drew the gun again and used it to push the boy into the back seat of a black Hummer.

Huffing from exertion, the short man returned from pulling Thomas Bradley's body behind the shrubs. He turned to Max's tawny frame and approached it.

The gunman with Xandra chambered a round in his gun.

Despite her training, none of it fully prepared her for this moment—the knowledge that she was going to die.

So many regrets.

Though it was likely that Ishmael Al Shihab was behind everything, she'd die never knowing why or how he'd managed to do it. Her ostensible gift of second sight hadn't helped her find or stop him.

"I hate ruining such a pretty face." The gunman leveled the gun at the bridge of her nose. "Such a pity." He brought the M-16's butt into the front of his shoulder, and took a breath.

Just then, in the distance, the short man started, and jumped away from Max's body.

Somewhere above, the sound of helicopter rotors beat the air causing tree branches to bend and sway.

In the split second it took for Xandra's captor to look up and away, she shifted her head to the right, grabbed the gun's barrel and pushed it in the opposite direction.

The gunman grunted, tightened his grip.

But Xandra placed a well-positioned kick to his "junk", as Wade was so fond of referring to it as, causing him to loosen his grip on the M-16.

She pulled it out of his hands by twisting it around and away from her.

Establishing her grip, she pointing it straight at his chest.

Unfamiliar with this particular kind of firearm, however, her finger rooted around for the trigger.

The helicopter's rotors grew louder and closer.

"So help me, I'll blow your head off," Xandra said to the creep whose gun she now held. "Now, tell me who you—"

A heavy blow to the back of her head.

Flecks of white dotted her darkening vision.

Before she lost consciousness, she felt her knees hit the ground, then her face. The sound of hurried footfalls rushed past her. Two thunks of the car's doors, and its engine turned over.

The last thing she saw through the narrow slit between her eyelids which she fought to keep open, was the car into which Mikey had been forced, driving away.

# EIGHTY THREE

NEMIDAN, TARIQISTAN
20 MILES OUTSIDE OF KISHWAR

EVEN WITH NVGs (night vision goggles) the abandoned streets of Nemidan yielded nothing more than derelict edifices, abandoned vehicles, and the crumbling mosque. Before US forces drove Massoud Haashir and the al Saif terror organization out of Nemidan and into the hills of Tariqistan, it had been a thriving city, though under radical extremist control.

As a parting gift, Haashir had bombed the city with Mustard Gas and various nerve agents four years ago. The body count didn't climb as high as Saddam Hussein's "Bloody Friday" attack on Halabja back in 1988, but it was every bit as merciless. Corpses of men, women, and small children as well as cats and dogs littered the streets.

Today Nemidan lay in ruins, dust and tumbleweeds blowing around its parched remains. Because it would cost too much to rebuild, and no one wanted to take up residency in a ghost town, it remained just that.

No one but terrorists like Ishmael Al Shihab, would want to be here, damned turncoat that he was.

Standing with Team 2, Staff Sergeant Jon Seaver of 6th Platoon, 1st Force Recon Company radioed the other two TLs (team leaders) who were standing by with their men, ready to move on his mark. They had waited until darkness fell upon the entire town, and clouds obscured the full moon's pale light.

"You see that, Sir?" SSGT Terry Roberts of Team 1 said over the radio. "South window, topside."

"Roger that." The silhouette of an armed man moved in the mosque's second floor, his gun prominent enough to discern. "Ishy's got friends with him."

"He's gonna be pretty lonely after we're done here."

It would've been too good to be true if Ishmael had been alone and unprotected. The presence of armed guards didn't really pose a challenge. Getting Al Shihab out alive was the tricky part.

"All right, ladies," Seaver said. "Facing the mosque, I want Team 1 flanking the left, and Team 3 on the right. Check in when you're in position."

A couple of seconds later they confirmed.

"I'll take Team 2 into the building and clear for Teams 1 and 3 to join. Got that?"

More affirmatives.

"All right, on my mark in 3...2...1...Go!"

Initially, the men of Team 2 were silent as they crossed the street. But as soon as they kicked the door open, all hell broke loose.

Weapons at the ready, Seaver's men rushed in, shouting as they filled the halls of the mosque.

Automatic gunfire rained down from the second floor balustrade.

But the recon marines were better equipped and trained.

About twelve seconds and six dead terrorist later, the quiet returned.

"Sir," Roberts of Team 1 said over the radio. "Perimeter's clear. I heard shots fired inside."

"Wait till I give the clear. Do not enter until I clear."

Seaver motioned for his team to spread out and look for Ishmael. With flashlights mounted, they stalked ahead into the shadows like panthers in the night. Sweeping the open meeting room, he only saw tattered curtains blowing in the breeze that entered through broken windows.

"TL2," said Rogers, Team 2's ATL (assistant team leader) who'd been bringing up the rear. "We got a problem here."

"What's your position?" Seaver said.

"Ground level, back at the second room."

Seaver doubled back and headed for the second, not once lowering his M-16's muzzle. "Do you have him?"

"Negative. Careful entering into the room," Rogers said. "You don't want to startle anyone."

Seaver arrived at the door, which was slightly ajar. "I'm coming in."

"Slowly, okay?"

When he stepped inside, he found an old CRT computer monitor running a Windows XP screensaver. He pointed his flashlight to the wall.

Instead of Ishmael, he found a room full of women, young and old, about six of them, sitting on the floor cowering and crying.

Rogers regarded Seaver and shook his head. "It's fugly, Jon."

The small room reeked of urine and excrement. The half dozen women and girls dressed in burqas were ragged, and their eyes dark-rimmed with exhaustion.

"What's that they're holding?" Seaver said, shining his light on them.

"Grenades." He tilted his head toward an elderly woman in the front of the group. "This one says they've been here since this morning, forced at gunpoint to hold these live grenades, with their safety pins removed. They're scared out of their minds."

The rest of Team 2 had completed their sweep of the small, dilapidated Mosque, and reported all clear, no sign of their target.

"All Teams, listen up," Seaver said, "Ishmael is not here, I repeat, IAS is not here. Team 1, I need four of you in this room, first floor second room. Do not come in hot. We've got locals trapped down here. They've put live grenades in their hands with pins removed. They'll go off, as soon the hostages get tired and loosen their grips on the strike lever. Secure ten grenades' levers with tape, or a rubber band if you have to, and bring the pins here. Team 3, call in the Sit-Rep."

They each acknowledged.

"Rogers, pull the hard drive from that computer and we'll see if there's anything useful."

In about half a minute, the members of Team 1 arrived. Seaver addressed them decisively. "Okay, real slow. Hold down the levers and carefully take their grenades. When you've got them, insert your pins, secure and stow them."

Rogers explained the procedure to the women in their dialect.

They responded with apprehensive nods of acknowledgment.

For the next ninety seconds, with hushed words, and calming smiles, the Recon Marines carefully pried the grenades from the victims' hands, and re-inserted the pins.

After they'd put them away, they offered the women and girls their hands to help them to their feet.

None of them reciprocated.

"Rogers," Seaver said, "Tell them it's okay, we're getting them out of here."

He spoke to them, took a step forward with a hand extended, but the oldest lady shook her head and recoiled. Then she began to speak at a rapid pace.

"What is it?" Seaver said.

"They can't move. She says that they've tied wires to their ankles. Thinks they might set off some kind of bomb if they do."

They lifted the hem of their skirts just above their ankles to reveal themselves shackled and daisy chained together with a quarter inch, vinyl coated braided cable.

Seaver nodded to Rogers, who went over to examine it.

Sure enough, the end of the cable lock was set as a tripwire for a Claymore antipersonnel mine, rigged to blow at the slightest tug.

Seaver clenched his jaw. "Sonofabitch..." Shaking his head, he radioed for Izzy "Pop" Barnes, Team 3's EOD (explosive ordinance disposal) tech, fresh out of Sapper School, which made him an expert in foot mobile breaching, demolition handling and IEDs. This M18A1 Claymore was the stuff he trained on in Sapper school, and would be easy for him to disarm.

Nevertheless, Seaver had a bad feeling about all this. From the start, this whole mission had FUBAR written all over it. It had been rushed, and in his opinion, not well-planned. In haste, they'd been inserted in a HALO drop into a questionable DZ, less than two hours ago. Would have been better to have arrived a day earlier, and surveilled the ghost town for hostiles for 24 hours before engaging. The mission was to slip in and kick some effin' terrorist ass, then nab IAS, who'd been presumed dead for three years.

All that effort, only to find this?

"Heard you found a live one, Sir," Sergeant Israel "Pop" Barnes said, eager to get to work—at least one of them got to do something they'd expected.

Seaver pointed to the mine. "Right there, Pop."

"Piece of cake." Barnes carefully made his way to the explosive device, taking care not to startle any of the hostages and accidentally trip it.

One of the hostages, a little girl about four years old, started to cry.

Being the father of a beautiful girl about the same age, Seaver felt compassion for her. *What kind of sick bastard ties a little girl to an explosive?* Thank God, his deployment would be over in two weeks. He'd already planned one of those surprise visits at Megan's school like some of those dad's had done on YouTube. He couldn't wait to hear her excited shrieks as she launched herself into his arms. Only this time, according to Rachelle, she'd be almost two inches taller and about eight pounds heavier.

Seaver knelt down before the girl, pointed to his heart, and with a warm smile, spoke tenderly in the same fatherly tone he used with Megan. "I'm Jon. We're going to get you home, okay?"

Her eyes wide, she nodded perhaps more in response to his tone than his words.

"Oh, hey..." Seaver reached into his pocket and pulled out a hand-sized plush animal—a brown puppy—with floppy ears. Dealing with locals, you always wanted to be prepared to make a connection. "I think someone needs a friend."

He handed it to her.

The fear on her face melted away and a wide grin replaced it. She held out her left hand and took it. With unmistakable sincerity, the little girl gave him an appreciative look. He'd won her trust.

"Sir," Barnes said, showing him the cable severed, and the Claymore disarmed and packed away in an M7 bandolier, "we're all set."

"Nice work, Pop," Seaver said, then signaled to Roberts that it was time to go.

Roberts, Barnes, and the other Recons gently guided the women and girls out of the room and into the hallway. There, Seaver led the way down toward the exit, where they'd rush them through the street and out to the city limits, back to the clearing over the hills where another helo would return for the dust off.

Without Al Shihab, unfortunately.

Taking point, Seaver walked down the Mosque's quiet hall with the exit in sight. Teams 1 and 3 had gathered outside and secured the path. As ATL, Rogers was once again Tail End Charlie, a term carried over from the Vietnam War, and guarded the rear of the train of Marines and civilians.

Through the mosque's sepulchral gloom, Seaver thought he heard a beeping sound coming way back from the room they'd just left.

He turned back to look.

In an instant, the mechanical whir of servos and panels swinging open filled the hall.

His instincts kicked in.

"Move out!"

Seaver stepped off the path, and pushed all the hostages out the door.

From within the walls and ceiling, muzzle flashes lit the room like a lightning storm. He never got more than a glimpse of the hidden automatic weapons sliding out of their panels, but he knew what had happened.

The marines covered the women, led them far from the mosque.

Out of instinct, Roberts whirled around and returned fire, but there were no human targets, only automated weapons programmed to lay down a blanket of fire all over the hall.

Barnes and the last of the women made it out.

Standing by the doorway, Seaver called out, "Roberts! Get out of there!"

But before he could react, a couple of rounds hit Roberts in the knee and thigh.

The ATL fell to the marble tile, which grew more and more pockmarked by the bullets raining down.

As Roberts hit the floor, Seaver saw a small figure in a black Burqa laying in the fifth degree of prostration on the ground, trembling in fear. Curled over on her face, hands and forearms, the little girl clutched the brown plush puppy toy in one hand, the other one balled in a tight fist.

In the brief interval in which the waves of gunfire ceased, Seaver ran over and grabbed both Rogers and the girl by their clothes. The girl, he hoisted onto his shoulder, and Rogers, he dragged across the smooth floor by the collar.

"Sir," Rogers said, blood pulsing from his wounds. "Get out of here before it starts up again."

"No one gets left behind," Seaver shouted, then gave a powerful tug.

Just then, the deafening gunfire resumed.

*Damn.*

He could barely see where it was coming from. Al Shihab was shrewd, he had to admit. All the more reason that bastard needed to be put down, and sent to hell in a body bag.

Just about a yard from the opening, the girl on his shoulder shrieked in terror.

Something clanked onto the marble floor behind him.

"Grenade!" Roberts groaned.

Unbeknownst to anyone, the girl had been clutching the unpinned explosive this whole time, too afraid to let go. But in all the chaos, she'd dropped it, releasing the lever. She was scared stiff, and Roberts was immobilized right next to it.

The next four seconds seemed to happen in slow motion.

Letting go of Roberts, Seaver used both hands to throw the girl over to Team 1's TL standing outside the door.

Meanwhile, Roberts tried to drag himself away with his hands but the blood on the floor kept making them slip. He shoved Seaver's leg. "Go!"

In the last seconds, time stood still.

Images ran through Seaver's head: Rachelle, Megan, the little girl with the plush puppy...the grenade, and Terry Roberts, staring up to him, his eyes wide with urgency and imploring him to get out.

In that eternal final millisecond, when all he felt was the love for his family and his best friend who could not move himself out of harm's way, Seaver prayed that his wife and daughter would forgive him...

...then threw himself on top of the grenade.

# EIGHTY FOUR

GARRETT COUNTY, MD
10:14 AM EST

SHE CAME TO because of someone shaking her shoulder. Through blurred eyes, she discerned the outline of a pair of black shoes and pant legs. A few blinks clarified her view and just as soon, someone helped her up into a seated position.

"Xandra..." Wade Masterson was looking at her with concern and a sense of distant urgency. "Are you all right?"

She rubbed the back of her head. "So that's what it's like."

"What?"

"Getting pistol whipped." She had received similar blows during training, but none that knocked her out.

"Where're the Bradleys, Agents Davis and Cooper?"

She tried to stand, but faltered. Wade caught her by the arm, and put a hand behind her back to steady her. "It was Davis."

"What happened?"

"She was in on it." As efficiently as she could, Xandra proceeded to recount the events, the explosion, Thomas Bradley's death, and Mikey's abduction." As she spoke, she saw the agents load Tom Bradley's sheet-covered body into the helicopter that had touched down nearby.

"Can you give a description of the people who took Michael?"

"They were wearing fatigues and ski masks. Two of them about your height, and one about mine."

"Any idea which way they took him?"

"I can't say for sure." She pointed down into a clearing in the forest. "I think they went off road."

In the background, two of the agents went over to Max and lifted him off the ground.

Xandra ran over. "Is he—?"

"Still breathing, Ma'am, but it doesn't look good."

She put her hand on Max's head. "Good boy..."

His eyes barely open, he whined and leaned his head into Xandra's touch. The precognitions she'd experienced had always been about humans, through their eyes, their memories, their futures. This time, she sensed something. A connection, not visual, not so much through second sight, but straight from his heart to hers. It took her by surprise. In that very moment, she wanted to break down and cry.

Max opened his eyes and gazed straight into hers, into her soul.

He was saying goodbye.

Wade leaned over her, his words hardly registering. "I'm taking the Suburban. You should go back with them, Xandra. It's safer, and you've been through enough."

"I have to help you find Mikey." She hadn't gotten this far to simply stop and go home. From the look in Max's eyes, he seemed to understand that.

Her heart ached, but she knew what she must do.

"I have to go, Max."

He leaned his head against her hand, and blinked.

She bent down, kissed his head, and said goodbye.

HALF A MINUTE later, the helicopter took off, leaving her standing on the ground with Wade. He climbed into the Suburban's driver's seat, where he found the keys she'd left.

"You said you could help me find him."

Xandra climbed into the passenger seat. "I hope you're more familiar with these parts than I am."

"What've you got?" He started the car and looked around the surrounding area.

"Something from Davis, just as she died."

"She talked?" Wade said, his gaze shifting between the dirt road, and clearing in the forest.

"It was a vision."

He shifted the Suburban into gear and drove it down the wooded path.

# EIGHTY FIVE

**BRADLEY DECLARES
NATIONAL STATE OF EMERGENCY**

BY THE ASSOCIATED PRESS
10:03 AM ET

After a statement by Vice President Philip Marsden earlier this morning regarding the terrorist attacks in various cities across the nation, President Jennifer Bradley, who was not available to appear due to a medical condition, declared a national state of emergency, as the NTAS (National Terrorism Advisory System) issued an alert for imminent terrorism threats to multiple targets, including the White House itself, which is currently on lockdown due to biohazard alert warnings.

Tempers flared over the internet as a mobile phone video from Cabotstown MD was removed. The video, depicting a scene of mass hysteria and violence after being infected with an airborne pathogen, went viral twenty-minutes prior to its removal from all social media sites. The White House Press Secretary stated that this measure was taken in order to contain and control a proper flow of information. However, downloaded copies continued to appear in defiance of government censure. This led to an unprecedented shut down of outlets including, but not limited to, YouTube, Facebook, Twitter, Yahoo.com, and thousands of blogs.

Declassified Intelligence reports indicate that certain highly populated parts of the country are in danger from this biological attack. The DHS (Dept. of Homeland Security), the FBI, CIA, United States and Tariqistani Military, as well the CDC have been mobilized in a concerted effort to locate any possible devices of deployment, as well as apprehend the perpetrators of these attacks, who are believed to be members of the al Saif terror group, which sponsors the FTM (Free Tariqistan Movement).

Meanwhile, along with support from federal and local law enforcement, the following cities have been added to a growing list of regions with mandatory quarantines imposed: New York, Los Angeles, Chicago, and Dallas.

The Army National Guard has been activated in those cities, where panicked citizens resisting curfews crowd the highways in an attempt to leave their cities. In an effort to contain, and prevent the spread of this virus, which CDC has designated L1N1 (its symptoms resembling a combination of Influenza, Ebola, and Rabies), all roadways and other possible means of exit and entrance to the high risk areas have been sealed off. The L1N1 virus is believed to be the same manufactured agent responsible for the deaths on Flight

1306, and this morning in Cabotstown, MD.

The CDC has issued the following statement: "We are urging all people of the United States to exercise extreme caution and good judgment. Remain indoors, and avoid likely targets such as public transportation, shopping centers, office buildings, etc."

In addition to the CDC's continued efforts to develop a vaccine and treatment, FEMA is preparing emergency medical overflow, and safe zone facilities.

As reports of unrest and riots emerge with residents demanding information, local law enforcement agencies have expressed concern that they are not equipped to deal with the widespread pandemonium anticipated to occur within the next 48 hours.

In the same White House statement issued by Vice President Marsden, he assured the nation that the Bradley administration is doing everything possible to find a cure, and stop the terrorist group from any further attacks.

# EIGHTY SIX

PRESIDENTIAL EMERGENCY OPERATIONS CENTER
(PEOC)
THE WHITE HOUSE - EAST WING
10:55 AM EST

IT MADE NO SENSE. Bradley simply could not accept the thought of dying without any understanding of how everything had happened. How did Ishmael plan to maintain power in Tariqistan, by simply killing the people there, and waging war with the United States through a domestic biological attack?

He could never pull it off.

And yet, there he was...sitting in some remote location in Nemidan sending threats to her, as if he didn't know that he'd soon be tracked down.

Frustrating as it was, she wanted nothing else but to be with Mikey, to hold him, and say how sorry she was for being such a poor mother to him, before leaving him forever. There was never enough time.

And now, there never would be.

The biological agent with which she'd been injected made breathing hard enough, with blood and fluids filling her lungs, but now the weight of regret pressed down on her, adding heartache to the struggle.

She'd erred in making decisions in haste. She'd erred in not trying harder to make time for her beloved son. For all the good she'd tried to do, she had failed. Was this to be her legacy to the nation, to Mikey?

The video conference alert chimed.

Forcing herself to be alert, she sat up and activated the screen. "Yes, General."

"Madam President, I regret to inform you that we did not find or apprehend Ishmael Al Shihab."

"What happened?"

"It was a trap, Ma'am. The Recon Teams went in and found no one but half a dozen civilians trapped and rigged to explosives. It became a rescue mission."

"Were they at least successful in that?" Bradley said, her head throbbing.

"Yes, Ma'am. But we lost Staff Sergeant Seaver, Leader of Team 2."

She lowered her head and rubbed her eyes. Another life lost because of faulty intelligence—because of her. She would have to contact Seaver's family tonight, if she lived that long. "I thought the intel was good."

"By everything we received," DCI Kendall said, "it was. Ishmael must have found a way to spoof and mask the IP packets of his transmissions."

"So he was just distracting us to buy himself more time." She shook her head, feeling even more ill than before. "Any idea where he is now?"

"We have other leads of like quality," Kendall said, "But they indicate numerous possible locations throughout the world."

"Including the United States?" Bradley said.

"Someone as high profile as Al Shihab would have a hard time getting into the States."

Cromwell joined in. "Ma'am, he's demonstrated that he can implement his attacks remotely and is able to consistently evade us. While I agree that finding and stopping him is the priority, we should not lose sight of the domestic situation. We have to prepare for the worst."

"General Fuller," Bradley said. "How are we with the National Guard?"

"Rolling out, Ma'am. I just wish we could keep a lid on the media for a day or two."

Bradley nodded in agreement. She imagined the troops entering the populated areas and trying to support local authorities in keeping order, and enforcing emergency protocols.

Where was Wade? Why hadn't he reported back about Michael yet?

"Thank you, Gentlemen." A wave of exhaustion rose over her. "I want reports as the situation unfolds, in intervals no less than every five minutes."

She ended the video conference and fell back into her bed. Time and the neurotoxin depleted her energy. On a scale of one to ten, ten being the worst, she'd rate the pain an eleven.

If there was no one else to consider, she would have ended it a while ago.

Still, Dr. Singh, who had continued working with her and the CDC, had told her privately, it would remain an option until the end. He had just arrived and was standing outside of the transparent tent.

She pressed the button on the intercom. "Doctor, we need to talk."

# EIGHTY SEVEN

GARRETT COUNTY, MD
10:57 AM EST

"I DON'T *KNOW* WHAT IT MEANS!" Wade shouted into the sat phone. "Just look it up and tell me what you find."

The trail of tire treads had vanished about ten minutes ago. Wade continued driving in the same general direction, wherever the car could fit between trees. During that drive he explained what had happened to President Bradley, the White House lock down, and Ishmael Al Shihab's threats.

Ishmael was supposed to be somewhere outside of Kishwar, near Tariqistan, how could she possibly help locate him while Mikey remained in grave danger? And what was the connection—if any—between this abduction to the outbreak here in America, and threats of the same in President Nasra Aamaal's country?

Wade had stopped driving to make the call to his contact, an analyst in the Secret Service investigative support division. He continued, his tone gruff enough to make Xandra wonder if his impatience would prove counterproductive. "All we have is a plaque with a symbol—an eagle, or some kind of bird, over a monogram, the letter B."

Xandra nudged his arm with her elbow. "That was just from a vision."

He shot her a quick glance, then started speaking on the phone again. "Are you sure?…Right. Broughman's…It's been abandoned how long?…okay, great! Thank you!"

He ended the call, activated the Suburban's GPS system, and entered the coordinates. "Could be a long shot, but it's all we've got."

"What exactly *have* we got?"

"Your vision? It was of a plaque that had been used years ago at a nearby abandoned mine. That might be where they've taken the President's son."

He revved the engine and shifted its gears.

Lurching forward, he turned to the left and sped up a hill.

"Hold on, Wade." Xandra gripped the side of the door to steady herself. "How do we know if that vision…? We could be wasting precious time."

"Which is exactly what we'd be doing if we sat around second guessing ourselves." He downshifted and accelerated even more, then glanced over to give her a subtle grin. "But everything's a choice, right? I choose to believe in your vision."

"Based on?"

"Track record? I don't know, maybe it's a gut feeling."

"Let's hope neither of us are wrong."

After about ten minutes of bumpy driving deeper through the woods, they arrived at a spot where ancient vines climbed and strangled the tree trunks and overgrown brush obscured the landscape. Other than that, the place was unremarkable.

Xandra looked to Wade. "Why are we stopping?"

"These are the coordinates."

"I don't see any mine shaft."

"Doubt they'd leave a welcome mat out." He keyed in a number and opened a secured panel on the door, and pulled out a gun, a pair of black tubes, and handed them to her. "

"What's this?"

"Sig Sauer P226 with subsonic rounds. Screw the suppressor on like this." He demonstrated by doing so on his own gun. "Element of surprise."

She finished attaching the suppressor, held it up, and regarded its extended barrel with concern. "Bulky."

"You'll appreciate how quiet it is, trust me."

Carefully, they opened their doors and stepped out of the car, guns at the ready. As they approached the clearing, Wade said, "You picking anything up?"

Xandra regarded him with a sarcastic smirk. "My antenna's broken."

"I didn't mean—"

Shots rang out.

"Take cover!" Wade shouted, and leapt behind a tree.

Xandra did the same, remaining where they could see each other.

Like heavy raindrops, the staccato of automatic gunfire sounded through the woods.

Wade fired one shot.

A body fell next to a tree about ten yards away from the clearing, where the Suburban sat.

Pulse racing, Xandra wiped her palms on her pants because they were so slick with cold perspiration. She could hardly keep a steady grip on her gun. She'd trained for marksmanship and some hand-to-hand, but not for a situation like this.

Her struggle with Davis had resulted in the rogue agent getting stabbed with her own knife, but Xandra wasn't sure she could be as decisive a killer as Wade, when it came down to it.

In the short interval between volleys, Wade indicated with his fingers that there were two more shooters. He pointed to a tree to the west, and behind a large tangle of vines to the north.

Silently, he mouthed, "Cover me."

She didn't quite understand, but before she could ask, he dashed across the clearing, shooting to the trees at the West as he dove and rolled onto the ground.

Instantly, she got it.

With a sustained burst of rounds, the gunman with a semiautomatic peeked around the tree trunk behind which he hid.

One clear *pop!* from Wade's direction took his target down.

A quick flash in her inner eye: One of the camouflaged men—the short one—with a rifle, taking aim.

She blinked and turned toward the vines to the north.

Wade was just about to stand.

Without even thinking, Xandra called out to him and pointed.

He took the shot.

The short man's head snapped back, as a spray of blood leapt up from his forehead.

But not before he fired off a round.

Wade let out a pained grunt.

"Wade!" There might have been more gunmen out there, but Xandra didn't think about it as she ran over to him.

He was holding his thigh, blood soaking his hand. "It's just my leg, no vital organs…"

"Can you walk?"

He shook his head tightly, and strained.

She pulled his jacket off and tied a tourniquet above the wound. Then she took out her cell phone. "There's no damned signal out here!"

Wade tried to laugh. "Watch your…language. One day, you'll be around Mikey and slip and cuss. POTUS is very strict about that."

His levity wasn't working. Xandra's heart raced even harder.

"Wade, where's the Sat Phone?"

"Back seat."

She ran back to the Suburban, retrieved it, and tried to make a call standing right at the open driver's door.

"Carrick!" Wade called out.

She was too focused on trying to make the call for assistance.

"This is a Sat Phone for pity's sake! There *has* to be a signal!"

"Listen to me, Xandra…"

The branches and leave of the trees encircling the clearing formed a canopy over them. But just past the tree to the west, a swatch of sunshine poured down into the shadows.

Xandra ran over to that clearing, watching the signal strength bars increasing.

Again, Wade called out. "Wait!"

She turned around and saw him with his face close to the ground, and pointing straight at the tangled vines around the overgrown shrubs. "What is it?"

"You can see it from here."

She stepped over the body of the short gunman, and over to Wade. Kneeling, she put her head down next to his. "What are we looking at?"

"Straight under those shrubs," he said. "It's like a handle or something, sticking out of the ground."

She gave him the Sat Phone. "Need to get you some medical attention."

"Didn't hit an artery, quit fussing." Again, he pointed at the spot under the vines. "That's what you need to look at."

Gun drawn, she went over. When she arrived, she crouched down avoiding Shorty's corpse, reached under the vines, and grabbed the handle, smooth and cold to the touch. Being what it was, she gave the handle a pull.

It didn't budge, but she felt some play.

This time, she pulled using her legs for leverage.

Whatever it had been attached to, gave.

To her surprise, the entire bush and vine tangle lifted up and fell sideways to reveal that they had been attached to the top of a trap door made of wood. She took one look and instantly recognized where she was.

# EIGHTY EIGHT

*THIS IS IT!* Xandra wanted to shout in triumph, but resisted. The hatch she'd just discovered revealed a ladder going down into a mine shaft. The inner walls of the vertical opening were lined with wood. On one side a rusted plaque hung. Just as she'd seen as Agent Davis died.

Etched into the rusted brass was that symbol.

An eagle's form juxtaposed over the monogrammed letter B.

"It's the plaque, Wade," she said. "Broughman's."

"All, right. We need to get a team over here to go down into—"

"Can't wait for that." She pointed her chin over to his leg. "How're you holding up?"

"I'll live."

"Good. I'll see you later, then." She reached over to Shorty's expired form, searched his clothes, found a magnetic security badge, and slid it into her pocket. *Might come in handy*. Then she grabbed the ladder and lowered a foot onto the rung.

Wade propped himself up on one arm. "I can't let you go down there by yourself."

"Can't stop me either." She took a step down into the shaft.

"Xandra, listen to me!"

She climbed down, leaving the hatch open to allow as much light in as possible. When she reached the bottom, the first thing that struck her was how cold and foul the air was. To the left and the right of the ladder, the low, narrow passageway stretched into the darkness, just wide enough for one person to crawl through.

Her chest tightened at the thought of getting on all fours and creeping into the void. With nothing but her gun and fool-hearted courage, she had to decide.

The worst part of it was the pitch blackness, not knowing what was ahead—a pit, snakes, bats, a murderer? At least in the dark-room, she had a safe light to illuminate the confines. Here, it was nothing but the unknown.

Heart pounding, breath shortening, she never considered her-self claustrophobic.

Now she wondered.

*Okay, just...breathe.*

She shut her eyes, siphoned a breath with great effort. If there was any chance that Mikey was in here, she had to put aside her anxiety and go forth.

She hadn't sensed this kind of fear since the power went out one night when she was eight years old. The entire neighborhood went dark around midnight and Dad had been away. It was Mom who comforted her, climbing into her bed, holding her and whis-pering that song:

*Even the darkness hides nothing from you,*
*And with Your hand you will lead me...*

And in the same reassuring voice Mom used backstage before Xandra would play for a competition or recital at Juilliard as a teenager, she heard her say, "You can do all things through Him who gives you strength."

"All right," she whispered, got down into a crawling position. "I can do this."

# EIGHTY NINE

HOLLAND TUNNEL
MANHATTAN ENTRANCE
NEW YORK
11:06 AM EST

IT WAS SUPPOSED TO BE his day off. The last thing Officer Derek Mullins wanted was to risk exposure out here. But everyone in the precinct had been called to help enforce the city-wide lock down and containment, at least until the National Guard arrived, which was supposed to be soon.

His buddies, Ortiz and Jones were among the others who watched the barricades on Varrick and Canal. In about three minutes, they'd come down and join him.

As per orders, barricades had been set up to block the entrance to the Jersey bound tubes, and under no circumstances was anyone permitted to cross them. Since the order had been issued, a surprisingly small number of people had come, most of them claiming not to have heard of the quarantine and lock-down regulations. Despite their gruff reputation, New Yorkers were generally decent and practical people. His concern wasn't so much unruly citizens, but the fact that he might be standing right at ground zero, if and when the terrorists struck.

His phone buzzed in his pocket.

A text from Julie.

**When r u coming home daddy?**

He smiled at the photo attached to his daughter's message. She was twelve years old, and thanks to good genetics from her mother, way smarter than he'd ever be.

**Soon as I can Julsie-baby**

**:( I'm scared…**

**Stay close to Mom. When I get back, we'll do popcorn and Netflix tonight, k?**

**K. Luv u.**

**U 2**

Just as he pocketed the phone, he looked up and couldn't believe what he was seeing.

A silver Ford Fusion barreled around the Varrick Street half loop and straight under the Holland Tunnel sign above the Broome Street intersection.

"Mother of—!" Mullins didn't expect anyone to cross the lines back up on Varrick or Canal Street before the turn. Blowing his whistle, he held up his hand. But the driver only accelerated past him, smashing through the plastic arm lowered to keep traffic out.

Mullins revved his bike and went after the car. He was just a traffic cop, what was he supposed to do, shoot him? How else could he stop the driver?

In an instant, the answer came in the form of a loud screech of brakes and the sickening sound of metal scraping and collapsing against concrete and brick.

He just caught a glimpse of it before it happened.

The driver spun out of control and smashed the front of his car into the concrete wall.

Derek stopped, leapt off his bike, and rushed over to the car. Its radiator was spewing steam, its undercarriage bleeding all kinds of automotive fluids.

When he got to the window, he found the driver with his face buried into the white airbag that had deployed.

"Hey, Mister!" Derek shouted. "You okay?"

The driver's shoulders rose and fell repeatedly.

Good.

Still breathing.

The bozo had been doing about forty-five when he smashed into the wall. Had to have been injured pretty bad.

Mullins got his walkie-talkie to call for an ambulance.

Just then, the driver lifted his head and turned to face him.

Startled, Mullins took a step back.

The guys' face, neck and hands, were black and blue, and he was bleeding from his mouth, ears, nose and eyes. It could have been from the impact, but he also recalled the briefing he'd received about what people infected with the virus looked like.

And this was it.

With uncanny speed, the driver opened the door and got out.

"Stay inside the vehicle, Sir!"

It seemed to get through.

The driver stopped.

For half a second.

Then he swung open the door again.

"I said remain in your vehicle!" Mullins drew his gun and with two hands pointed it at the driver.

The bloody man bared his teeth like a wolf, then turned to the tunnel entrance.

*Aw man, this sucks!*

Mullins walked around to impede the man's path. "Not another step!"

But the man ignored him, and with one quick swing of his arm knocked Mullins off his feet.

Stunned, Mullins got back up and aimed his gun. In all his years as a 'friggin' traffic cop', he never thought he'd hear himself say the words: "Stop, or I'll shoot!" But he didn't know of a better way to convey the threat.

The dazed driver craned his neck to look Mullins in the eye, then resumed his slow walk.

"Dammit." Mullins fired a warning shot. The sound ripped through the tunnel and resounded.

It jolted the man who was obviously infected.

He began to run at an incredible speed.

Was he going to have to chase this sucker down, shoot him before he made it to New Jersey and infected more people?

A string of expletives flew from Mullin's lips. He'd promised Julie that he'd stop cussing. *I'll have to try again tomorrow.* He called in the situation and requested backup from the Newport side of the tunnel. But on his bike, he'd overtake the infected person with ease.

And then what?

He ran over to his bike and started it up.

In the distance, there was a growing commotion back around the barricades by Canal and Broome Street. Crowds shouting, car horns, blaring.

He radioed to the officers up the road. "Ortiz, what's going on up there?"

No response over the radio.

Only shots fired.

A swarm of cars and pedestrians flooded in like white water rapids through the entrance. There must have been hundreds—

men, women, children, all pushing and shoving past the cars that jammed their way into the tunnel.

Before Mullins could do anything, something or someone knocked him to the ground. The next thing he knew, he was gasping for breath, and getting crushed under a human stampede.

# NINETY

SITUATION ROOM
THE WHITE HOUSE
11:16 AM EST

THE SHIFTING OF BLAME wasn't overt, but he could detect it in the subtext of every department that contributed to the intel. The fact remained, however, that he, Evan Cromwell, the National Security Advisor, had presented the intel as reliable, and had based his recommendations upon it.

Now, with a heightened sense of urgency, the hunt for Ishmael Al Shihab was to extend to all reaches of the globe. From a remote location, the terrorist had been able to infect the President, members of the White House, and rural towns like Cabotstown. For all Cromwell knew, Ishmael could be anywhere, even here in the United States, sitting right under their noses.

His head felt like an anvil, perhaps from dehydration or hunger. No one here in the Sit Room had tended to any basic needs for the past couple of hours. All eyes, ears, and minds were so affixed to the incoming information from the military, intelligence, CDC, and local law enforcement agencies that thoughts of food and water were all but forgotten.

Vice President Marsden was truly out of his element. He sat there holding his head in his hands, at an utter loss. Though he'd observed Jennifer Bradley at her best in crisis situations for the past four years, he never seemed to possess her drive and leadership. He knew how to ask non-specific questions, but the unspoken consensus was that he didn't really know how to grab the proverbial bull by the horns. He kept deferring to the recommendations of the various department heads.

One report that came in seemed to leave him speechless.

Based on vector research and the L1N1 virus's current rate of infection, if another similar bioweapon were to go off in like Los Angeles alone, the entire state of California would be infected in less than a week, and the entire West Coast three days later. Within the month, half of the United States population would be infected or dead.

While Cromwell pondered the implications, everyone on his side of the table stood up to get a better look at the television sets with the news playing. What he saw next made his neck muscles constrict, sending a lash of pain into his head.

From the cockpit of a helicopter, Allan Coleman of New York's Channel 4 News reported as the camera took an aerial shot of the scene. Not since September 11, 2001 had Cromwell seen anything like it.

"As you can see below," Coleman said, "thousands of New Yorkers are lined up in cars and on foot at City Hall, by the entrance of the Brooklyn Bridge, demanding passage. The National Guard as well as the NYPD are trying to enforce the city wide quarantine and lockdown, but I'm concerned they won't be able to contain this."

"Our affiliates report that as many as two hundred people have already broken through barriers at the Holland Tunnel and are being held in place by armed law enforcement officials at the New Jersey side."

The view switched back to Kate Chang, Channel 4 News anchorwoman.

"Allan, I'm seeing armed soldiers and military vehicles down there." A quick zoom in of a tank with a pair of National Guardsmen with rifles drawn.

"Hopefully there won't be any need."

"Isn't that just a little excessive?" Mitch Donovan said. In Cromwell's eyes, Bradley's Chief of Staff never had much of a stomach for anything military. The executive order to activate the National Guard was probably making him sick.

"This whole damn thing will turn on a dime," General Fuller said. "You don't really think everyone is going to simply obey the rules, and not try to exempt themselves, do you? Never underestimate the power of human self-interest. We're looking at a global Pandemic here. It's not a question of if, it's a matter of when."

Donovan glowered at him. "I don't know if the President shares your cynicism, General."

"She's the one who authorized this."

"Only if absolutely necessary."

Evan had to diffuse the situation and rescue Donovan from making the President look completely feeble. "It's a precautionary measure, Mitch. That's all."

"No, it's a statement about the faith this administration has in the people." Donovan jabbed a finger at the screen that showed crowds swarming the tanks like bees in a hive. "This has got Tiananmen Square written all over it!"

"Now *that's* excessive," Fuller said. "And melodramatic."

But Donovan ranted on. "Mark my words. History will judge us!"

Cromwell stepped over to whisper to Donovan. "Mitch, we're all on edge. Could you go and see how the President is doing, find out if she's in any condition to get on a conference call for an update?"

"If I didn't know you better, Evan, I'd think you were trying to get rid of me."

Cromwell put a hand on his shoulder. "Trust me, if that were my goal, things would be much different."

"I was on my way out for some fresh air anyway—fresh as it can be in a quarantined White House. I'll tell you this, though.

When Bradley sees the news, the tanks, the soldiers, she's going to be pissed. I know for a fact—"

A round of gasps went up.

Everyone in the Sit Room gathered closely around the television monitors.

"It's all hitting the fan!" General Fuller said.

On the screen, the camera zoomed in to the situation around the Brooklyn Bridge. The crowds were going berserk, climbing on the tanks, assaulting the soldiers, overturning jeeps. In a massive wave, they all surged forward, climbing over everything and everyone in their path.

"Oh my God," Allan Coleman said from within the newscopter's cockpit. "I think some shots were fired."

"Are you sure?" Kate Chang said.

The camera zoomed in again and focused on soldiers positioned on the pedestrian walkway about a hundred yards behind the tanks. With their rifles aimed, they were firing into the masses, the recoil of their weapons clearly visible. But it did nothing to deter the people from running across the bridge over to Brooklyn, the fourth largest and most populated city in the nation.

Donovan crossed himself. "Lord have mercy."

# NINETY ONE

ABANDONED SHAFT
BROUGHMAN'S MINE
GARRETT COUNTY, MD
11:22 AM EST

EVEN THE DARKNESS hides nothing from You.

Peering into the crawlspaces to her left, then to her right, Xandra couldn't decide which one to use. If she knew for certain that she'd find Mikey here, it might be worth the torture of squeezing through these tubes like a sewer rat, and braving the dangers of collapse, fall, and suffocation.

Not to mention cardiac arrest.

Left or right?

*And with Your hand You will lead me.*

She was nearly about to give up and climb back out, when she put her hand in the tunnel on the right. Then, clear as the midday sun, she saw something in her mind's eye.

It was one of those powerful visions in which she could walk around.

It was a room with very little in it but a door, a concrete wall with a heavy glass window separating it from the adjacent room, a table, and a chair. She could hear the computerized beeping sounds, see the lights reflecting in a man's pupils as he stared into a monitor.

Looking down at the hands, the knees, the shoes...she knew she was looking through Mikey's eyes. This had happened once before—a shared vision—with Dad, a few years ago, but it had been about a memory. Was this also a memory, the residual effect of something in Mikey's past?

No. Somehow, she knew.

It was happening right now, in real time.

Then it stopped.

Before she could talk herself out of it, she crawled into the tunnel on the right.

The deeper she went, the colder the air grew. The ground was wet and slippery, and an offensive odor filled the tube. She could swear something had crept over her hand, and on her back, but ignored it as best she could.

After an interminable few minutes, her hands and knees were wet, freezing and aching.

But right ahead, something made her heave a breath of relief.

Light.

Somewhat diffused, it leaked into the tube through the bend at its left side.

She crawled over, looked past the bend.

About fifteen feet ahead was the end of the tunnel and an open space illuminated with incandescent light.

A man coughed, and hacked up a clam.

Assault rifle in hand, he turned to the opening in the wall.

Xandra ducked behind the bend.

Had he heard her? Seen her?

For the next minute or two the man could be heard pacing around. Xandra didn't move, hardly breathed. When it seemed enough time had passed and the man was gone, she moved slowly to the bend.

A quick stolen glance showed the area clear.

Nevertheless, she moved cautiously toward the exit, her gun pointed straight ahead. *Might have to shoot him, if he returns.*

She didn't like the thought of it.

"Even if it's to protect someone you care about?" Wade had said, the first time they spoke in the West Wing.

Another few paces forward.

The sound of the man's voice stopped her cold.

The passage was too narrow for her to turn around and, she was too far to back up around the bend.

As quickly as she could, she crawled forward to the opening.

Just as she got there, the man's face appeared before the opening at the end of the passageway.

"Hey!" he shouted, eyes wide with surprise.

With all her strength, Xandra launched forward, and struck the man in the side of his head with the black suppressor attachment of the Sig Wade had given her.

It struck him right at the bridge of his nose. Judging by the crunch and vibrations, she'd just broken it. The guy fell back and groaned.

Xandra climbed out.

Exploiting his stunned state, she retrieved the gun he'd dropped, turned it over, and using it like a baseball bat, clubbed him in the head. With that singular stroke, the disarmed man lost consciousness, his jaw slack.

Straightening out, and now holding two guns, she made her way to the only door in this subterranean vestibule.

Maybe it was the adrenaline rush, or the lack of oxygen, but seeing that she'd subdued a man who had to be at least a hundred pounds heavier gave her quite a rush. And she hadn't even fired a round.

Kneeling, she searched the man's pockets.

She grabbed his walkie-talkie and pocket knife, then checked his other pocket.

*Hello!*

Zip ties.

Convenient.

She took one, and bound the guy's wrists behind his back.

Then the ankles.

Just then, the guard began to stir.

His eyelids fluttered.

"Hmmm? What...?"

Eyes not quite fully open, he started to struggle with his restraints.

Xandra sighed impatiently.

She grabbed the guy's rifle, and once again struck him across the head, sending his face into the dirt again. "Down-stay."

Satisfied that she'd taken care of him properly, she went to the door. The clean lines of stainless steel contrasted sharply with the stone walls, rather went with the lighted sconces that illuminated the petrified antechamber.

She took out the security badge pilfered from Shorty, and waved it over the clack sensor mounted on the wall.

To her relief, the lock disengaged, and door opened.

Taking great pains not to make any noise, she slowly opened it.

A warm gust of air evacuated the room. Though it carried no physical scent, in her mind it evoked the briny spray of the ocean, the deck of that Nineteenth Century ship.

She stepped inside and found herself in a narrow hallway, the only light shining through the other end. Whoever designed this place must have been a snake.

With the Sig firmly gripped in her hand and M-16 slung over her shoulder, she slipped into the corridor.

# NINETY TWO

SITUATION ROOM
THE WHITE HOUSE
11:35 AM EST

THE OUTLOOK WAS BLEAK. Reports of mass hysteria from all over the country filled the news channels on the televisions mounted on the Sit Room's walls. Evan Cromwell fought to remain composed as Mitch Donovan, who had returned with a report that President Bradley was not doing well, argued with just about everyone who opposed pulling the National Guard from high risk areas in the country which hadn't yet erupted in riots.

The National Security Advisor had been so involved in the heated discussions he almost missed a call from his assistant. His support staff came over to alert him, then directed him to the Top Secret secure telephones in one of the "Superman" tubes, a cylindrical privacy phone booth. Cromwell entered and slid the curved transparent door shut. "This better be important."

"I wouldn't call otherwise, especially today."

"What is it?"

"It's him, Sir. Al Shihab. I don't know how, but he's on a secure video line and demands to speak with the President."

According to the CIA records, Ishmael had been selected three years ago as an asset not only for his ability to work easily in

Islamic and Western circles, but because of his vast technical skill-set, including hacking into network and telecom systems. It came as no surprise that he had found a means of patching into the White House Situation Room.

"Have Homeland and NSA run a trace," Cromwell said.

"Already on it."

"Patch it into VTC1 in the Sit Room. I'll take it from here."

He asked Donovan to inform Bradley, then alerted the NSC, Joint Chiefs, and cabinet members, and everyone else that Al Shihab would be on the line.

"Any way to verify that it's really him?" Cromwell asked Douglas Kendall.

"Possibly by what he knows. Regardless, we need to keep him on the line in order to trace him to his real location. After what happened with our Recon Team in Nemidan, I wouldn't trust a word he says."

"And yet, we seem to be subject to his whims and demands, because no one has been able to locate and stop him!" Cromwell didn't feel particularly good about raising his voice at the director of the Central Intelligence Agency, but given the circumstances, his frustration should be understood.

Additional opinions exacerbated the ensuing debates, the dissonance rising in volume to the point where hardly anyone could be heard over one another. This went on for a while until the door swung open, and a strong voice interrupted.

"Atten-hut!"

Everyone in the Sit Room rose to their feet and snapped to attention.

To Cromwell's amazement, President Jennifer Bradley walked in with a slight stagger, but her head held high. She wore her typical blue suit. The makeup could not completely conceal the dark rings under her eyes, but she exuded confidence.

"Ma'am, I don't understand," Cromwell said. "Are you all right?"

"Against the advice of my physicians, I have decided to join you all." She took a seat and the others did likewise. "In case you're wondering…Yes, I am dying. But I am not contagious, according to Dr. Singh and his staff. Ishmael was telling the truth about one thing, he didn't infect me with the same strain of the virus that's out there. In any case, while the White House is still on lockdown, my particular quarantine has been lifted."

Clearly relieved, the Vice President smiled at her from his seat on her right. "It's good to see you, Madam President."

She nodded her appreciation.

Then to Cromwell. "I understand that IAS is on the line."

"Ma'am, it's possible this is simply another diversionary ploy."

She coughed weakly, and tried to speak, but her voice was dry and raspy. After a sip of water that had been placed within reach, Bradley said, "I'll give him two minutes to get to the point."

"You got it." Cromwell gestured to the wall across the room opposite the President. A pair of monitors rose out of the console, the video conference camera between them spun around to face her, and the panel beneath it lit up to read: "MIC ON."

"All right." Straining through the pain and fatigue, the President of the United States sat tall and dignified. "Put him on."

# NINETY THREE

SITUATION ROOM
THE WHITE HOUSE
11:35 AM EST

IT WAS THE MOST DIFFICULT THING she'd ever had to do. Jennifer Bradley felt her life draining with each passing moment. She'd spent the past couple of hours coming to terms with her impending death, but could not stop thinking about Mikey.

Last she'd heard, Wade had just witnessed the deadly rage of a couple of outbreak victims just outside of Cabotstown. But no sign of her son.

Now they'd lost contact.

*Please, just let my boy be all right.*

She kept repeating it in her head, even as her strength faded.

But then came the news that Ishmael was trying to contact her.

She would not be remembered as the President who lay in bed, while her people came under attack. She had to be here in the Sit Room, even if these were her final minutes.

So she had ordered Dr. Singh to give her something to keep her alert. He conceded and administered an injection of Narcan, a drug typically used to counter the effects of a heroin or morphine overdose. In this case, she was experiencing the same shutting down of the central nervous system, respiratory system. The Narcan was only a temporary measure, but that was all she could hope for at this point.

Bradley nodded to the video conference screen. "Put him on."

Before the entire Situation Room, the image of a man who had been on the video after she'd been struck by the hummingbird drone appeared on the screen.

"President Bradley, so pleased to see you."

"You have declared war on the United States of America. Whatever your political aspirations, you've painted a bright red bullseye on your own back."

He gave her a patronizing smile. "For a dying woman, you're looking remarkably well. Ah, but it's just a matter of time before the unspeakable agony sets in. You will be begging to be euthanized like the dog that you are."

"We found Bin Laden, and we will find you."

"As you did in Nemidan? Come now. How will your administration explain that? It is time for you to accept the fact that you, Jennifer Bradley, have failed. Even if you find me, it will be too late."

A twisting pain in her lower back made her grimace. She drew a deep breath. "We will not allow you to threaten President Aamaal. Tariqistan is—"

"Are you truly that dim?" His eyes flashed with incredulity. "I care nothing for Tariqistan."

"What about your demands, FTM, Al Saif?"

"*Their* demands. I merely issued them to keep you distracted. You see, while you were busy looking through Kishwar and Tariqistan's surrounding regions, I was closer than you could ever have imagined."

Cromwell was in the tube, but forgot to shut the privacy shield. "Get on that trace, now! Where's he calling from?"

"Ishmael," Bradley said, "why target innocent civilians?"

"Why am *I* targeting innocents? Oh, Jennifer, don't you think that's a bit hypocritical? I had been working with the CIA and about to turn Haashir over to you. The intel was correct, he did indeed possess the WMD's Saddam sent for him to hide. I was just weeks away from obtaining them, killing Haashir, and turning everything over to you."

Ben had been right after all. She should not have acted in haste with Operation Nighthawk. Her head light, a wave of nausea engulfed her. "Why didn't you contact us? Our reports say you missed three check-ins. You had to know what that meant."

"Where is the trust, Jennifer? I was loyal, dedicated, more than competent. And in turn..." His lip twisted, his gaze smoldered. "My son was just a little boy! My wife...They loved America, we all did! And you didn't even have the decency to send a human asset to check, to verify. Instead, you send a Predator Drone to do your dirty work from thousands of miles away!"

"It was...a mistake," Bradley said, her strength diminishing. "We truly believed...you had turned."

"It was YOU that turned, Madam President! Against your own asset. I sacrificed everything to help you."

"It was tragic. And nothing I can say will—"

"In less than five minutes, I will send the command codes to deploy the L1N1 virus—as your CDC has named it—in New York, Chicago, Los Angeles, and Dallas. You've already seen its effects in a small area. Once the infection spreads in these metropolitan centers, there will be no stopping it."

"What good does it do you to kill so many innocent people?"

"Only the satisfaction of shaping your legacy as the president whose people paid for her sins."

Bradley pulled her chair closer to the table, stood, and set her hands down on it to steady herself. "The grievance you have is with me, not them."

"You're right, of course. My grievance *is* with you." He set his lips and gave it a second or two of thought. Then he looked back to the camera. "I had to watch him die, do you have any idea what that's like? One moment, Odin was healthy, happy. The next, he's burning up in flames, his body shattered and spread across the ground in pieces. He was just four years old!"

Jennifer held his gaze, fighting back the tears welling up. With a hard snarl, she said, "No child should have to suffer and die like that." It was never her intention to harm the boy and his mother, Bradley had no idea it would happen. But she was the one who gave the green light for the drone strike.

"Before my very eyes, you took my son from me, President Jennifer Bradley. So yes, my grievance is indeed with you." He turned to look away from the camera, then back. "Now, I intend to have it redressed accordingly."

"What do you...?"

He stepped out of view for a moment, then returned.

What she saw struck her so hard, she let out a gasp. All at once, everything made sense—where he'd been all this time, what he intended to do. Until this moment, Jennifer Bradley did not know the true meaning of panic. Up on the screen, Mikey stood there eyes wide with fear in the clutches of Ishmael Al Shihab.

# NINETY FOUR

ABANDONED SHAFT
BROUGHMAN'S MINE
GARRETT COUNTY, MD
11:41 AM EST

HE CUT THE TRANSMISSION to the White House, confident that his scrambling and masking script would send their network analysts on a wild goose chase all over the globe. Though, if they had even a bit of intelligence, they'd have figured that Michael could only be less than an hour from the Bradley Ranch.

He'd have to act quickly.

"Best not to struggle, Son," Ishmael said, still holding Michael Bradley tight, with the tip of a Ka-Bar under his chin. "It will only hurt more."

"I'm not your son!" Michael said, and wrestling to free himself from his grip. "My mother is the president of the United States."

"Yes, I know."

"And you're just a stinking terrorist!"

Ishmael tightened his grip around the boy's neck. It would be priceless to witness the expression on the President's face when he administered the justice due her. Even in her Judeo-Christian culture, she must appreciate the Old Testament concept of "eye for an eye."

The video camera was set.

In just a minute, he'd reestablish the connection and administer the execution before Bradley in real time. But first, he would make her suffer the torment of waiting haplessly.

Since they'd considered him an Islamic terrorist, he would make sure not to disappoint. A gruesome beheading would deliver just the right amount of horror befitting her punishment.

"It is time, Michael." Taking care not to shed any blood prematurely, he pulled him before the camera.

"Get your dirty hands off of me!"

Back in his lab, the chime sounded.

He turned his head back.

The boy lifted his foot, and with surprising force, stomped his heel down into Ishmael's foot.

A searing pain went through it.

But Ishmael had experienced far greater pain than this. To him, it was a mere annoyance. Grabbing Michael by the hair, he yanked his head back.

He was just about to scold him, when their eyes met.

Michael's were blue and wide, full of fire. "What did I ever do to you?"

It had been three years since he'd had such close contact with a child, so it took him by surprise. A strong sense of compassion, as he once had for Odin, filled him with irrational remorse.

"It's not your fault," Ishmael said, trying to sustain the rage needed to carry out his plan, for he was not an innately violent man—not with children, anyway. "But we must all learn and experience the age-old axiom our parents and teachers have taught us: Life isn't fair."

Once again, back in his lab, a tone from his computer chimed.

An entry alert.

He'd given strict orders to Racine not to enter without prior authorization. This interruption would be dealt with severely.

Enough delays! One hand still restraining the President's son, Ishmael reached for a black hood, and prepared to reconnect the video stream. "Let's get this over with."

"What are you going to do?" Michael said, trembling in his grip.

For just a moment, Ishmael considered what he was about to do. If after all these years of clawing his way out of the cesspool in which Bradley had dumped him, would killing her son bring Odin and Aiza back? Would he feel any better after he took the life of this boy who was as innocent as his own son? And how would that make him any better than the Americans whom he planned to wipe out?

*Don't over-think this!* It was a matter of principle, something he'd resolved long ago. Too late to alter his course. Doing so would render everything he'd worked for meaningless.

With one hand pressing the knife into Michael's neck, and the other grasping the video control switch, he stretched his thumb over the button.

Without warning, the door to the room in which he stood flew open. Before he could see who had entered, he heard the voice of a woman.

"Drop the knife! Do it, now!"

# NINETY FIVE

ABANDONED SHAFT
BROUGHMAN'S MINE
GARRETT COUNTY, MD
11:47 AM EST

XANDRA POINTED HER GUN at the man holding Mikey at knife point. He had a deep Middle Eastern complexion, but his features seemed more European. The jeans and black T-shirt made him look more American than anything else.

"I said drop it!"

"You're too late," he said.

Immediately, she knew. This was the person Tempest had told her about, the man she'd sought to stop. All the intel she'd gathered through means both natural and preternatural brought his true name to her lips.

"Ishmael."

"Take another step, and I'll slice open the boy's Carotid Artery." He put the blade in the very spot. Mikey flinched, suppressing a yelp.

With her gun aimed right at Al Shihab's head, she could surely make the shot.

"Are you certain you can stop me in time?" he said, the strain in his grip jiggling the knife at Mikey's neck. A tiny red streak trickled down his fair skin.

"Xandi...?"

"Ishmael, listen—"

"No, *you* listen! You are going to put your weapons down, and—"

With the Sig still pointed at him, she crouched down and slipped the M-16 strap off of her shoulder.

"Drop them *both*!" Ishmael snarled.

It took only a fraction of a second to decide.

Xandra shifted slightly to the right.

Then fired off a round.

Even with the suppressor, the crack was loud and jarring. It hit him in the right shoulder a couple of inches from Mikey's head.

The knife fell from his hand.

Releasing the boy, Ishmael reached for his wound with his left hand.

Mikey squirmed out of his grip as he staggered back.

Xandra took that opportunity to rush Ishmael. With the gun still in her fist, she pounded his bleeding wound.

Face contorted with rage, he cried out in pain.

His left hand shot out, grabbed her by the throat with a powerful grip.

Xandra dug her nails into his hand until they broke his skin. At the same time, she pummeled his right shoulder with her gun.

That brought him to his knees, but he pulled her down with him.

He rolled her over, slammed her back onto the floor, and knelt over her.

Gasping for breath, Xandra felt his foot come down hard on her wrist, pinning it down with the gun. In a deft move, he used his left hand and twisted it out of her grip.

But as soon as she found her breath, she swung her legs up and clamped her knees around his neck. Before he could establish a grip on the gun, Xandra turned sideways, throwing his weight down to the floor, where his head hit the concrete.

The gun fell out of his hand and slid over in Mikey's direction.

Watching with such intense trepidation, the boy didn't seem to notice.

Limbs flailing, Ishmael managed to find his knife.

The blade moved so fast toward her leg she couldn't stop it.

Slicing through her pant leg, it carved a superficial line in her thigh. Burned like the devil, but she kicked at his wounded shoulder again.

Ishmael blocked it with his left arm, and in a flash was on top of her.

With his elbow, he delivered a heavy blow to her temple.

Silver flecks danced before her and for a second or two, everything else went dark. Stunned, she blinked repeatedly until his fogged outline became clear.

The knife in his left hand was driving straight down at her throat.

# NINETY SIX

11:55 AM EST

THE KNIFE CAME DOWN so quickly, Xandra couldn't get her hands up in time to stop it. Out of instinct she shut her eyes, threw her arms up anticipating a brutal series of stab wounds, resulting in one fatal slash.

But then, a gunshot rang out.

Ishmael's body jerked back.

Xandra opened her eyes.

As her eyesight cleared, she saw him get to his feet.

Xandra turned her head toward the sound of the gunfire to find Mikey standing with the Sig in his hands, a wisp of smoke rising from the muzzle.

Ishmael, staggered over to the boy.

Dazed, Xandra tried to reach out and grab his ankle.

But she missed. She tried to get up, but the pain and dizziness in her head weakened her too much.

Mikey pointed the gun at him again, squeezed the trigger repeatedly.

Nothing happened.

He couldn't get another shot off.

Blood oozing from his chest and gasping for breath, Ishmael yanked the gun from the boy and tossed it aside. He then grabbed the boy by the collar and shoved him into the room with the large glass window. Gripping the steel door frame, he swung himself inside.

A heavy stainless steel door slid shut with a deep boom, sealing the room off.

With great effort, Xandra made it to her feet and limped over to the door. Fist pounding the smooth surface, she could tell it was made of solid steel, several inches thick. The window frame was constructed with a few layers of thick glass.

"Mikey!" she said, slapping the glass which absorbed so much of the impact it made practically no sound.

Ishmael fell into one of the chairs, his shirt soaked in blood.

He rolled over to the console, tapped a button which made his labored breathing audible over an intercom on Xandra's side. "Who...are...you?"

"It's over, Ishmael. You need medical attention or you'll bleed out and die."

Slowly lifting his eyes to meet hers, he gave her a look of despair. "I died three years ago."

"What?"

"Never mind, just...go away." He pressed a few more buttons, and swiveled his chair around turning his back to her. Stretching his quivering hands out to Mikey, he gestured with his finger for him to come over to him.

Mikey backed into a wall, shaking his head.

"Fine..." His shoulders making tiny pulses with each weakening gasp, Ishmael's head drooped and he turned halfway to reach for a video conference camera. He pointed it to the back of the laboratory at Mikey. "We'll take the long road."

Xandra found the gun on the floor that Mikey had used to shoot Ishmael, retrieved it, and found it jammed—it had failed to reload. She quickly popped out the jammed round, reseated the magazine, and chambered a fresh round. Making sure that Mikey was clear of the line of fire, she pointed the gun at the window.

# NINETY SEVEN

11:59 AM EST

THE WORST PART OF DEATH by a gunshot wound was the cold. Ishmael could scarcely operate the equipment because of the tremors and his fast fading consciousness.

Over the intercom, he heard a series of gunshots, and the dull report of shots fired. They left a few marks on the opposite surface of the glass-clad polycarbonate, bullet resistant security window. At UL protection Level 8 however, nothing short of a 12 Gauge could come close to penetrating it.

That accursed bitch! He now realized who she was.

*The President's photographer.*

He couldn't help but laugh, though it hurt exquisitely. Of all the people in the world to find him and attempt to stop him, it had been her. It didn't matter, she was neither important, nor a threat any longer. Nothing short of an excavator or jackhammer would get her inside his lab. Cerberus provided him with everything he needed. All in exchange for the virus. The cure and vaccine, however, would be wiped out with his computer's hard drive as soon as the weaponized canisters in his target cities deployed.

But first, he had to complete his most important task, lest he expire without accomplishing it.

With a tap of a button on his iPad, the video conference screen came to life. Before him appeared President Bradley. They had patched her into her private office by the White House Situation Room.

"Ah, there you are." His head grew almost too heavy for his neck to hold up. "I daresay, you're looking as well as I feel."

"What have you done with my son!"

From behind him, the boy called out. "Mom, are you okay?"

Ishmael's breaths grew shorter. He'd seen this numerous times with friends who had died in his presence. Now it was his time. With whatever strength remained, he lifted his eyes to confront her.

"This is a most touching reunion. But I'm afraid the end of our time here draws nigh."

"Listen to me…you bastard…My son—"

"You will watch him…die…"

"Don't do this!"

"Madam President…" He pointed to the iPad and pressed a button. "…in exactly five minutes…a weaponized virus will be released…into all the cities…And as it does…a Sarin hybrid will be released in here in this lab…providing a slow…agonizing death…for your son."

"Look, I'm sorry about your wife," Bradley said, barely containing her distress.

"It's all right, though…In about…four weeks…like the great pharaohs of ancient Egypt…you'll be joined in death…by more than half of North America."

"And your son, Ishmael. It was a mistake. Don't do this!"

For the first time in his life, he saw her weak, helpless.

*Good.*

She deserved to know how it feels to watch her son die, and not be able to do anything about it.

"Mom!" Mikey looked around the room.

A euphoric wave came over Ishmael.

His breaths grew smaller with each attempt to draw air into his lungs.

And then, one final surge. "I looked, and behold, an ashen horse..."

"Mikey, get out of there!" Bradley called out.

"...and he who sat on it had the name Death; and Hades was following with him."

"It's locked, Mom!" Michael paced frantically around the lab searching for an exit. He came upon the second auxiliary door. Nothing but the correct access code would allow him to unlock it, though. And that code was so complex, it had to be saved in an encrypted text file with all the other passcodes on Ishmael's desktop computer.

"...Authority was given to them over a fourth of the earth..."

"Mikey!" the photographer called out, over the intercom. "Look for a—"

Ishmael shut the intercom.

"...to kill with sword and with famine and...with PESTILENCE!"

"Xandi, help me!" Mikey turned and stared at Ishmael with terrified eyes.

But Ishmael only saw the smiling face of Odin, holding his Ironman action figure.

In that last moment of awareness, a chasm of despair yawned open, ready to swallow him whole. Though he had succeeded in exacting his vengeance, the satisfaction he'd derived from this lasted for but a fleeting moment. After all was said and done, he had gained nothing.

It had been meaningless...*chasing the wind...*

*Vanitas vanitatum...*

Ishmael slumped back in the chair.

...breathed a final sigh...

... and pressed the button...

The countdown began.

# NINETY EIGHT

12:05 PM EST

HE WAS DEAD.

Judas, Ishmael Al Shihab, whatever his name really was, the man who had tried to murder Michael Bradley sat completely still in his chair, a vacant shell, eyes as empty as his soul.

But Mikey remained trapped in the lab, frightened as a caged animal, while the command codes triggered a countdown to deployment.

There had to be a way to get him out.

"Michael!" Xandra shouted.

But he didn't look up, he was looking at the video conference monitor, tears in his eyes.

She banged against the window, waved her hands to get his attention.

He looked up, pointed to his ears and shook his head.

Ishmael had deactivated the intercom.

Xandra made a button-pushing gesture, hoping he'd understand that she meant for him to find the switch and re-activate it.

But in this desperate game of charades, he didn't manage to find it.

Suddenly, he lifted his head and pointed over her shoulder urgently.

At the same moment, the door creaked open.

Xandra turned around.

Standing in the doorway was the guard who she'd subdued and bound. He'd somehow escaped and now stood holding the M-16 she'd left on the floor.

He pointed it at her.

But with a response so quick, it surprised Xandra herself, she fired one round, striking center mass.

The guard fell to the floor with a heavy thud.

Her first kill.

Contrary to what she'd expected, she felt neither remorse, revulsion, nor gratification…Nothing.

"…happened, Xandi?"

He did it! The intercom was back on.

She turned around, and for the first time since she found him, she felt hopeful. "Mikey, are you all right?"

"Yeah. I'm okay." But his frightened eyes told a different story.

"I promise, I won't leave you. Now listen, can you find a way out? How about that door back there?"

"It's locked."

"Try punching in some numbers on that keypad, while I look for another way in!"

"Okay." He walked over to the keypad at the back exit door and made beeping noises on the locking system.

Was that a vent above him? A metal grill near the top of the wall behind him certainly implied it. She traced an imaginary route that lead to the air vent in the room in which she stood.

More crawling.

Good thing she wasn't a claustrophobe.

Thirty seconds later, she was on her belly slithering through the cramp ventilation shaft, going in the general direction of the sealed lab. The surface was cool and smooth, nothing like the dank tunnels on her way in. But with multiple junctions, it was a maze.

For a brief moment, she wondered if Wade had been able to

call for help. Even if he had, it would take some time for anyone to arrive.

Time which Mikey didn't have.

Neither did the targeted cities.

She continued through the vent until she came upon an intersection from Hell.

Disorientation set in. Of the four possible directions, which way led to Michael?

She banged on the sheet metal and shouted, "Michael! If you can hear me, answer me!"

She waited…

And waited.

Then repeated her message.

This time she heard a faint reply followed by a tapping of a grill. "*Over here!*"

Taking the vent to her left, Xandra commando-crawled as quickly as she could to the sound. But when she arrived, she found that on her side of the grill, it had been fitted with thick iron bars, like those of a prison cell.

"Damn!" She slammed the bars in futility, though she could see Mikey between them, and down below.

He glanced up, their eyes meeting.

"There's an iPad with a timer counting down," He said. "It's down to four minutes, but I think I might be able to stop it."

"DON'T touch anything!"

"But I know about iPads and stuff!"

"Please, just wait for me."

"Fine!"

"What about that other door?" she asked. "Which way?"

Mikey sat down in a chair pointed to his right.

Xandra made her way in that direction, trying to stave off an anxiety attack from being trapped in so tight a space.

# NINETY NINE

BREAKOUT ROOM
WHITE HOUSE SITUATION ROOM
12:06 PM EST

SHE WAS THE LEADER OF THE NATION, ostensibly the most powerful individual in the world but at this moment, the most helpless. While everyone in the Sit Room coordinated efforts to prepare for the impending outbreak, and to control the riots flaring up throughout the country, teams from numerous agencies were on their way to Wade Masterson's reported location. The density of the forest impeded their efforts, however. They would eventually find him, but there was no guarantee that they'd reach Mikey's actual location in time. He had told her about Xandra, but there wasn't any way for her to get to him.

President Jennifer Bradley sat at her desk in the Breakout Room, a small, private conference room just outside of the main White House Situation Room, its windows fogged for privacy. Michael had reactivated the video conference link.

She watched in despair as her little boy paced the locked room, in which Ishmael's still body remained slumped in the chair. Then he came to the camera, and rolled the chair aside on its casters.

"Michael," she said, the fever sapping her strength. "Keep

away from him."

"He—he's dead, Momma. I shot him." Mikey leaned in close to the camera, and glanced aside at Ishmael's corpse with revulsion. "I had to do it, I'm sorry."

"Okay, don't worry about that now." She pulled herself closer to the camera, sniffling and bravely wiping away her tears.

In a furtive tone, he whispered, "Mom…I'm scared."

She reached out and touched the image of his face on the desktop monitor. "Momma's so sorry."

"I'm going to die, aren't I?"

She didn't want to say it, but if Ishmael had been truthful about the Sarin hybrid that would soon be released into that room, there was little hope, unless he could get out. "I'm here with you, Mikey."

"Wait…you don't look too good. Are you sick?"

"Don't worry about me. I'm just a little tired. Now listen. Xandra is—"

"Don't lie to me. I can tell. It's like when Daddy was sick." He blinked, his lower jaw shaking visibly. "You're dying."

"Mikey…"

He broke down and wept. "I didn't mean it, Mom, honest! I'm sorry about what I said."

Seeing him but not being able to gather him up in her arms was almost worse than not being able to see him at all. They were only supposed to be apart for a couple of days. And now…"You're sorry? For what? What are you talking about?"

"The last time we were together." He sniffled, then sat tall. "I got mad at you for not coming with me to the Ranch, and…and, I said that I hated you. I didn't mean it. I'm so sorry I said that. I love you!"

"My sweet boy…" Too weak to prevent it, Jennifer began to cry. It had been the last time they were together, after all. "I know you didn't mean it, Momma knows. I'm sorry I didn't spend more time with you. You deserved so much better. Please, forgive me, Mikey. I love you."

So many regrets, so much self-recrimination. Had it all been worth it, the security of the Nation, the support of foreign allies, the fight against terrorism, all at the cost of her family?

If only she could hold him one last time, kiss his fair head, snuggle next to him in his bed and tuck him in. She never imagined saying goodbye this way, so distant, so impersonal.

Their eyes met.

He was looking around the desk. "Mom?"

"Yes, sweetie?" She could hardly open her eyes but when she looked at the screen, he was glancing back and forth between an iPad on the desk, and another computer monitor. "I think I see something."

# ONE HUNDRED

12:07 PM EST

SHE CURSED THE STEEL GRILL covering the ventilation shaft and kicked at it. It was bolted down and all Xandra managed to do was put a slight dent in it. On its other side was another steel door, similar to the one through which Ishmael had pushed Mikey through before trapping him inside.

It would take another minute to get back there, only to be faced with the same problem.

Xandra turned to face the grill and placed the muzzle of her gun at its outer edge. With one shot in each corner, the grill came free, and Xandra pushed out of the ventilation shaft landing on her feet.

She went to the door only to find it locked with a hand scanner. There was no way she could get in.

Urgently, she banged on the door. "Michael!"

A click on the speaker on the side of the door. "Is that you, Xandi?"

"Yes. Can you unlock the door for me?"

"I don't know."

"We need to get you out of there."

A brief pause, then his voice returned. "There's no lock, only a panel with a keypad—like a telephone's."

"Okay, try these numbers..." she pictured the keypad, its letter and numbers, then transposed and spelled out a few inane sequences.

A faint series of beeps sounded on the other side of the door as he tried them.

None of them worked.

"What does the timer say, Michael?"

It seemed like an eternity before he replied. "3:21...and counting...Wait, I think I saw something on his computer."

Xandra heard him, but was already onto her next idea.

Aiming the gun at the hand scanner mounted on the side of the door frame, she shot it, breaking it open. Inside, a tangle of multi-colored wires mocked her, daring her to try to make sense of them. She had no idea how to hotwire a security system, though. What was she thinking?

"There's a folder on his computer Xandi," Mikey said over the intercom. "It's got a whole bunch of files. But you have to type a password to get in."

Concentrating with all her might, she pressed her back against the wall and slid down to a crouch. She'd never been able to invoke this permutation of second-sight, it had always come unannounced. But she had to try.

Please...let it work...

*The darkness clears.*

*Before her lies the desk, the iPad counting down, the computer screen.*

*Multiple text document windows are open.*

*The mouse pointer flits around between file icons, unsure which to try clicking.*

*One file starts to glow with a golden highlight.*

*Hellhound.txt*

"That one, Mikey!"

"What?"

"Hellhound, that's the one!"

"Wait, how did you—?"

"Please, just open it."

A quick silence.

"It wants a password!"

*Come on! Doesn't help getting this far only to be stopped by a password.*

She focused on her inner sight. Within seconds, she was back in the lab perceiving through Mikey's eyes.

*The iPad countdown…2:08, 2:07, 2:06…*

*A photograph of a young boy, and of a woman—his mother.*

Come on, come on, give me something, anything!

*And then she sees it.*

*A hardcover book, cloth spine facing out, bare and devoid of a dust jacket.*

*First, the author's name: Melville*

*Then the title in gold inlaid letters: MOBY DICK*

*All at once, everything floods back into her mind.*

*The ocean spray.*

*The harpoons on the wall*

*The rail lined with the whale's teeth.*

"Michael, how much time?"

"It says 1:43!"

"Enter this password: M-O-B-Y-D-I-C-K"

A few more precious seconds pass.

"It didn't work, Xandi!"

*He moves the pointer to another file. To Xandra's amazement, it's called DoorCode.txt*

"That's the one, you have to open that one. That'll give you the codes to open the door and get you out of there. Hurry!"

*He looks to the screen, where his mother watches, her face laced with anxiety.*

*"Please, Mikey...listen to Xandra. Get out of there before it's too late."*

12:09 PM EST

"That man set a timer," Mikey said, sorry that he would disobey his mother. "And when it counts down to zero, it'll kill a lot of people."

"No, no, no, Mikey. Listen to me..." Mom's eyes were open wide, she looked almost hopeful, but scared too.

Over the intercom, Xandra continued to ask him to open the DoorCode file. The timer now read 1:10

```
1:09
1:08
1:07
```

"Mom, it might kill you, and Mr. Wade, and Xandi, too."

"Don't worry about me, Michael, open the file, find the code, and get out of there!"

```
0:58
0:57
0:56
```

He thought about Dad, how much he missed him, his big smile when coming home from deployments, running into his big, strong arms. And he remembered how he'd done everything to save others, even though it meant risking his life.

*Greater love has no man than this, that a man lay down his life for his friends.*

"Good bye, Mom. I love you so much."

"No, wait! Mikey, don't—!"

He pressed the power button switched off the video conference camera.

His entire body trembled, but he had to do this.

*It's what Dad would do.*

```
0:44
0:43
0:42
```

"Xandi, I need another password!"

# ONE HUNDRED AND ONE

12:09 PM EST

SHE COULDN'T BELIEVE IT. Michael Bradley had made the bravest choice anyone could make. It made Xandra proud, and terrified, and ashamed all at the same time.

"Give me another password to try, Xandi. Quick!"

She got up and put her face near the intercom, considered the elements of her visions. At a frantic pace, she prompted him to try: Melville, Whale, Ahab, Queequeg, and even Ishmael...

"Nothing! None of them work!"

Xandra slammed the wall with her hand.

"Only twenty seconds left!" He said.

At a loss for what else to do, she aimed her gun at the door, slid her finger around the trigger, knowing it was futile.

*A tall mast...*

*Whale's teeth on the rail*

*And then, a shiny brass bell with the engraving, clear as day...*

# ONE HUNDRED AND TWO

12:09 PM EST

IT WAS NO GOOD. Everyone out there was going to die. And so was Mikey. He just couldn't get to the codes in the document without the right password.

Disheartened, he glanced at the clock.

```
0:17
0:16
0:15
```

"We're not going to make it, Xandi..." He slapped his hand on the desk.

"It's Pequod!" Xandra shouted over the intercom. "Mikey, the password is Pequod!" She spelled it out for him.

He leapt up, typed it in, got one letter wrong

```
INCORRECT PASSWORD
```

"UGH!" He tried again.

```
0:11
0:10
0:09
```

"Yes!" Right in the center of the page was the six digit passcode for disarming the weapon that would kill millions of people.

0  2  1  3  0  9

"Got it!"

"Hurry," Xandra said.

He grabbed the iPad, touched the override button, and typed in the command code on the countdown app.

0:03
0:02
0:01

# ONE HUNDRED AND THREE

12:10 PM EST

DEAD SILENCE.

That was all Xandra got through the intercom. By her esti-
mate, the clock must have counted down to zero by now.
"Mikey…"

"WE DID IT!" He shouted, his voice tinny and distorted over
the intercom's speaker.

"Are you sure?"

"Yes!" His voice was jubilant. "It stopped right at the last second and I can see the word DISARMED on the screen. We
stopped it!"

All the weight lifted from her. They'd prevented Ishmael's
WMDs from deploying. Not the CIA, not the US Military, just her
and Michael, a photographer and a young boy—a hero like his
father. She let out a long breath.

"You're a genius, Michael!"

"No, *you're* a gen—" a shrill beep interrupted him. "Oh no…"

In an instant, the joy drained from her and transformed into
dread. A prickly chill spread to her extremities. "Michael, the
door code!"

"Something's hissing, Xandi."

The Sarin hybrid.

She slapped the steel door. "Go to the computer, and try to open that document! We have to open this door!"

"No…it'll kill you too."

"Michael Bradley, you listen to me! Go to the computer!"

But he didn't respond.

As the room filled with the Sarin hybrid, all she heard was his violent coughing.

# ONE HUNDRED AND FOUR

12:14 PM EST

SHE'D CRAWLED THROUGH THE MAZE of air ducts and found her way back to the room outside the lab, where the guard she'd shot lay dead. But Xandra paid no attention to the body. As soon as her feet touched the ground, she ran over to the large window.

Mikey was sitting before the teleconference camera, his head barely held up as he leaned back into the chair. Frustrated tears falling from his eyes, he was clicking on the controls repeatedly. When he looked up and saw Xandra, his face was as white as salt, his eyes red. Between weak, blood-producing coughs, he spoke.

"Can't...turn it back on..."

She pressed her palm against the window. "You have to open that file, and get the key codes."

"I just...wanna say goodbye...to my mom..."

"Hang on, Mikey...I'm going to get you out of there."

With an angelic smile, he almost looked like he was going to sleep—if not for the abrupt grimaces that each stab of pain evoked. His chest quavered with each breath. "Say goodbye...to her...for me, Xandi, okay?"

"You are *not* going to die down here Michael. Do you hear me?"

But what could she do? Even if she crawled back out of the mine shaft, to get help, would he even live long enough to be rescued? The Sarin hybrid was lethal, and working at a merciless pace.

"Thank you, Xandi."

"No, Michael...Look at me."

"And...give Max a hug...

...for me..."

Feebly, she slapped the bulletproof glass with her palm. "Get the door codes...please."

His head reclined against the chair's back.

The trembling stopped.

The life in his eyes departed.

Xandra was not aware of anything but the implosion of her heart, her sobs muffled by her hand...

...and the sound of someone approaching the door behind her.

# ONE HUNDRED AND FIVE

"HE WAS A HERO," Xandra had told President Bradley, the first time they'd spoken since she emerged from Ishmael's pit. But no words could comfort Jenna. And she hadn't said a word in response.

Xandra must have been in shock during the rescue. She could scarcely remember being taken outside and airlifted back to Andrews, where she'd been cleared for any infection. She learned later that a team of armed FBI agents, CDC staff in hazmat suits, and a crew with equipment for breaking into Ishmael's lab had arrived just seconds after Mikey breathed his last.

When they'd finally gotten inside, cleared the room of the Sarin, and retrieved Mikey's body, specialists seized all of Ishmael's computers and lab specimens.

To the military and intelligence community's despair, they'd found neither a stockpile of weaponized bio-chemical agents, nor delivery devices. They did, however, find and decrypt documents with a map and plans of where Ishmael had arranged to plant the canisters with remote detonators over the course of two years, without anyone noticing. None that were set in major cities had deployed, thanks to the sacrifice of Michael Bradley who would forever be remembered as the youngest American hero.

They also discovered documents with the exact genetic markers for a vaccine and treatment for L1N1. Apparently, Ishmael had wanted an insurance policy against the virus. Already, the drugs were being manufactured and distributed.

The total death toll was reported to be about five hundred and seventy four, with hundreds more in critical condition, but the treatment seemed to be working. And the vaccine showed great promise.

President Bradley and the White House staff who'd become infected responded well to the medication and, though exhausted and weak, returned to work a day later.

In the forty-eight hours since the initial Cabotstown attack hit the news, riots and bedlam threatened to burst forth, in the wake of the quarantines, media and border lockdowns. But when the world learned of Michael's sacrifice, just about everyone put aside their outrage and pulled together.

Candles, flowers, and wreathes were laid by the White House gate with photos of Michael Bradley. Men, women, and children of all nations and faiths gathered in prayer vigils. All around the capital and the nation, flags flew at half-mast.

As in the days following the attacks of September 11, 2001, the nations of the world joined hands as one global family. Heads of state from numerous countries called to offer their support and condolences, not only to President Bradley, but to the United States as a whole. If anything good could possibly have come of this, it was the solidarity of humankind, if only for a fleeting moment in history.

# ONE HUNDRED AND SIX

ARLINGTON NATIONAL CEMETERY
10:50 AM EST

THE SUN SHONE WARMLY UPON HER SHOULDERS as she performed on her Montagnana the poignant *Sarabande* from Bach's Sixth Suite for unaccompanied cello. Unaccompanied, save for the cooing white dove in the tree branch that stretched out over Michael Bradley's casket enshrouded by Old Glory, the American flag. A photo Xandra had made of him smiling with an arm around Max, rested on a stand. Erica Gordon was on duty in Xandra's place, making photos of the ceremony.

Seated before the casket, in a black suit, Bradley held her head high though she could not stop herself from a few sniffles, and dabs of the handkerchief. Though her sister and brother sat with her, the President seemed alone, even with Wade Masterson sitting stoically with crutches on the grass in the row behind hers, his PPD agents nearby.

As Xandra played the final chord of the Bach, there was nary a dry eye in the assembly. She could hardly contain it herself. Even Wade slipped a hand under his dark sunglasses to wipe a tear.

The uniformed pall bearers standing by lifted Old Glory above the Casket as the chaplain proceeded to give a short homily, his kind countenance and consoling smile softening the sting somewhat.

Xandra quietly got up and went to put her instrument back in its case behind a tree.

"You okay?" A soothing voice said behind her as she fastened the case's clasps.

"I don't know." She turned around and there stood Jake Rittenhouse, with Max on a leash, his bandaged left foreleg in a sling. "Thanks for being here, it's good to see you both." She reached down and rubbed Max's ears.

Jake came over and opened his arms, as she stood and buried her head in his chest to cry.

"I just don't understand," she said, with a sniffle. "How could such terrible things happen, to such a good, innocent boy? How could God allow this?"

His arms enveloped her, and when he spoke his voice comforted her. "I often wonder that myself. And you know, we've been asking ourselves that question for as long as humans have walked the Earth." He looked over to Michael's casket. "But I'm grateful that in all that darkness, sometimes the light of a single, beautiful candle shines, short as it may burn."

Xandra considered the evil that threatened to destroy the lives of millions. Michaels' sacrifice had triumphed over that darkness. Those who joined hands with blood-thirsty terrorists like Ishmael Al Shihab, and with the Machiavellian members of Cerberus had to be stopped. From this day forth, she would do everything in her power to do just that.

Jake put his hand on her back, and gestured to the ceremony. "Shall we?"

The Pastor was concluding his homily as Xandra and Jake stood in the back with Max amidst the oaks and the dogwoods.

"Behold, I tell you a mystery. We shall not all sleep, but we shall all be changed, in a moment, in the twinkling of an eye, at the last trumpet. For the trumpet will sound, and the dead will be raised imperishable, and we shall be changed.

"Death is swallowed up in victory. O death, where is your victory? O death, where is your sting? But thanks be to God, who gives us the victory through our Lord Jesus Christ. Therefore, beloved, be steadfast, immovable, always abounding in the work of the Lord, knowing that in the Lord your labor—dear Michael Bradley—is not in vain. Amen."

About twenty yards away, seven Marines lifted their rifles and fired off three volleys. Then a bugler played Taps as the pall bearers proceeded to fold the flag and present it to President Bradley.

In a plot Bradley had originally reserved for herself, Mikey was to be laid to rest beside his father. The casket rested on a brass bier above the grave, and the guests proceeded to line up and pay their final respects by laying flowers on it.

Xandra joined the end of the line with Max at her right, and Jake on her left.

By the time they arrived, Jenna Bradley was the only person remaining. She sat in the chair staring out at the casket that seemed too small to actually be there. Jake went ahead, placed a flower on it, bowed his head, and said a quiet prayer.

The President had not spoken with anyone the whole time, so out of respect, Xandra refrained from approaching her. She and Max went over to Mikey's casket.

Sorrow twinged Xandra's heart, her eyes welled up. Max sat and gave a mournful whine, his tail swaying slowly, his eyes moving from Xandra to his friend's coffin.

Placing her white carnation with the rest, she stood there recalling his sandy hair, bright blue eyes, and the strength and courage in those final minutes of his unjustly curtailed life. Having attended more than her share of funerals of beloved friends and family members who died too young, she anticipated that sinking sense of despair to revisit her. Perhaps it would be best to leave before she broke down.

But as she touched the cool lacquered surface of Mikey's coffin, a surge of inner light overwhelmed her senses like a crown of beauty for ashes, a joyous blessing instead of mourning, festive praise instead of despair.

The white light gave way to a lush garden with grass greener and sweeter than any she'd ever set foot on, with skies so vast you could see clear through the universe.

And just over the babbling brook whose water sparkled like gems, Benjamin Bradley stood fully decorated in uniform, laughing in delight as he knelt down, spread his arms wide, and caught an ecstatic Mikey running, then leaping into his arms.

A sublime warmth enveloped her. It mattered not if the vision was actual or symbolic. The questions she'd had about her gifts, her purpose had just been answered. All doubt had been removed. Instead of sinking into months of sorrow, she would look forward to another day.

Because there was so much more to do.

www.ingramcontent.com/pod-product-compliance
Lightning Source LLC
Chambersburg PA
CBHW020500260626
47156CB00006B/1808